THERE'S ONLY *One* PARIS

THERE'S ONLY *One* PARIS

Tales from our Times

APRIL LILY HEISE

There's Only One Paris

©2020 by April Lily Heise

ISBN: 978-0-9920053-4-4

First Printed in 2020

Cover design: April Lily Heise & Mats Haglund
Cover Photo: Viacheslav Lopatin
Interior Art: April Lily Heise
Author Photo: Pascale Vincent Marquis

TGRS Communications

Contact: jetaimemeneither@gmail.com
www.jetaimemeneither.com

"There's only one Paris, and however hard living here may be, and if it became worse and even harder, [the city does] a world of good." — *Vincent van Gogh*

Table of Contents

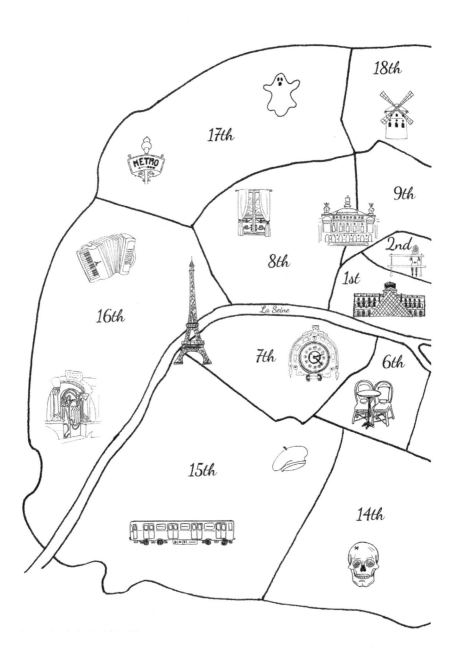

18th

17th

9th

METRO

8th

2nd

1st

16th

La Seine

7th

6th

15th

14th

20 arrondissements

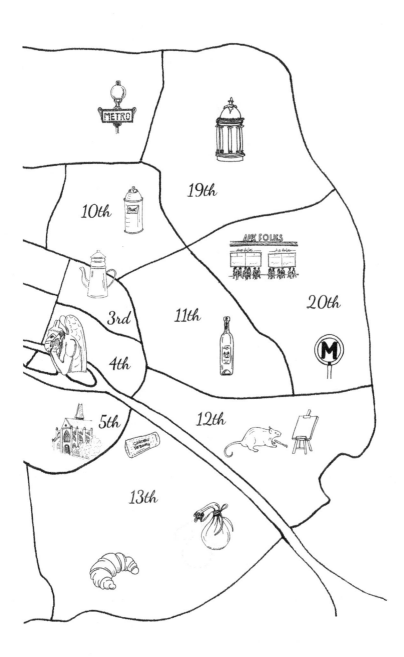

Le Métro
1st & 2nd Arrondissements

"Nooooo!"

Sasha ran and launched himself into the *Métro* car just as the buzzer sounded. He was immediately tugged backwards. The corner of his shoulder bag was caught in the closing doors. He freed it with a hefty yank, allowing the doors to shut properly. The train set off.

"No! I mean yes! I wasn't saying no to you," Sasha shouted into his phone as he regained his footing. "Yes, I've got it…"

There were two empty flip-down seats next to him. He lowered the closest and plunked himself down.

"I'm on my way now. I should be there shortly." He then removed a handkerchief from the zippered pocket of his satchel and dabbed his brow. He'd worked up a sweat on his race to catch the train. Well, considering recent events, it didn't take much for Sasha and his level of anxiety to surge.

"Il n'y a qu'un seul Paris… Paris… Paris…"

Oh no! Sasha grumbled to himself. No wonder that section of the *Métro* car was empty. He'd been in such a hurry to catch the train, he hadn't paid any attention to the state of where he was landing.

"Paris… Paris!"

Most Paris *Métro* cars were divided into sections comprised of groups of stationary seats alternating with open areas. The latter had poles for standing passengers to hold on to as well as flip-down seats which could be used when the car wasn't too full. Sasha was in one of these, and there, just a few feet away from him, was a musician. She was accompanying her passionate singing with a concertina, a mini accordion. The resulting tune was so loud Sasha could barely hear the person on the other end of the phone.

"What was that?" he yelled into his cell.

"There's only one Paris...!" the subway performer bellowed, switching into English.

Oh brother! I hope she gets off at the next station! Sasha bemoaned as he was trying to make out the instructions provided to him over the phone.

Petite in stature, but *grande* in voice, the musician had a dark brown bob atop which was a bright red beret. She was dramatically pressing the tiny keys on her accordion which, in turn, wheezed out a melody to go along with her crooning. Something about her look, and her emotional expressiveness, evoked the great French songstress Edith Piaf.

"I'm sorry, could you repeat that?" Sasha hollered. He plugged his free ear in an attempt to close off the annoying background noise. "I can't hear you very well."

As they approached Pyramides Station, the Line 7 conductor made an announcement which further added to Sasha's audible difficulties. He glared up at the *Métro*'s built-in speaker then over to the musician. With any luck she'd be getting off at the next station.

"What time did you say?" Sasha asked, frustrated. He couldn't handle any further stress right now. He was already on the brink of a nervous breakdown. "Yes, yes. As I said, I'm on my way now. You'll definitely have it by 4:30."

Sasha held his phone away from his ear to check the time. It was 12:40, he had plenty of time. The *Métro* pulled up to

Pyramides Station. A few people got off. The performer was not one of them.

"*There's only one Paris...!*" she belted out once again.

Sasha was trying to concentrate on his call, but he was getting increasingly annoyed by the musical distraction.

"*Il n'y a qu'un seul Paris...*"

Sure. There's only one city in the world *like* Paris, Sasha reflected on the lyrics of her song. But there are many different 'Paris-es' within the city. He possibly knew this better than anyone. He wasn't simply considering the city's 20 *arrondissements*, its administrative districts. Each of these had its own distinct personality. But beyond these larger borders, each *arrondissement* had a multitude of sub-districts, its *quartiers* or neighborhoods. Within these were a myriad of specific places, from historic sites to colorful markets and from local cafés to picturesque parks, which also influenced that neighborhood's spirit. Then there were the types of people found in each *quartier*; its residents, other Parisians or foreigners passing through. In middle of all this was the Seine River, much more than a mere border between the Left and Right Banks. Finally, there was Paris's extensive *Métro* system, where Sasha currently found himself—it had a whole life of its own. The sum of all of these individual components made up this 'one and only' Paris. But how were these very strange times, with a worldwide pandemic, affecting Paris? What were the short and long term repercussions of the virus? Besides the effects of the current state of the world, Paris was also changing in so many ways and at a rapid pace. Would the city always be this 'one and only' Paris?

"*Paris... Paris!!*" enthusiastically concluded the musician.

Good! Sasha huffed as he was pulled from his thoughts and back to the present moment. He was ready to give her 20 euros just so she'd shut up.

With one hand holding out a small leather pouch, about the size of her palm, and the other pressing away on the accordion's keys, the musician made her way through the carriage soliciting

15

spare change for her tune. Now that the noise levels had gone down, Sasha unplugged the ear that was not glued to his cell.

"Oh yes, it was a very close call," he told the person on the other end of the line. He was opening his mouth to add something when a squeaking accordion note went off in his newly unplugged ear. He swung his head up and saw the smiling face of the musician. *Shouldn't she be wearing a mask??* he admonished. He supposed it would be hard to sing with one on, nevertheless, she was spewing her germs around with each and every energetic *Paris!*

"*Une petite pièce pour la musique, monsieur?* Spare some change for the music, sir?" she asked, rattling her pouch under his nose.

Yes... if you go away and leave me alone! Sasha screamed in his head. Exasperated, he jammed his hand into the pocket of his jeans, removed all the change he had and tossed it into her pouch.

"*Merci, monsieur!*" she acknowledged cheerfully. She then continued down the carriage to canvas and cajole the rest of the passengers. Sasha took a deep breath, relishing in the return of a blissfully serene ambiance.

"Yes. A very, very close call indeed. But I've got it here," he said as the train pulled into the platform at Palais-Royal-Musée-du-Louvre Station. "Right here," he added, patting the pocket of his jeans. The *Métro* car doors flung open.

Wait a second... Sasha patted his now empty pocket. Panic instantly washed over his face. It *had been* right there. Right there with his spare change.

The musician!

The *Métro* buzzer sounded. The doors started closing. Sasha sprang up and leaped out just in the nick of time. He narrowly missed getting his bag caught once again. Teetering to recover his balance, he looked down the platform and over the sea of commuters.

Which way did she go?

People were rushing in every direction creating the effect of a tropical cyclone. His head was spinning, caught in the eye of the storm. Just then he spotted the red beret, bobbing up and down like a buoy in these choppy commuter waters. It floated with the wave of passengers flowing down a tunnel to the right.

Sasha had no choice. He dove into the crowd. He had to reach that musician. He had to retrieve the valuable object that she now had.

Meet Me at the Louvre

"MEET ME AT THE LOUVRE.
AT OUR WORK. 5 PM."

David picked up his bag from the X-Ray machine and walked towards the escalator. It was Wednesday 4:45 pm. The Louvre was open late on Wednesday and Friday evenings, time frames that attracted only a fraction of the crowds that paraded through the world-famous museum during the day. Indeed, as David descended into the vast hall, he noticed only a few patrons milling through the basement level. This airy space was cast in beautiful natural light courtesy of the 673 panels of triangular glass overhead.

Added to commemorate the 200-year anniversary of the first French Revolution, Architect I.M. Pei's controversial Pyramid also served as the new main entrance to the Louvre and created a common entry point to the museum's three wings. Convenient as this was, it didn't help David when he reached the bottom of the escalator. Those three wings spread over 45,000 square meters (53,819 square yards) and contained over 35,000 works of art. Of those thousands of pieces, which 'work' was the cryptic text message referring to and in which wing was it found?

David looked right towards the Denon wing. It was home to most of the museum's blockbuster works. That seemed too predictable. He looked left towards Richelieu. The polar opposite to Denon, it was the museum's least visited wing. Possibly. Then, with determination, he forged straight ahead towards Sully. The Classics. Yes, that made sense.

He bounded up the short staircase leading to the entrance two steps at a time and removed his ID card from his wallet as he approached the ticket control. The museum was free for European nationals under 26 years old. He took off his backwards baseball cap, lowered his protective face mask and presented his ID to the ticket agent who examined the date, compared his face to the younger version on the card, then waved him on.

The Sully wing occupied the oldest sections of the sprawling former palace of the French royals. Therefore, it fittingly contained many of the museum's oldest artworks. After a few short turns, David was surrounded by high stone walls. The Louvre was originally constructed as a fortress to guard the western side of a massive defensive wall that King Philippe Auguste built around the city in the late 12th century. From the early 1500s, this fairytale-like castle was gradually torn down to make way for a new Renaissance palace—one which ended up taking four hundred years to complete. When the Pyramid was added in the 1980s, other large scale projects were also undertaken at the Louvre, including digging up much of the space beneath the palace's courtyards. This was how the impressive remains of the Medieval fortress were rediscovered and subsequently restored.

David now found himself in what was that ancient castle's moat. The space instantly brought back a wave of vivid childhood memories. How many times had he raced down this corridor, imagining what it must have been like back in the Middle Ages? Gazing up at those mammoth towers, he could almost see the valiant knights and archers defending the city from their heights. He also enjoyed hunting down the symbols and initials carved into some of the stones by the workmen who'd built the fortress. This primitive graffiti had left a mark on David in more ways than one.

David followed the walkway around the tall walls until he reached a staircase, which he ascended. A well-preserved Egyptian sphinx stood guard in a fork of the stairs. A left turn would take him to further Pharaonic art, but David turned right. The person he was looking for was more likely in the other section.

At the top of the stairs David found himself amidst a crowd. No, not a hoard of photo-snapping museum-goers, but rather a group of muscular athletes, almighty gods and graceful goddesses. He was in the Department of Greek, Etruscan and Roman Antiquities. Time had not always been kind to these sculptures. Most of them were missing arms, legs, heads or more. The Louvre's most famous 'wounded' work was at the end of the room: the *Venus de Milo*. The refined Greek statue wooed viewers with her delicate perfection and mysterious smile. But instead of returning her grin, David frowned in disappointment. His first hunch turned out to be wrong. The person he was seeking wasn't in front of this 2,100-year-old masterpiece, nor was he anywhere in this entire section.

Our work? Which work?! David huffed. All he'd received was that vague text message. David had tried calling him when he'd arrived at the Pyramid, but the line just rang and rang and finally went to voicemail. His phone was usually on silent mode and even if it wasn't, cell phone reception in certain parts of the museum was patchy, at best. David had no choice but to carry out his search the old-fashioned way; on foot and with his own eyes.

Before leaving the Sully wing, he popped into the Salle des Caryatides. A former royal reception room, it was named after the four female sculptures carved by Jean Goujon in 1550 who appeared to be supporting the musicians' gallery. One could easily imagine a Renaissance ball being held in the elegant room. Today though, gown-clad dancers have been replaced by some of the Louvre's finest Roman copies of Greek sculptures. David knew the person he was looking for immensely loved this room. Despite this, he was nowhere in sight. He was not admiring *Artemis, Goddess of the Hunt,* caught in mid-action, removing an arrow to strike, nor was he marveling at *Sleeping Hermaphroditos,* a dual-sexed mythological character who was resting peacefully in a corner, on an incredibly realistic marble mattress sculpted by Bernini in the 1600s.

Proceeding on his quest, David backtracked and found himself in the long room where the Sully wing merged with the Denon wing. It was home to more sculptures from Antiquity, with an eclectic mix of Herculean gladiators, drunken Bacchuses, selfish emperors and oversized stone vases. These gems of the Antiquities culminated at the top of a grand staircase with the monumental *Winged Victory of Samothrace*. The awe-inspiring heroine was poised as if she was about to take flight. Frozen in stone, she would not reach the summits of Mount Olympus, yet, through her impressive fashioning, she had reached the pinnacle of sculptural arts instead.

At the top of a small set of steps to the right, Botticelli's alluring *Venus and the Three Graces* were beckoning David into the Department of Italian Painting, but before falling to their temptation, he slipped into the Galerie d'Apollon, located on the other side of the *Winged Victory*. He'd read that these opulent rooms had undergone extensive renovations, unveiled just before the lockdown had begun. Now was his chance to see the results of the restoration. Covered from floor to ceiling in gilded carved wood and allegorical paintings created in the 1660s, these sumptuous rooms served as a model for the Hall of Mirrors at Versailles. David was more attracted to these rooms' artistry than to the former royal jewels on display.

Okay, enough with the distractions, David scolded himself. At this rate, he could easily traipse through most of the museum by its closing time and not even find who he was looking for. He circled back past the *Winged Victory,* and snuck a peek at Botticelli's doe-eyed beauties as he breezed past them and entered *la Grande Galerie*.

It was impossible to not be completely awestruck by this astonishingly long and gorgeous gallery. Conceived between 1595 and 1610, it connected the section of the 'new' Louvre palace, dating from the 1520s to 50s, to the Tuileries, which was an entirely separate palace built in the 1560s by Queen Catherine de Medici. The latter building was tragically ravaged by a fire set by the Revolutionaries of the Commune in 1871 and was subsequently torn down. Practically a museum within a museum, *la Grande Galerie* held many of the Louvre's most renowned paintings, namely those by the Italian masters of the 14th to 17th centuries. Giotto, Ghirlandaio, Mantegna, Raphael, Caravaggio… all of them were talented men, but not the one David was on the hunt for.

The most famous Italian painting in the museum was not hanging in this seemingly endless hall of fame, but in a side room. David ducked into this and the first thing he heard was a woman calling out: "Oh look, Mabel! There she is!"

'She' was none other than *La Gioconda*. Known in English as the *Mona Lisa,* Leonardo da Vinci gifted the small portrait, painted on a board of poplar wood, to the French King Francois I before the artist passed away in 1519. Lisa Gherardini, and her enigmatic smile, have been bewitching viewers for over 500 years; however, her fame has been dramatic amplified in recent years thanks to social media. Bypassing the long line of guests waiting to have a close-up look at the painting, David, in fact, quickened his pace to get out of this manic room as soon as possible. Although it was filled with many overlooked masterpieces, David knew the person he sought would not be in here, he was merely using the room as a convenient shortcut to where he might actually be.

David now found himself in an ornately decorated vestibule which, to fully enjoy, one had to look up. Its ceiling was emblazoned with the depictions of four great rulers of France, chosen to represent the country's major art movements: Saint-Louis for the Middle Ages, Francois I for the Renaissance, Louis XIV for the Classic period and Napoléon I for the 'modern' era. On either side of the vestibule were two galleries, each one containing artworks created in that so-called 'modern' era instigated by Bonaparte. That said, 'modern' meant something entirely different to David than these giant paintings. On one side were the emotional Romantic paintings of Théodore Géricault and Eugène Delacroix, like the latter's legendary painting *Liberty Leading the People*, which paid tribute to the second French Revolution of 1830. On the other were the hyper realistic Neoclassical works by Jean-Auguste-Dominique Ingres and Jacques-Louis David, which instead honored the Emperor and Imperial values.

David took a minute to scrutinize his namesake's most acclaimed work, *The Coronation of Napoléon*, an excellent example of both Imperial propaganda and 19th-century Photoshop. Completed in 1807, the work restaged the Emperor's 1804 coronation at Notre-Dame and included certain personalities who weren't in attendance at the actual event, like Napoléon's own mother. The audacious artist even sneaked himself into the work, which is what young David liked most about the enormous painting. This cheeky act had possibly influenced him more than David realized. Since the painting was of personal significance, David had thought he might find his target here. Unfortunately, he wasn't sitting in front of the colossal work, nor was he anywhere else in these two large rooms.

David was starting to get impatient. He doubted he'd find him in Denon's other important sculpture room, the Michelangelo Gallery. As its name indicates, it contained the Louvre's two sculptures by the Italian master, *The Rebellious Slave* and *The Dying Slave*. David knew that his target's favorite Michelangelo sculptures were not at the Louvre, but in museums and churches of Florence and Rome. So there was no point in going to that gallery, even if it did have other wonderful works, like Antonio Canova's incredibly romantic *Psyche Revived by Cupid's Kiss*. David sighed and made his way back to the central foyer so he could access the Richelieu wing.

Despite its lower visitor numbers, Richelieu contained some splendid works. David strode up its entrance stairs, flashed his ID card at the bored ticket agent and went down a dimly lit corridor. He rounded a corner and was suddenly bathed in lovely natural light, similar to what he experienced beneath the Pyramid. He'd arrived in la Cour Marly. The space used to be an outdoor courtyard until it was covered with a glass ceiling during those extensive renovations in the 1980s. The luminous gallery displayed French sculptures from the 17th and 18th centuries originally commissioned for outdoor gardens. The atrium provided the works with a setting akin to their intended homes while also protecting them from the elements. David knew the person he was looking for was extremely fond of the room's star pieces, the *Horses of Marly* by Guillaume Coustou. However, David's thorough check of the room's many nooks was yet another flop.

His frustration was mounting. How was he supposed to miraculously *guess* which work the message had been referring to? He was about to throw in the towel when he had a hunch. *Ah ha!* Which way would be the fastest to get there?

He took the stairs on the left and found himself in the Napoléon III Apartments. Now, David was quite sure his target wouldn't be in these glamorous state apartments designed for this subsequent Emperor's high level entertaining, but he was using them as another useful shortcut. At the end of the series of rooms, opulently decked out in red velour drapery and seating, huge gilded mirrors and dazzling crystal chandeliers, was a staircase going up.

A few minutes later David arrived in the spacious room completely dedicated to the Medici Cycle, 24 paintings by Peter Paul Rubens commissioned by Marie de Medici and depicting the Queen's life and 'struggles.' David shook his head. *Struggles?* What did that queen know about life's difficulties? What did she know about the social problems of the time? He put his grudges and lofty idealism on the side and returned his focus to the room. Even though he personally didn't like the topic of these paintings, David had to admit that Rubens was an amazingly gifted artist. It was a shame, so few visitors made it over to this part of the museum to enjoy these works. And today, this was an even bigger shame... because the person he was looking for was not among the handful of guests who were currently in this room!

David collapsed onto a bench. *Now where?* David gazed helplessly up at the work in front of him. Entitled *The Education of the Princess*, it illustrates how Marie—*supposedly*—received divine education from the gods Apollo, Athena and Hermes. David hadn't received any divine intervention from the multitude of gods he'd passed on today's trek through the museum, that was for sure!

Education. David's eyes traveled to the bottom of the painting where there was a Greek style bust lying on the ground. Something about it spoke to him. No, the person he was looking for hadn't been among those Greek and Roman sculptures. However, there were other sculpted figures throughout the museum... and it was true, one in particular had indeed played a role in David's own education. This line of thinking gave him a new idea. *Of course! Why hadn't I thought of that before?*

David raced out of the room and rushed down a marble staircase. He weaved through more French sculptures, this time from Middle Ages through the Renaissance, and ended up in rooms showcasing the works of ancient Mesopotamia. He skirted past *The Code of Hammurabi* and through the stunning gateway in the Cour Khorsabad, featuring gigantic human-headed winged bulls carved in the 8th century B.C.E.

These were another childhood favorite of David's. The mythical creatures had not only enlivened his imagination, they had also opened his eyes to the world and its many diverse cultures. He actually knew little about his own heritage. His father was a rare pure Parisian, whose ancestors were likely among the troublesome Revolutionaries who'd burned down the Tuileries palace. However, his mom's background was more cosmopolitan. Her great grandfather had been a Senegalese *Tirailleur,* a rifleman who'd fought for France in WWI. Thanks to his sharpshooting skills, he made it through the gruesome war alive. When he was discharged at the end of the War, he decided to stay on in France rather than make the arduous journey home. With each new

THERE'S ONLY *One* PARIS

generation, fewer and fewer stories from 'back home' were passed down. This might be part of the reason David tended to cast aside everything from the past and instead look firmly towards the future.

He sped through a series of rooms containing more pieces recovered from historic sites in the Middle East and entered one filled with fragile artworks protected inside glass cases. Scanning the room, his eyes came to a sudden halt at a case in the far corner. *Bingo!*

David walked towards the case and stopped. He put his hands on his hips and loudly cleared his throat. This succeeded in getting the attention of the man seated in front of him. He turned to face David and his eyes instantly lit up.

"Oh, there you are, David. Better late than never."

"Well, you weren't exactly specific about *where* we were supposed to meet!" David said exasperated.

"I knew you would find me," answered the fifty-something-year-old before returning his gaze to the object in his hands.

"But Dad, I've had to roam through the whole museum in order to find you!" David exclaimed.

"Good, I'm sure the museum was happy to have you back," he replied with a sly smile.

Hey wait a second, thought David, struck by another realization. *Seriously?* This had all been a ploy? Yes. That's exactly what he'd connivingly intended all along. That sneak! David looked back down at his dad. He was sitting on one of those small folding stools, sketchbook in hand.

"I miss the good ol' days, when we used to come sketching together," his dad commented wistfully. "I really wish you hadn't dropped out of art school, David."

"I don't go by David anymore. Remember?? It's D-Zyne now, *Deeee Z-eye-ne*," he corrected. "That place wasn't teaching me anything I couldn't learn on my own. I don't need an institution telling me what is or isn't art. I'm much more creative doing my own style."

"I'm not really sure you can call that spray paint stuff 'art,' but if you insist..." David was noticeably irritated by his dad's reply. Sensing he'd gone a little too far, he added; "But that doesn't matter, I'm just happy to see you."

David's stance was softened by his dad's pale grey eyes. He hadn't seen him since before the lockdown. They'd gotten into a big argument last year when his dad found out David hadn't re-enrolled in art college. But that was last year, a lot had happened since then. Maybe he shouldn't be so hard on him, he meant well after all. That said, David was sick of getting into these art debates with him. His dad was a staunch classicist and David didn't really see the point in copying all this old art. David had swapped oil paints for spray cans and stretched canvases for building walls. For him, street art was real art. Today's art.

"This is where it all started. This is where I first brought you, all those years ago."

David looked at his dad's sketchbook. On the page was a simplistic figure, armless, just like the *Venus de Milo*.

"Maybe you don't remember that far back, you were only three or four. But I wanted to start with the beginning, with this work, the Ain Ghazal statue, the oldest artwork in the Louvre. Can you believe it's 9,000 years old? Although, humans have been using their creativity and making art for much longer than that; since the dawn of time. We can move forward into the future, David, but we should never forget the past."

As much as he'd done it begrudgingly, David had to admit, he'd actually enjoyed his trek through the museum. It brought back so many memories and at the same time had also reminded him why he'd become an artist; why he'd followed in his father's footsteps. It was nice to be back... and it was nice to see his dad. So much of humanity had stood the test of time. David felt as invincible as those gladiators and the other heroes he'd just viewed. However, he was not invincible, and his dad was even less so. Even if they didn't agree on what constituted art, it could still bring them closer together once again.

"Next time I could bring another sketchbook and folding stool? I was thinking of some Greek art. How about the *Venus de Milo*? Are you free next Wednesday, same time?"

"I'll think about it," David replied, not wanting to sound too keen. "But if I do come, don't be expecting me to change my style or anything."

"Fair enough," replied his dad, extended the pencil in his outstretched hand. David shook it. This substitute handshake sealed the deal.

David looked down at his dad's drawing and then back up at Ain Ghazal statue. Damaged by time and the elements, it was modern in its own way.

This got the wheels turning in David's head. *Perhaps the new and old could coexist?*

In Search of Lost Time at the Palais-Royal and Galerie Vivienne

Although it varied slightly depending on the time of the year, the colonnade's series of repeating shadows always slanted in the same direction in the morning. Capucine preferred to see this sight, one she'd taken in daily for the last 30 odd years, in this particular light.

Well, almost daily. If it were raining cats and dogs, she'd forgo her morning ritual. And there were those few short holidays she and Robert had taken, once to the French Riviera (too hot), and another to Belgium (too cold). Well, then there were all those months at the hospital, but she didn't like thinking about them.

It took exactly 262 steps to get there. One day she'd counted. 262 steps from the door of her apartment, down the stairs (luckily, she only lived on the second floor), along Rue de la Banque, right into the Galerie Vivienne, then to the left to reach Rue Croix-des-Petits-Champs. She would then have to wait for a gap in the steady stream of traffic so she could cross over and duck into the hidden Passage des Deux Pavillons. She then had to go down its set of steps, across quiet Rue de Beaujolais, and through the iron gate, minding the little step, which was worn down in a gentle curve after centuries of foot traffic.

A further eight steps would take her to the Galerie Beaujolais, the northernmost covered arcade of the Palais-Royal. On a grey day the play of light was less remarkable, but on this late September day, the soft morning sunlight created a domino effect cascading down the full length of the passageway. However, just because she'd entered le Jardin du Palais-Royal, it didn't mean she'd arrived at her final destination. She still had 27 more steps to go.

Originally built in the 1630s for Cardinal Richelieu, King Louis XIII's prime minister, the Palais-Royal was expanded over the years, particularly in the late 1700s when the regal residence's private gardens were boxed in by buildings and these columned arcades. Visiting the tranquil space today, one could hardly imagine it was once the bustling heart of Parisian shopping and entertainment, which had since shifted to around the Opéra Garnier.

Struck by the sun's rays, Capucine squinted as she stepped into the enclosed gardens. After some initial trial and error, she'd come to the conclusion that 11 am was the perfect time of day to come. This would spare her the lunchtime sandwich eaters, the mid-afternoon kids let loose from school and the *apéro* hour *pétanque* players (French 'bocce ball').

The only time of year when the pretty park was uncharacteristically busy in the morning, was late winter when the magnolia blossoms popped out. But this was a relatively new phenomenon. In recent years during that two-week period she'd noticed a considerable upswing of people, fancy 'smartphones' in hand, taking an absurd amount of photos. She didn't really understand what all the fuss was about. When the subject had come up last year during one of the few conversations she had with fellow park-goers, apparently those thousands of photos went onto a thing called 'Instagrin' or something like that. Anyway, the oohing and aahing photographers usually descended upon the park in the afternoon, so she wasn't all that bothered by this brief invasion.

Five steps from her destination, suddenly Capucine froze. There was something seriously wrong.

There was *someone* on her bench.

She stood there, as rigid as the manicured trees which lined the garden. Her already squinting eyes were reduced to tiny arrow hole slits through which she was launching a barrage of poisonous evil eyes. Her defensive efforts seemed to have absolutely no effect on the abominable 'invader.'

After what seemed like an eternity, the intruder finally noticed Capucine.

"*Bonjour Madame!*" he greeted her cheerfully.

Capucine intensified her war stance.

"Would you like to take a seat?" suggested the young man, looking over at the rest of the bench. There was clearly ample room on it for this little old lady, much more than the meter required with the new social distancing rules. Nevertheless, he slid over to the very edge of the bench and made a 'Vanna White' arm gesture, matched with an equally gleaming smile, over at the vast space available to her. Capucine didn't budge.

"What a lovely day!" he said as he loudly inhaled the crisp morning air. "The park is splendid in autumn, don't you think?"

No! Capucine thought. *It isn't splendid at all with this obtrusive man on my bench!*

"I almost prefer the park at this time of year," he continued nonchalantly. "Springtime is also nice, however, in the past few years the magnolia blossoms have been attracting way too many people!"

"I couldn't agree more!" The statement popped out of her mouth before she realized what had happened. She couldn't 'consort' with the enemy!

"What's the point of taking all those photographs, when you can sit here, on this lovely bench, and simply savor their beauty," he said with another wave of his arm, this time up in the air from his seated vantage point. Capucine couldn't help but follow his gesture up towards those magnolia branches. It was true, her bench was perfectly positioned to enjoy them and, actually, the whole north end of the park.

Capucine scrunched up her toes. Even if she was going just 'to the park,' she still wore her pumps. She was only meant to walk 262 steps, then she would be sitting down. Standing on these uneven pebbles was not part of her usual routine! She took a few steps forward in order to relieve her cramped toes.

"Have you noticed that the leaves on the chestnut trees are starting to turn?" he went on, pointing up at the branches, seemingly oblivious to Capucine's displeasure and discomfort.

She turned around to check, but with her bad knees she wasn't able to crouch down enough to get the right angle. She had no choice but to sit down on the bench so she could see what he was referring to.

"No, those aren't chestnut trees, they're lindens," she corrected.

"Ah okay, thank you!" he said without acknowledging that Capucine had finally sat down next to him. "I grew up in an apartment, so I don't know my trees very well."

"So did I, but it's something you can learn," she said curtly.

"Yes, that's true," he replied thoughtfully. "Like the saying goes: 'we can learn something new every day'!"

"I suppose so, but once you pass 80, those little details don't seem to matter much anymore."

"Eighty?! But *Madame*, you don't look a day over 65!" he proclaimed sincerely. She pretended not to be flattered, however, her glacial frown was defrosting and her dagger eyes had retreated.

"My name's Lucas," he took the liberty of introducing himself.

"Lucas?" she questioned. "I assumed your name would be... different."

"Born and raised in *la Region Parisienne, Madame...*"

"Madame Dubois."

"Madame Dubois, *enchanté!* It's a pleasure to meet you!"

34

Well, at least he had good manners despite growing up in the suburbs, Capucine thought to herself.

"Do you work in a restaurant around here or something?" she asked, nodding her head in the direction of the two Michelin-starred establishments on the north side of the park.

"No, no. I'm quite fond of Le Grand Véfour, but I don't work in the restaurant business," replied Lucas, unfazed by her presumptuous question. "I actually run a bookshop."

"You run a bookshop?" she said, surprised yet trying not to seem too interested.

"Yes, it's nearby. I needed some fresh air, so I came to the park for a short break."

"Which bookshop?" she quizzed. "I've lived here in the district since, well, since long before you were born... in *la Region Parisienne.*"

"You'll surely know it then," replied Lucas. "*A La Recherche du Temps Perdu*, the bookshop at the end of the Galerie Vivienne."

"*A La Recherche du Temps Perdu?*" she repeated, taken aback. "Yes, I know it. I know it very well." she added after a moment of silence. Capucine turned her gaze back towards the garden. *A La Recherche du Temps Perdu.* In Search of Lost Time. That's what Capucine now spent most of her days doing.

***

It had been hard losing Robert. They'd been married for 51 years. Even though he hadn't been overly affectionate, he was a good man. He'd spent his whole career working at the Central Post Office, a colossal building located a few blocks away. As a *fonctionnaire*, a French civil servant, he qualified for an HLM, *un habitation à loyer modéré*, a state sponsored apartment with low rent, otherwise they would never have been able to afford to live where they did, right in the heart of the city.

They'd had a simple, yet happy life. They had two kids, a boy and a girl. They were both good students. They went to university, got jobs, got their own apartments, got married... got on with their own lives.

After their children moved out, although Capucine still had the household to manage and meals to prepare, she suddenly had a lot more time on her hands. She ended up occupying these extra hours with reading, a new passion which came about rather by accident.

She usually did her errands along la Rue Croix-des-Petits-Champs, where one could find a bakery, greengrocer's, butcher's and other small shops. To reach it, she would always take the shortcut through the Galerie Vivienne, the same route she would later take to the Palais-Royal Garden. However, one morning, it must have been in 1988 or 1989, she had an appointment close to the Opéra Garnier, so instead of turning left down the main section of the Galerie Vivienne, she turned right.

Admittedly, she knew there were some other stores at the far end of the early 19th-century shopping gallery, but since she rarely went that way, she'd hardly given them any notice. As she reached the end of the passageway and descended its small staircase, her purse caught something resulting in a loud clatter behind her.

Whipping around Capucine was mortified to see a dozen or so books strewn across the Galerie's beautiful mosaic-tiled floor.

"*Mon dieu!*" she exclaimed, bending down to pick up the books.

"Please, don't trouble yourself!" called a man's voice from inside the shop. "Let me get those."

In an instant the owner of the voice swooped down to collect the fallen books. As she looked up, Capucine's gaze met a set of piercing blue eyes, hovering a mere few inches away from her own.

"I'm terribly sorry," said Capucine, her cheeks flaring as she hopped up and turned away in an attempt to mask her embarrassment. "If I damaged any of the books, I would happily pay for them."

"There won't be any need for that, *Madame*," he assured her. "These are used books which have already been knocked about a

good deal during their lifetime. They only cost a few francs each...
but the entertainment they provide is priceless."

Capucine dared let her eyes meandered over to the stack of
books in his hands. The title *Au Bonheur des Dames* jumped out at
her.

"Ahh, a classic Zola!" enthused the bookseller, noticing her
shifting gaze to the cover of *The Ladies' Delight.*

"How much is it?" she asked.

"Eight francs," he replied upon checking the amount written in
pencil inside the front cover. Capucine rummaged through her
handbag. She pulled out her change purse, but was dismayed to
find that it contained only a few *centimes.*

"I'm afraid I only have large notes on me, but I live nearby, I
will come back another time for the book."

"Please, take it now!" he implored, forcing the book into her
hands. "Someone else might have bought it by the time you return.
You can pay for it the next time you're passing this way."

"But, but, but..."

"I insist!"

"That's very kind of you, Mr..."

"Swann, Mr Swann," he answered.

"Very well, Mr Swann, *à très bientôt.* See you very soon," she
said, then she gave a courteous nod and carried on her way.

"With pleasure, *Madame.* With pleasure!"

That very afternoon Capucine dove into the book. The hours
flew by as she devoured Zola's riveting prose. It took the fading
afternoon light to startle her out of her literary trance. Robert
would be home soon, she'd better get down to making dinner. The
time-consuming *boeuf bourguignon* she'd intended on making
would have to wait for another night.

The next day she couldn't resist returning to her book, but she
immediately felt guilty. *I should really go and pay Mr Swann for it,*
she thought. Capucine didn't like having debts. Before sliding on
her coat and pumps, she found herself in front of her dressing
table, applying some lipstick, sprucing up her hair and spritzing on

a dash of perfume. *Was this really necessary to go around the block... to a bookstore?* She called herself out. *Well, it never hurts to be at one's best.*

Capucine couldn't explain it, but her heart rate quickened as she walked under the passageway's glass roof in the direction of the shop. Yesterday she'd been too flustered to see what it was called, so when she arrived in front of the bookstore, she craned her neck up at its sign: *A La Recherche du Temps Perdu*. Even someone not very literarily minded, like herself, knew the title of Marcel Proust's epic seven-volume saga, obviously the inspiration for the shop's name.

The little tinkle of the bells hanging on the door handle announced Capucine's arrival.

"*Ah! Bonjour Madame!*" Mr Swann greeted, raising his head from a book. "How nice to see you again so soon!" Capucine blushed. She glanced around the shop in an effort to avoid Mr Swann's sparkling eyes. All around her were hundreds if not thousands of books. The ones that lined the upper bookshelves had worn leather spines, these must be the more precious ones. Whereas on the tables and in the bins were the used, modern paperbacks.

"I hope you are enjoying the Zola," he said, regaining Capucine's attention.

"Oh yes, it's an excellent book, which I must duly pay you for," she said. She pulled out her change purse and placed precisely eight francs on the counter.

"Thank you for your promptness," he said, putting the money in the till. "Isn't it a lovely day?"

"Why, yes. Now that you mention it, spring is decidedly in the air," replied Capucine, trying to remain formal.

"You could take your book to the park," suggested Mr Swann.

"That isn't a bad idea," reflected Capucine. Le Jardin du Palais-Royal was so close, yet she hadn't spent much time there since the children were little. Tucked away within those buildings it was so quiet, plus it had plenty of benches. It was the ideal setting to read in peace while also enjoying the balmy weather.

"Be sure to come back when you need a new book, *Madame*..." Mr Swann's sentence trailing off as he fished for her name.

"Madame Dubois."

"Happy reading, Madame Dubois!"

And so began Capucine's daily trips to le Palais-Royal. She always went at 11 am and always sat on the same bench, the one which she had carefully staked out. While Robert was still working, these outings were reserved for Monday to Friday, however, when he retired she added on the weekend. She only shortened her Sunday sessions if the kids and their families were coming over for lunch. Even when she babysat her grandchildren during their school holidays, she kept up her routine, bringing them along with her to play in the park while she read, always with a watchful eye in their direction.

Her voracious new appetite for literature needed to be fed and Capucine could be found at least once a week at *A La Recherche du Temps Perdu*. She continued to remain cordially formal to Mr Swann, but her fondness for him was growing with her rapidly expanding collection of books.

Of course this 'crush' was absurd. She was a married woman, after all. She loved Robert and was entirely faithful, nevertheless, she couldn't debate Camus with him. Mr Swann had first turned her to literature and then succeeded in broadening her scope. After a few years, Capucine slowly left behind Hugo, Sand and Flaubert to enter the 20th century.

"With all the time you're spending in le Palais-Royal, it's really high time you read some Colette!" declared Mr Swann many years later.

"Why is that?"

"The writer lived in le Palais-Royal, I think in the 1920s," Mr Swann elaborated. "She wrote about it in her book *Trois... Six... Neuf*."

"Do you have it in stock?"

"Let me take a look," he said, scanning his tables. By now Capucine knew how the shop's collections were organized, but she secretly loved how Mr Swann's face transformed as he concentrated, brow furrowed, in search of a particular title.

"You're in luck!" he beamed, producing a worn book with curled page corners.

Six...Neuf. Six.... Nine. No, these specific numbers had brought no 'luck' at all to Capucine. When she turned 69, her husband, then 72, was diagnosed with cancer. Despite his prognosis, he remained upbeat. It was now the 21st century! They had fancy new treatments these days. The doctors would surely be able to help him. And they did. For a time.

Naturally, during Robert's health concerns Capucine put her hobby on hold. When Robert went into remission after his first chemo treatments, he seemed strong enough for Capucine to have some time for herself, nonetheless, she couldn't bear to go to the bookshop. Not now.

Sadly though, eight months later Robert's condition had worsened and he was admitted to the hospital. Things weren't looking good and any veils of optimism had been pushed aside.

"Read to me," murmured Robert after they'd spent the first few days in painful silence, save for the regular visits of the overly perky nurses.

"Excuse me?" Capucine asked, puzzled by his request.

"Read to me," he said, raising his voice to a more audible level. "Why don't you read me one of those books you always have your nose in."

And so they spent the next five weeks in the company of *The Count of Monte Cristo*, *Le Père Goriot* and *The Hunchback of Notre-Dame*. Robert took his last breaths during *Les Misérables*, Capucine by his side, like Cosette was to Jean Valjean.

***

One day, in the weeks that followed, Capucine found a small, thick package in her mailbox. As she carefully opened it, a book and folded letter slid out.

Chère Madame Dubois,
Une pensée pour vous. / A little thought for you.
~ C. Swann

She turned over the book to read its title: *Voyage au bout de la nuit. Journey to the End of the Night* by Céline.

News of Robert's passing must have spread around *le quartier*. Although it had never been discussed, she was quite sure she'd caught Mr Swann looking down at her left hand on one of her first visits to the shop. He therefore knew she was married and never made any advances, despite the spark that continued to flicker between them. She was touched by his thoughtful gesture, but she was not ready to fill her heart with her favorite pleasure, anything or *anyone* else, just yet.

***

"Madame Dubois, it's been ages!" exclaimed Mr Swann when he looked up to find Capucine at the door of his shop. "I've been worried about you!"

Almost a year had gone by since Robert's diagnosis and her last visit to the shop. Although Capucine wasn't finished mourning, she had finally got around to Mr Swann's touching gift, which reignited her desire to read.

This didn't mean she was completely ready to go back to living. She took her time. Now and then, Mr Swann's passionate descriptions of the book he was encouraging her to read brought a look of joy to Capucine's face. On another visit, she even laughed. The two of them seemed to be getting closer and closer, however, as the years passed, neither took that extra step in the other's direction. No invitation for lunch or coffee. No suggestion to meet up at *her* bench in the Palais-Royal.

***

"Mr Swann is missed by many," Capucine eventually managed to say after several minutes staring at the linden trees.

"Yes, he was a fine man," said Lucas. "His sudden death was a shock to us all."

"The worst was not being able to say goodbye," added Capucine, somewhat misty-eyed. Capucine had been one of the lucky ones, one of the few elderly who'd not been hit by the virus. Her children had forced her to stay indoors and had even arranged to have groceries and the occasional meal delivered right to her door. She'd terribly missed her outings to the park and to *A La Recherche du Temps Perdu*, but knew it was in her best interest to stay home. Mr Swann, who couldn't be kept from his beloved shop, even if it was not open during the lockdown, did not meet the same fate.

"You know, I think I remember seeing you in the shop once," said Lucas.

"Oh really?" she answered dubiously.

"I did a three-month internship with Mr Swann while I was working on my Master's," explained Lucas. "It must have been five or six years ago. My uncle's a Tunisian poet, so I had started doing my dissertation on poetry, however, during my time at the shop, Mr Swann slyly converted me to 20th-century French literature. In the mornings I spent my time researching at the library and in the afternoons I worked at the bookshop. One day I arrived early, actually around this time of day. Mr Swann was so enraptured in conversation that he didn't even notice me come in. He was talking to a smartly dressed woman, about your height, who was holding a copy of Marguerite Duras's *The Lover*."

The memory hit Capucine as hard as Quasimodo ringing the bells of Notre-Dame.

Yes. At one point, around five years ago, Mr Swann *had* tried to drop stronger hints of his admiration. This was done in true Mr Swann style, through a series of 'romantic' book suggestions which culminated in Duras' *The Lover*. Mr Swann had just finished a fervent introduction to the book and was about to say something else, something that seemed important to him, when he was interrupted by a cough coming from the direction of the shop's entrance. Mr Swann and Capucine swung around to find a young man standing meekly at the door and the moment was lost. Forever.

Capucine was indeed extremely fond of Mr Swann, but she really didn't know how to handle the situation. She didn't know if she was capable of loving him, of loving anyone but Robert. So she avoided the shop for a few weeks and when she did return, Mr Swann pretended as if nothing had ever happened.

"It was during my internship that I got to know Mr Swann and fall in love with his shop," said Lucas.

"It's good to know his memory and his shop will live on, through you," said Capucine. "You seem like a fine young man." She added, the hostility she unrightfully displayed to him at the beginning of their encounter had vanished.

"I will do my best," he pledged. "The shop has stayed pretty much the same, but I've expanded with some non-fiction and some art books. We've just received a great new release on women artists of the 19th century, in case the topic could be of interest."

"No, thank you. I think I'll stick to literature."

"Well, we definitely have plenty of that, so I expect to see you soon!"

Capucine gazed around her park. Maybe the leaves on the linden trees were turning. She thought about the 262 steps it took to get here, and the 148 steps it took to get to the shop. She had spent too much precious energy, these past months, these past years, in search of lost time. She could not rewrite the volumes of her life, but she could turn over a new page.

"With pleasure, Lucas, with pleasure."

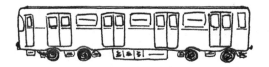

Le Métro

3rd & 4th Arrondissements & the Seine

Ah ha! There she is.

Sasha could see her red beret bouncing through the crowd up ahead. He just needed to catch up with her. Then he'd calmly explain that something incredibly important had been amongst the coins he'd just tossed into her pouch. Heck. If she seemed reluctant to give it back, he was more than willing to give her some extra money in exchange for it. Anything she wanted. The object she had was priceless.

She hopped up a staircase to reach the platform of Line 1. He wasn't that far behind her, however, she spryly reached the top of the steps well before he'd even set foot on the bottom. Her agility was certainly in part owing to her youth, but also in part thanks to all the time she must spend in the *Métro*. It wasn't like Sasha was very old, he just didn't take the *Métro* nearly as much as he used to. His current fatigue also slowed him down.

When he was halfway up the stairs, Sasha heard an all too familiar sound—the whooshing of an approaching Line 1 train.

Darn! Sasha cursed. He'd been hoping to catch the musician before she got on the next train and started playing again. He scrambled to get to the top of the steps. A sleek, modern train soared past his line of sight. It sent a gust of air down the stairs, making it even harder to climb up the last few steps. Sasha reached the platform as the green and white train came to a smooth halt at the far end. This was roughly where he spotted the musician and her red beret. *Boy, she was fast!*

Sasha knew he wouldn't have time to reach her, especially since so many commuters had disembarked onto the platform and were now blocking his way. However, he wasn't too worried. Line 1 trains weren't divided up into carriages, like the older trains found on many of the other lines, including Line 7, the line they'd just been on. Sasha could walk all the way through the train to reach the musician 'entertaining' at the other end.

The doors snapped shut and the train set off, the force of which sent Sasha shuffling back a few steps. He grabbed hold of a pole to steady himself. With his two feet now firmly on the floor of the train, he tried to take his first step forward. Gravity would have it otherwise. *Geez! This was like trekking through the Sahara during a windstorm!* Maybe it was going to be trickier to walk through the train to reach her than Sasha'd previously imagined.

By the time he made it past the first section of seats, he was getting the hang of this 'desert walking.' Sasha looked on ahead. Sure enough there she was. The musician, whom he likened as a *petite* Piaf, was singing her heart out at the front of the train.

"Louvre-Rivoli — Louvre-Rivoli," announced the automatic recording as they neared the next station. The train's speed suddenly reduced. Sasha was thrown backwards, skimming a nearby Spanish-speaking couple holding souvenir bags from the Louvre. He regained his footing when the train stopped at the platform. Sasha was about to take another step forward when the doors flung open and a boisterous group of school children piled on. They were around nine or ten years old and were clutching art activity booklets. Like the Spaniards, they too must have just been at the Louvre.

As much as he thought fostering a love of art in children was a good thing, these museum-going kiddos had created a wide barricade ahead of Sasha. They were children. He was not comfortable pushing past them. Plus, with everyone being attentive to social distancing, his quest was made all the more difficult.

The next station was Châtelet, a much dreaded, yet incredibly useful station. Five of Paris's 16 *Métro* lines and three of its five *RER* lines (the Réseau Express Régional, suburban trains) met at the twin Châtelet-Les-Halles Station. This made it not only Paris's largest subway station, but the largest subway interchange station in the world. A whopping 750,000 travelers passed through it every weekday.

As they neared the station, Sasha had two simultaneous, but contrasting, wishes: that the kids would get off there and that the singer would **not** get off. It would be virtually impossible to find her if she got a head start into this station's insane maze of tunnels which somehow connected all those different *Métro* and *RER* lines. As they stopped at Châtelet, one of his wishes came true. The other did not. The musician was still on the train, but so were the kids.

The train hurtled on. Sasha tried to shimmy around the excitable students and their order-shouting teachers. He'd made little progress by the time the train pulled up to the next station, Hôtel-de-Ville. Outside of this station was Paris's central city hall, which governed all of the 20 arrondissements. Notre-Dame Cathedral was also not far. He highly doubted the students would be getting off here, they didn't look like they were on an all-day sightseeing trip of the city.

"There's only one Paris...!" Sasha could vaguely hear Petite Piaf's words above the brouhaha of the school group.

The train pursued on its journey east. Above their heads were the beautiful, tranquil streets of the Marais, so much calmer than where Sasha was currently stuck. After Saint-Paul Station the train's speed slowed and the track curved. They were approaching Bastille Station. *Could the rambunctious kids get off there, please?* Sasha silently begged.

This time it looked like his wishes would be granted... or at least one of them.

As the kids' chaotically tumbled off the train at Bastille, so did the singer. In a flash, she darted into a stairwell that was right in front of her.

Noooo! cried Sasha, unable to believe his misfortune. He instinctively jumped off the train and managed to skirt past the students while their teachers were herding them together. He jetted down the stairs. Bastille Station had two other lines. *Which one was she heading for?*

Sasha barreled down the steps and rounded a corner. Where was that red beret? The performer could have taken a variety of passageways. Straight ahead was a long corridor that led to Bastille's two other lines, numbers 5 and 8. That would make the most sense. But just as he was about to join the flock of other commuters heading that way, something colorful caught his eye to the left. It bopped down some steps. *The red beret!*

There was no signage above the stairwell, so it must be the exit staircase for a platform. When commuters took certain *Métro* lines frequently, they eventually got to know these shortcuts. Sure enough, as Sasha descended the steps, he found himself on the southbound platform of Line 5. On any other day he would have been tempted to take the short detour over to the other platform to have a look at the historic details it contained. Beneath some information panels were large stones marking the former location of la Bastille. The rest of the stones of the formidable fortress and symbol of the first French Revolution had long since disappeared from the site. As fascinating as these were, today Sasha had no time for such leisurely pursuits.

As he was craning his neck up to see where the musician had gone, he heard the screeching tires of the train. A moment later it rounded the corner and came into the station. *Darn!* Petite Piaf had already make it far down the platform. He'd hop onto the train wherever it pulled up. Like Line 1, the number 5 also had newer trains without separate carriages. Despite this similarity, Line 5 didn't seem to go as fast as the driverless, automatic number 1.

With the practice he'd done on the previous train, Sasha was confident he could catch up to her rather quickly this time around. The train journeyed beneath the southern Marais. Sasha didn't waste any time. He immediately set off down the train in the direction of the musician. Sasha's confidence was further bolstered by the virtually empty train. *Excellent!* He should reach her, if not at the next station, certainly by the following one. In fact, he'd already walked through almost a quarter of the train and now he could make out some of the words to her signature song.

"Il n'y a qu'un seul Paris..."

The train started climbing and soon they were above ground at the Quai de la Rapée Station. Sitting in an obscure location right on the banks of the Seine River, it was certainly one of the least frequented stations on the *Métro*'s vast network of 302 stations. Just as the doors next to Sasha were about to close, two long pointy objects entered the train. Two athletic types followed, hopping onto the train just as the doors slammed shut behind them. *Rowers?* There must be a rowing club somewhere nearby down on the River's banks. Proud of being able to catch that train, the two sportsmen gave each other a 'high five' with their oars. *There's nothing celebratory about this!* thought Sasha angrily. How was he supposed to get around this new obstacle?

The *Métro* left the station and sailed along an iron bridge high above the water. Sasha would have normally enjoyed looking out at the pretty view one could admire on this stretch of Line 5, however, he was too busy trying to navigate his way around the rowers. When they saw him approaching, they clumsily tried to move their gigantic oars at the same time, this only made matters worse. The oars were caught in bars of the *Métro* pole! Sasha felt like he was stuck in the middle of a jousting match!

While this skirmish was still very much underway, the train arrived at Austerlitz Station. Although he was busy battling it out with the cavalier rowers, Sasha noticed something red hopping off the train. *Why was she getting off here?!* There weren't many people on the train, perhaps she hadn't made much money on her first song?

Sasha struggled to escape the lance-oars. He broke free and luckily got off the train just before the doors slammed shut. He spotted the red beret capering down some steps.

Where could she be going now?

Coup(e) de Chance in the Upper Marais

— FERMÉ —

Jane stared at the closed sign in disbelief. Her eyes then descended to the other sign posted on the door. This listed the shop's opening hours as Tuesday to Friday 2 pm to 7 pm, Saturday 10 am to 1 pm and 2 pm to 7 pm. It was 2:45 pm on a Thursday, so the shop should technically be open.

Jane suppressed her mounting fear by reminding herself that this was France after all. The French had a more lenient approach to fixed hours—and to rules in general for that matter. In fact, the first time Jane had visited the shop it was also closed, but everything had worked out in the end.

She cupped her hands around her eyes and peered in through the window. Yes, it was indeed still 'her' shop. She had to admit, she'd been worried about it since the outbreak of the pandemic. So many businesses had been affected by it. Many had, or still might, close down. Would her absolute favorite shop of all time, on the whole entire planet, manage to survive?

Her eyes traveled up past the dreaded *Fermé* sign and stopped on a pink sticky note attached to the other side of the glass. '*De retour bientôt*' it announced in quick, but tidy handwriting. *Retour* was very close to the English word 'return,' and Jane knew that the expression *à bientôt* meant 'see you soon,' so based on this reasoning, she deducted that the shop owner was out on an errand or other business and would be back soon. *Whew!* False alarm. She could easily occupy herself for a half an hour or so and return *bientôt*. The shop was in the heart of the beautiful Marais district and Jane always liked going for a stroll in the neighborhood after she first stopped in at 'her shop.' Today, this meander would just have to be before.

One of the oldest areas of Paris, the Marais had thankfully escaped the wrecking ball which destroyed vast swaths of the city to make way for the new designs for the capital imagined by Emperor Napoléon III and Baron Georges-Eugène Haussmann, the Prefect of Paris, in the mid-19th century. Most of this urban planning was focused around the Opéra Garnier and western Paris. Jane headed down the street she was currently on, Rue Barbette, and took Rue Payenne south. Like most of the streets in the Marais, these were lined with elegant mansions constructed from the mid-1500s to early 1700s, when the area was popular with Parisian high society. A number of these had been converted into museums, however, some were still private residences, either as individual homes or sectioned up into apartments.

Jane loved contemplating who once and who currently lived in these elegant homes, like the ivy ladened building she'd just stopped to admire. Hidden behind large stone walls, the mansion was certainly built for an aristocrat, perhaps even a count or a duchess. The French Revolution would have put an end to their ownership and, sadly, over the course of the 19th century many were converted into workshops. By the time the mid-20th century had come around, much of the area was in such a dismal state that these historic homes started to be torn down. Fortunately, in the early 1960s this tragic destruction was halted by the Minister of Culture, André Malraux, who safe-guarded the district. It was gradually cleaned up and, as they advanced into the 21st century, the Marais had once again risen in prominence and was now one of the poshest neighborhoods in the city.

A window was open on the second floor of the building. Jane crossed the street so she could get a better look. She reckoned it was the apartment's living room as she could see a wooden-beamed ceiling, a sizeable crystal chandelier and a gilded mirror in the background. Catching sight of these items was all it took for Jane's imagination to start running wild. What other beautiful objects could this apartment contain? It was this passion for antiques and curiosities that kept Jane coming back to Paris time and time again.

***

Jane had had a lifetime love affair with second-hand shopping. This had begun during her childhood as her grandmother and her friends held 'garage sales' to make money for their church to feed those in need in Kansas City. The items for sale came from donations from church members and neighbors. It just so happened that her grandmother, who lived only a block away from her own house, had the only garage in the group and therefore it was in it that the objects for their frequent sales were stored.

Every time there was a sale, young Jane would spend hours carefully perusing the donated wares. She was fascinated by all the different types of clothing and accessories in these donations. Seeing her avid interest, her mom and grandmother would give her a few coins to purchase a couple of items at each sale. Her spirited eyes would literally sparkle as she examined the wide array of objects, especially foreign ones, which she would not have otherwise been exposed to. Where had they come from? What were they used for? What was the story behind each object? Jane's curiosity had been irreversibly piqued.

Passing her driving test was a particularly important milestone. This achievement meant that Jane could then travel to sales further afield. She discovered tag sales, flea markets and estate auctions. At each one she was always keen to seek out the best bargains. When she moved out of her family's home, got her first place and was a young professional on a budget, she found many used household items at these sales that could be re-purposed or painted to look brand new, all for next to nothing.

When she started earning a good salary, she used her extra income to travel; first to the Caribbean Islands, then to the Far East and Europe. No matter the destination, she was always 'on the hunt' for antique stores and flea markets. This was how she developed her love for her favorite European city: Paris.

She was simply glowing during her first visit to Les Puces de Saint Ouen, the sprawling flea market on the edge of Paris. The largest second-hand and antiques market in the world, Jane was like a kid in a candy shop browsing its never-ending stands. As much as she loved the vast bazaar-like market, it was on her third or fourth trip to Paris that she first went to *her* shop.

As she was traveling more and more, Jane also began reading an increasing number of travel guides and magazines to inspire her future trips. In one publication a specific article caught her eye. It was about a small shop in Paris called *Coup(e) de Chance*. From the photo included with the article, it looked like just the sort of place she'd adore. Jane carefully clipped out the article and saved it for her next trip to Paris.

Jane was curious about what the name meant so she took out her French-English dictionary. After some digging, she figured out that it translated as 'a stroke of good luck', however, the 'e' in brackets created a double meaning. By adding an 'e' to the end of the word *coup* it becomes *coupe*, as in a champagne coupe or glass. This gave a little hint towards the sort of goods sold in the shop. The name also perfectly embodied the experience of second-hand shopping, the best finds always came by a stroke of good luck.

It must have been nine or ten years ago now, nevertheless, Jane remembered that first visit like it was yesterday. She unfolded the clipping from her pocket to double check the address written in tiny block letters at the end of the article. Yes, she was on the right street, Rue Barbette in the 3rd arrondissement, but when she arrived at #7 (lucky number 7!), she was confronted with a darkened shop front. She cupped her hands around her eyes and peered in through the window. Yes, it was a spitting image of the photo in the magazine clipping. She leaned back and examined the door, that's when she noticed the *Fermé* sign.

It was a Monday. It would take Jane a few more trips to Paris before it stuck in her mind that some shops were closed on Mondays if they were open on the weekend. Being small, these boutiques were usually staffed solely by the owner, who needed at least one day off per week. Jane was certainly disappointed at seeing the closed sign after the months of her building anticipation over visiting this particular shop. She'd just arrived in Paris and could come back the next day—and make sure it would be within the hours listed on the small placard beneath the closed sign.

The next day she arrived shortly after the advertised opening time. As soon as she set foot inside, it was love at first sight. Although the shop was quite small, it was overflowing with wonderful objects. Jane was in awe as she admired the neatly arranged shelves of French country kitchenware, linens, home décor items and school supplies. It was a quirky combination of things that somehow worked together. Jane wasn't sure quite how long she'd been in there. She was lost in her thoughts and it took some time to see everything that was on display. The space was packed to the brim and its layout encouraged customers to wander around and around, poking through the piles. This was nothing new to Jane. She was truly in her element. She loved deciding which items she would purchase—which honestly would be all of them if she could have her way. Unfortunately, she was hampered somewhat by the fact that whatever she bought had to travel across the Atlantic in her bags. As she gained more experience from each trip, she became very adept at packing light so she would have room for all the purchases she made during her travels.

She distinctly remembered the items she bought on that first trip to her shop. Among these were two kitchen towels, some coffee pots, three *allumette* (match) holders and a small mirror.

She just loved the aesthetic of the old-fashioned metal coffee pots, simple yet elegant. The *allumette* holders sparked her collection of matchboxes she would pick up on her travels around the world (and for free no less!). The small mirror was decorated with a group of children launching sailboats on a lake in a mountain scene which was reminiscent of the toy sailboats that could be rented in some Parisian parks. Whenever Jane would look at these splendid objects, she would be transported virtually to Paris, and to her shop. Her collection of French items grew with each visit, yet she was always eager for her next visit and for the new treasures she would acquire.

Unfortunately, this year she would not be able to come in April, as she usually did. The pandemic kept her away from her beloved Paris and from her cherished shop. However, as soon as she was able to, which was September, she booked her trip. She didn't care if she had to do a virus test a few days before flying out, it was worth it.

In the end, coming in fall wasn't such a bad thing as she'd recently read that it was a popular time for *vide greniers*. Literally translated as 'attic emptying,' these neighborhood sidewalk sales allowed Parisians to sell their used odds and ends and were the closest thing in France to North American yard sales. The autumn was also good for *brocantes*. Run by professionals, these street sales were a step up from *vide greniers*, and were, in essence, mobile flea markets. Jane was also looking forward to tracking down a few of these during her two-week stay. But priorities first; a visit to *Coup(e) de Chance*.

***

Jane didn't want to drift too far from the shop's location on Rue Barbette. However, she did go as far as Place des Vosges. One of the loveliest squares in Paris, it was bordered by refined red brick townhouses, a rarity in the Parisian cityscape dominated by beige limestone. She resisted the temptation to people-watch from a bench in the alluring park found in its center or grab a coffee at the classic bistro, Ma Bourgogne, which presided over one corner of the square. Either activity would delay her return to *Coup(e) de Chance*. So, she decided to amble down the small streets north of the square. These eventually led her to the Picasso Museum, which was housed in one of the grandest historic mansions of the Marais. She wondered if the *avant garde* artist would have approved of his work being displayed in such a classical building. Jane felt compelled to visit this museum on a previous visit, but anything modern just wasn't her cup of tea.

The maze of narrow streets surrounding the museum were packed with contemporary art galleries. This was even less Jane's 'thing,' but since she had a little more time to kill, she peeked in at some of the displays. After a few, Jane came across one hosting a street art exhibit. Forget understanding Picasso! This urban art form was even less comprehensible to her.

On the wall outside the gallery were a few works that seemed to have been done in conjunction with the exhibit. One of these did capture her attention: a spray-painted classic Greek statue. It was a gladiator who was wearing a heavy duty gas mask and was holding a discus which had been filled in with tiny green viruses. It was like this heroic athlete was flinging away the virus. If only it were that easy! *Peculiar, but timely,* she reflected.

As she was examining the work, she noticed it was signed 'D-Zyne.' *What kind of name was that?* she puzzled, shaking her head. Even if Jane was hesitant about this so-called art, it did handily remind her that she needed to book a ticket to the Louvre. She hoped there would be some available, but as there still weren't many tourists in the city, she didn't think she'd have a problem.

She looked down at her watch. It was 3:15 pm. To play it safe, she'd walk around another block or two before returning to the shop. The more she strolled through the area, the more Jane noticed an increased number of designer clothing shops since her last visit. *The neighborhood was really getting trendy,* she thought. What did that mean for the nostalgic *Coup(e) de Chance*? This weighed on her mind as she circled back to Rue Barbette. Entering the street, she was relieved to see the lights on at #7. Brimming with excitement, Jane opened the door and stepped inside. The shop owner looked up from behind the counter and, despite the fact she was wearing a mask, Jane could see joy flood over her face.

"Madame Jane! You're back! It's so good to see you!"

"*Bonjour* Claudette! I'm so happy to be here!"

The two women greeted each other very warmly, like long lost friends. On that first visit to the shop all those years ago, Jane had been too shy, and too engrossed in what she saw, to speak with the shop owner. However, on a subsequent trip, and bolstered by having heard Claudette speak English to some other clients, Jane had built up the courage to strike up a conversation with her. This was just the first of many they would have during the hour or so Jane would inevitably spend in the shop.

"When did you arrive in Paris?" asked Claudette.

"Yesterday... and with a virtually empty suitcase!" enthused Jane.

"Wonderful! That's just what you and I both need," replied Claudette. Before she could elaborate, they were interrupted by the ringing phone. "Ah, would you excuse me for a moment?"

"Of course! I'll take a wander around," said Jane, who immediately was absorbed in the shop's new arrivals. Her eyes marveled over polka-dot enamelware, egg cups in every shape and size, chocolate bowls and various canister sets labeled with the French words for flour, sugar, tea and coffee. Several tin and ceramic water pitchers called out to her, but Jane had to restrain herself, she'd bought a white pitcher on a previous trip. Did she really need another one? She took her time sorting through some of the smaller items of school supplies, including petite boxes of white chalk and decorative cards with whimsical characters on them. In the past she'd also purchased card stock, which inevitably made their way into Christmas packages for her friends as a unique

Parisian gift. She was picking out a handful of these when
Claudette hung up the phone with a long sigh.

"Is something wrong, Claudette?" asked Jane as she walked
back over to the counter. The French were generally more reserved
than Americans when it came to divulging personal information.
Nevertheless, there was such a good rapport between them that
Jane felt she could ask.

"That was the bank," started Claudette. "They'll approve one
more loan, but said it would be the last."

"I thought business was good? What about all the great press
you've had? Doesn't that send you customers?"

"Yes, it does, or well, it did, in the past. However, with this
pandemic carrying on, foreign visitors aren't coming, especially
Americans and the Japanese. Also, being closed for two months
earlier this year was very tough. What's more, the area is getting so
chic. Have you seen all the luxury boutiques popping up? How can
I compete with shops like that? My landlord is eager to have me
leave so he can raise the rent. He can probably triple it for the likes
of Chanel and Louis Vuitton! If I miss one payment, he'll be here
the next day, ready to shut me down."

"But there still must be a market for antiques?"

"Yes, I believe there is, but if my shop was down in the south
end of the Marais, in le Village Saint-Paul where there are lots of
antique shops, I would reach more potential clients who go
meandering from shop to shop. Up here and on this small side
street, most customers come because they have been here before or
have read about it in an article. Maybe it's time, time I moved on
to something else."

"Claudette! You can't just give up and close down your
wonderful shop!"

"But, what else can I do?" Claudette looked down at her desk
with a heavy heart. Just then her computer lit up and a chime went
off, announcing the arrival of a new email. This also caused Jane's
face to light up.

"If your customers can't come to you, you can go to them."

"What do you mean?"

"Why don't you set up an online shop? That way it doesn't matter where someone is in the world, they can still order a piece of France from you. Online shopping has become even more popular during the pandemic. The Internet is not exclusively for big websites and chains. Small shops can sell online too."

Claudette mulled this over for a minute. "That's certainly a good idea and is a way of reaching both current and new customers. But there's one problem, I'm hopeless with computers."

"You don't need to be good with computers. It's much easier these days. Besides, I could help you."

"You would do that?"

"I'd love to! I'm not a computer whiz, but I can get by. After retiring I took a few IT courses at my local library, one lesson was actually on how to build an easy website. It also covered how to create an online shop."

"Well, it appears like today it's my turn to have a *coup de chance*, my own stroke of good luck!"

"Yes, Claudette, you deserve some good luck after all the happiness you've given me over the years, actually every day. No matter where I look in my house, I can find items from your shop. They bring me so much joy, as I'm sure they do to all of your customers."

"Shall we brainstorm and celebrate this at the end of the day over *une coupe*? *Une coupe de champagne* that is!" suggested Claudette.

"Deal!" accepted Jane.

The two women's smiles, covered by masks, still came through in their eyes. As much as the 'new' could often render the 'old' obsolete, it could also help save it—and provide a *coup(e)* of luck just when it's so desperately needed.

Our Lady of Hope: Notre-Dame

Daniela distinctly remembered her first trip to Paris. She was ten. It was her first trip ever, outside of her city, outside of her country. It was her first time on an airplane or riding in a taxi. It was her first time staying in a hotel. The first time her palate was treated to different and delectable flavors; her first croissant, her first crêpe, her first *mousse au chocolat*, so thick her spoon could stand straight up in the bowl without falling over. While the whole trip was memorable, one memory in particular was forever etched on her mind.

***

She thought they'd never reach the top. Around each bend were more stairs, and more and more! *Come on, Daniela!* her father said, cheering her on. *We're almost there!* Her whole body was trembling by the time she placed her foot on that last step. But, reaching the top, the sight directly in front of her, made it shake even more. Clinging to the corners of the stone balustrade were monsters, one seemingly much more terrifying than the next. A burly dog with the head of a wild boar about to release a vicious bark. A scaly dragon on the verge of spitting out a deadly gust of fire. A half-goat half-human figure with pointy horns spying down on the plaza below. She tightened her grip on her father's arm. He gave her a reassuring pat on the head. Then suddenly, amidst these ferocious faces, appeared an angelic one, right next to a gigantic bird, leaning down with its open beak, ready to bite her head off. But the beautiful lady was not afraid. She just stared back at Daniela, through the protective metal barrier, which she was ever so gently pressed up against. Daniela felt immediately comforted. It was like the lady was saying; *'Don't worry, little girl. Everything is going to be okay, you're safe here.'*

Then, the reassuring woman curled her lips in the faintest smile and let her gaze wander. Daniela followed her eyes as they journeyed across the glistening river and over the grey rooftops to reach their final destination: a tall, pointy structure. The moment was suddenly broken by Daniela's father, one hand tapping her shoulder, the other pointing emphatically in the direction of that tower. When she looked back over, the mysterious woman was gone. To Daniela, it felt like she was an angel who'd flown back to heaven.

Had I come to Paris in search of this angel? Daniela now thought. *Even if I found her, would she be able to save me? Would she be able to make a miracle happen this time?*

***

Daniela's mother was a renowned cellist. Despite the restrictions of the Iron Curtain, she still managed to have a noteworthy career and even performed abroad a few times. She'd met Daniela's father, a sound engineer, during a rehearsal at the Great Guild Hall in Riga. She used to joke that it was love at first 'arco,' the act of drawing a bow across strings. Whatever it was, she had struck the right chord and from then on hadn't stopped 'conducting' him, nor anyone else close to her.

Soon after they were married, she got pregnant with their only child. She decided to take a few years off when Daniela was born.

However, after Daniela started school, her mother decided not to return to the Latvian Symphony Orchestra. She said she couldn't handle the stress, but Daniela always suspected there was another reason. Even playing in smaller ensembles and giving private lessons, she was still very high strung, especially when it came to Daniela's practicing.

Much to her mother's dismay, Daniela hadn't inherited her mother's musical talent. She wasn't a bad player, she just wasn't a virtuoso. Yes, her mother knew this, yet refused to acknowledge it. She remained bound and determined that Daniela should follow in her footsteps. And it seemed like this determination was the reason why the whole family would make that trip to Paris.

***

It was 1995. The chamber orchestra Daniela's mother was performing with at the time had been invited to a festival in Paris. *Parīze*. From the perspective of a ten-year-old, it sounded magical. The kind of word a fairy godmother would say as she waved her magic wand. Would this city cast a spell on her too?

Their country was no longer under Communist rule, nevertheless, times were tough. Money was tight, but her parents had squirreled away every spare *lat* they could so all three of them could go to Paris. It would be a little family vacation, although Daniela's mother seemed to be secretly hoping the trip would also have some miracle effect on her daughter's musical skills.

The date of their departure quickly approached. They piled into a taxi at the crack of dawn to head to the airport. Arriving in Paris, they went straight to their hotel to drop off their small old-fashioned suitcases. The room was cramped, wallpaper was peeling off the walls and a musty smell prevailed, but they weren't there for long. The concert would be taking place the next day. Today Daniela's mother had to get to rehearsal straight away, so they grabbed a baguette sandwich at the bakery next to the hotel and inhaled it as they rushed through narrow, cobbled streets; each seemingly identical to the street they had just traveled.

They crossed a bridge and suddenly arrived in a vast open square. There were no cars, yet it was packed; with people milling about, groups following umbrellas and individuals snapping photos. Everyone seemed to be heading in the same direction, the one Daniela's parents were leading her in. She looked up and saw their destination. Was it a castle or a church? *It's Notre-Dame*, her dad leaned down to whisper in her ear. Notre-Dame. Our Lady.

Made of a creamy beige stone, sporting two giant towers and covered in a multitude of statues, it was very different from the brick or onion-domed orthodox churches like they had back home. The concert was being held in the garden behind this legendary place of worship. It was a great honor to play here, Daniela's father explained as they watched her mother disappear through the park's gate. While they waited for the rehearsal to end, the two climbed up exactly 387 steps into the church's great towers. This is where Daniela came face to face with those monsters and her angel, or maybe she was her fairy godmother. Our Lady. Her Lady.

***

The concert was a great success. Unfortunately, Daniela couldn't say the same about the miracle for her cello-playing skills her mother had hoped would come true in Paris. Our Lady had not cast a magic spell on Daniela. Her mother persisted, got fed up, then went back to her persisting. If only Daniela would practice more. If only she would concentrate harder. If only she could just follow in her mother's footsteps.

When she was finishing high school, her mother pulled some strings to get Daniela into the Latvian Academy of Music. She actually excelled within this new environment, removed from her mother's constant criticism. However, no matter how well Daniela did, it was never good enough for her mother. She wasn't top of the class. She didn't receive any of the special awards or accolades upon graduation. She wasn't immediately selected for the National Orchestra, like her mother had been.

Now here she was, in her mid-thirties, stuck in a lackluster career, with a failed marriage, a failed life. She hadn't needed a miracle when she was 10, she needed one now.

***

Maybe it had been a far stretch to think coming back to Paris would help save her. Daniela was actually supposed to have come a year ago. In March of last year her wavering marriage finally tumbled into an unsalvageable abyss. Mārtiņš and she had been married for eight years, they didn't have any children. They kept busy with their respective careers. They gradually fell out of love.

She had some professional commitments and couldn't get away immediately, in spite of these, she still needed something to look forward to so she booked a flight for later in the year. She'd heard that September was a nice time to visit Paris and she vaguely remembered that their family vacation had also been in autumn. Returning around the same time of year might rekindle some magic, or, at the very least, spark some pleasant nostalgia. High on her priority list was climbing those towers again. To be honest, she didn't really expect her guardian angel to be there waiting for her at the top, her secret childhood fairy godmother, ready to reassure her once again. However, she was sincerely hoping the experience would inspire her.

Then The Fire happened. It felt like Daniela's marriage certificate and wasted Academy of Music diploma had also gone up in smoke with the Cathedral's spire and roof. Traumatized by the Cathedral's tragedy, and how it mirrored events in her own life, Daniela just couldn't bear going to Paris at that time. Luckily, she was able to change her ticket, but it would have to be used within a year.

She was dragging her feet and almost decided against going altogether. Then the pandemic hit and concerts were completely put on hold. Any travel plans were also put on hold. Her whole life seemed to be put on hold. European borders finally began opening up over the summer, but Daniela was still reluctant. Then, on a whim, she booked a last minute flight, just a week before her credit was going to expire. And that's how she ended up back in Paris, 25 years after that first and only trip.

***

Daniela couldn't say she actually remembered much as she walked from her hotel near the Opéra Garnier, coincidently the home of the French National Academy of Music, over to Notre-Dame. Map in hand, she took a meandering route which first led her through some lovely covered passageways. Not pressed for time, Daniela lingered at a few window displays and popped into a charming old school bookstore where she picked up a used copy of *The Hunchback of Notre-Dame*, in English. She doubted she would have all that much time for reading during her short four-day stay, however, it could keep her occupied on the plane ride back to Riga.

Happily discovering the hidden garden of the Palais-Royal made her haphazard path all the more enjoyable. She then passed through the Louvre's courtyards, which were nice to see since she hadn't intended to visit the inside on this trip. Daniela reached the banks of the Seine, whose waters were shimmering serenely in the late afternoon sun. Soon she could see the Cathedral's towers peaking over the rooftops of Ile-de-la-Cité. She was almost there.

Rounding a corner, she entered a large square, which she immediately recognized to be the one she had visited as a child. Yet something was noticeably different. This time there were no people milling about. No groups following their umbrella-waving tour guide. Much of the plaza in front of the Cathedral was barricaded off, she assumed, due to the restoration works on the wounded church. In spite of this, the Cathedral was still grandiose, and from this exact vantage point, there was little evidence of the fire. Daniela took the time to get reacquainted with Our Lady, who, even at this distance, was still so much closer than it was back in Riga.

Although the front plaza was closed off, she thought the little park behind it, where her mother had played that concert all those years ago, might still be open. The closure of the plaza required Daniela to crossed a bridge over to the Left Bank and traveled the length of the Cathedral to the next bridge where she could crossed back onto the island.

Fermé. Closed read the sign on its gate. Daniela would have to make do with the view from the bridge she just crossed. However, from that perspective the damage to the spire-less, roofless building was much more apparent. Her melancholic gaze floated over the flying buttresses, currently braced by wooden supports to prevent them from collapsing, and up to the towers. Those horrid monsters were still there, but where was Her Lady? Where had she gone?

I've lost everything! thought Daniela. *Not just my angel, but my career, my husband, my mother's esteem.* It seemed all she had left were the monsters in her mind, which were constantly haunting her. A tear streamed down her cheek and tumbled down, down, down into the Seine. Those waters looked ever so tempting right now. That could be an easy escape from her failed life.

"*Elle est très belle, n'est pas?*" a voice said, interrupting Daniela's dark thoughts. She swung around to find a man leaning against the railing of the bridge a few paces to her right. She stared at him blankly, the extent of her French being, *bonjour, merci* and a few words of music terminology.

"She's beautiful, isn't she?" he repeated in English.

"Yes, very," Daniela replied, wiping her eyes to erase any evidence she'd been crying. She desperately hoped he hadn't noticed.

"Every time I cross this bridge, I stop to admire the Cathedral," he said, an indication that he most likely lived in Paris. "She's still standing, she didn't give up despite all that happened."

"I suppose that's true."

"Blessed is the one who perseveres under trial because, having stood the test, that person will receive the crown of life that the Lord has promised to those who love Him," quoted the man.

Daniela gave him a quizzical look.

"James chapter 1, verse 12," he specified.

"You know the Bible much better than I do," she complimented.

"Actually, it's thanks to Our Lady," he started. "She's always given me hope."

"Is that so?" she questioned, inviting him to elaborate.

"I came to Paris 15 years ago. I'm from Sri Lanka and my country was caught up in a brutal civil war to which I lost countless friends and family members. I had to get out, it was a question of life or death. I had a distant cousin in Paris. It wasn't easy, but he helped get me here. I didn't have papers, I didn't know what I was going to do, but I managed to get a job in a restaurant right there, at the foot of Notre-Dame."

"Oh really?"

"Yes, Our Lady was looking out for me. The days were long at the restaurant, made even longer by my commute from my apartment far out in the suburbs, but I was grateful to have work and a roof over my head. To be able to get back on my feet. One morning, I arrived about twenty minutes early so I decided to go inside Notre-Dame. I'd been raised a Buddhist and had never been in a church before. Not only did I have a great sense of peace about being in that majestic Cathedral, but from that moment onwards, I was always overwhelmed with tears when I visited. I think it was because the Holy Spirit always touched me there. It's a sacred place. I started leaving early for work so I could have my moment of peace in the Cathedral before my tiring work day would begin. She kept my hope alive."

"Did you convert to Christianity?"

"I was considering it. Once my French was good enough, I took some catechism classes, which is how I got to know the Bible. It was a meaningful experience. It helped me recall some of the teachings of The Buddha who said: 'Hope is the one thing that is stronger than fear.' I realized that, despite what had happened to me and to my country, torn apart by religious differences, that I didn't need to put a label on my faith. I just had to believe in that hope, completely and without question."

"I guess that's a good way of looking at things."

"I carried on visiting Our Lady and she kept her watchful eye on me. I eventually got my papers sorted out. I met a wonderful woman, we got married and now have three kids. I went from washing dishes to head cook. It isn't the career as a doctor I'd aspired to have as a young boy in Jaffna, but I'm alive and remain hopeful for a brighter future."

"Do you still work there, at that restaurant?"

"Sadly, it had to close after the fire. Being so close to the Cathedral, it had extensive smoke and water damage, which, of course, paled in comparison to the damage inflicted on Notre-Dame."

"You must have been devastated."

"I was and still am. I was in a state of shock as I stood helplessly by, watching the flames devour her. But she's still standing. I have to live by her example. I lost my job, but under her protection, I got a new one, not far, over on Ile Saint-Louis. That meant I could still pay tribute to her on a daily basis. However, as a result of the lockdown and restaurants having to stay closed for so long and being in an area normally frequented heavily by tourists, now obviously missing, the owners had to close down permanently. So I lost that job too. I started panicking, I had my family to take care of. Then I remembered Our Lady. She had guided me in the past. She could do it again. Through word of mouth in the area's restaurant circles, I landed a new job two weeks ago. And I still get to walk by her every day."

"That's a beautiful story. I'm glad everything worked out for you."

"'There is surely a future hope for you, and your hope will not be cut off,' Proverbs chapter 23, verse 18," he added. "I see sadness in your eyes. Whatever is troubling you, don't lose sight of hope."

"I will try my best."

By now the sun was hovering just above the uneven horizon made up of trees, rooftops and bridges. To the right, the Cathedral had a peachy glow and beneath their feet the Seine's gilded waves bobbed lazily to and fro. The temptation to join them had drifted.

"Well, I'd better get on my way, my shift is about to start," he said, setting off down the bridge. "Have a nice evening."

"Thank you, you too... Wait!"

"Yes?" he asked, turning back around.

"What's the name of the restaurant you work at? I'd love to try your cooking."

"*Les Deux Tours*. The Two Towers. It's just over there," he replied, pointing down the road she'd walked up earlier.

"Thank you. Maybe I'll see you later!"

He waved and went on his way.

The Two Towers, Daniela repeated to herself. Stunned, she realized she had indeed found her guardian angel. Her fairy godfather, in fact. She got the miracle she needed. She had lost all hope, but now thanks to him, her hope was gratefully found and restored.

Paldies. Merci. Thank you, once again, Our Amazing Lady.

Picnics & Surprises along the Seine

"*Santé!*" Echoed five voices as five glasses came together in unison.

"It's *soooo* good to see you guys!" Skye gushed.

"Yes, finally!" agreed Erin.

"No more virtual *apéros* for us," declared Pearl.

"Or at least we hope not!" added Amelia.

"Cheers to that!" said Rose, raising her glass again.

The cosmopolitan quintet was made up of an American Midwesterner, an Irish lass, a half French-half South African, a French Canadian and a Corsican, who adamantly insisted on the regional distinction instead of being called 'French.' Her family were staunch supporters of the island's quest to gain independence from France.

The young women instantly clicked when they'd met three years ago at the small publishing house where they were all working. Although they'd moved on to other jobs, their friendship had remained and the friends never missed their monthly get-togethers. That is, until this year, when the quarantine had kept the fabulous five apart. Some of them had gone home before the lockdown was imposed and hadn't returned immediately when the restrictions had been lifted. Therefore, it wasn't until now, late-September, that they were finally reunited. Since the weather was still lovely, they decided to meet over a picnic along the Seine.

To make the most of their evening, the young women had each snuck out of their respective offices a little early in order to arrive at their favorite picnic spot by 6 pm. Well, almost everyone. Rose, the Corsican, was always late, so true to form, she rolled up at 6:20.

Their spot was located on the Quai de la Tournelle, a section of the riverbank on the Left Bank which extended between le Pont de l'Archevêché, the bridge behind Notre-Dame, and le Pont de la Tournelle, the next bridge to the east. This location gave them a nice view of the elegant Ile Saint-Louis and the back of the Cathedral. Still scarred by the fire, the grand lady of Paris was admittedly not exuding her former splendor, but she was beautiful nonetheless. On early autumn afternoons, this location also caught the setting sun at a nice angle. Plus, it wasn't far from Pearl's apartment in the Latin Quarter; handy in case anyone needed to use the bathroom.

Since Pearl, the *Québécoise*, lived so close, she was also in charge of bringing her tin camping cups, some reusable plastic plates and a blanket, which was now overloaded with the various goodies they'd each brought. The tempting casual feast included several oozing cheeses, mini *saucissons* (sausages) made by Rose's Corsican uncle, veggies and dip, a bunch of grapes, a few baguettes and a sinful bag of thick-cut mature cheddar & chive chips. The addicting chips were the first thing everyone devoured, including Erin, whose own staunch nationalism, that for a united Ireland, usually made her snub anything British.

"I knew I should have bought two bags!" joked Skye, the Midwestern, emptying the last of the crumbs into her palm.

"Don't be sad," Erin teased. "I brought a surprise." She opened her bag and removed a large plastic container. "I got up early... so I could make a batch of my famous triple chocolate brownies!"

"I think I've died and gone to heaven!" exclaimed Rose, already drooling at the sight of the container.

"Have you had any news from Jules, Amelia?" Pearl queried. Erin shot her the evil eye, but it was too late.

"Nope…" Amelia sighed, looking out at the Seine.

"I can't believe he just disappeared like that!" fumed Skye, always the opinionated one. "What a loser! Who breaks up with someone at the start of a pandemic?"

"Are you sure he didn't get the virus?" Erin asked.

"Yes, he's alive and well, according to his updated Instagram posts," answered Amelia, rolling her eyes.

"Well, it's probably for the best," said Rose. "If he can't handle some bad times, then he won't be reliable in the long run."

"True, but still," Amelia sighed. "It wasn't the greatest of times to be alone. At least I had you gals to cheer me up during our video chats."

"Cheers to friendship!" proclaimed Skye.

"To friendship!" the others repeated in unison as they raised their glasses.

"I've been trying to find out if my colleague Pierre is still single," said Rose. "He's really cute, but he's a hardcore hypochondriac."

"Poor guy, didn't you say he had serious asthma or something like that?" asked Erin. "Cut him some slack."

"Actually, he's been noticeably happier these days, so I suspect he's dating someone," Rose replied.

"Ladies, thanks for your offers to help, but I can manage just fine on my own," defended Amelia. "I've just downloaded a new dating app."

"Forget about those dating apps," Skye interjected. "It's much better to meet someone in person."

"Easier said than done!" complained Amelia.

"You should really go back to dancing," suggested Pearl. "That's where I met Xavier. There are tons of cute guys who come out. Plus, since they dedicate themselves to dancing once or twice a week, that shows they can manage at least a minimum level of commitment, something Jules certainly couldn't."

"Perhaps…" replied Amelia wistfully. As much as she loved dancing, she wasn't sure if she was all that keen on the idea. That's where she'd met Laurent, her boyfriend before Jules. They had been together for over a year and she definitely didn't want to run into him, twirling his new girlfriend around on the dance floor.

"Just think about it and text if you'd like to join us next week," said Pearl. "Try something different, be spontaneous!"

"Okay gals... who's ready for a brownie?" asked Erin, waving her container in an attempt to put an end to their Inquisition of poor broken-hearted Amelia. She removed the lid, releasing an intoxicatingly sweet aroma of rich chocolate. In a matter of minutes there was nothing left in the container but a few crumbs.

In spite of the sugary pick-me-up, Amelia's spirits had only mildly lifted. She gazed out at the River. The sun was still in the sky and a golden shimmer sparkled across the Seine's surface. It was sometimes hard being the only single in her group of happily coupled-up friends. They'd all seemed to have met their *âme soeur*, their soulmates, and she was left with the castaways, the dancers sitting in the chairs in the corner that nobody else wanted to dance with... who, in turn, didn't want to dance with her. The River's waltzing waves didn't seem to have any answers for her.

"Sorry gals, I've got to call it an early night," Amelia announced, suddenly hopping up from the blanket. "I have a lot to do tomorrow."

Before her friends could object, Amelia blew them all kisses, scooped up her bag and put on a protective face mask.

"I'll be fine!" she called over her shoulder as she headed east along the riverbank. She would walk to the Austerlitz Station to catch *Métro* Line 5. This would connect her to Line 1 at Bastille which would take her to Concorde Station and back home to the austere 8th district.

By now more people had gathered along the riverbank. Amelia's eyes wandered over the festive crowd, small groups of people enjoying the soft early autumn air, bottles of wine and each other's company. Unfortunately, her eyes also fell upon several affectionate couples. *Where oh where would she find a new and better 'Jules'?*

She crossed under the Pont de la Tournelle and looked up to the statue of Sainte Geneviève. One of the patron saints of Paris, the young nun is said to have saved the city from Atilla and the Huns back in 451 AD. *Come on, Geneviève! Can't you do something for me?* As hard as Amelia stared at the statue, it seemed doubtful the spirit of the saint could save her from the barbarians of today's dating world!

Soon after the bridge, the riverbank became the Tino-Rossi park. The south part of this had small plots of flowers, bushes, weeping willows and some outdoor sculptures whereas the stretch along the Seine had several rounded alcoves. These half-moon areas were bordered by a few tall steps, which descended to the River's edge. These 'amphitheaters' were often used for open-air dancing and one of them was currently filled with a dozen or so couples dancing salsa.

Maybe I really should take up Pearl's offer to join them at the dancing club, Amelia considered as she approached the dancers. Just then her foot kicked a small object and sent it flying towards them. However, it didn't make it all the way to the dance floor... because it hit someone sitting on the steps first.

Oh no! thought Amelia, mortified. *What should she do? Turn and scurry the other way? Pretend she didn't know what had happened?*

The victim flinched. He reached down to pick up the projectile and turned around. There was no way she could hide now! A slender man with short dark hair stood up, looked at her and raised his hand. Between his index finger and thumb was a wine cork.

"*Je suis vraiment désolée!* I'm terribly sorry!" Amelia called out as she walked towards him to apologize. "My foot..."

"It's no problem at all," said the stranger as he jumped up to the top of the steps. "No harm done!"

"Okay, good, I am really very sorry," she muttered, now standing in front of him.

"Well, if you want to make it up to me, you could join me on the dance floor," he said with a twinkle in his eyes.

"Um, I was just heading towards the *Métro*…"

"Just one song!" he pleaded. "My dance partner didn't show."

"Well, okay, I guess…" she said, her inhibitions melting away thanks to the warmth this stranger exuded. She also had to admit, her cork-victim was rather good looking.

"What's your name?" he asked as he ushered her down to the dance floor.

"Amelia, and yours?"

"Julio," he answered.

Arggh. Julio. That was very similar to Jules, thought Amelia. *Honestly though, she couldn't really hold that against him. He hadn't chosen his name, nor did he have anything to do with the dreaded Jules.*

"Amelia, that doesn't sound like a very French name," he commented as he swung her around on the dance floor.

"You're right. My mother is French and my father is South African. She wanted to call me Amélie, but he wanted a more international name, so they compromised. Julio doesn't sound very French either!"

"Ha ha! You've got me there," he replied with a chuckle. "I'm from Venezuela."

"Ah, so that's why you're a good dancer!"

"And perhaps your nationality makes you so good at shooting corks. You must be from South Africa's wine region."

"Actually, I am!" she answered. "I'm from Franschhoek. My mom's from Bordeaux, she was hired as a wine consultant at a vineyard in the Franschhoek area. My father was a young apprentice there, they fell in love and she stayed on. Now, here I am back in her homeland."

"What a romantic story!"

"Yes, I suppose it is," replied Amelia, certainly blushing beneath her mask.

Their chipper chatter had already taken them into the second song. The third one simply flew by. Amelia couldn't remember the last time she'd had so much fun, she'd completely lost track of time.

At the end of the next song there was a pause in the dancing as the host went to change the sound system's playlist.

"I should really get home," said Amelia.

"What a shame," said Julio. "Where do you live?"

"Over near Place de la Concorde."

"Ohhhh... posh," he teased.

"Oh, I couldn't normally afford to live in the 8th. It's my aunt's place. She works in fashion and is currently working over in New York City," explained Amelia.

Just then a cruise boat floated by. Its passengers waved to the dancers. Julio looked over and waved, but not to those friendly passengers.

"I have an idea! I'm friends with some of the staff of the Batobus and I know the captain of that boat. The next station is just up ahead. We can get a free ride over to the stop near your place! You won't need to take the subway that way."

"Umm, ahhh..." Amelia hesitated.

"Quick, it's docking!" he said, pulling her hand.

Don't be such a stick in the mud! Amelia scolded herself. There was no reason not to go along with Julio and his ingenious idea. *Really, what nefarious thing could happen on a Batobus?* she reckoned.

Weaving through the clusters of picnickers, Amelia and Julio darted over to the dock. There are various boats which cruise the Seine. Most visitors take hour-long cruises on sightseeing boats or longer dinner cruises, but the Batobus, a hop-on-hop-off water taxi, offers tourists and locals alike a different way to travel around the city while enjoying the sites along the River. Nearing the jetty, Julio waved his arms to get the captain's attention who, in turn, waited for them. They hopped on board as the deckhand unwound the rope from the pilings. They were off!

"*Hola!*" Julio greeted the captain, who made a little salute gesture back. "This is Amelia. Amelia, meet Marc."

"*Bonsoir!*" greeted Amelia. Marc winked at Julio and waved them on, signifying that there was no need to stop and chat with him. Julio looked like he was happily in good company.

They'd gotten on the Batobus at its easternmost stop, le Jardin des Plantes. So, from here, the boat turned around to cruise back towards the west. The sun was just dipping under the horizon. This must be the last sail of the day as the Batobus general stops at dusk. Gliding on the Seine at twilight and the evenings can be very romantic.

Julio guided Amelia to the very back of the boat where there was a small outdoor deck. There were only a handful of other passengers on the boat and they were all seated inside, so Julio and Amelia had the deck to themselves, therefore, they also lowered their protective masks. *Wow! Julio's smile was even more sparkling than his eyes!* The thought made Amelia's cheeks redden.

"This is a great way to see the city!" said Amelia, attempting to create a distract from her momentary embarrassment.

"Is this your first time on the Batobus?" asked Julio.

"Yes, actually it is!" she replied. "I did take one of those larger boats when I first arrived in Paris."

"When was that?" he asked.

"Three years ago. How about you? How long have you been here?"

"Just over two years," he replied. "I came to do my Master's and I hope to stay. The economic situation in my country is pretty bad right now. However, it might not be easy to get work papers after I complete my Master's."

"That's too bad," she said. "I'm lucky enough to have a French passport, so I am spared the daunting ordeal of getting a residence permit. I've heard horror stories about the Préfecture."

"Oh, it's all worth it in the end, to be able to stay in this marvelous city," he reflected. "Do you hope to stay on here?"

"Yes, absolutely! I plan to stay forever!" she confirmed enthusiastically. "And one day I'm going to have an apartment along the Seine, like one of those, over there on Ile Saint-Louis.

It'll be just like in *La Traviata*. I would be singing my heart out as I take my last breath. What a way to go!"

"Well, I hope you can achieve your dream of the apartment, but not the tragic ending, at least not any time soon," he remarked. "So you're a fan of opera as well as salsa?"

"Yes, if I could sing, I would have become an opera singer," she replied. "Since I'm not vocally gifted, I content myself with enjoying opera from a seat in the audience instead. How about you?"

"I've actually never been," he admitted. "Caracas has a gorgeous opera house, but times have been tough there for a while. I've been meaning to go ever since I arrived in Paris."

"The new season is just starting, we could go together if you like?" she suggested.

"That'd be great!" he said. "Hey look, the lights of Notre-Dame just came on. Isn't she beautiful?"

"Yes, it's a magical building. All of Paris is magical, especially at this time of day."

"I agree. The magic of Paris is more undeniable at night and from the vantage point of the River. Did you know that there's only one Unesco World Heritage Site in Paris and that is the Banks of the Seine? No individual historical building in the city has that distinction."

"No, I didn't know that. That's very interesting."

"The Seine is unique in France," commented Julio. "Unlike most of the other rivers in the country, it doesn't originate from a larger river or lake, but instead begins northwest of Dijon at a place called Source-Seine. It then flows northwest through Paris and empties into the English Channel between Le Havre and Honfleur."

"What a special river."

They floated alongside the north side of Ile-de-la-Cité, the island upon which Notre-Dame sits. From this angle they had an even better view of another prominent site of the island, the Conciergerie, the palace of the French kings before they moved to the Louvre. With its turrets and towers, it conjured up images of what Paris looked like in the Middle Ages.

"We're coming up to my favorite bridge!" Julio exclaimed, pointing ahead of them. "Le Pont Neuf. Did you know it's the oldest bridge in Paris despite being called the new bridge?"

"No, I didn't!" confessed Amelia.

"Yes! It was built in the early 1600s," informed Julio. "It was the first bridge to span the whole River and the first built without houses."

"Cool!" said Amelia. She craned her neck up to admire the wonderfully lit bridge as they cruised under it. "Yikes! Those faces are a bit creepy though!"

"Yes, they are a little scary. They're called *mascarons*. There are over 380 of these stone masks on the bridge. Each one represents a different forest or field divinity from ancient Greek mythology."

"How do you know all of this stuff?"

"Well, I used to work for the Batobus, a part-time job during the first year of my Master's. That's how I got to know these guys," said Julio pointing towards the captain.

"Ah ok, but there doesn't seem to be a guide on here."

"No, there isn't, but sometimes the staff member who announces the stops relays some historical tidbits. I'm a history buff so I studied up on the sites along the boat's route."

"You seem to have many talents," observed Amelia, with a smile.

"As do you!" he replied, moving a little closer to her. "Great dancer, walking encyclopedia of opera, a beautiful smile." He took her hand and spun her around. She laughed and her long dark, curly hair blew softly in the evening breeze. She felt so free. Still holding Amelia's hand, Julio pulled her a little closer.

"Escale du Louvre. Fermato del Louvre. Parado el Louvre. Louvre Stop." The multilingual announcement interrupted the moment.

"Is this where we're getting off?" asked Amelia, taking a step backwards, away from Julio. *This is crazy,* she thought. She'd just met the guy and he'd literally whisked her off her feet. Something had to be wrong... or maybe it was the workings of Sainte Geneviève?

"No, we'll get off at the next one," said Julio.

After a few passengers descended, the boat set sail again. They leaned back against the railing, silently taking in the enchanting vista. The sky was transitioning to a royal blue. The lights of the monuments were coming on one by one. This was when Paris truly became the City of Light. The Louvre seemed to go on forever on their right and on their left the Musée d'Orsay, with its two huge glowing clocks, proudly stood guard over the River.

They approached the Assemblée Nationale, the French Parliament. This democratic building was born out of the First Revolution and was straight across from the Place de la Concorde, the largest square in Paris and where the heads of the French royals and revolutionary dissidents went rolling over two centuries ago.

"You see those large blocks?" asked Julio as they went under the Pont de la Concorde.

"Yes," replied Amelia.

"They were from the Bastille Prison!" he said, revealing another one of his fascinating facts.

"Interesting," exclaimed Amelia. "I always wondered why the prison was no longer in the Place de la Bastille!"

"That bridge is historically interesting, but we're actually coming up to the most beautiful one of all, or at least, in my opinion. We'll be getting off the boat just before. The station is coming up."

The boat veered to the right towards the dock.

"Awwww... I don't want this moment to end!" said Amelia savoring the last seconds before they reached the riverbank.

"No need for it to end!" Julio suggested coyly. "We could go for a little walk along the River, if you like?"

Amelia hesitated. Her mind naturally drifted to everything she'd intended to accomplish that weekend. Would staying out a little longer really hold her back from her to-do list? Did she really even need to do her laundry first thing tomorrow morning? Couldn't it wait? Couldn't she try living in the moment? Just this once? He was not Jules. Julio seemed to be dancing to a very different beat.

The Batobus hit the dock. Julio grabbed her hand. They had to hurry to get to the exit before the boat pushed off again.

"*Gracias, amigo!*" Julio called out to Captain Marc.

"*Merci!!*" added Amelia. They hopped off the boat and it pulled away, leaving them all alone on the tranquil riverbank.

"Wow! I see what you mean! The bridge is totally gorgeous from here!" said Amelia gazing up in awe at the ornate bridge, decked out in candelabrum, lions, Pegasuses, water nymphs and other sculptures.

"It's called le Pont Alexandre III," said Julio. "It was built for the World's Fair of 1900 and named in honor of the Russian Tsar. Yes, it may be gorgeous, but not as gorgeous as you."

She smiled, but quickly looked back at the bridge. She was not yet able to accept his complimentary words.

Twilight was turning to darkness and the lights reflecting upon the water appeared to be straight from one of those Impressionist paintings hanging in the Musée d'Orsay. The rhythm of the water lapped softly against the *péniches,* the converted barge houseboats which were moored nearby. Nighttime along the river had the most intimate feeling. Amelia thought about the many who'd gone by that specific location over the centuries and for so many different reasons. Life, death, war, escape, joy, despair and wanderlust are just a few of those reasons one could imagine. Lest we forget love.

"I think I'll take you up on that suggestion of a little stroll," she finally said, turning to Julio. She was releasing her inhibitions, or at least some of them.

"Great!" he cheered. "Which way would you like to go?"

THERE'S ONLY *One* PARIS

"Surprise me!" she said, embracing the spontaneity the River and its banks had inspired. She would simply go with the flow, the flow of the Seine and that precious moment she was sharing with Julio. He took her hand and they walked, not off into the sunset, but into the twilight, venturing bravely into the unknown.

Le Métro

5th, 6th & 7th Arrondissements

Sasha hurdled down the stairs, into the brave unknown of the *Métro* system. Well, somewhat known, as there were only limited options one could take at Austerlitz Station. It served the Gare d'Austerlitz, a proper train station with intercity trains, the *RER* C suburban train and the east-west Line 10. Considering this small selection, he assumed Petite Piaf would be headed for the last one.

Indeed, as he reached the bottom of that first set of stairs, he saw the musician duck down into a stairwell. Above this was a sign reading Line 10. At least he didn't have to wonder which platform she'd be on. This was the start of the line, so trains only departed in one direction: west. Nevertheless, there were so many steps! Down, down, down he went. Beneath his feet the ground began to tremble. *An approaching train!* Sure enough, just as he was getting down to the platform an old-school *Métro* train pulled up. He checked for the red beret. There it was, about midway down the platform. Petite Piaf turned and looked towards the approaching train. Her eyes rested for a minute on Sasha. She squinted. Had she recognized him?

Sasha hopped into the first car and paused to catch his breath. He had to confess. Yes, he was a bit out of shape. He'd been working so hard the past few months, he hadn't prioritized regular exercise. Last night's events, and the subsequent sleepless night he'd had, reduced his stamina even further. Despite this, he was determined to reach the *Métro* performer. So much was riding on the tiny object in her pouch!

Around a quarter of Paris's *Métro* lines still had these older trains. Each carriage had four open sections, with poles to hold onto and flip-down seats. These were interspersed with stationary seat sections which had two sets of four seats that faced each other. The carriage Sasha currently found himself in wasn't very full, so he easily maneuvered his way to the other end. He was ready to open the doors and zoom over to the other car as soon as they pulled into the next station: Jussieu. Only one more car to go after that to reach her. It should be easy.

Sasha was going over in his head what exactly he'd say to her, he didn't want to come across as a weirdo. The train stopped on the platform. As Sasha stepped towards the doors, they flew open and a loud crowd barged in. *Oh no!* Jussieu Station was adjacent to a large campus of the University of Paris. The new term was just beginning. The group of chanting university students who filled the second half of this *Métro* car had to be doing some sort of activity for frosh week, the orientation for new students. Be that as it may, Sasha wondered why these kids weren't in class at that very moment. He then wondered why they were gathered in such a large, densely packed group. That was how the virus was spreading again! Sure, they were wearing masks, but all that loud singing, arm in arm, was certainly not very safe!

The train chugged through the 5th arrondissement passing more university campuses, the quaint Rue Mouffetard market street and the Latin Quarter. It took several stations for Sasha to snap out of his horror-stricken daze and develop a new game plan. Petite Piaf had likely moved down a carriage. He had to get past these potential virus spreaders and catch up to her! It was risky, but in order to get closer to her, his new strategy was to jump out of this carriage at the next station and run all the way past the next car so he could reach the following one to jump on. That would bring him up to the carriage behind the one he believed Petite Piaf must be in.

They'd just left Cluny-la-Sorbonne Station and were entering the 6th district. Odéon Station was next. Sasha braced himself and, as soon as the door lock released, he held his breath and shimmied through the rowdy students. He dove out the doors and bolted down the platform. He jumped into the second car as the buzzer was sounding. Huffing and puffing, he ignored the curious looks sent his way by the surrounding passengers. Maybe they thought he was yet another *Métro* performer? The one Sasha was looking for had just left them. He teetered through the jiggling car to get to the other end and peered cautiously through the back window.

"There's only one Paris...!"

Standing in the middle of the carriage, Petite Piaf was still belting out her tune. However, Sasha could tell she was approaching the end. He was getting all too familiar with the song, having heard it over and over again.

The train pulled into Mabillon Station, just up the street from picturesque Place Saint-Sulpice and nearby the legendary cafés of the Saint-Germain neighborhood. Sasha made his move and hopped through the first doors of the next car. Petite Piaf's car.

"Paris... Paris!" she triumphantly concluded. A elderly lady seated near the musician clapped and rummaged through her handbag for some change. The performer graciously accepted her coins then moved down to the far end of the carriage in search of other donations. Sasha made his way towards her. He was one seat section away. The train slowed and came to a halt on the platform. Petite Piaf swung around and saw Sasha. She froze. A passenger on the platform released the door handle and climbed into the car. Sasha opened his mouth to recite the speech he'd so carefully rehearsed in his head before being rudely interrupted by the singing students. But, before he could even utter a word, the musician rushed off the train. She dashed into the nearest passageway and was out of sight in a flash.

"*Attendez!* Wait!" he shouted after her, in vain. He just needed to get her to stop and listen to him. Just as the buzzer rang, he flew off the train and sprinted after her. He could not let her escape!

Sèvres-Babylone was another interchange station, but it only had one other line, number 12. Therefore, it was rather predictable where Petite Piaf was going. Nevertheless, she had a decent head start on Sasha.

He jogged up and down some stairs and he was confronted with a fork in the passageway. Which direction could she have chosen? North or south? Sasha heard the rumble of an approaching train. He would have to make a decision. And quick. This station was roughly in the middle of Line 12's route. That said, the most popular stretch of the line was to the north. This reasoning sent him barreling down the steps on his right just as the train whooshed into the station. Up ahead was the red beret. He'd made the right choice. Reaching the bottom of the stairs, Sasha heroically sprung into the Line 12 train, just before the doors slammed shut.

"*Mesdames, Messieurs, je vous prie de bien vouloir patienter pour régulation,*" a muffled voice cracked through the *Métro* car's speakers.

After all that rushing, now the train would be held up because of traffic! grumbled Sasha upon hearing the announcement. He then realized this delay would actually give him a minute to catch his breath and assess the situation.

Line 12 didn't have any interchanges for several stations. The train would travel under the elegant streets of the 7th district, skirting the Musée d'Orsay and the Assemblée Nationale, the French Parliament, before journeying beneath the Seine to reach the Right Bank. This would give Sasha the chance to catch up with her. This time he could not, and *would* not, let her slip away.

While the *Métro* was still stationary, it would be easier to move forward a carriage. Sasha started to walk through the one he was in, but didn't reached the far end before the buzzer suddenly sounded again and the doors locked. He'd have to wait until the next station in order to make his next move.

So close yet so far away! That felt like the motto for his whole life, until now. This very bizarre year had been disastrous and depressing for so many. However, not entirely for Sasha. The lockdown had provided him with an unusual opportunity, one that could now advance his career and change the course of his whole life. That is, if he could get his priceless object back.

The train slowed as they neared Rue du Bac Station. He returned his attention to the present moment and walked up to the carriage doors. If he was really quick, he might be able to double the next car and go straight into the one Petite Piaf was in. But on second thought, it might be better to get her towards the end of the song. She wasn't quite there yet. *Patience, Sasha, patience.*

When the train came to a stop, he hopped out and jogged over to the middle of the next carriage. He reckoned he didn't need to make it all the way to the end of this car. At the next station he only had to reach the first door of the following one. He could do this.

"There's only one Paris...!"

Sasha could faintly hear Petite Piaf's melody wafting down from the next carriage. The train reduced its speed. Sasha stepped up to the doors. As soon as the lock released at Solférino Station, he jumped out. He turned to jet down to the next carriage, but was blocked by a nanny pushing a double stroller, waiting to get onto the train. How was she going to get on with that mammoth beast? More importantly, how could Sasha get around it?

He shuffled to the left then to the right as she did the same with the oversized stroller. He eventually managed to scoot around her, but then ran straight into a man standing right in the middle of the platform. He didn't have time for apologies, the doors were about to close! So he bulldozed past this second obstacle and charged onto the train.

Il n'y a qu'un seul Paris..."

Sasha stared down the carriage. There she was. Two seat sections separated him from his future. Just then a thought crossed his mind. What if she sees him and bolts again? His eyes darted around his *Métro* car section. *Yes! There!* Tucked into a nearby seat was one of those free newspapers they give out in front of *Métro* entrances in the mornings. At that very moment, Sasha didn't care if there might be nasty germs on it. He snatched it up, opened it wide and hid his face behind its pages.

Sasha figured that Petite Piaf would be finishing her song just after the next station. Then she would go around the carriage soliciting coins. When she reached Sasha, he'd lower the newspaper and make his plea. They would be in between stations, so she couldn't escape. In the meantime, Sasha nervously tried reading the newspaper. He'd randomly opened it to the *Arts & Culture* section. One headline announced the opening of a new exhibit of a Japanese artist who did paper sculptures. Another talked about the rise of street art around the capital. A third piece was an interview with a noted art historian, a certain profession Conroy, about her new book on 19th century women artists. These were all topics Sasha was keen on, but his hands were trembling too much. There was no way he could focus on the text.

"Paris... Paris...!"

Thankfully they soon reached Assemblée Nationale Station. From the corner of his eye, Sasha could see that a few people got off and got on. He only cared that one person in particular was still on his car; and that was Petite Piaf. She wrapped up her tune. The doors closed. She pulled the pouch out of her pocket. Sasha was ready.

"Mesdames, Messieurs, vérification des titres de transport," announced one of the passengers who'd just gotten on the train.

Sasha apprehensively lowered the newspaper. At either end of the carriage were two clusters of three or four *Métro* controllers, here to conduct a spontaneous inspection of everyone's tickets.

Uh oh. This wasn't good news for Petite Piaf. And therefore it would also not be good news for Sasha.

Lunch on the Rue Mouffetard

Philippe concentrated hard, his hand gripped the mouse. He barely managed to hover it over the printer icon long enough to make a successful click. His eyes darted eagerly over to his little-used printer. He heard the ink cartridge sputter to life and get to work, very, very slowly.

"*Allez*... come on..." he huffed impatiently. The bells of nearby Saint-Médard chimed 11. That gave him two hours, which should be more than enough time to do everything he had to do. Well, that is, as long as he wasn't held up at any of the shops.

He looked back at the printer. After a minute Philippe acknowledged that staring at it would not help it work any faster, so he turned back to his list. He didn't want to forget anything. Just then something popped into his mind. He picked up a pen and scribbled at the end of his list: *fleurs*. Flowers.

The printer let out an emphatic, whirling clunk and, with great effort, spit out a single piece of paper. A recipe. Philippe snatched up the sheet and cross referenced the ingredients with his list. Everything seemed to be in order. He stood up and went over to the mirror. He smoothed down his thinning hair and straightened his shirt. He really shouldn't have put on his lunch attire as he still had the cooking to do. Inexperienced though, he wasn't used to 'all this.' *Tant pis*, oh well. He could put on an apron once he returned from the market with all the necessary wares.

He threw on his suit jacket, slid his wallet into his pocket and headed towards the front door of his apartment. His right hand followed its natural reflex for the keys in the lock, but it retracted at the last minute. *The list!*

Philippe jogged back over to his desk, grabbed the little piece of paper, shoved it in his pocket and returned to those keys, this time removing them from the lock. Out on the landing he pushed the elevator button. In moments the doors of the tiny lift slowly clanked open. It was so puny there was barely enough room for two people.

Down on the ground floor, Philippe tumbled out of the elevator, hurried through the entrance hall and yanked open his building's main door. As he exited onto Rue du Fer à Moulin, he was blinded by the blaring sunlight. It was yet another balmy late-September day. Perhaps they could go for a stroll after lunch, but one step at a time. He first needed to purchase everything he needed for *le déjeuner.* Lunch.

Philippe squinted as he crossed the busy Rue Monge. He passed the lovely Fontaine Bazeilles as he walked up the short tree-lined Rue de Bazeilles, where he quickly met the second of the pair of identical fountains, la Fontaine Guy Lartigue. Woven into the melodies of the gurgling fountain water, was some live music. Its volume increased, along with the number of people, as he neared Saint-Médard. The beautiful late Gothic church presided over the small square which stood at the base of the Rue Mouffetard. Affectionately called 'la Mouffe' by locals, Philippe's life revolved around this vibrant market street located in the 5th district of Paris. Today, it was of primordial importance as it was where he would be procuring the essential, and very precise, items on his list.

Narrow, crooked and steep, Rue Mouffetard is one of the oldest streets in Paris. As the saying goes, all roads lead to Rome, well, this is actually the case for this 2,000-year-old street. It starts in the Place de la Contrescarpe, an attractive square which was once on the edge of Roman Paris; then called Lutetia or Lutèce in French. It descends down a sizeable hill, taking a southwesterly course in the vague direction of Italy and thus Rome. The ancient route then meanders through la Place d'Italie, or 'Italy Square.' Over the centuries this road has been modified and split into different streets, with modern day Rue Mouffetard stopping just past Saint-Médard.

Philippe had reached the foot of the church. He glanced up at its flying buttresses, then his eyes traveled down to its entrance. This was the exact spot where he'd first met today's special lunch guest, a mere few weeks ago. But that was on a Tuesday. Today was Sunday... and the square was currently abuzz with a lively swing band and a sea of dancers. Sunday—the busiest day on the street. *Oh mon Dieu.* Dear God. *Why hadn't that crossed his mind?!* Now that he was retired, there wasn't much of a difference between weekdays and weekends for Philippe.

He swallowed hard. This was going to be challenging. But it was all worth it.... for *her.* He pulled the list out of his pocket and, very carefully, sashayed through the dancers to reach his first stop.

***

He had adamantly resisted over and over. More than one friend had urged Philippe to try online dating. To begin with, he wasn't very tech savvy. He was a retired *Métro* train driver, after all. That job didn't require complex computer skills. He just had to know which lever would open and shut the doors, make the train go, slow down and stop. And what to do in case of emergency, of course. Therefore, all this online stuff was rather daunting for him. But, just like for many singles, the lockdown had been very lonely for Philippe. So unless he got up enough courage to talk to the pretty lady who came for her morning coffee at the same time he did at his neighborhood hangout, le Café Mouffetard, or unless he gave into his son Jean's persistent offer to set him up with his mother-in-law's sister (the one who fell asleep at their wedding), he really saw no other option.

"It's easy!" said his friend Gilles, a recent convert to online dating. "You still have that old laptop your son gave you, right?"

"Yes, but..." Philippe protested. He wasn't sure he even remembered how to turn it on. And, the fact Jean had shown him dozens of times how, made no difference. He was very proud of his son's career path and current job at the prestigious Opéra Garnier, but was also too proud to ask him yet again for help.

"I'll come over and get everything set up!" Gilles insisted. Philippe knew better than to refuse his strong willed best friend. Gilles somehow always got his way, at least he had with Philippe for the last 60 odd years. They'd met back in elementary school. They'd gone to the same middle school and high school, however after passing their 'bac,' their baccalaureate exam required to complete French high school, they'd pursued very different career paths. They'd got married, moved out of *le quartier,* had families and got divorced. Now, they found themselves back in the 5th district, coincidentally both living in the same apartments they'd each grown up in.

Gilles invited himself over one night with a bottle of Saint-Emilion. He knew Philippe had a soft spot for this particular red. It wasn't just any bottle of Saint-Emilion either. It came from this excellent Bordeaux-focused wine shop next to where Gilles used to live while he was married, over in the 11th district. Indeed, Philippe's eyes lit up when his friend set the bottle down on the table. This helped him put aside his reservations over the idea, at least for the time being.

Philippe went to get two glasses from the kitchen as Gilles removed the towering pile of junk mail covering the laptop. He deftly turned it on, opened a browser window and typed in the name of the dating site which had worked so well for him. After he'd poured out the wine, Philippe was ordered to put on a smart shirt, comb his hair and smile, as Gilles snapped a few photos with his 'high tech' smartphone. Philippe looked on in awe as Gilles magically transferred the images to the computer (how did he do that without connecting a cable?!) and uploaded them to his new dating profile.

"There's a hobbies section, shall we say you like cooking?" asked Gilles. "That attracts the ladies."

"Well, I prefer eating to cooking," Philippe replied honestly.

"Oh, come on, Philippe, I know your ex-wife was the cook of the house, but your mom must have taught you a few recipes before she passed away last year."

Philippe was a little embarrassed to admit to his *gourmand* friend that his meal plan alternated between prepared dishes bought at the local butcher's, the Greek delicatessen, the Italian specialty shop and then leftovers from each of those. Occasionally, he'd throw into the mix a frozen meal from Picard, France's high quality, frozen food chain. He had been tempted to start ordering from one of these bike delivery companies that had become so popular during the lockdown; however, he couldn't remember how to download apps onto his 'not so smart' phone. Again, he was too ashamed to confess this to either Gilles or his son in order to solicit their help.

Gilles ignored Philippe's hesitation and returned to filing in the profile boxes. Then, moments later he finished with a triumphant 'click.'

"*Voilà!*" he announced victoriously. Philippe sheepishly leaned over to have a look at the screen. He was surprised to see a confident, not bad looking Frenchman of 66 wise years smiling back at him.

"Oh, I put a filter on the photo, I think it looks pretty good!" Gilles boasted. Philippe sighed. All those years spent selling glossy magazines at his newsagent's shop had taught Gilles a thing or two about portrait photography.

"So, what do I do now?" Philippe asked naively.

"We wait for some matches," replied Gilles, taking a sip of his Saint-Emilion. "Don't worry, I'll coach you through all the rest. Well, that is, until you get a date, then you're on your own."

***

Gilles was a man of his word, perhaps a little too much so. It seemed like every day he was calling to touch base, which did admittedly come in handy when Philippe forgot his login details. Gilles taught Philippe how to 'like' profiles he found interesting and gave him some conversation starters which were not too cheesy or lame. Their efforts started paying off. Philippe had a few chats going and within two weeks, he had his first dates lined up. However, he was still very new to this and was learning by trial and error.

The first lesson he learned was to *not* rendezvous at le Café Mouffetard. All his other regular buddies are still teasing him about the first (and only!) woman he'd brought there. She was a buxom brunette from Brittany who made it known, before their drinks had even arrived, that she spent most of her Saturday night's at various swingers' clubs. That was NOT what Philippe had had in mind when he'd let Gilles add 'open-minded' to his dating profile!

His second date was equally disastrous, but for entirely different reasons. This time he wisely suggested meeting at a café in Place Monge. This was another lovely square near the Rue Mouffetard, but was far enough away to have altogether different locals. At first sight, he was very charmed by the cute Kiwi who arrived and then he instantly fell under the charm of her New Zealander accent. However, the only words out of her dainty mouth were gushing praise of her Italian hairdresser, Luciano, who had a salon a few paces away on Rue Monge. It was nothing but 'Luciano this' and 'Luciano that.' She was obviously infatuated with *Luciano il Magnifico*. It was true, she had a wonderful haircut, but it seemed like it would take a much bigger weapon than a pair of scissors to release her ties to the Italian stylist.

The third time's the charm, right? For a reason he couldn't quite pinpoint, Philippe had a good feeling about this next meetup. There was something familiar about her photo, despite the fact that it was taken from a distance and she was wearing sunglasses. On the given day, as Philippe was approaching the designated meeting point, he stopped dead in his tracks. There, right in front of the entrance to Saint-Médard, was her, the lady he saw everyday at le Café Mouffetard. Now, he understood why her photo had caught his eye and why she'd suggested meeting in front of this little-known church, she was also from the neighborhood. She was wearing a smart yet relaxed navy blue skirt suit with a burgundy colored top and had a coordinated silk scarf tied around her neck. Her face lit up when she saw Philippe. This gesture seemed to acknowledge that she too recognized him from their regular café. He hoped she hadn't seen him with the swinging Breton nor heard his friends teasing him about her!

They settled down at a table on the spacious café terrace in front of Saint-Médard and got to know each other. Philippe discovered that Yvonne, a retired nurse, was also divorced. She had a daughter who was a teacher at a middle school in the 14th district, near the Catacombs. Yvonne was part of a *pétanque* ball club which met in the park found within the old Roman arena, les Arènes de Lutèce. She liked going to the L'Epée de Bois cinema, found midway up Rue Mouffetard. Once or twice a month she also went to Le Bowling Mouffetard. Did he know it? Perhaps they could go there together sometime.

Their coffee date had gone so well that, before they parted ways, Philippe suggested they go for dinner the following Thursday. He took her to one of his favorite places, La Grange, a charming Savoyard restaurant with wooden beams and old-fashioned tools decorating the walls. The successful evening of laughter and gooey fondue led to a third date. This time he took her to another favorite, la Bourgogne, where they got to know each other even better over a *cassolette fromagère*. She obviously had an appetite and not just for good food, but for life and living— exactly the kind of positive energy that Philippe needed right now.

Their next date started off with a few lively rounds at the bowling alley. She totally whipped his butt, so he treated her to a victory dinner at le Café Tournbride, another friendly local bistro where they had French onion soup paired with a bottle of Riesling wine. Philippe got a little more adventurous for their fifth date by taking her to the edge of the 5th arrondissement to Les Deux Tours, a restaurant which boasted lovely views of Notre-Dame. Sitting on its terrace on that mild September evening, everything was just perfect, Philippe couldn't have been happier. He gazed up at the Cathedral, its wounded rooftop and missing steeple camouflaged by the plane trees which lined the Seine, and thanked Our Lady for bringing such a special woman into his life. It was at this moment that Yvonne put forth her fateful request.

"I do enjoy eating in these lovely restaurants, however, I recall reading in your profile that you loved cooking. Perhaps you could cook for me next time? I'd absolutely love to try one of your specialties!"

Philippe was left tongue-tied. Staring into Yvonne's sweet and sincere sea-green eyes, how could he possibly say *non?*

***

"*Pas de problème!* It's no problem at all!" asserted Gilles when Philippe explained his dilemma over the phone the next day. "I'm coming over tomorrow night!"

Philippe hung up the phone and breathed a sigh of relief. It was Gilles who had gotten him into this mess by putting that information down on his dating profile. The very least he could do was help get him out of it.

The next day Saint-Médard's bells had just finished tolling seven times when Philippe's doorbell rang. He swung open the door to find Gilles holding several bags of groceries.

"*Bonsoir mon ami!* Good evening my friend!" cheered Gilles. He marched past Philippe and went straight into the kitchen. He set the bags on Gilles's small breakfast table and began removing their contents: a carton of eggs, a baguette, a few brown paper bags and a bottle of wine.

"Here, you can start by opening this," ordered Gilles, handing Philippe a bottle of Sancerre. "Then go get that archaic laptop of yours."

Philippe did as instructed, pouring a half glass of the chilled Loire wine into two glasses. He set the bottle down and went off to accomplish his second mission.

"I thought it would be better for you to learn something yourself," he went on. "So I bought you an early birthday present!"

"But it's September and my birthday is in April!"

"A very, very early present!" Gilles busily typed away on the computer's keyboard.

"*Voilà!*" he concluded with what was becoming his trademark triumphant last click. An irretrievable click, just like on that first fateful night after Giles set up Philippe's dating profile.

Philippe looked at the image and words which popped up on the screen: 'Master French Classics with Chef Lise.' It was a virtual cooking class tutorial, one of the many which had been born out of the quarantine. So many people learned skills online during this period while they were stuck at home. Gilles was among them, Philippe was most certainly not.

"We're going to do the first class together!" declared Gilles. "I thought omelettes would be nice and easy for you. Do you have two aprons?"

What had he gotten himself into? thought Philippe, mortified. Gilles was now loudly rummaging through the kitchen cupboards in search of the other items they'd need for the lesson. Philippe opened the linen drawer, and pulled out two of his mom's old aprons.

"Which one do you want?" offered Philippe. One was pink with ruffles on the straps and the other was emblazoned with the words 'Trois Etoiles Mi-*chat*-lin' (three Mich-*cat*-lin stars) below which was an apron-clad cat holding a wooden spoon.

"Here put this one on, it might bring you luck," snickered Gilles, handing him the one with the cat chef. "And it brings out your big brown eyes!"

Aproned up, Gilles pressed play on the tutorial. Professional chef Lise and amateur chef Gilles made it all seem so simple! Gilles was so skilled in the art of cooking, he might as well have been teaching the class himself. Philippe bet that Gilles could even flip crêpes with his eyes closed. In less than 20 minutes they were sitting down with two fluffy omelettes, sprinkled with parsley and served with a side of green salad.

"*Santé!*" Gilles raised his glass enthusiastically. "See, that wasn't so hard! The recipe is included too, in case you need a reminder on the day of. If you want to be a little creative, you could add in some other ingredients to the omelette. That would impress your *chérie*, your sweetheart, even more."

Gilles heartily dug into their 'team' effort. Philippe wasn't as entirely convinced he'd be able to pull off this omelette feat. Nevertheless, he had to admit, the video tutorial had helped... and the omelette was actually rather tasty.

***

It was D-Day. D for *déjeuner*. Lunch. Philippe embarked on his monumental mission imagining those brave soldiers hitting the Normandy beaches on that history changing day. Today would also be unforgettable for Philippe, but for entirely different reasons.

Philippe started off dodging the dancers swaying through the square. Just then the bells of Saint-Médard chimed once, 11:15. He hoped to be back home by noon. The lower part of the Rue Mouffetard was home to the 'market' section. It was packed with the perfect assortment of shops selling produce, bakery items, fish, meats, fresh pasta and libations. Scattered amongst the food stores were some other vendors selling a variety of items from scarves and hats to household odds and ends.

He looked down at the list he'd so meticulously copied out. He would have to make several different stops. To his left was a large fruit and vegetable vendor. He might as well start there.

Ever since Gilles had suggested dressing up the omelette with some other ingredients, the idea had stuck with Philippe. He'd see what was in season, which was usually proudly displayed in the bins outside the shop. His eyes scanned this week's new arrivals. Squash? Too much work. Artichokes? Even more work! Swiss chard? Not everyone's cup of tea. Chanterelle mushrooms? They wouldn't require much prep work, plus he recalled Yvonne mentioning she was fond of them. *Parfait!* Perfect!

Luckily, the line was moving swiftly and soon it was Philipe's turn.

"*Autre chose?* Anything else?" asked the vendor after he put a large handful of mushrooms into a paper bag.

Philippe checked his list. "Yes, some mixed greens, cherry tomatoes… and some grapes."

"Which sort of grapes?"

"Whichever… those," he said, pointing to the closest ones. In his nervous state Philippe couldn't focus on making too many decisions. Paid up, he went a few doors down to his next stop: the cheese shop. One of the best in Paris, it also had a unique, beautifully painted facade. However, here he wasn't lucky. The line snaked out the door. So Philippe decided to try again on his way back home. Hopefully the line will have gone down by then as it was an essential stop.

Next up, the bakery. Its line was advancing speedily enough, that is, until the person in front of Philippe decided to order a takeaway piece of *quiche lorraine* and a *croque monsieur*. These would need to be heated and thus take up the sales assistant's time. Philippe tapped his foot. The few minutes' wait seemed like an eternity.

"*Une tradition,*" Philippe ordered an old-fashioned style baguette, known at most bakeries as *une tradition,* when his turn came up. "*Et six macarons.*' He'd watched several baking tutorials from the package Gilles bought for him, but today he felt like he could only manage to succeed at just one recipe!

"*Quels parfums?* Which flavors?" the bread seller asked.

Whichever... *un mélange*... a mix." Once again, he was in no mood for decision making.

He left the *boulangerie* with his carefully wrapped package and baguette and continued up the street. Something colorful caught his eye. *Les fleurs!* The flowers! He was in front of the florist, which miraculously didn't have any line at all. Philippe rapidly picked out a pretty bouquet he'd give to Yvonne. Then, he grabbed some sunflowers to decorate his table.

Ladened down with his new purchases, it was a little tricky to weave in and out of the crowds on the street, which were quickly multiplying. His favorite wine shop was a little further up so onwards he trekked.

"Philippe! Philippe!"

He looked over in the direction of the voices. *Oh no!* He was outside le Café Mouffetard. He should have avoided passing in front of his local haunt. Sitting on the terrace were three of his coffee buddies, waving enthusiastically for him to come join them.

"*Désolé mes amis!* Sorry friends, I can't today."

"Ohhh.... Philippe has a date!" said one, whistling.

"Is it with that *belle bretonne?*" asked another. They were never going to let up about that swinger from Brittany.

Blushing, Philippe waved them off and went on his way.

The coast was clear at the *cave à vin*, the wine shop, no big line and no other pestering friends. There was just one other customer whom *le caviste* was advising. Philippe tried to wait patiently, but his level of anxiety had risen with each new stop. He glanced over at the hundreds of bottles on display, all hand picked by the owner, Jacques. He'd know the best wine to go with their lunch.

"*Bonjour Philippe!*" Jacques kindly greeted when he was finished with the other customer. "Is everything ok? You don't look well."

Philippe would normally have been in the mood for some friendly banter, but not today.

"Well, I'm in a bit of a hurry. I'm cooking lunch."

"Oh really?" replied the *caviste*, noticeably surprised. This wasn't something he normally heard from this regular customer.

"I know, I know... an old dog CAN learn new tricks," said Philippe.

"What are you preparing?"

"An omelette."

"Plain or with something?"

"With chanterelles. Then we'll have some cheese, so something that pairs well with both would be ideal."

"I would suggest some Pouilly-Fumé, that should be a good match for everything."

"Excellent. Do you have a bottle *au frais*?"

"Yes, let me get that for you," Jacques ducked into the back room and removed a chilled bottle of this renowned wine, also from the Loire Valley, from the fridge and wrapped it in tissue paper. "Do you need a bag?"

"No, I can put it in this one."

"Perfect." Jacques handed him the wine in exchange for Philippe's 20 euro bill. He slid the bottle delicately next to the produce and took his change.

"*Bon appétit!* Enjoy your meal!"

"*Merci Jacques!*"

Philippe left the wine shop and looked at his watch. It was 11:50, he was making good time, but still had to stop in at the *fromagerie*. Just as he was going back down the street he remembered his buddies sitting outside the café, did he have time to go around to avoid them? Not really, so instead he attempted to shield his face with the bouquets of flowers as he hurried by.

"*Bon appetit*, Philippe!" his friends shouted after him, just as he thought he'd made it safely past them without being noticed a second time. Oh well, enjoying a special meal with Yvonne was worth being the brunt of his gossipy friends and their jokes.

Philippe was relieved to see that the cheese shop's line had diminished greatly. Nevertheless, the customer ahead of him seemed to be inviting half of Paris over for Sunday lunch. Ten or

15 cheeses later, it was finally Philippe's turn. He ordered some aged comté and a generous wedge of brie de Meaux.

"*Autre chose, monsieur?* Anything else?" asked the cheesemonger.

"Non...." Philippe started, but his intuition urged him to double check his list. *The eggs! The cream!* That was a close call! These were more vital to the meal than the cheese and this cheesemonger had the best quality dairy products of any kind.

Now his grocery list was complete. He exited the *fromagerie* as Saint-Médard chimed once. That meant it was 12:15 pm. He was a little behind schedule, but the omelette should only take a few minutes to prepare. However, before that, he'd have to tango his way through those dancers once again, on his way home.

In front of his building Philippe juggled his bags so he could get his keys out of his pocket. He could never remember his door code, so he used an electronic fob. He shuffled inside the tiny lift, its two-person maximum capacity now taken up with all his shopping.

As Philippe went to push FOUR, such was his state of anxiety that he accidentally hit the alarm button, thereby setting off an eardrum splitting alarm.

"*C'est pas possible!* This isn't possible!" he shouted as he stabbed the button repeatedly until it eventually shut off. It seemed like the whole of Rue Mouffetard knew he was cooking lunch. Now all of his neighbors, or at least those who'd peeked their heads out of their apartments to see what was going on, would also know.

As Philippe stumbled out of the elevator and onto his landing, he managed to open his front door without any further disaster. He went straight for his dining room table where he tossed his keys and the flowers. He took the rest of his shopping bags into the kitchen.

"Okay, Philippe, concentrate," he commanded. He looked up at the kitchen clock. He had 40 minutes. That should be plenty of time. He removed all his purchases from the bags. He then carefully unwrapped the two cheeses and placed them onto a plate. It was better to let them breathe, that way the brie would be oozing perfectly when they got around to the cheese course.

He put the lettuce and cherry tomatoes into a colander which he placed into the sink and turned on the tap to rinse. *The recipe!* It was on the table in the other room. He left the water running as he raced to get it.

He snatched up the piece of paper, but then the flowers caught his eye. He should really put the sunflowers into a vase. He grabbed them and opened the buffet to take down the right sized vase. It was covered in dust, it probably hadn't been used since before his mother had passed away.

He took it, and the recipe, back with him into the kitchen. When he arrived, he was surprised to notice that the floor was wet. *The tap!* He'd set the colander on an angle, which covered the drain and caused water to splash everywhere. He reached through the fountain mist, getting the sleeve of his impeccably ironed shirt drenched in the process. As he was turning off the tap, his arm hit the colander, catapulting lettuce and cherry tomatoes all over the already damp kitchen floor. This was NOT what Chef Lise had meant by a 'tossed' salad to accompany the omelette!

Philippe flung the sunflowers into the sink and cautiously stepped backwards to reach the tea-towel drawer. As he did so, he landed squarely on a cherry tomato. He skidded across the floor, and only managed to save himself from tumbling over by gripping onto the counter. He caught his breath and assessed the situation. It could be worse, much worse, but time was ticking by, and quickly. He had to get a move on.

He yanked some tea-towels out of the drawer and threw them on the floor. He mopped up the watery mess, and put the troublesome tomatoes into a small bowl. By some divine intervention, it seemed like most of the lettuce had remained in the colander, so he would still have an *'accompaniment'* for his omelette after all. Floor dry and void of visible hazards, he got back to the recipe, albeit now on a crumpled and smeared sheet of paper.

He grabbed an apron, threw it on and banged around in his cupboards for a medium bowl, whisk, spatula and frying pan. These he carefully organized for efficient cooking. He cracked the entire six eggs into the bowl, added in some cream and whisked ferociously, as Chef Lise's instructions commanded. In the meantime he turned on the burner to get the pan heated up. When it seemed like it was hot enough, he poured the battered mixture into the pan.

Returning the bowl to the counter, he noticed another brown paper bag. *The mushrooms!* Since they were an addition and weren't listed on his recipe, Philippe had forgotten all about them. He tossed the lettuce into a salad bowl and dumped chanterelles into the colander and went over to the sink to rinse them off. *The sunflowers!*

This time he turned off the tap first, took out the flowers and plopped them into the still dusty vase, which he then rushed to the dining table. Reaching the table, he saw that it wasn't ready either. He scooped up the scattered letters and junk mail and shoved them into a cabinet drawer before darting back into the kitchen. As he approached it, he could smell something burning. *The omelette!*

He dove into the kitchen and snapped off the burner switch. In his pan was a crispy brown mess. Just then the fire alarm went off, he rushed to open the kitchen window and swung his hands wildly in an attempt to diffuse the smoke. Smoke... his lunch had just gone up in smoke!

Since he'd only bought precisely what was on his list, there were no more eggs. So he couldn't even make another omelette if he wanted to. Horrified, and before he had time to come up with a backup plan, his doorbell rang. He looked up at the kitchen clock. It was 1:05 pm. He swallowed, hard.

Dazed, confused and utterly defeated, Philippe went to the door and opened it. Standing on the landing was the pristine Yvonne, whose pretty smile faded when she saw Philippe. Just then something to his right caught his attention. In the mirror by the door, was the reflection of a distraught 66-year-old man, hair disheveled and sprinkled with a few yellow petals, one damp sleeve rolled up and wearing a very kitschy cat apron. It was a far cry from the put-together, attractive man Gilles had photographed a month or so before.

Yvonne caught a whiff of the smoke. Her smile returned.

"Shall we go out for lunch?" she asked sweetly. "I noticed that le Café Mouffetard has omelettes on special today. I just adore a good omelette. Then we could go dancing in the square. How does that sound?"

"*Parfait*, Yvonne. That would be just perfect."

The Café on Place Saint-Sulpice

"*C'est libre, Monsieur?*" Lauren asked politely. It looked like the table was free, however, the belongings of the patron at the next table seemed to be spread across the entire row.

"*Ah, oui, oui,*" the man replied flustered as he was suddenly pulled from his daydreaming; gazing out at the square. He looked down over his sprawling collection of sturdy reusable grocery bags and clumsily slid the ones occupying the chair of the 'free' table over onto the one next to him. He looked up at her and smiled.

"*Merci,*" she said, returning his smile. As she set her own tote bag down in the newly liberated one and sat down in the chair next to it, Lauren couldn't help but wonder what was in all of his crumpled bags. They seemed a bit heavy, perhaps they contained the same thing that was in hers?

Lauren's eyes scanned her table and then the ones around it. No menus. Just as she was about to flag down the waiter, she noticed the QR code taped to her tabletop. Ah, yes. She still hadn't gotten used to this new way of accessing menus, brought in to reduce virus germs from being passed around on print menus. She took out her cell phone and held it over the code.

"*Ah! Ça ce fait comme ça!*" That's how it's done!" her café neighbor exclaimed. "I'm hopeless when it comes to technology."

Lauren forced a thin smile in reply. She didn't really feel like chatting. Plus, she couldn't tell whether this older gentleman, with a balding head crowned by tufts of wild Albert Einstein-esque white hair, was crazy or just a bit eccentric. It seemed like ever since arriving in Paris, she'd become a weirdo magnet! Walking down the street, standing in line at the *boulangerie*, sitting in the park, waiting to get her visa at the Préfecture... no matter where she was, an oddball would pop out of the woodwork. She quickly looked down at her phone to peruse the café's virtual menu, hoping also to dodge a possible conversation with her apparent café acquaintance.

"I always get the same thing here, so I don't really need to check the menu," he went on, gesturing down at his half finished glass of white wine. "The Sancerre. It's impeccable. Never disappoints. There's nothing quite like the feeling of this golden nectar of the gods gently tickling your throat... and with the glorious backdrop of this sublimely serene square. Divine. One could even go as far as qualifying it as heavenly!" He finished his eulogy by lifting up his glass and toasting to the square.

It was true, beautiful Place Saint-Sulpice was worthy of a poetic toast. The spacious square nestled within the Saint-Germain district was overlooked by most tourists, however, it was much loved by the residents of *le Rive Gauche*, the Left Bank of Paris. Dominating its easternmost end was the square's namesake: l'Église Saint-Sulpice. The Neo-Classical church was the second largest in Paris. It was slightly smaller than Notre-Dame, but technically it had taken longer to build as its construction was paused several times due to lack of funding, revolutions and other reasons. It was finally finished in 1870, however, shortly thereafter the Franco-Prussian War, Napoléon III's failed attempt to prevent the various German Kingdoms from uniting as one country, broke out. Paris was under siege for four months and some enemy mortar shells hit and damaged one of the church's two already mismatched towers.

In the center of the rectangular space in front of the church was the graceful fountain of 'Les Quarts Points Cardinaux.' Its name was something of a play on words in French. The four sides of the fountain roughly face the four cardinal points—north, east, west and south—and, each proudly displayed the statues of a prominent 17th-century French bishop, who are, still to this day, generally mistaken for cardinals.

Cardinals, bishops, Lauren wasn't too bothered about their classification. She prayed to all four religious men to please stop sending weirdos her way. This was obviously divine punishment for not attending mass for many years, well, actually decades.

"*Avez-vous choisi?* Have you decided?" Luckily the waiter arrived to take her order and, in the process, quieted the overly chatty, overly friendly stranger.

"I'll have…" It was a more complicated choice than it seemed. She'd actually been contemplating the Sancerre, that is, before the unusual stranger gave his unsolicited, albeit exuberant, recommendation. It was a lose-lose situation. He was bound to give his opinion whether she followed his suggestion or whether she went for another type of wine. "*... je prends un kir.* I'll have a kir."

Maybe ordering something entirely different, in this case the popular French *apéritif* made of white Burgundy Aligoté wine with a splash of cassis liqueur, might throw a wrench in her neighbor's conversational plans. Indeed, her order did catch him off guard, providing Lauren with just enough time to slyly retreat back into the safety of her own bubble. Avoiding his gaze, she went about removing the numerous books from her bag. She set them down on the table and pondered which one she was going to read over her kir.

"Hemingway! Joyce! Fizzzzgerald!" he exclaimed in what Lauren now noted was well-spoken but slightly accented French. "All extraordinary writers, but no! So old now! So passé! So timid! Where is Ginsberg, Burroughs or Kerouac?"

Oh brother! Lauren bemoaned silently. She now totally and utterly regretted coming to the café. Nevertheless, she was sick and tired of being holed up in the tiny apartment where she'd spent way too much time this year. Well, almost a year. Little could Lauren have imagined what this year in Paris would have in store when she arrived last November.

***

Lauren was finally able to allot herself a year to write—a goal she'd been chasing for twenty-odd years. After graduating with a dual-major in literature and politics from the University of Moncton, Lauren easily got a job for the Canadian government thanks to her bilingualism. Most people didn't know that Canada had French speaking regions outside of Quebec. She happened to come from one of these, the region of Acadia in the small east coast province of New Brunswick. She moved to Ottawa for the job, one she thought she'd do for a few years, just long enough to pay off her student loans. Then, somehow she was celebrating her 40th birthday in a classy French restaurant down the street from the National Parliament buildings. She did like her job, however, that milestone birthday got her thinking back to that book she'd so strongly dreamed of writing back in those idyllic university years. Thanks to her seniority, Lauren would be able to take a year off and her cushy job would be awaiting her return. She'd get nothing done if she stayed home. Since she was well ahead on her mortgage payments, she could afford a small budget to do her sabbatical year abroad.

What better place to go than Paris, the city that had inspired so many writers before her? Unfortunately, as inspirational as the city *can* be, November, with its interminably grey and rainy days, was certainly the least inspirational month of the whole year in the City of Light. One might think a Canadian would be able to hack chilly weather, however, the cold in Paris wasn't like back home. It was a humid, bone-penetrating cold, particularly aggravated by the bad (or nonexistent) insulation in the decaying apartment building she was staying in. This was located one street away from the Place Saint-Sulpice and was probably older than the church itself.

She'd thought she'd given herself a big enough budget, however, with the weak Canadian dollar, her loonies (the affectionate name of Canadian one-dollar coins) fell short of the amount required for the one-bedroom apartment she'd envisioned. Plus, it was harder to find an apartment for rent than she'd expected. A friend had given her some tips on how to find one directly from the owner. But this was where she'd encountered her first weirdo! Or rather weirdo**s**!

One landlord was taking a nap on the bed of the rental apartment when she arrived. Another was gnawing on a chunk of sausage the whole time (didn't the French only eat at the table??). And a third looked (and smelled) like he hadn't showered in about a year. While they were touring the equally stinky apartment, he actually paused in the bathroom to use a can of air freshener as deodorant. In the end she resorted to going through an agency. It was, thankfully, not run by weirdos, however, it only had one place her budget could afford, a tiny *chambre de bonne,* a former maid's quarters. These small spaces were the rooms located under the rafters of many Parisian buildings. If Hemingway had managed to be creative and productive while shivering away in the drafty *chambre de bonne* he used as his office, which was situated a short walk away on the other side of the Luxembourg Gardens, so could she. She accepted it right away.

By the time she'd sorted all of that out and was settled into her new place, it was already December and the city was aglow with holiday lights. The festive ambiance warmed Lauren and she finally got down to writing. She typed her way through the holidays, slipping out only for a Christmas meal at the Closerie des Lilas, one of Hemingway's favorite restaurants found on the south side of the park, and to attend a New Year's Eve concert held right here at Saint-Sulpice Church. And, true to form, in both places, she had oddballs sitting next to her. These locals talked her ear off as they went through their entire life story, however, they were enjoyable experiences nonetheless. Actually, she had to confess to herself afterwards, it had been nice to talk to someone. She'd been so focused on her 'project' that she hadn't taken the time to try to make any friends. That was not the goal of this trip.

Her lifted spirits, and revitalized inspiration, were quickly washed away with January's rain clouds. Little by little she became less and less productive. Things should have improved in February with the arrival of warmer and longer days, but by that time, all anyone could talk about was this fast spreading virus.

When the quarantine seemed imminent, Lauren anguished over what to do. She could go back to Ottawa, but she'd paid a full year's rent upfront in order to secure her dismal lodgings. Plus, she'd been looking forward to this year, and what a shame it would be to give it up for what would probably be a short-lived crisis. She could manage to stay held up in her shoebox for a month, couldn't she? Besides, that was pretty much what she'd intended to do all along, wasn't it? To not leave the house and write all day long. Isn't that what Hemingway had done? Yes, but the vast difference was he'd been able to take inspirational walks in the park and he spent most of his evenings in cafés, the very two things which were now forbidden, albeit temporarily.

At the beginning of the quarantine she *was* actually productive, then a month turned into two. Her output also changed two-fold—a two-fold decrease, that is. Soon she found it more and more tempting to click on the Netflix icon on her laptop rather than on the word processing one. She made her way through all the latest American TV series and even a few French ones. She had a particular fondness for *Inspecteur Marcel*, a show about a police inspector who investigated mysterious crimes around Paris. This gave her a much needed window into the city beyond the one-kilometer radius authorized by the country's strict lockdown. Despite this virtual escape, she was sorely lacking human contact.

As happy as she was when the quarantine finally ended, she ⁃ ˙ 't quite get out of the funk she was in. She would stare at her computer screen for hours and only manage to write a few lines, or maybe a whole page on a good day. She took stock at the end of the summer and realized she'd barely reached 20% of her year-long goal! This is when she had to look reality in the face and admit the truth. She had writer's block. And bad. She still had two and a half months left in Paris, but if she was going to get anything accomplished, she'd have to get out of this deep rut first.

She attempted to fill in this hole by going back to the basics. She'd planned on setting her novel in Paris of the 1920s, so she spent the first two weeks of September burrowed in her rooftop den rereading all the books from the Lost Generation. She hadn't read most of them since university, but she believed this would help her get under the skin of the character and the era. Since the weather was nice, she eventually decided to do some of this reading outside. She'd tried reading in the Luxembourg Gardens, but every time she went, the same weirdo managed to find her! He'd sit down beside her and describe all the different symbols he could 'read' in that day's clouds.To evade him, she tried the Palais-Royal Garden. She'd discovered this pretty park after she'd stopped by an old bookstore located in a nearby historic passageway. There she picked up a used copy of Hemingway's *The Sun Also Rises* and F. Scott Fitzgerald's *Tender is the Night*. Settled down on a nice bench, she had to shrug off yet another annoying oddball, a man who sat down beside her and was ranting on about how the first French Revolution had been sparked in that very place. She tried switching benches and sat down next to an elderly woman who, in turn, wouldn't stop glaring at her with disdain. This lady seemed to think she owned the entire bench!

She then tried the Parc Monceau, thinking that this posh park would certainly be free of freaks. But no! This time a bizarre character sat down next to her and went on and on about how Lauren should be reading under a tree in the more obscure Buttes-Chaumont park. If this kooky lady preferred that other park so much, why wouldn't she leave Lauren alone and go over there! *Enough!*

These episodes got Lauren thinking. Maybe zany characters were more attracted to parks? Could be. So she decided to shift her outdoor reading locale. The café terrace overlooking the square seemed harmless enough. But looks can be deceiving. Even in the discreetly chic neighborhood of Saint Germain, there was no escaping the weirdos.

***

The waiter set the kir, and a small dish of complementary olives, gracefully down on Lauren's table. This provided another useful distraction from Monsieur Chatty, however, she feared he was absolutely intent on conversing with her.

"*Santé!* Cheers!" he chimed from his table, tipping his glass in her direction.

"*Santé,*" she half-heartedly reciprocated.

"Did you know that when Alan Ginsberg came to Paris in 1957, he lived just a few blocks from here?" he asked, enthusiastically picking up the conversation interrupted by the waiter.

"No, I didn't know that," Lauren replied politely, trying to keep it simple.

"Oh yes," he carried on passionately. "Over on Rue Gît-le-Coeur, near Place Saint-Michel. He stayed in a dive hotel which they nicknamed the Beat Hotel, you know, for the Beatnik generation."

"Yes, I know of the Beatniks…" she started to reply, but before she could say that she'd studied literature, he carried on with his tirade.

"Those were the days!" he declared wistfully. "Sure, the Lost Generation writers spent lots of time in cafés and altered the course of 20th century literature, but the Beatniks were also part of a movement. They helped trigger the revolutionary decades of the 1960s and 70s. Sure, some French people also played a part in this, like Jean-Paul Sartre and Simon de Beauvoir. They were

headquartered at Café de Flore just up the block from here. So
much was going on at that time, forget the 1920s!"

headquartered at Café de Flore just up the block from here. So
much was going on at that time, forget the 1920s!"

"Did you know Ginsberg while he was living here?"

"Me? No. I was but a mere boy in the 50s. I first came to Paris
from Milan in 1968, a big year of revolt, not just here, but across
the globe. It was definitely an exhilarating time to be here, but I
would have rather been born ten years earlier. That way I could
have been a real Beatnik myself."

Ah, so he's Italian, Lauren noted. *I guess that explains why
he's so expressive.* This brought him down on the weirdo scale, but
only a few precautionary notches.

"1968? That must have been an exciting time to be here
despite being too late for the Beatniks."

"Terribly exciting! Maybe too exciting. By day cobblestones
were flying over the protest barricades and by night clothes were
flying off those free-spirited Sorbonne students high above the
street in their *chambres de bonne!*"

Oh no, chambres de bonne... like where she was staying!
Lauren blushed. She hoped he wouldn't go into too many vivid
details about those particular exploits! She was quite sure she
didn't want to imagine him without his clothes, even if it was a
younger version of himself.

"So did you come to Paris for your studies?" she asked, trying
to steer the conversation onto a more prudish track.

"Yes, although those were quickly set aside for the *cause*. The
unrest brewed, but not like weak French coffee, it was quick and
powerful... like real coffee made in an Italian espresso pot! The
flame was ignited at the beginning of May and, over the following
weeks, the turmoil rapidly bubbled up with each student sit-in and
each new factory strike. The Latin Quarter was the epicenter of
this revolution. It's true, there was some unnecessary violence on
both sides and maybe a few too many cars were set on fire and
shop fronts destroyed, but it was the time... the time to stand up
for our rights!"

Lauren looked in the direction of the Sorbonne, which was a few blocks away across the park, not far from where 'Hem' had lived and worked. Although it was the headquarters of the University of Paris, the university was actually spread across dozens of buildings around Paris, with a high concentration over in the 5th district as well as in 6th, where they currently were. It was hard to imagine these elegant and peaceful streets erupting in violent protests. She looked back to the tranquil Place Saint-Sulpice. It was a Thursday and on the other side of the square some people were setting up some white stands. The large square was often used for art fairs and antique sales, there must be one taking place that coming weekend. *Their equipment would be useful for barricades*, thought Lauren. *Hey! Wait a second!* Was she getting into the revolutionary spirit herself?

"Over a million people marched in the general strike of May 13th, unlucky number 13… for the French government, but not only it! The upheaval brought down *le Grand Charles*. It was the beginning of the end for President Charles de Gaulle."

"That does certainly sound like a very exciting time," replied Lauren, who'd actually enjoyed the Italian's riveting description of the events of this influential period in French history. She couldn't help reflecting how current times showed parallels, including the French Yellow Vest movement and the demonstrations, taking place around the world, against racism and police brutality.

"There were peaceful protests then too, and a lot of solidarity was displayed by all walks of life. I still remember some of our chants and slogans. 'It is forbidden to forbid,' 'Be realistic, ask the impossible,' 'I love you! Oh, say it with paving stones!' or, my personal favorite, 'Enjoy without hindrance.' Cheers to enjoying life without hindrance! *Santé!*"

"*Santé!*" replied Lauren, more enthusiastically than she had for the first toast he'd proposed. That sounded like a great motto and she realized it was something she had, unfortunately, not been doing since she'd arrived last November.

"*Mai soixante-huit,* or May of 1968, should really go down in history books as France's fifth revolution! Actually that's the title of my latest book," revealed the ardent Italian. He reached into one of his many bags and produced a white and red covered book. He set it on Lauren's table. "Here, for you!"

"Oh, thank you," said Lauren, surprised by his impromptu gift. She picked it up and turned it around to read the back cover. "So you're a writer?"

"Not a writer," he corrected. "a philosopher who occasionally communicates his thoughts through words. Had we been back in the times of Socrates, there would be wise men orating on the streets, and the public would stop to listen. That's how revolutionary ideas got around, via word of mouth. However, in contemporary times all of that seems to be done only in print... or actually now on those little phone screens. My teenage granddaughter is glued to her phone, but there's still hope for my little 10-year-old grandson. Maybe I can pass the revolutionary torch on to him."

This thought momentarily silenced the passionate Italian. Lauren could almost see his train of thought, accompanied by his gaze, traveling over to the square. His pensive state was broken by the scattering of a flock of pigeons, previously patiently pecking away on the square before a young boy came to chase after them.

"And what is it you do, kind fair lady?" he asked, returning his attention to Lauren.

"It's Lauren."

"Ah, Lauren. I'm Giancarlo and it's my greatest honor to meet you. So what is it you do, kind fair Lauren?"

"I'm a writer too," she replied without thinking. "Well, um... an aspiring writer. I came to Paris to write."

"Ah, I now see why you are reading those books," he commented, taking a sip of his Sancerre. "Came to Paris, you said. I thought I heard a little accent. Are you from Quebec?"

"No, Acadia..."

"Acadia! Then you too must have some revolutionary spirit in your DNA!"

"That might be a bit of a stretch."

"Oh, but your ancestors stood up to the British when they wouldn't pledge allegiance to their crown. A daring act which led to many being deported. A large portion of these embarked on an exodus to the then French-ruled Louisiana where they became known as *les Cadiens*, or the Cajuns. A feisty bunch, that's for sure."

Feisty wasn't the exact adjective normally used to describe Lauren, however, all this talk was firing up her imagination. Was it just a coincidence that all of these odd characters gravitated towards her? She'd wanted to come to Paris to be inspired. She had even said to herself that she couldn't do this back in Ottawa, back in her cozy home in the suburb of Barrhaven. But now that she was here, she'd been rejecting the inspiration the city was giving her. Maybe her book wasn't meant to be set in the 1920s at all. She took a sip of her kir, which was now almost finished, and looked back over at the Italian.

"Shall we have another glass?" he suggested with a mischievous grin. "To toast to the success of your book, *chère* Lauren?"

"That would be great, Giancarlo," she accepted, her resistance fading along with the afternoon sunlight. Drenched in a honey golden glow, the square was at its prime at this hour. The workers had made progress with setting up their 'barricades,' some antique dealers had shown up ready to unpack their boxes of vintage treasures for what was now obviously going to be a *brocante* sale and even more kids had spilled out of a neighboring school and were zipping around on their foot scooters or simply chasing pigeons.

"Waiter, waiter! Two glasses of Sancerre!"

She smiled. Giancarlo had gotten his way. And, she finally felt free enough to give into the moment; to give into Paris. She would be open to its inspiration, but perhaps only some, not all, of its weirdos.

This story is dedicated to Lauren Hume and Giancarlo Pizzi.
Two lovers of Paris who disappeared this year, not directly from
Covid, but in part due to the strain it put
on the healthcare system.

L'Âge Mûr at the Musée d'Orsay

"*Mesdames, Messieurs, je vous prie de bien vouloir patienter pour régulation,*" a muffled voice cracked through the *Métro* car's speakers, notifying passengers that the train was held up because of traffic.

Hearing the announcement made Aurélien fume. *I'm totally going to be late! This was such a bad idea!*

It was 1:40 pm. He was cutting it way too close. He just might manage to arrive in the nick of time, *if* he was lucky. This was supposed to be 'fun,' and now it felt like he was back at school, racing to slide into the classroom before the professor arrived.

Just then the door of his section swung open and an accordion-wielding musician hopped in.

"*Mesdames, Messieurs… un peu de musique pour votre trajet!* Ladies and gentlemen, some music for your journey!"

Seriously? Could things get any worse?! griped Aurélien. He immediately shuffled to another section of the carriage to get away from the music, he really didn't need anything else to add to his already highly agitated state.

"Il n'y a qu'un seul Paris…" the singer began.

Only **one** *Paris, huh?* huffed Aurélien. *If that was the case… it was currently a very bad one!*

***

It had all started a year ago, to the day. Aurélien's boss, Cécile, had requested a meeting. That was definitely a bad sign. It was only the second one-on-one they'd had since, well, his job interview. Word had gotten around that there would be some layoffs. It seemed like Aurélien was going to be among the first sent to the chopping block.

He had to confess. While he'd been a 'good' employee these past seven years, he wasn't exactly passionate about his job. He arrived on time. He submitted his reports by their deadlines. He was amiable to his colleagues, but, in true French work style, kept his distance from them. He always passed his annual performance assessment without any issues and, consequently, received the standard pay rise. But let's face it, he just wasn't that passionate about mortgage loans. This was not his 'dream' job by a long shot. *How had he ever ended up there?*

***

— RUE DU BAC STATION —

Enfin! Finally! One more stop! Aurélien grumbled as he went over to the *Métro* car doors in anticipation. The stress of being late and the accordion music were doing his head in.

Then, just as they were pulling out of the station, the train stopped again, this time right at the mouth of the tunnel. The *Métro* driver's voice was barely audible over the blaring accordion. He looked at his watch again. 1:47 pm.

Sighing dramatically, he glared out the window, anything in order to distract him from his current situation. In fact, something did capture his attention, something colorful on the tunnel wall. Some stretches of the *Métro* tunnel walls were plastered with street art, or rather graffiti tags. This one was different. On the wall was the replica of a statue of a man, eyes closed, one hand on his chest, the other behind his head. Even though his studies were now far in the past, Aurélien immediately recognized it as a Michelangelo, one of the Louvre's two sculptures by the Italian master. This was *The Dying Slave*. However, instead of all white, the wavy section of rock at his feet was filled with tiny green virus symbols, which traveled in a swirl up and around his body and into the ties around the figure's chest and wrist. On his face was one of those heavy-duty gas masks. At its base, the 'work' was signed D-Zyne.

The Dying Slave. A Slave to the wage. That was Aurélien. Could a return to art be his own savior?

***

Sure enough, when he'd entered Cécile's office for that fateful meeting, doom was hanging heavily in the air. She didn't beat around the bush. With the automatization of his sector, having an actual person do rate calculations and simulations was less necessary. So they were 'offering' him his walking papers, along with half of the team, which made him feel a tiny bit better. They were proposing him *une rupture conventionnelle*, a type of layoff agreed by both parties in which the employee would qualify for two years of unemployment benefits. In his case, to encourage employees to accept, the company would also be giving a very generous payout. *Where did he sign?*

At first Aurélien took the layoff as *un coup de chance*. Yes, it really seemed like a stroke of good luck. It would give him a chance at a fresh start. He felt quite confident that, with his solid resume, he could find a new job in his or a related sector *sans problème*, without a problem.

After a three-week holiday hopping around the Greek Isles with his girlfriend, he returned to Paris energized and ready to tackle his job hunt. He spent hours sifting through job websites. He signed up for email alerts. He sent off dozens of resumes... but he was only getting standard copy-and-paste rejection emails in reply —if he got any reply at all. When he last looked for a job, seven years ago, Aurélien's situation was quite different, and not only because of technological advancements.

He was now 48, which meant, professionally speaking in France, he was practically prehistoric, or, at best, from the Stone Age. He was too experienced, too unmalleable, too expensive... or so he assumed those recruiters must be thinking, based on the radio silence he was getting. Nevertheless, he did have some friends around the same age who'd recently landed new jobs. Why wasn't he even being called in for an interview? No, not one.

His initial optimism waned as the weeks tricked into months. He was crawling out of bed later and later. He didn't bother shaving every day. The dishes were piling up in his kitchen, as were the wine bottles in his recycling bin.

He got something of a wake up 'call' four months into unemployment when his girlfriend rang to say that things weren't working anymore. There was no point in having any discussion, she added. She'd had a chance encounter at her favorite café over on Place Saint-Sulpice and had been swept off her feet by a new suitor. She wished him the best of luck, and added he would need it.

Shortly afterwards, the lockdown was announced. He'd been spending so much time at home already, this didn't change Aurélien's routine very much. In fact, at first it provided him with the ideal excuse for not looking for a job and for lazing around on his sofa, watching episode after episode of *Inspector Marcel* or simply wallowing in his own self pity. His sink and his recycling bin were teetering dangerously on the brink of overflowing.

Things hadn't changed much either after the end of the lockdown, that is, until he had an unexpected visitor in early September.

"*Degueulasse!* Gross!" balked Clarisse, upon entering his apartment and waving a hand in front of her nose. She and Aurélien had been friends since middle school. After sensing that he wasn't doing so well, she decided to pop by to check up on him. This visit confirmed her worst fears. After brushing baguette crumbs off the sofa, she plopped down and listened to Aurélien's woeful story.

"Aurélien, you didn't like your job and you didn't really like the previous one," noted Clarisse, always the wise one. "Why don't you use this time to figure out what you really want to do? Didn't you first study art history? Why don't you attend some art talks or something? Immersing yourself in some culture might give you some fresh perspectives. At the very least, it'll get you out of the house."

Aurélien had studied art history—for one year. Then, he finally gave into his parents, who'd been pressuring him into studying something more practical. Now, 20+ years later, look what position his business degree had put him in: jobless, inspirationless, girlfriendless... okay, maybe it wasn't fair to blame the last 'less' on his studies, too.

***

— SOLFÉRINO STATION —

As soon as he heard the little click of the door's lock release, he flipped up the handle and jumped out of the car. Once on the platform, he swung his head back and forth in search of a sign leading him to the correct exit and in doing so, he smashed right into a fellow commuter, also in a hurry. The 40-year-old, dressed in jeans and a dress shirt, rudely barged past him and jumped into the carriage.

"*Bonne chance!* Good luck!" Aurélien mumbled under his breath. The pushy fellow passenger would have to contend with the ear-piercing accordion player. Returning his attention to the task at hand, Aurélien looked up at the *Métro* signal clock. Its yellow lights flashed 1:52 pm. He had eight minutes. Could he make it in time?

***

In the days after Clarisse's impromptu visit (and counselling), her words of wisdom were running laps around his mind. She had a point. Although he might not make a complete 180-degree turn career wise, some cultural outings could help shift his negative mindset—and his self-neglect. What's more, his unemployment status granted him free entrance to most museums. Therefore, the diversion would only cost him the price of a *Métro* ticket and even those he got at a discount due to his unemployment status.

Late one afternoon, he popped into his neighborhood *fromagerie*. The *fromager* was beaming, he'd just received a fresh stock of some exceptional goat cheese which Aurélien simply had to try. *Mais bien sûr!* But of course! Leaving the cheese shop, he unconsciously gravitated towards the wine shop. Since the scolding from Clarisse, he'd made a concerted effort to get his alcohol consumption under control, however, such a prized cheese absolutely deserved the perfect wine pairing. His wine merchant suggested as a bottle of Muscadet, a light white from western Loire Valley. He would just have a glass. Or two.

Leaving the wine shop, he stopped in at his newsagent's. His natural reflex, to pick up the latest edition of *GQ*, was intercepted by a small white and blue magazine: *L'Officiel des Spectacles*, the weekly listing of Paris's cultural offerings. He was surprised to see the magazine was still in print, he would have assumed it would be yet another victim of technology! He placed a one-euro coin in front of the newsagent and slid the little booklet in his bag, next into the bottle of Muscadet.

That evening, while nibbling away on his *chèvre*, he couldn't resist the temptation to check his ex-girlfriend's Facebook page. He immediately noticed that something was different. The picture he'd taken of her, all tanned and smiling on a cobbled street in Mykonos, had been replaced with a new photo. There she was, smiling broadly, in Venice of all places, arm-in-arm with another man. It had to be her café-encounter Romeo. Aurélien flung his phone on the coffee table next to his picnic dinner. He then ripped off a chunk of baguette, copiously smeared it with goat cheese, topped up his glass of crisp wine and burrowed himself into the sofa.

That's exactly where he found himself the next morning, or rather afternoon. On this day in Aurélien history, he'd achieved an unemployment wake-up time of 12:55 pm. A new record. Okay, it seemed clear that he hadn't really gotten his wine intake under control.

"Aurélien, pull yourself together," he chided as he raised his head from the sofa cushion, sat up and brushed some baguette crumbs off his face. His hazy eyes surveyed the contents of his coffee table: an empty bottle of Muscadet, the axe murderer remains of his goat cheese, the end piece of now stale baguette and something white and blue. *L'Officiel.* He snatched up the tiny magazine and flipped to today's date.

"Ah ha!" he declared when his finger stopped on the words: 'Musée d'Orsay, free tour with admission ticket, 2 pm.' It was 1:05 pm, he could make it there on time. With renewed determination, he tossed the magazine onto the apocalyptic coffee table and bolted for the shower.

It should normally have only taken him 20 minutes to get from his apartment in the 14th arrondissement near the Catacombs to the Orsay Museum. But the *Métro* gods were not on his side that afternoon. As he hopped down the steps to the platform, a train was just pulling out of the station. The next one wasn't for another six minutes, an eternity by Paris daytime *Métro* standards. To keep from getting annoyed or antsy, he distracted himself with thoughts of what awaited him at the museum: Monet's delicate water lilies, Renoir's rosy-cheeked ladies, van Gogh's undulating clouds and Degas's dainty little dancers. Yes. It would be nice to revive his love of art.

Sadly little of this joy was still showing on Aurélien's face as he jogged up Rue de Bellechasse, the time was flirting dangerously close to 2 pm. Arriving in the plaza in front of the museum, Aurélien jetted towards the shortest line, neglecting to see it was for special card holders only. Reaching the revolving entrance doors, the security guard raised his eyebrow when Aurélien presented his unemployment card. The guard pointed to the list of cards which granted skip-the-line access. An unemployed card was not among those cited, but rolling his eyes, he waved Aurélien through anyway.

More card flashing got him past the ticket controller, who sent him in the direction of the tour desk. It was hard not to stop in awe when one first enters the Musée d'Orsay. In the 1980s the former Belle Epoque train station had been converted into a museum. This provided a new more spacious home for the French State's collection of mid-19th to early-20th century art that was previously crammed into the tiny Jeu de Paume museum. The Orsay's soaring main hall, with its gigantic arched ceilings adorned with elegant iron rosettes, still reminded one of the building's original *raison d'être*, or function. One could still almost hear the train whistles and feel the clouds of steam hovering in the air. However, at that moment, Aurélien didn't have time to admire the building's stunning splendor. He quickened his pace and craned his head up at the huge clock which presides over the hall. It was 1:58 pm. He'd made it. Proud of his victory, he whipped around and... *Wham!*

"*Oh la la!* I'm so sorry!" he apologized, horrified that he'd just crashed into someone.

"Aurélien?" asked his run-in victim, who seemed unscathed by the incident.

"Bénédicte?!" Standing in front of him was his first-year university crush.

"Wow, it's so nice to see you!" she cheerfully replied. "What's it been... 20 years?"

"Something like that..." he managed to spit out while trying to catch his breath and regain his composure.

It was more like 25 years, actually. After Aurélien had switched degree programs, they'd run into each other occasionally around the Sorbonne, but he never worked up enough courage to ask her out. After he finished his degree and got his first job at a mortgage broker's, he started hanging out less and less with those original university friends. He'd see Bénédicte's name on the occasional group email with invites to 25th or 30th birthday parties (this was way before the days of Facebook), but over the years, as everyone settled into their professional lives, these emails eventually dried up. Beautiful and bright Bénédicte had also drifted to the back of his mind.

"How are things going?" she asked, with one eye on the clock.

"Ahhh, things are fine. No, they are great!"

"Still working in mortgages?"

"Um, ah, something like that..." he fumbled, not wanting to get into the details of his current unemployment woes.

"Shouldn't you be at work right now?" she asked, puzzled.

"Ahhh, I took a day off..." he blurted without thinking.

"Ahh, I see," she replied. "I'd love to chat, but I really have to run."

"Me too, I have a tour to get to."

"Oh really? So do I," she said while slowly steering them in the direction of the tour desk.

"What a coincidence!" he exclaimed as they neared the desk. "Which one are you attending?"

"I'm not really *attending* a tour, per se ..." Bénédicte started.

"Professor Conroy, there you are!" shouted a frantic woman from behind the tour desk, waving a clipboard wildly at Bénédicte.

Aurélien's mouth dropped as Bénédicte turned her head to the tour group organizer, giving her an 'I'm coming' gesture.

"There's only one tour in French starting at 2 pm. I'm so pleased to see you're still interested in art, Aurélien, and especially given the topic of my tour."

Aurélien's eyes drifted over to the desk, where there was a large sign advertising the tour of the day:

— *ARTISTS FEMMES: UN AUTRE REGARD* —
— *WOMEN ARTISTS: ANOTHER VISION* —

His eyes darted back to Bénédicte, or rather to Professor Conroy.

"Oh, yes... yes... of course. I can't wait," he stammered as visions of Monet's bobbing water lilies, Renoir's luscious ladies and van Gogh's curvaceous clouds pranced out of his head as quickly as Degas's little dancers.

"*Messieur*, please register so we can start the tour," ordered the tour organizer, shoving her clipboard at Aurélien. He duly jotted his name and email address down on the form, while the organizer herded together the others who'd already signed up for the tour.

"*Mesdames, Messieurs*, what an honor it is to have Professor Conroy with us today," started the tour organizer. "Art History professor at the Sorbonne, author of six critically acclaimed books and renowned expert on women artists of the 19th and early-20th century, I am certain you will have an enlightening tour with Professor Conroy."

The tour attendees all clapped to welcome their accomplished guide. Aurélien was in a state of bewilderment, first from running into Bénédicte and then at the description of her illustrious career.

"Thank you so much for such a glowing introduction, Karine," began Bénédicte. "As the title of this special tour indicates, we will be looking at some key works produced by women artists that are rightfully displayed in this prestigious museum. We will see how the works and careers of artists like Rosa Bonheur, Mary Cassatt,

Berthe Morisot, Eva Gonzalès and Camille Claudel helped change the course of art history and paved the way for more gender equality in the art world. These female artists were quite daring for that time period. There's no better place to do this than in front of the artworks themselves. So, without further ado, please, follow me."

As the tour proceeded, Aurélien had more and more trouble concentrating, but it was not because of Berthe Morisot's blurry brushstrokes. He was enraptured by Bénédicte. She had always been top of the class, so Aurélien wasn't surprised that she was so knowledgeable, it was her passion for the subject that hypnotized him. Soon he was hanging on her every word.

Bénédicte plunged the tour attendees into the movement and realism of Rosa Bonheur's *Ploughing in Nevers*, a scene of a farmer arduously preparing his fields for autumn with the help of his cattle. The group peered into Mary Cassatt's *Girl in the Garden,* quietly observing the young subject of the painting sewing amidst vivid flowers and greenery. They joined the glamorous theater-goers of the Belle Epoque in Eva Gonzalès's *A Box at the Theatre des Italiens.*

Aurélien would never look at Impressionism the same way again. His perspectives were changing in other ways as well.

"For our last work, I would like to show you one of the museum's most important sculptures," announced Bénédicte, as she escorted the group back down to the museum's lofty main hall. They did not go to the ground floor, but instead to a side mezzanine. Passing by the works of Auguste Rodin, Antoine Bourdelle and Aristide Maillol, they came to a halt at an imposing composition in bronze.

"This is *L'Âge Mûr* (*Maturity*), one of Camille Claudel's finest works," introduced Bénédicte. "Claudel can be admired for her ingenious talent, for her struggle as a woman artist and for all the challenges she went through during her tumultuous relationship with her mentor, Rodin. Working on a state commission secured by Rodin in 1895, Claudel produced this work soon after their breakup. In it we see a middle-aged male figure, interpreted as Rodin, entering the embrace of old age, depicted as an elderly woman. Behind him on her knees, is youth reaching out for him, trying to hold him back, this is Camille. She not only captured the intensity of the moment, of her experience, but also her soul. Finished on the eve of the new century, one could even say it illustrates the trials and tribulations these brave women went through to usher in a new era for female artists."

The group broke into thunderous applause at the conclusion of the tour. Obviously Aurélien was not the only one who'd been enraptured by Bénédicte. He waited in the background as some of the attendees passed on a few personal words of thanks to Bénédicte. When they'd all gone, he meekly stepped forward.

"That was amazing, really," he humbly praised.

"So, does that mean you'll take days off to come to the museum more often?" Bénédicte suggested with a wink.

"Well, actually I have a confession to make. I'm currently unemployed. So, right now, every day is a day off."

"Oh, I'm really sorry to hear that, Aurélien," she replied with sincerity.

"Seeing you in action makes me think I should have carried on with my art studies all those years ago!" he joked, trying to lighten the atmosphere.

"It's never too late!" she correctly affirmed. No, it wasn't too late, not for a lot of things in his life.

L'Âge Mûr. Was Aurélien ready for his own age of maturity? Would he have enough courage, like these audacious artists, to forge his own new path? Whatever that may be?

"Would you like to grab a coffee?" asked Aurélien in an attempt at his first bold new step. "It would be nice to catch up a little more."

"I'm afraid, I can't," she said. "I have an appointment with one of my Master's students. Speaking of which, I should head out so I'm not late."

"Ah okay, no problem, you're obviously very busy," he stammered, somewhat embarrassed for having dared to ask in the first place.

"But if you're free next Wednesday, I am giving a talk on Camille Claudel at the Rodin Museum. Why don't you come?"

"That sounds great."

"2 pm, on the dot," she teased in reference to their run-in at the beginning of the tour as she turned to rush off to her meeting. "See you then!"

He gazed up at the museum's gigantic clock. Yes, he would be on time—on time for his own life, instead of wallowing it away, instead of letting it pass him by. He was ready to reset his personal life clock.

Le Métro
8th, 9th & 10th Arrondissements

Just as Sasha had presumed, Petite Piaf didn't have the permit normally required for musicians to legally perform in the *Métro*, otherwise she would have been displaying it. The group of controllers was on her like bees to honey. Sasha was busy watching this when the other batch of controllers approached him.

"*Monsieur, votre titre de transport,*" requested one of them. Sasha didn't react.

"*Monsieur,* your ticket or transit pass, now," demanded another controller who was twice the size of the first one. Sasha snapped out of his hypnotic trance fixated on Petite Piaf. He rummaged through the pocket of his satchel for his ticket. The train was journeying north and was currently beneath the Seine River as it crossed from 7th arrondissement to the 8th.

Sasha could hear Petite Piaf trying to talk her way out of a fine. The train's speed decreased as it neared Concorde Station. Petite Piaf's tone increased. She'd launched into a speech about her right to be an *artiste*. She should be able to express her creativity wherever and whenever she liked. She added fervor to her monologue by dramatically waving her arms.

"Yes! The Revolutionaries were right to take action! Off with their heads! Off with the heads of authoritarian tyrants!"

Her fiery words were firing up the hulky controller. He left the seemingly harmless Sasha and stomped through the carriage towards the disruptor. The train came to a stop at Concorde. The walls of this particular platform were covered in tiled letters which spelled out the Declaration of the Rights of Man and of the Citizen, a document established in 1789 near the beginning of the first French Revolution, the one Petite Piaf was alluding to in her rhetoric. The choice of this station for an homage to this important document was no accident. High above them was Place de la Concorde, where the main guillotine had been in that Revolution. During those turbulent times the square was also briefly renamed Place de la Révolution.

"*Vive la Révolution!*" cried Petite Piaf as she raised her arm in a valiant gesture resembling the heroine of Delacroix's painting *Liberty Leading the People*, hanging a short distance away at the Louvre. The doors of the train shot open and the modern-day revolutionary dashed off the train. Sasha's eye bulged at her audacity. He then raced after her. He couldn't let her charge over the barricades without him!

The red beret flew up the escalator. Sasha was trailing around half the escalator length behind her. Some shouting echoed up from the platform, but he didn't dare turn around to see if the controllers were in hot pursuit or not.

When he got to the top of the escalator, Sasha was confronted with a number of passageways. In addition to Line 12, from which they'd just descended, Concorde Station had two other lines, numbers 1 and 8. They'd already been on Line 1 earlier on, so he would take his chances with number 8. Fortunately, his hunch was right. As he entered the long corridor leading to it, he spotted the red beret bouncing through the crowd up ahead. He picked up his speed.

Arriving at Line 8, Sasha once again had to guess which direction she'd taken. Unlike other stations, here at Concorde an open bridge went above the tracks of Line 8. This provided a handy lookout for scanning the full length of both platforms. *Ah ha!* He easily caught sight of the red beret. Petite Piaf was already at the far end of the platform for the train heading northeast. The nose of the train peeked through the mouth of the tunnel and advanced along the platform. Sasha scurried down the steps and jumped into the first carriage before the train set off.

It was turning out to be much more difficult to retrieve his vital property than Sasha had anticipated, but he really had no choice. He had to get it back. Nevertheless, Line 8 would be a challenge. At a length of 22 kilometers (13.6 miles) and with 37 stations, it was the longest line in the whole of the Paris *Métro* system. It took an arched trajectory across the city from southeast to southwest. They were now in its busiest section. This first skirted the posh 8th arrondissement, with its chic shops, embassies and historic mansions, then it traversed the popular shopping and business district of Opéra and Grand Boulevards. Forget the influx of passengers, what made this line a huge concern for Sasha was its bounty of interchange stations and, consequently, their abundance of potential escape routes for Petite Piaf.

Since she was at the other end of the train, Sasha would aim to advance one car per station in order to reach her. Leaving the train each time would also allow him to make sure Petite Piaf was still aboard. The idea crossed his mind to remove a 20-euro bill from his wallet. Maybe waving that in her face would get her to stop and listen to him. He contemplated this as he switched carriages, each time getting closer to Petite Piaf and his prized possession. By the time he got to Bonne Nouvelle Station, he had his own *bonne nouvelle*, or 'good news.' He spotted the red beret in the next car. He'd make his move at the next station: Strasbourg-Saint-Denis.

Although there were only three lines intersecting at this station, it somehow felt like the most manic in the whole network. This was likely due to its location. The station was at the junction of Rue Saint-Denis, located in the 2nd district and one of Paris's two traditional Red Light districts, and the Rue du Faubourg Saint-Denis, an ethnically diverse part of the 10th arrondissement which bordered the Canal Saint-Martin and two of the city's largest train stations: Gare de l'Est and Gare du Nord. Although both streets and their surrounding areas were rapidly gentrifying, they were still a bit rough around the edges. This grittiness seeped down under the street and into the *Métro* station. In fact, the platforms for Lines 8 and 9 were popular with homeless people who often hung out there for hours, if not the whole day.

The train slowed into the station. Sasha stepped up to the door. Line 8 had semi-modern trains, the same as those found on Line 7. The doors of these trains opened by pressing a large button, instead of the flip-up levers found on older trains and the automatically opening doors on modern trains. As much as Sasha didn't relish the idea of touching the germ-ridden button, his finger was nevertheless resting on it. He wanted to be ready to press it as soon as the train came to a stop at the station.

"Il n'y a qu'un seul Paris..."

Good, thought Sasha. Petite Piaf wasn't quite finished her song and would therefore not be descending at this station. Sasha eagerly pressed the button. The doors flew open.

"Bonjour! Monsieur! Cher Monsieur! Hello! Sir! Dear Sir!" In front of Sasha, completely blocking the opening, was a scraggly looking couple. Not wearing protective masks, arms interlocked and holding a can of beer in their free hands, they staggered onto the train. Their putrid stench was soon to follow. Sasha recoiled to the back of the car. Before he could even attempt to flee, he was cornered.

"Monsieur, une petite pièce pour manger? Spare some change for something to eat?" asked the woman, waving her beer can in his face. *Something to eat?!* There were definitely many homeless people in need in Paris, however, these two seemed to be spending their 'spare change' on one thing and one thing only: beer.

The closing *Métro* doors woke Sasha up to his current reality. He'd just missed his chance to hop over into the next carriage!

"There's only one Paris... !"

Whew! He could just make out Petite Piaf's melody still drifting down from the next car. Like he'd guessed, she hadn't intended to get off at the last station. That said, she'd soon be coming up to her conclusion. He absolutely had to get off at the next station.

"No, actually I don't!" Sasha answered honestly.

"Come on, sir, you don't even have a few coins for us?" asked the man, taking a chug from his can.

"I gave it all to that singer, the one in the next carriage!" Sasha hollered back.

"We'll take bills too... or restaurant vouchers!" chimed in the lady with a hiccup.

This is unreal! thought Sasha woefully. He had to get out of this mess, and fast. They were approaching the next station.

"Well, in that case, let me take a look," he said, regaining his cool. "Just step back so I can get my wallet out."

The two bums exchanged a victorious glance and clinked their beer cans together, thinking they were about to score. They took a few steps backwards. The train began to slow.

"A little further, please," Sasha instructed, shooing them away with his hand. "And a little to the right. Okay, perfect."

He started to reach into his satchel. Their grins widened with glee. A passenger standing on the platform pushed the magic button. The doors slid open. Sasha catapulted out of the car. He turned around and waved at the stunned hobos. Proud of himself, he turned his head to the right. There, around ten paces away, was Petite Piaf. At the sight of Sasha, her eyes and mouth widened. She hightailed it down the nearest set of stairs.

"*Attendez!* Wait! I just need to talk to you! It's very important!" he shouted after her. They were at République. Forget the punny other interchange stations on Line 8. This was the big kahuna. Five intersecting lines. Dozens of underground passageways. Hundreds of steps. Thousands of places for her to escape or hide.

He had to hit the pavement. Now.

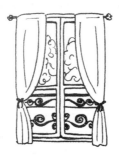

A Palace on the Parc Monceau

"*Le voici, Madame.* Here you are."

Cara looked out the taxicab window. Yes, this was pretty much how she'd imagined it.

"*Gracias*, um... *merci*," she fumbled, handing the driver a 10-euro bill.

She picked up her purse and got out of the posh vehicle, which inadvertently fit in perfectly with her current surroundings. There certainly were not Mercedes taxis in Buenos Aires. Cara's capital city was often referred to as 'the Paris of South America,' but now that she was finally visiting the 'real thing,' she sensed they were worlds apart.

She returned her attention to the address she'd been given: 2 Rue Murillo. The taxi had dropped her off on the corner with Avenue Ruysdaël. There, in front of her was an almost freestanding house, well, actually not just a house. It could easily be classified as a mansion. To Cara, it seemed more like a palace.

It was made of the same beige stone she'd observed from the window of the cab on her ride over from her dingy 1-star hotel near the Gare du Nord train station. Four stories high, this building had regal triangular pediments above its windows which were dressed in handsome wrought iron grills. The main entrance appeared to be via a columned portico; however, she'd been instructed to use the entrance on the other side of the building.

"Madame Vidal?"

Cara's reverie was broken by a voice calling her name. A man in a chic business suit was leaning out of a door on Rue Murillo. She packed up her dreamy thoughts for later, acknowledged the man with a little wave and walked towards him.

"*Monsieur Cohen, enchanté*," he introduced as he returned her wave. People weren't shaking hands these days. "Nice to meet you," he added, switching into English.

"And you also," she replied. "I'm sorry, I only speak a few words of French, but with my Spanish I can usually get by."

"That's not a problem at all," he assured her with his impeccable manners and English language skills. He'd stepped out the door and held it open for her. "Please, do come in."

She entered the building, whose modest former staff entrance had been heavily modified since the building's construction back in the mid-1800s.

"My sincere condolences for your loss," he offered.

"That's very kind of you," she answered. "Aunt Jeanne was 105, she'd lived a long and full life."

"Undoubtedly she had. Please, follow me, it's on the first floor," he said, guiding her over to the modern elevator. A lift didn't seem necessary for going up only one story. She complied, nonetheless. It took a minute for the doors to close. Cara shifted her gaze over to the elevator's buttons.

"How was your flight?" he queried, trying to fill the awkward silence.

"Not too bad, but I'm still a bit jet lagged," she answered. In all honesty though, she was more than a 'bit' jet lagged. She'd made the mistake of having too long of a nap after she arrived yesterday and then couldn't fall asleep at bedtime. She finally drifted into a deep slumber around 5 am only to be jolted awake by her alarm at 9. Despite her extreme fatigue, she dragged herself out of the lumpy bed. She didn't want to miss her 10:30 rendezvous with Mr Cohen.

"Yes, it does take some adjusting to get used to the time difference," he sympathized. The elevator quickly arrived at the first floor. They stepped out onto a landing, off of which was a short corridor. Cara noticed a large wooden door, but they walked past it to a second one, found at the end of the hallway. Mr Cohen took a set of old-fashioned keys out of his pocket, unlocked the door and held it open for Cara.

She took a few steps through the entrance and stopped suddenly, taken aback by the sight of the room's grandeur. Beneath her feet stretched light parquet flooring, its polish muted slightly by a layer of dust. Although the white walls had faded over the years, their intricate stucco moldings still gave them a sense of elegance. This was augmented by imposing marble fireplaces at each end of the room, above which were two large gilded mirrors.

"Splendid, isn't it?" commented Mr Cohen, noticing Cara's awe.

"Yes, it's marvelous," was all she could manage in reply.

"As you might be aware, the building used to be one single home," described Mr Cohen. "This is a very special area in Paris. The park just beyond used to be a pleasure garden built before the French Revolution by the Duke de Chartres. He was a cousin of King Louis XVI and actually the father of the post-revolutionary King Louis-Philippe. When the Duke de Chartres's father died, he took over the more prestigious title of the Duke of Orleans and became the owner of the Palais-Royal. He was entrepreneurial and enclosed the Palais-Royal's gardens with buildings used for shops, cafés, entertainment facilities and more. However, before he embarked on that project, he created this vast park. Instead of following in the tradition of a *jardin à la française* or formal French garden, he opted for a more natural English style garden. It's quite beautiful. You might like to have a look for yourself, after we've finished here."

In fact, courtesy of its large windows facing the park, the room had a wonderful luminous aura. Cara wandered over to the windows to get a better glimpse of the garden. From this vantage point all she could see was green, green, and more green, but when she focused, she noticed small pathways and a few people strolling. Cara felt much more comfortable with this natural vista than the glitzy interiors she currently found herself in.

"During the mid-1800s, with the expansion of Paris under Napoléon III and Baron Haussmann, the former royal garden was reduced in size and renamed le Parc Monceau. The remaining land was divided up and sold to real estate developers. Highly coveted, these plots were quickly filled with luxurious mansions commissioned by the most influential bankers and industrialists of the era: the Rothschilds, the Ephrussis, the Camondos, and also your ancestors."

As he spoke, Cara cautiously drifted around the room. She reckoned it had originally been a grand reception room for entertaining. It had since been configured into a double living room with a dining and formal sitting area. Cara's eyes glided around the room, stopping to linger on the occasional ornately carved antique, elaborate lighting fixture or bronze sculpture. One of the mantlepieces had a gilded clock, frozen at 3:35. Next to this was a dried-up floral arrangement, a further sign that the apartment had been unattended to for many years, if not decades.

"Maurice Vital, Vital spelled originally with a 'T' instead of a 'D', I think he must have been your great, great grandfather, made his fortune in supplying building materials for the Periere brothers extensive railway networks around France. However, the 1929 stock market crash sent ripples across the globe and the company he'd founded, then managed by his grandson, your grandfather, went down with the sinking financial ship. The family was forced to divide up their sumptuous palace into several apartments, keeping the loveliest section, half of the noble first floor which overlooked the park, for themselves."

Cara knew little about her family history. It wasn't something her father had been interested in talking about. Even Aunt Jeanne had rarely spoken about their childhood in Paris. *What must it have been like to play in such an opulent room? Were they even allowed to? Most likely they would have been sent with their governess out to play in the park instead,* Cara reasoned.

"Things became even more difficult as the 1930s progressed. After the financial crisis, there was the rise of Nazism in neighboring Germany. Your grandfather had the foresight to leave France before it was too late. A friend who worked at the Préfecture removed any indication of their Jewish origins from their records. Your grandfather packed up the family, sealed up the apartment and left the keys with my grandfather. They fled to Argentina in 1938, just before that country started tightening its borders to foreigners. I believe that's when he made the slight modification to the family name and bought the horse ranch you still live on, is that correct, Madame Vidal?"

"Yes, I believe that's all correct."

"As far as I know, when your grandfather passed away, your aunt and your father made a swap. She got the apartment in Paris and he got full ownership of the ranch in Argentina," said Mr Cohen.

"Yes, he's since passed away and I have possession of the ranch. Aunt Jeanne was never very interested in it. She spent most of her time in Buenos Aires, where she kept an apartment. When I was a child I remember that she would go off to Paris for several months out of the year. However, I don't know if she was able to come back after she fell and broke her hip when she was in her eighties."

Cara gazed around the room, effectively a precious time capsule. It was truly magnificent, but could she afford to keep it? And did she want to?

Cara put her personal debating on hold as Mr Cohen was already at the room's entryway, ready to proceed with his tour of the apartment. She followed him down a long corridor, off of which were several rooms.

"This would have been your grandfather's study," said Mr Cohen when they entered a room lined with bookshelves. In the center was a large mahogany desk. It had an uncluttered surface, save for a pen holder, a few paper weights and an old-fashioned desk lamp with a stained glass shade.

"Ecole de Nancy. The lamp," he clarified. "It was an important school of Art Nouveau artists that were active in eastern France at the turn of the 20th century. It, like a lot of the furniture in this apartment, is worth a lot of money. Should you wish to sell it, or any of the other contents."

As polite as he was, Cara knew very well that Mr Cohen must be aware of her own financial situation and must have assumed she'd come all this way to sell off what she'd inherited. Truth be told, that was precisely what Cara *had* intended. That is, until she entered the space. Her heritage was here, in France and in this opulent apartment, but her heart and soul were firmly rooted in her family's adopted home, where she was born and raised. Once so prosperous, Argentina's economy was now in dire straits. This was further aggravated by the pandemic, during which time the country had come to a virtual standstill. Cara was additionally impacted because less travel meant fewer tourists were coming to stay at their ranch. This vital supplementary income helped it stay afloat. Without it, she didn't know how much longer she'd be able to hold on to the family ranch.

Mr Cohen had momentarily let himself get distracted by some of the book titles, so Cara couldn't resist opening the desk drawer to take a peek inside. It contained a few letters, the top one was a handwritten note on a sheet of refined letterhead, with the monogram *Cohen et fils, Expertise Immobilière et Notaire,* Cohen and Sons, Real Estate & Notary Experts, centered at the top. Cara quickly scanned the letter, addressed informally to *Chère Jeanne* (Dearest Jeanne) and signed *Affectueusement, Frank* (Affectionately yours, Frank). That seemed a bit overly friendly for a notary and especially for the times. The 'Mr Cohen' now perusing the bookcase was André, so Cara concluded that this 'Frank' must be his father. Cara had always found it strange that beautiful Aunt Jeanne had never married, perhaps there was a reason for this? She closed the drawer as gently as possible, hoping Mr Cohen hadn't noticed her snooping.

"What a wonderful collection of books," he complimented as she approached. "Zola, Dumas, Hugo... Proust himself lived in a few different apartments surrounding the park. I believe he wrote parts of his opus *In Search of Lost Time* while residing in the area. My apologies, Madame, I digress. I've let my passion for literature get the best of me. I really should never have taken over my father's notary business and instead pursued my literature studies, but perhaps those dreams will be for another lifetime. Shall we continue?"

Cara enjoyed seeing this 'human' side of Mr Cohen which also stoked her imagination about the truth of the life and interests of her Aunt Jeanne. She'd always seemed both energized and saddened after returning from her trips to Paris. Papa never understood why she insisted on going to Paris since she claimed to be so happy while she was there, yet was so glum upon her return. There may very well have been a specific reason for her melancholy.

Their tour continued to the apartment's three bedrooms, much more sober than the previous, public spaces, yet these still maintained a classic elegance. The last room was the all-white bathroom, which had a huge clawfoot tub with vintage faucets and a large marble sink.

They circled back to the front of the apartment where Mr Cohen led Cara into a sizeable kitchen with fittings that would make Julia Child proud.

"There you have it," announced Mr Cohen. He reached into his pocket and removed the set of keys he'd previously used to unlock the door. He placed them on the table. "You can take all the time you would need to decide what you would like to do with the apartment. All you need to do is come by my office while you're in Paris to sign some paperwork. Your aunt was very clever and switched the apartment over into your name while she was still alive, with the stipulation that it would go to you only upon her death, Madame Vidal. That way you do not need to pay France's extremely high death taxes. However, you should know that the property taxes are quite high. If you were to keep the apartment, you would be assessed around 2,000 euros per year. Plus the building's monthly maintenance fees and contributions to any renovations are likely to be at least 3,000 additional euros every year. If you were interested in selling the apartment, I do have a number of ready parties. It could easily be sold within the week you are here. For now, I'll leave you to think about all of this."

Mr Cohen removed a business card from his wallet and set it next to the keys. "I believe you have my contact details, but my cell phone number is also listed here on my card. Feel free to call me if you need anything."

Cara was speechless. She managed to mumble a *'merci'* as Mr Cohen went on his way. As soon as she heard the front door close, she slumped down onto one of the chairs around the kitchen table.

How could I ever cover 5,000 euros? And every year?! Cara agonized. It was a colossal task made even more difficult in these uncertain times. Cara needed to clear her head. Back home she'd do this by going out for a ride. Since she was too far from her horses, the best she could do was go for a walk in the park. Yes, that would help.

Cara picked up the keys and Mr Cohen's business card and made for the door. It took her a minute to get the knack of locking it, but she eventually figured it out and took the stairs to the ground floor. She turned left out the door, then left again to reach one of the regal entrances to the Parc Monceau. Its mammoth gilded gate echoed the chicness of the residences which encircled it.

She veered to the right upon reaching the first of the park's pathways. Centuries' old trees shaded the path, chirping birds and the occasional fluttering butterflies added to the serene ambiance.

Cara was instantly calmed and relegated her dilemma to the back of her mind, at least for the time being.

Since it was a weekday, the park wasn't too busy. As she walked, Cara noticed how stylish the other park-goers were. Many likely lived in the grand homes surrounding the park. Nannies pushed well-dressed children in designer strollers. A fashionable couple were walking hand-in-hand in front of her, posh sweaters effortlessly resting over their shoulders like they were straight out of a magazine ad.

The picture of these classy people was complemented by romantic bridges, a curious small-scale Egyptian-esque pyramid and other interesting *faux* ruins from antiquity. She passed by a Roman-style colonnade bordering a pond, beyond which was a colorful old-fashioned carousel. How she would have loved to ride that as a child. She wondered if Aunt Jeanne had ridden it when she was a young girl? And, how many times had Jeanne walked this very path?

Cara continued on her amble, completely lost in her thoughts. The path eventually came full circle and she found herself in front of the regal gate she'd entered through. Cara took a seat on a nearby bench. From here she could see the Vital Palace and the tall windows she'd gaze through earlier.

How can I manage to keep it? Cara mulled over. Her life was at her ranch, but since she'd turned 50, Cara had been thinking ahead to her future. It would be all too easy to accept the eagerly awaiting buyers Mr Cohen had alluded to and return to Argentina with enough money to live comfortably for the rest of her life. Nevertheless, as much as she loved the ranch, it was hard work. *Wouldn't it be nice to share my time between the plains of Argentina and elegant Paris?* The idea was certainly growing on her. But how could she realistically make it work?

She was pulled out of her deliberating by an all too familiar smell. She looked over at the entrance to the park. On the other side of it was parked a truck with a long, covered trailer. Out of its back door, a man was unloading ponies. Even with her feeble

French skills, Cara could tell by the advertisement on the side of the trailer that these were for children's rides in the park. The scent of home and also the airs of change.

This gave Cara an idea. She took out her cell phone and Mr Cohen's business card.

"*Allô?*"

"Hello Mr Cohen, this is Cara Vidal."

"Oh, hello Madame Vidal, nice to hear from you so soon. Have you already decided what you'd like to do with the apartment?"

"Actually, I have a question."

"Please, go ahead."

"You said that the base costs of keeping the apartment might be around 5,000 euros per year."

"Yes, it would be about that."

"How much could such an apartment go for if rented out?"

"It's a lovely apartment and in such a prestigious location. You could easily get 3,000 euros a month, if not more. However, keep in mind, if you do go for this option, you would not be able to use the apartment yourself."

"I understand, but if I were to rent it to a diplomat or business person who would only need to stay for a year or so, that would earn some money to cover the following years and at least prolong the decision of whether or not to sell it."

"Yes, I suppose it would. Although, you might want to do a few renovations. Spruce it up a little. That will cost some money upfront."

"Perhaps I could sell that Art Nouveau lamp and a few of the other antiques?"

"Selling some of the more valuable pieces could certainly bring in a few thousand euros. Why don't you decide which items you might like to sell and we can meet back at the apartment in the coming days."

"Thank you very much, Mr Cohen, that's awfully kind of you."

"Given our family connections, I really don't mind assisting you with this, Madame Vidal."

"When we meet again at the apartment, why don't you select a few of those books you were admiring in return?"

"I would be more than honored to have that original copy of *In Search of Lost Time*."

"Consider it yours. I'll be in touch shortly."

Cara hung up and reflected on what Mr Cohen had said. Spending some time going through the apartment, and its contents, would help her piece together her family history, and help keep its legacy alive.

Cara glanced back up at the palace and, for the first time since her arrival, she felt she'd returned home. Even if it might just be for a little while, it was still home.

Hidden Plans for the Opéra Garnier

Elodie quickened her pace. It was 8:50 am. She scurried as fast as she could up l'Avenue de l'Opéra. Due to the time of day, she had to weave in and out of the throngs of suit-clad office workers on their way to the posh offices which populated the elegant avenue and its side streets.

Unlike most of the other wide boulevards that were laid out in Paris in the mid-19th century, there were no trees lining l'Avenue de l'Opéra. Branches and leaves would have blocked the view of the building that had instigated the creation of the street itself. A whole section of 'old' Paris had to be torn down in order to build a straight street between the royal residence of the Louvre and the crown jewel of this 'new' Paris—the Opéra Garnier.

Even though she'd seen it countless times, as she neared the majestic building, Elodie couldn't help but marvel at its extravagant facade. Before her were the busts of great composers, clusters of gleeful dancers, dedications to the various arts and gilded allegorical figures. If a person carefully examined all the decoration on the front of the Opera House, just above the central row of columns, they could spot the repeating initials N and E. These letters were a nod to the commissioners of the opulent *Académie National de Musique*, the National Academy of Music, Emperor Napoléon III and Empress Eugénie.

It may have been commissioned by the imperial couple, nevertheless, the monumental building ended up being named in honor of its architect, Charles Garnier. Famous the world over, le Palais Garnier was not Paris's first opera house. Founded in 1669 by Louis XIV, the Paris Opera has been housed in various buildings over the course of its 350-year history. In fact, it was an 'incident' at the previous opera house which sparked the building of this new one.

Built in 1821, the Palais Garnier's predecessor was located a short distance away, on Rue Le Peletier. On January 14th, 1858, the Emperor and Empress were on their way there when Italian anarchist Felice Orsini tried to bomb their carriage. Although the Bonapartes were unscathed, thanks to their iron-lined carriage, the strength of the blast left 156 people injured, eight fatally, and blew out the glass of neighboring buildings. A new opera house was deemed in public interest and necessary for the safety of the head of state.

Considering this event, it isn't surprising that a very special entrance was built for the Emperor and Empress, which Elodie was now in front of. Found on the west side of the Opéra Garnier, and emblazoned with the Napoleonic eagle, it had a curved ramp, designed so the Emperor's carriage could travel up it and straight into an enclosed entrance. This meant he could safely attend the opera without ever having to set foot out in the open. Clever as it was, the Emperor never got to use his ultra-safe entrance. The building was completed in 1875, five years after the disastrous Franco-Prussian War which led to Napoléon III's downfall. Elodie's destination just happened to be right above the Emperor's designated entrance. She flashed a card at the security guard as she darted inside.

Most visitors' voices fall to whispers as they enter the Opera House. As much as the facade was utterly stunning, the Opera's grand staircase was so sumptuous it literally took your breath away. Despite being in a hurry, Elodie lingered for a quick minute to take in its mesmerizing grandeur. This was the first time she

156

could access the building since the lockdown. Absence made her appreciate its intricate details that much more.

She walked up the regal staircase slowly as she admired its architectural accents. She took in the ornate columns and balconies, as well as the use of gold ornamentation and candelabras; all perfect examples of the excesses used in the 'palace's' overall design. These features also spoke volumes about the expectations of the Emperor, his desire to be noticed and to be remembered for what he did for Paris and his noble subjects. She gazed up at the meticulously painted ceiling overhead, complete with soaring angels. She could only imagine what it might have been like to glide up this spectacular staircase back in the late-19th century, wearing a magnificent dress, furs and jewels. She guessed that only the very wealthy or nobility were afforded this pleasure. It was the place to *be* and *be seen* at the time.

For grandiose reasons, some staircases were built to stand out and really attract the elegant eye. They command not only a person to notice the flamboyant architectural details, but also for other patrons to observe the fascinating people ascending or descending them. They are an attention grabber, if you will. Garnier's grand staircase reminded Elodie of another one that became well-known: the one built into the Titanic. That was also a grand staircase and was meant to be a design centerpiece of that ill-fated vessel, as ill-fated as Napoléon III's military campaign against Prussia.

It was 9:05 when Elodie pushed open the doors to her final destination: the Opera's Library-Museum. It was home to over 600,000 documents, from performance programs to music scores. Since starting her research for her Ph.D. dissertation in architecture, Elodie had gotten to know its impressive collections extremely well. Perhaps too well. In fact, the day before the quarantine was announced, she'd come across a very curious exchange of letters, a chain of correspondence between Charles Garnier and a certain Monsieur Blanc.

Since the lockdown prevented Elodie from coming back to the library in person, she searched online to find out just who this Mr

Blanc was. She felt like she was in an episode of the series *Inspecteur Marcel,* which she would watch when she took breaks from her own investigating. As she dug online she discovered that the cost of the Opera House was much greater than anticipated. It actually became the most expensive building constructed in France at that time. All together it cost the modern equivalent of a colossal 313 million euros. One of the main reasons for this towering expense stemmed from the fact that the plot of land chosen for the enormous building was very wet. Despite months spent trying to pump out the water, they eventually had to resort to building a large cistern to hold the water. This is the legendary 'lake' which was still found beneath its depths. The 25 by 50 meter (80 by 262 feet) reservoir was off limits to the public, but was used by firemen for training exercises.

The building wasn't complete when Napoléon III fell from power, but it was well-underway. Since France's coffers had been drained by the costly Franco-Prussian War and subsequent reparations to Germany, there were not enough state funds to finish the Opera House. So, the government borrowed 4.9 million gold francs from François Blanc, a wealthy French financier and real estate promoter.

The letters Elodie had come across clearly showed the growing professional relationship between Blanc and Garnier. After completing the Paris Opera, the architect was hired by Blanc to design a concert hall for his casino in Monte Carlo, Monaco. This would later become the official Opera House of the Côte d'Azur principality.

One specific letter had caught Elodie's attention. Although it wasn't plainly spelled out, it seemed to make reference to a special request Blanc had made to Garnier, something that would remain just between the two of them. A secret passageway. And Elodie was determined to find it.

Her heart was practically beating out of her chest as she strode down an aisle lined with bookcases, in the direction of the documents section.

"*Bonjour Jean!*" she greeted the distinguished looking, 40ish librarian, sitting behind a large solid oak desk. Although he was somewhat reserved, he was still approachable, and they'd developed a nice professional friendship since she'd started coming to the library.

"*Bonjour Elodie*, so nice to see you!" His face lit up when he lifted his eyes from his copy of *Opera Magazine* and saw who was there.

"Jean, let's catch up later over a coffee," Elodie blurted. She knew he would want to chat; it had been months since they'd last seen each other. However, at this very moment, she couldn't handle any small talk. She was too excited. "But first, I need to see Garnier's floor plans for the Opera House. Especially the final ones, any that show close up details or potential last-minute modifications. Please, Jean."

"Sure thing," Jean replied. "I'll be right back." Five minutes later he returned bearing a stack of oversized file folders.

"I know you don't need reminding, but please make sure you don't get any dust or dirt on them," he duly added. He slowly set the precious documents down on one of the large examination tables.

"Of course!" Elodie said. She knew the drill by now. Setting her purse down on a chair, she removed a small pouch containing a pristine pair of white archival gloves which she put on gingerly. Despite bubbling over with excitement, she carefully opened the first folder and went about scrutinizing the plans for any clues to the whereabouts of a secret passageway.

***

"Hungry?" asked Jean, smiling down at Elodie.

"Huh?" Elodie was completely lost in the collection of plans.

"It's almost 2," he informed her.

"Oh my!" she exclaimed. She'd been so focused on her quest that she hadn't noticed the hours flying by. Jean could tell she was a little hesitant.

"Let's go grab a sandwich and you can tell me what you're looking for," he suggested. "Maybe I can help?"

"Okay, sounds good," she agreed. She figured since she hadn't discovered anything on her own that morning, she could probably use some assistance this afternoon.

Elodie removed her white gloves, returned them to their pouch and scooped up her purse. Then the pair headed towards the exit.

In addition to being surrounded by offices, the Opéra Garnier was in the heart of Paris's main shopping district. This meant there were a lot of chain eateries in the area, however, Jean knew where there was a hidden local bakery. What's more, it was also a previous winner of the best baguette in Paris contest. As they were on the late side of lunch, there was fortunately no line so they were able to quickly procure their sandwiches on award-winning baguette.

"Shall we go eat these in the Palais-Royal Garden?" proposed Jean.

"If you don't mind, could we just sit on the Opera House steps?" requested Elodie anxiously. "I really want to get to the bottom of the curious documents I found as quickly as possible."

"Sure, no problem," he accepted reluctantly.

"Don't worry," said Elodie. She was keenly aware of his very strong aversion to anything dusty and dirty, like outdoor steps. "I have one of those free newspapers they give out on the subway in my bag. We can sit on its pages."

His furrowed brow relaxed and they found a place on the Garnier's steps, far enough away from the few others who'd had the same idea as Elodie. In between bites, Elodie spilled the beans on what she had discovered and explained the mystery she hoped to solve.

"Well, I do know there are a few official secret passages, like the narrow one that goes from the lake all the way up to the fourth floor," started Jean. "But I suppose it isn't out of the question that there are others."

"I scoured all the old plans this morning and didn't find any clues," said Elodie, frustrated.

"If there's anyone who might have actually noticed something unusual or out of place, it's Michel," answered Jean.

"Michel?"

"Michel, the old custodian," he clarified. "He knows the building like the back of his hand. He's been working here forever. Okay, maybe not *forever*. He wasn't working here when the Opera House first opened, but he's been here for at least 40 years. I believe he's retiring soon."

"It wouldn't hurt to ask him," said Elodie.

"Okay, I'll help you find him, but then I really should get back to work," Jean said, looking at his watch. He must be the only Frenchman who respected the actual time-frame of an hour-long lunch break.

After finishing up their sandwiches, they went on the hunt for Michel. They started by roaming the various foyers. Not one detail of the opulent interiors had been overlooked by Garnier and his troop of gifted artists and artisans. Every surface was adorned with sculptures, paintings, crystal, mirrors and gold. Everything was gold! Gold paint, gold gilding, and gold candelabras. Throughout the world gold seemed to always denote wealth, power and importance. The global effect of these glamorous rooms made you feel like you were at a miniature Versailles. Beautiful as these rooms were, there was no Michel.

They checked the more intimate Rotonde du Glacier and Rotonde des Abonnés, round public vestibules located under the auditorium. No Michel. They even popped into the Salon Florence Gould, named in honor of the famous American philanthropist. Still no Michel. This left them with the maze of storage and rehearsal rooms found behind the scenes, which would be a nightmare to search through, or the building's largest room, the vast 2,000 seat auditorium. This is where they decided to continue their search. Jean heaved open the large door and the pair were suddenly enveloped by warm golds and sensual reds, colors chosen to accentuate the beauty of the audience members. Overhead was Marc Chagall's whimsical ode to opera featuring 14 scenes from the works of Mozart, Puccini, Bizet, Verdi and other musical masterminds. Even though the building had so many references to opera, since opening it has also been used for ballet. Today, most operatic performances took place at the modern Opera House, located in Place de la Bastille and built in the 1980s to commemorate the bicentennial of the first French Revolution, just like the Pyramid of the Louvre.

"Michel!" Elodie called out. Her words echoed through the cavernous room.

"No use in doing that," advised Jean. "Despite this room's amazing acoustics, Michel's hard of hearing."

"Poor guy. That means he can't even make the most of the place where he works."

"Oh, sure he does," Jean insisted. "Maybe not audibly, but visually. You can often find him sitting at the back of the auditorium during ballet rehearsals. Actually, there's one about to start, which is why there aren't any tours taking place in here right now."

"Zzzzzz … Zzzzzz …"

"Hey, what's that?" Elodie asked upon hearing what sounded like loud snores, amplified by the room's acoustics. The two followed the deep nasal noises towards the back of the auditorium. Sure enough, the snores guided them straight to a snoozing Michel, slouched down in one of the room's plush red velour seats.

Jean cleared his throat loudly, but this had no effect on the dozing Michel. Jean and Elodie looked at each other. Jean was too polite, Elodie would have to take matters into her own hands. She shooed Jean out of Michel's line of sight. From her pocket, she removed the crumpled receipt from her lunchtime sandwich.

Standing behind Michel, she leaned over and tickled his nose with the receipt, then jumped backwards. Well-mannered Jean put his hand over his eyes. How utterly embarrassing it would be if they got caught!

Michel awoke with a start and quickly took the rag in his hand and began wiping down the wooden frame of the seat in front of him.

"Oh, there you are, Michel!" said Elodie, stepping forward as if she'd just arrived. Michel turned around, smiling pleasantly and polishing ferociously, as if he'd been at it for ages. "We need your help with an important matter!"

"What's that?" Michel asked. He stood up with some difficulty and clung to the chair he'd been sitting on. "How can I help?"

"We want to find a secret passageway..." Elodie then gave him a brief rundown of the story. While she was provided the details, some dancers appeared on stage, out of costume and in casual practice leotards and tights. The rehearsal was about to begin.

"If this Monsieur Blanc was that wealthy, he would have had one of the best private boxes," concluded Michel. "There's the Presidential Box, originally built for the Emperor. It wouldn't be that one, but there are several others that are almost as prestigious. If he'd commissioned Garnier to make him a secret passageway, it would likely be in one of those."

"That makes sense!" said Elodie. "Any idea which one?"

"Yes," he said pointing across the room. "That deluxe box over there has a perfect view of the stage. Plus, it's next to the wall, so it would be ideal for a secret passageway."

"*Allons-y!* Let's go!" she cheered.

Jean looked hesitant. He checked his watch again.

"I should really be getting back to work," he said.

"Come on, Jean! Please!" implored Elodie. "It's the first day you're open to the public. There were barely any people at the library this morning. And, if your colleagues really needed you, they could always call you."

"*Bon d'accord,* okay," Jean agreed reluctantly. No sooner were Elodie and Michel marching towards the door. "Only five more minutes!" he added as he trailed after them.

Exiting the auditorium, they went up a set of stairs. Michel guided them to the left and stopped in front of the last of that level's private boxes. Elodie pointed up at the door, completely stupefied.

"F.B.," she read out the initials painted on the door in faded gold. "François Blanc."

"This must be it!" exclaimed Jean, pleased he'd tagged along after all.

Michel pulled a massive keyring from his pocket. It seemed to contain every type and size of key you could imagine. He selected an elegant old-fashioned brass one; the master key for the boxes. He slid it into the lock and gently pushed open the door. The trio tiptoed inside like shy young dancers.

"Places!" shouted the choreographer, startling the three amateur sleuths. Elodie crept up to the edge of the box. It certainly had the perfect view of the stage. The dancers lined up and the choreographer motioned to the rehearsal pianist to start. The music was from Merante's *Sylvia,* which had actually premiered on that very stage in 1876. Although, considering the backdrop which had just been installed, it looked like they would be doing a contemporary version of this classic ballet.

"I would imagine if there was a secret passageway, it would be over on this side," Michel suggested, breaking Elodie's engrossed spell.

"That makes sense," said Jean. The three of them proceeded to investigate the walls in search of any unusual crevices or openings.

"*Hmmm...* I don't see anything out of place," commented Jean.

Elodie ran her fingers up and down the trim. She stopped near the bottom.

"Hey what's this?" she asked. The spry and youngest of the group, Elodie agilely crouched down to inspect her possible find.

"It's a small keyhole! Michel, are there any very small keys on your keyring?"

"I think so," he said, riffling through his huge collection. "*Ah ha!* I've always wondered what this one was for.*" He held up a tiny key. No more than an inch long, although it was tarnished from age, it didn't look like it had been used much.

"Let's give it a try," Elodie proposed. Michel handed her his clunky set of keys and she carefully inserted it into the lock. It fit! She slowly turned it to the left and a section of the wood paneling creaked open. The trio gasped.

"We found it," whispered Elodie, in awe.

"Maybe we should go tell the Director about this?" suggested Jean trepidatiously, always one to err on the side of caution.

"Let's just have a quick look first," Elodie insisted. Michel unhooked a small flashlight from his belt and shone the light inside. Elodie peered over his shoulder. At first the space looked more like a closet.

"What are those?" asked Michel. On the ground to one side were scattered pieces of torn up paper. Elodie bent down to pick them up.

"They're old programs," she noted. "I wonder why they're ripped up?"

"That's strange," said Jean, trying to read the text on the pages. Elodie skimmed through them quickly.

"They all seem to feature the same lead dancer," noted Elodie, "A certain Cléo Deschamps."

"Cléo Deschamps!" gasped Jean.

"Do you know of her?" asked Michel.

"Oh yes!" he answered. "She's something of a mystery. As I'm sure you both know, or at least have seen in the paintings of Edgar Degas, there were various categories of ballerinas in the 1800s. At the bottom were *'les petits rats,'* the little rats, young dancers generally from poor families and often with somewhat... um... flexible morals. Wealthy benefactors would often attend rehearsals and were doted on by some of the girls who were trying to secure the protection and financial assistance of these influential men.

"Of course, not all the dancers resorted to this dubious system. The best ballerinas, who were striving to be chosen as lead dancers, were much more cautious. They often had a mother or an aunt who would also attend rehearsals, to keep a watchful eye on their family's valuable asset. Cléo Deschamps fell into this latter category. With exceptional beauty and skill, she was quickly spotted and was soon on track to become *le danseur étoile*, the star dancer, of the Paris Opera. In fact, she was supposed to be the star of Merante's *Sylvia*, but she suddenly disappeared. Completely vanished. And no one knew what had happened to her."

"It seems like Monsieur Blanc was particularly interested in Cléo," observed Elodie. "I wonder if he was her benefactor?"

"Or maybe he was trying to woo her, hence the passageway?" suggested Michel. Jean and Elodie looked over at the custodian, surprised by his interest in the affair. He shone the light around the secret alcove. His flashlight stopped on the ground. "Elodie, is that a little lever down there?"

She set the programs down on one of the box's velour seats and got down on her hands and knees. She worked her fingers around the edge of the board Michel was referring to.

"Ah ha!" she proclaimed as her fingers slid under a recess. She pulled the boards, which easily came up in one grouping. "A trap door!"

Michel leaned over and shone his light down. "Stairs." Indeed, his flashlight revealed a very narrow spiral staircase.

"I wonder where they lead to?" Elodie looked over at Michel and Jean.

"With my bad hip I won't be trying those stairs, but here, you two can go," said Michel, handing Jean his flashlight. "I'll wait here."

"It looks pretty dusty," observed clean-freak Jean. Not only did he have an aversion to dirt and dust, he also rather disliked claustrophobic places. These phobias most likely resulted from the time his father took him down into the tunnels of his workplace, *le Métro*, and they got a little lost *and* dirty. He thought they'd ended up in the Catacombs! His father didn't seem too bothered, but the incident had forever left its mark on poor Jean.

"Come on, Jean," Elodie persisted. "We'll go tell the Director right afterwards, I promise."

"Okay, fine," he complied, his degree of curiosity outweighing his aversions.

"Just holler if you need anything," said Michel as he went over to sit by the edge of the box to watch the rehearsal. With a renewed spring in his step, he returned to what he had obviously intended to spend part of his afternoon doing. His passion for dance made Elodie wonder if Michel had been a dancer in his youth. A *'petit rat* himself?

Elodie turned towards the steps and carefully descended them one by one, Jean followed closely behind, shining the light on the stairs. They seemed to go down about the equivalent of three stories, then stopped on a small landing. Here, there was another door. The word *'Loges'* was written on it.

"The dressing rooms," said Jean. "Just what I thought. Benefactors were allowed to attend the rehearsals, however, visiting a prima ballerina in her dressing room was a very coveted privilege and not an easy one to obtain."

"Look! More torn up bits of paper!" said Elodie, reaching down to pick them up. "*Hmmm...* it seems like there are two types of paper. Here, I'll give you the beige pieces and I'll keep the light pink ones. Let's try to figure out what they are."

The two spent a minute attempting to assemble their puzzles of paper.

"Mine is a cheque," concluded Jean. "For 10,000 francs!"

"Wow, that's a lot of money!" declared Elodie.

"Don't forget these would be *'ancien francs,'*" clarified Jean. "Old francs from the 1800s. Their monetary value was different from the francs used in France before the euro was rolled out in 2002."

"That may be true, but it still sounds like a substantial sum!" said Elodie.

"Yes, I'd imagine that's equivalent to around 50,000 euros today," said Jean. "Have you figured out your papers?"

"It seems to be a letter," said Elodie, holding the pieces together.

Cher M. Blanc,

Thank you for your complimentary letter, the bouquet of beautiful roses and your over-generous gift. However, I am afraid I am unable to accept it. I am in love with Gaston and we are running away together tonight, after the performance. We have pledged ourselves to each other. Do not try to find me.

A dieu,
Cléo

"Wow!" exclaimed Elodie when she had finished.

"I guess that solves it," concluded Jean. "Blanc had been pursuing her and even got Garnier involved to help him. Garnier was corruptible, but Cléo wasn't."

"But the mystery still isn't completely solved," said Elodie. "Where did Cléo and this Gaston go?"

Jean turned the flashlight around the space.

"Look!" he said. "The passageway continues."

"Let's see where it goes," suggested Elodie.

The pair followed the passageway, which started as a straight corridor and then made a right-angled turn. At the end was a small door, closed by a latch. Elodie flipped it up and the door came ajar. They were in the Rotonde des Abonnés! Of course! From here, one could discreetly slip in or out of the passageway. The vestibule was just beneath the grand staircase, so one could conveniently exit the building from here.

"Cléo must have discovered the secret passageway," said Jean.

"Yes, and she turned its intended purpose around in her favor," deduced Elodie. "Instead of Blanc using it to court her, she used it to escape with Gaston!"

"Clever Cléo!" stated Jean.

"But who was this Gaston?" wondered Elodie out loud. "Do you think he also worked here at the Opera?"

"That's a good guess. Cléo would have rarely left the building with her intense schedule," said Jean. Just then his face lit up, struck by an idea. "I know how we can find out! Follow me!"

"Great!" chimed Elodie. She scurried after Jean who was already jogging up the grand staircase and back in the direction of the library.

As he pushed open the doorway, the other librarians raised an eyebrow, as if to say 'where have you been?' But Jean didn't even make eye contact with them as he rushed in the direction of his desk. He quickly sat down in front of his computer, put in his password and did some frantic typing.

"What are you looking for?" asked Elodie.

"We've recently digitized the staff records dating all the way back to the Opera House's opening in January 1875. I can do a keyword search by name. *Voilà!* There have been three Gastons on staff... and one stopped working here in the fall of 1875! That's exactly when Cléo disappeared!"

Jean clicked on the profile. "Gaston Ledoux."

"What was his job?"

"He was in charge of raising and lowering the massive stage curtain! On the sidelines, he must have spent hours admiring the lovely Cléo from a similar vantage point as Monsieur Blanc."

"Wow!"

"Wait a second," said Jean. "Ledoux.... That name sounds familiar."

Jean quickly plugged in a new search.

"Two names have come up for Ledoux: Gaston Ledoux... and Michel Ledoux!" declared Jean.

"Michel?" questioned Elodie.

"Yes, our Michel!" confirmed Jean.

"Let's go find him!" said the ecstatic Elodie. The pair zoomed back out of the library, passing the puzzled, and disapproving, other librarians.

Michel was right where they'd left him, enraptured by the dancers, fingers drumming on the box's ledge along with the music, like tiny footsteps of *les petits rats*.

"Michel!" called Elodie. Startled from his trance, he sat up straight.

"So what did you find?" he asked.

"Before we get around to that, we have a question for you," said Jean. "Do you know if you had a Gaston in your family? An ancestor?"

"*Hmmm*, why yes," he replied after a minute's reflection. "My great grandfather was called Gaston."

Jean and Elodie exchanged glances.

"My family used to run a ballet school out in Normandy, but my parents decided to move to Paris," continued Michel. "I always had fond memories of watching those *petits rats* practicing at the school. I guess that's why I ended up applying for a job at the Opera House."

"Why didn't you try to become a dancer?" asked Elodie.

"Look at me!" he said, gesturing to his broad shoulders. "Alas, I don't have the right physique!"

Elodie and Jean smiled. Despite his sturdy size, dance nonetheless flowed through Michel's veins.

They knew he'd be thrilled to find out the true story about his great grandparents… and at that moment, they also knew exactly what the team should get Michel for his retirement present: a lifetime season's pass to the Opéra Garnier.

New "D-Zynes" for the Canal Saint-Martin

"*Tu fais quoi?* Whatcha doing?"

"Whatcha doing?"

"Whatcha do…."

"*Dégage!* Get lost!"

"Whatcha…."
"Can't you see I'm busy, kid?" said the young man in a muffled voice.

"Yes, but whatcha do…." The curious little boy wasn't going to give up that easily.

"Art!" shouted the young man after he'd pulled the mask down from his mouth.

"But doesn't art hang on walls, inside?" the boy persisted.

"Sometimes it does, sometimes it doesn't. Haven't you ever seen outdoor sculptures, like in parks?" retorted the artist as he stood up from his crouching position. He was dressed in ripped jeans, a black t-shirt smeared in various colors of paint and a camouflage-style hoodie. His look was completed with a backwards baseball cap.

"Well, yes, but you're not making a sculpture," the boy innocently, and correctly, noted.

"No, I'm not, smarty pants," replied the artist, increasingly annoyed by the boy and his pestering. "This is called 'street art.' Now buzz off."

"Oh, but it isn't on the street," observed the boy.

"It's not *on* the street.... It's *in* the streets, meaning out in the streets!" bellowed the artist as he waved his arms wide to emphasize his point, his right hand brandishing a spray can. "There's plenty of it around the Canal, haven't you seen any before?"

The boy pondered this question for a minute before responding; "Yes, I suppose so, but I guess I've never seen anyone making it before."

"Keep your eyes peeled. You'll see lots of street art around here, as well as in places like Belleville, Montmartre and down in the 13th district," informed the artist, calming down a little.

"Why are you doing art in the street?" asked the boy.

"It's not art in the street, it's *street art*," he corrected.

"Why are you doing street art?" persisted the boy.

"It's a statement," said the artist, proudly. "Art doesn't have to just be in art galleries and museums. Street art is for everybody. It speaks to the people, to the times we live in. It can address social issues too."

"Oh. What's this art you're making about?"

"It isn't finished yet... because you're distracting me!"

"When will it be finished?"

"Come back tomorrow."

"Okay. Why are you wearing a mask like that? It isn't like the masks my parents and the teachers at school have to wear?"

"It's because of the paint fumes," answered the artist. "They can be dangerous if you sniff them. So, since you're not wearing a mask, tyke, maybe you should scram."

"What's your name?"

"D-Zyne."

"That doesn't sound like a real name."

"It's my street artist name. We usually choose another name, one which symbolizes who we are as artists," he replied. "D-Zyne, like design, or *designer*, like the verb to draw. What's your name, kid?"

"Alex."

"Okay, Alex. Do you have any hobbies?"

"Ahhh… Badminton?"

"Okay, and what's your favorite color?"

"Blue."

"Then we could call you Bad Blu. But 'blue' spelt 'B. L. U.', that has more character. Bad is short for badminton and in English the word means *mauvais* or *méchant*."

"But I don't think I'm *mauvais* or *méchant*," protested Alex anxiously.

"That's not the point," said D-Zyne exasperated. "Your street art name has to have personality."

"Okay, Bad Blu, that works."

"So you run along now, Bad Blu, and think about what kind of street art you might like to do yourself."

"Okay," replied Alex, his eyes lighting up. "I'll stop by again tomorrow, after school."

"Catch ya later, Bad Blu." D-Zyne stuck out his elbow in this new form of a 'handshake.' Alex grinned and lifted his small one to return the greeting.

"See you tomorrow, D-Zyne!"

The smile stayed on Alex's face as he crossed the street and walked along the Canal. He'd been on his way home from school when he'd encountered D-Zyne. He'd never met an artist before, nor anyone remotely interesting for that matter. Well, there was that writer who came to his school once to read some of his storybooks, but Alex couldn't remember his name and that was quite a while ago anyway. He supposed his grandpa was interesting, he was always full of stories too, but that was different. He was definitely not cool like D-Zyne was.

This impromptu discussion with D-Zyne made Alex more aware of his surroundings. Now that he thought about it, there *was* a lot of this street art in the neighborhood. He'd already noticed the large mural of a girl with colorful bubbles for hair, he liked that one. He kept on the lookout for more artworks as he took his usual route home north along the Canal.

It was a mild September afternoon and quiet along the pretty waterway, the complete opposite to how it was on weekends and evenings when its banks were brimming with strollers and picnickers. Today, there were only a few scatterings of people well-spaced out along the water's edge. Some were chatting in small groups of friends, others were sharing a bottle of wine and a few solitary souls were reading or simply admiring the shimmering waters.

The 4.6 kilometer (2.86 mile) canal was built in the early 19th century by Napoléon I in order to bring fresh water into the city center. It also connected with a series of other canals and waterways that snaked throughout northern France. Today, these are predominantly used by pleasure boats. Like other canals and small roads in France, the Canal was bordered by tall plane trees, intended to provide shade for travelers. These were just starting to turn orange, announcing the arrival of autumn.

Nearing a bend in the Canal, Alex passed by a row of colorful shops selling clothing and artsy household items made by local designers. He reached the raised stairway bridge which allowed for foot passage above a canal lock. Alex climbed this and paused for a moment when he reached the top. He looked out at the slow, glistening water to see if a boat was approaching, he enjoyed watching them go through the lock, but something else caught his eye. Down below on the side of the old lock-keeper's station, there was a large spray-painted mural. More street art. Alex remembered D-Zyne's instructions. He was meant to think about what kind of street art he'd like to do. Alex pondered this on the rest of his short journey home.

He followed the Canal for another two blocks, passing a guitar-player serenading his girlfriend and an elderly couple soaking up some rays on a sunny bench. As a houseboat floated by, Alex waved to its driver and wondered what it was like living on a boat. He'd only been on a boat once, when his class had taken the boat cruise which went up and down the Canal. He especially liked the part when the boat went through the underground tunnel, kind of like the tunnels of the Catacombs, but for boats instead. The cruise was fun and all, but he wasn't sure he'd like to spend all his time on a wobbly vessel.

He veered right onto Rue Louis Blanc, then walked past a few buildings until he arrived at the door of the modern apartment complex his family lived in. Entering the foyer, he said *bonjour* to the building's concierge, busy mopping the foyer floor, and took the elevator up to his family's 5th floor apartment. Built in the 1970s, his building wasn't very fancy, like many of the buildings in this part of Paris, nevertheless, the upper floor apartments boasted nice views of the Canal and the southwest of Paris.

Once inside, Alex kicked off his running shoes and tossed his backpack on the other side of the entryway. He knew nobody else would be home yet, as his sister's middle school got out later than his elementary school and his parents were rarely home before six. He resisted the urge to play some video games, deciding instead to do his homework right away so he could give what was on his mind his full attention. What kind of street art could he, Bad Blu, do?

***

"Alex, à table! Dinner's ready!"

Alex's doodling trance was interrupted by his sister shouting from the kitchen. He put down his coloring pencils and went to take his usual spot at the dining room table. He scrunched his nose when he saw what was on the plate his dad set down in front of

175

him. *Uggh*. Green beans again? At least there was roast chicken to mask their icky flavor.

"So how was your day, Alex?" asked his mom, once everyone was seated.

"Fine. What are social issues?" he asked, trying to get some answers to what had been on his mind since his encounter with D-Zyne. His sister rolled her eyes and pushed a few green beans around on her plate with her fork while her other hand was secretly scrolling her phone screen under the table. His parents exchanged curious glances.

"Is that something you learned about at school?" his mom prodded.

"No, I was just wondering."

"Well, social issues refer to problems in the world, like people who don't have a place to live or food to eat. It can also be about racism, like those protests we saw on the news. Or it can be about equal access to healthcare, like we talked about during the pandemic, remember?"

"Sort of."

"Maybe this is a topic he can discuss with your father when he comes for lunch this Sunday?" suggested Alex's dad, aiming his sarcasm at Alex's mom. "That's just the kind of topic *nonno* Giancarlo could go on about for hours!"

Alex's mom glared at her husband and his sister giggled. *Nonno* Giancarlo was famous for his utopian and revolutionary rambles.

"Well, at least my father is obsessed with making the world a better place. That's more than I can say about your mom. Ever since your father passed away, all she can talk about is her charming wine-seller!" criticized Alex's mom.

"Well, you don't seem to mind the nice bottles of Bordeaux she's always bringing over," countered his dad. "And neither does *nonno* Giancarlo. I bet we'll get to hear an exuberant eulogy of her bottle of Côtes-de-Bourg this coming Sunday."

"That's all beside the point. I think it's nice Alex is interested in social topics," said his mom in the defense of both little Alex and her idealistic father. "Unlike someone else who only seems to care about... TikTok! Lucie, you can put your cell phone away right now or I'm taking it for the rest of the night."

Startled, Lucie slid her phone beneath her right thigh. "What are you talking about? I'm not always on my phone like you're constantly accusing me of!"

That was all it took to divert the conversation away from Alex's question. While his mom and sister bickered about phone rules and regulations, Alex's attention was drawn out the window and to the twinkling lights of the Parisian horizon beyond. Just then a light went off in his head. *Yes, that's it!* Alex picked up his fork and scarfed down the remains of his dinner, right down to the last green bean. The faster he finished, the faster he could be excused so he could work on his new designs.

***

Alex found it very hard to concentrate at school the next day. He was so excited to go find D-Zyne and show him the design he'd come up with. Despite his enthusiasm, Alex realized he had to keep his project top secret. His teacher, Madame Cohen, almost caught him doodling. Twice. Then at lunchtime some of his classmates saw him sketching on his napkin and tried to steal it. A small ruckus ensued which was, thankfully for Alex's sake, put out by the cafeteria's strict supervisor before the other boys were able to get their hands on his drawing.

Geez, were these the kind of 'issues' D-Zyne had to go through to make his art? Alex wondered as he discreetly slid the napkin into his school bag upon returning to his classroom. The afternoon proceeded without incident, however, the hours went by excruciatingly slow. It seemed like an eternity before the school bell finally rang. Alex hopped up out of his seat, stuffed his notebooks and pencil case into his bag and was out of the school's main door in a flash.

Alex followed his regular route home knowing that this would lead him past the place where he'd met D-Zyne the day before. He rounded a corner, entering the small lane from yesterday. He stopped, frozen. It was empty. There was nobody in sight. Alex frowned, then resumed his walking, maybe the spot was a little further ahead than he'd remembered. As he reached the end of the deserted street, his eyes rested on the wall of the last building, a rundown structure which seemed to be ready for the wrecking ball. Its decrepit state had been given new life by the dozens of street artists who'd left their mark on it. Alex was sure this was where he'd encountered D-Zyne.

But where was he?! D-Zyne had promised to be there! Before Alex got too glum about the artist's absence, he realized that D-Zyne might not know exactly what time school got out. He didn't look all that old, not a real adult like his parents, but Alex reckoned he'd been out of high school for a couple of years now.

Alex turned back to the wall to admire D-Zyne's completed work. On the wall was the image of a statue, one Alex remembered seeing on the trip his class took to the Louvre last winter, before the quarantine. It was really old, he vaguely recalled that the guide said it was Greek or Roman, something like that. D-Zyne's statue had a face, but didn't have any arms, nor a top for that matter! She was only wearing a sort of loose wavy skirt, like a sheet. Actually, no, not a sheet…. It was unravelling at the bottom and this cloth went along the base of the building. The way it was depicted, it eventually turned into a roll, a giant roll of toilet paper. Alex now remembered all the toilet paper shortage jokes from the beginning of the lockdown. D-Zyne had filled the roll in with dozens of little green virus symbols, like the emojis his sister sent in her phone messages to her friends. Alex looked back up to the painted sculpture's face which had on a gas mask, similar to the one D-Zyne had been wearing yesterday.

"So, what do you think?"

Alex spun around to find D-Zyne leaning on an electric foot scooter. He'd had been so absorbed with the art that he hadn't heard him whiz up. Today, D-Zyne wasn't wearing his gas mask, he had one of those cloth ones. It looked liked he'd painted it himself with more of those tiny virus symbols. He lowered it down over his chin and grinned at his potential protégé.

"It's super cool!"

"Thanks, Bad Blu," he said, putting out first his right elbow to 'shake,' then his left, adding in sort of a secret handshake element to it, like they were part of the same street artist clan. "Come up with any ideas for your own work?"

"Yep!" Alex answered enthusiastically as he fumbled through his bag. He pulled out his napkin doodle and held it out to D-Zyne.

"No, I don't want to see it on paper, I want to see it here, up on the wall."

Alex was stunned. He'd never used a can of spray paint before.

"Don't worry, Bad Blu," said D-Zyne. "I went home to get you a mask, that's why I was a bit late. Here, I'll teach you how it's done and then you can get to work."

These words thawed Alex's fear. He set his school bag down against the wall. He let D-Zyne put on the gas mask and teach him how to use the spray can.

"See, it isn't that hard," said D-Zyne. "Now it's over to you, Bad Blu. Get on it before the police show up! Ha ha! Just kidding, little bro! They don't mind when we use abandoned buildings like this one."

Alex got over his scare provoked by D-Zyne's joke and looked down at the different colored spray cans he had to choose from. He picked up a brown one to start with and approached the wall with confidence.

***

179

"Okay! I think I'm done!" Alex said as he removed the gas mask, put the paint can he was holding on the ground and stepped back proudly.

"Whoa, Bad Blu! You're a mean street artist!"

"But, but, yesterday I told you I wasn't mean."

"Yo, Blu, chill out. It's a compliment! Mean also means great."

"Oh, okay. Thanks!" he said, relieved. "So, you like it?"

On the wall, next to D-Zyne's modern *Venus de Milo*, was the image of the Eiffel Tower with a happy face in the center. It was wearing a mask, not a gas mask, but a simple surgical one. At its base was a row of stick-figure children, all painted a different color, touching elbows just like the handshake D-Zyne had taught him.

"Love it, Bad Blu. Well done. I think you got this."

Alex beamed. "These are different kids from around the world. The Eiffel Tower brings them together and keeps them safe."

"I see that. You've got social issues and you've got Paris. Keep up with those ideas, Bad Blu."

"I'll try! Will I see you again, D-Zyne?"

"Well, I'm not always working in this area, but remember like I told you, keep your eyes peeled. Stay aware too, little guy." D-Zyne noticed Alex's disappointment with his answer. "You gotta fly with your own wings too, Bad Blu. You can do it. You're learning to express yourself and what you believe in. But just so you know, you can't paint on just any building, okay? And definitely not inside your house, unless your parents are cool with that. But, I really doubt they are! My parents certainly aren't!"

"Okay."

"Before you go, let me snap a shot of you and your work. I'll share it on my Instagram!"

This made Alex beam even brighter. He couldn't wait to show his sister. That is, after dinner when she was allowed to use her phone.

"Thanks a lot, D-Zyne!"

"See ya around, Bad Blu!"

Alex's glow remained ablaze the rest of his walk home. He loved his initiation into street art and social issues. In his bag was a flyer for this new academic year's after-school options. Perhaps there was an art class?

Le Métro
11th & 12th Arrondissements

Tumbling down the *Métro* stairs, Sasha was confronted with his worst fears, no sight of the red beret. He was instead faced with République Station's myriad of passageways and stairwells. He had to think rationally. If someone wanted a quick escape from where they'd just been, which line would one take? The closest one. This happened to be Line 9. She seemed to know all the shortcuts. He didn't have any time to lose.

Following the signage, he proceeded to race up and down several short staircases, then found himself on the Line 9 platform, but heading west. That was the direction they'd just come from. That wouldn't make sense at all.

However, from this new vantage point, Sasha had a view of both platforms. *Voilà!* There, on the other side, virtually right across from where Sasha was standing, was Petite Piaf. The screeching of the *Métro* tires forewarned the imminent arrival of a train. She saw Sasha, stuck her tongue out, giggled and waved. *If only she knew why he was chasing her!* thought the tormented Sasha. *It was no laughing matter!*

He rushed back down the stairs, but then had to figure out how to get to the other side. The ceiling trembled above his head with the approaching train. He scanned the various tunnels. *That one!* He spotted an obscurely placed sign for 'Mairie de Montreuil.' He darted for it, dashed up the steps and dove into the train. The buzzer sounded. They were off.

This is going to give me a heart attack! wheezed the breathless and exhausted Sasha. Not only was this physically exerting, his head felt like it was going to explode with all the stress! He collapsed onto a folding seat. He needed a moment to regain his composure, or at least to the best of his ability given his current circumstances.

Come on, Sasha! Rally! You haven't worked so hard for this long for to let it all go down the drain, or rather, into the abyss of the Métro. His pep talk gave him some renewed momentum.

The train wasn't very busy. After the next station, Oberkampf, there wasn't another interchange station until Nation. He didn't know exactly how many train cars she was ahead of him, however, he should be able to catch up to her before then.

Pulling into Oberkampf, Sasha surged quickly out of the carriage and shot down to the next one. He did the same at the next station, Saint Ambroise. When he reached the far end of this new car, he peered through the window.

"Il n'y a qu'un seul Paris..."

Ahhhh! There she was. Fantastic. He stepped up to the door, ready to make his move. The train's rumble decreased as they approached Voltaire Station, named in honor of the great thinker of the 18th century Enlightenment era. If only Sasha could be enlightened enough to get his precious item back. *Focus, Sasha, focus!*

Before the train had come to a full stop on the platform at Voltaire, his phone rang, dragging Sasha out of his intense state of concentration. Shakily, he pulled his cell out of the pocket of his shoulder bag. *On no!* It was the last person he wanted to talk to right now, but he felt compelled to answer nonetheless.

"*Allô?*" he replied nervously.

"*Oui, oui ! J'arrive!* Yes, yes, I'm coming!" he whimpered. " I ran into, um, a little delay."

The voice on the other end of the line didn't sound happy at all, but what could Sasha do? The only thing he could do is catch up to that musician so he could retrieve his important object.

"Of course, I have it!" he fibbed. "Yes, yes, I know. I'll definitely have it to you by 4:30. I promise."

As he hung up the phone he noticed the time. It was almost 2:15. His eyes bulged. How had more than an hour already gone by since that fateful coin toss? While he was transfixed on the time, the doors slammed shut at Voltaire.

Darn! He'd missed his chance to get into Petite Piaf's carriage!

Sasha quickly glanced into the other *Métro* car. The musician was no longer in it. Panicked, he flipped his head over to the platform which was flying by his eyes. No red beret. This observation gave him some hope, he assumed she must have moved onto the next carriage.

The train carried on with its journey through the up and coming 11th arrondissement. On the streets above were an increasing number of hip cafés, small designer boutiques and innovative restaurants. The train slowed as it came into Charonne Station where Sasha quickly shifted to the next car. Working his way to the other end he could already hear the words which he now knew all too well.

"*There's only one Paris...!*"

He'd have to be more daring at the next station, Rue des Boulets. *Don't screw this up by being un boulet!* he scolded. Although the word *boulet* technically meant 'ball,' as in cannonball or the ball of a ball-and-chain, it was also slang for imbecile. He quickly devised a clever and completely new plan of attack, he had to get his item back and delivered on time. The train came to a halt when it reached the platform. With calm assurance, Sasha exited and then jogged up to the following carriage. But this time, instead of going into the first section of the car, he went straight for the one Petite Piaf was in.

The buzzer sounded. The doors closed.

Petite Piaf was facing the other way, singing for the benefit of a pair of Eastern European-looking tourists. Polish? Ukrainian? *What were they doing up here in the 11th, where few tourists ever ventured?* Sasha pondered. *They must be lost.* Sasha put aside his thoughts and concentrated on the red beret.

"*Paris... Paris...!*"

The musician cheerfully concluded her tune with a little twirl. Her joy quickly dissipated when she saw Sasha. This time though her song ended on a deflated note from the wheezing accordion, like a punctured tire. They stared at each other for what seemed like the longest split second. Then Sasha went to open his mouth.

"*Vous êtes vraiment un boulet!* You're such a ball-and-chain!" she huffed using the proper definition of the word *boulet*.

"But I just need to talk to you for a minute, it's…"

"Leave. Me. Alone!" she shouted at him. Seeing her consternation, the man of the Eastern European couple jumped out of his seat.

"Hey, mister, you leave girl alone!" he ordered, coming to her defense.

"But, but, but…"

"No buts!" he commanded as he made a punching gesture with one fist into the other palm. He looked pretty tough and was much, much bulkier than average-sized Sasha. He certainly didn't want to be at the other end of those fists. The tension mounted as the train's speed descended.

"She has…"

"I don't care what she has," he said, advancing towards Sasha who in turn stepped backwards until he was pressed up against the flip-down seats closest to the door. "She good singer. She do no wrong."

The train pulled into the platform at Nation.

No, she hasn't done anything wrong, but she has my…"

The doors flew open and out flew Petite Piaf. Both Sasha and the muscle man looked over at the flash of red. Sasha used this as a convenient distraction to escape as well. He jetted after her.

"You leave that girl alone!" was all Sasha could hear as he barreled down the tunnel. But he wasn't trying to do her any harm! All he wanted was his important possession back. Despite his mounting despair, he charged onwards.

Located in the northeast part of the city, Place de la Nation was the meeting point of the 11th, 12th and 20th districts. Underneath the large square was this mid-sized interchange station. There were three other lines Petite Piaf could be heading to. The *RER* A suburban train was the least likely option. Line 2 took a similar yet more northerly path than the one they'd just come from, so this made it improbable as well. They'd already been on Line 1, so that left Line 6. Although it started and ended on the Right Bank, the half-moon trajectory of this line spent much of its time over on the Left Bank. Checking for her there first would also be the easiest option. Like he'd encountered with Line 10 at Austerlitz, Line 6 started here at Nation, so he wouldn't have to guess which platform to search for her on.

Sasha jetted down the tunnel to Line 6. He thought he might have seen a flash of red duck into the staircase up ahead, but he couldn't be sure. He jogged up the stairs, but then slowed his pace down. If that had really been her, he wanted to catch her by surprise and on the train so she couldn't run away as easily.

He pressed himself against the wall and tiptoed down the steps. Reaching the platform, Sasha edged along the wall until he arrived at a snack vending machine. He discreetly peered around it. *Thank goodness.* She was indeed there, albeit already at the far end of the platform. He couldn't risk her seeing him. So he decided to wait here for the train to come and, once again, painstakingly work his way through the train cars to reach her. Actually, he figured they'd likely meet in the middle after a handful of stations.

Unlike the previous close calls he'd had in catching the *Métro*, this train took its sweet old time to arrive. An absolute eternity for anxious Sasha. A drop of sweat trickled down his forehand. He was tempted to take out his handkerchief to dab his it, yet he was too petrified to move. Sasha was starting to feel like he was in an episode of *Inspecteur Marcel*. As much as he liked the show, he knew he'd never be cut out for that kind of stress-intensive job.

The train finally tooted into the station and those waiting on the platform got on board. Sasha waited a minute. He didn't want her to spot him. When he heard the buzzer sound, he hurriedly jumped into the first carriage. They were off.

Picpus, Bel-Air, Daumesnil. The train worked its way beneath the quiet streets of the mostly residential 12th district. Sasha didn't come over to this part of town much, except for the occasional stroll along the Promenade Plantée or to browse the shops and art galleries of the Viaduc des Arts. He remembered the article he saw earlier on in the *Métro* newspaper, about a new exhibit that would be taking place in one of those galleries. Maybe in a few days' time, when he'd sorted out all his current problems, Sasha would come see it. Correction, not *when* he'd sorted them out… *if!* He still hadn't retrieved his very important object.

Sasha was advancing through the train cars. At Dugommier Station he heard the first hint of Petite Piaf.

"There's only one Paris…!" She wasn't quite finished her song. He'd try to hop over onto the carriage at the next station, Bercy. This time, his previous idea of tempting her with a 20-euro note resurfaced. He took out his wallet. But instead of a 20-euro bill, he removed a 50. That would be more enticing. Besides, the valuable item she had was worth much more than that.

He took a deep breath and as the train slowed, he got ready for this new offensive. As soon as the lock released at Bercy, he flung himself out of the train and into the first door of the neighboring car. But he wasn't the only person who got on at Bercy.

Uh oh. Petite Piaf suddenly had more to battle with than simply Sasha.

A Young Vintage in the 11th

"What are you looking at?"

"What? Me?! I'm not looking at anything!"

"Didier, you can't lie to me. All this morning you've been creeping over to that window every chance you get! Actually, come to think of it... you've been acting strange all week!"

"I have no idea what you're talking about! You must be imagining things!"

Valérie didn't dignify this with a reply. She simply rolled her eyes, sighed and went back to unpacking the new shipment, which had just arrived. She bent down to remove the bottles from their cardboard box. *Ow!* She straightened up and rubbed her lower back. She'd gradually been coming to the realization that there were just some things, physically speaking, that she couldn't, or shouldn't, do anymore.

"Would you get away from the window and come over here to help me, please?"

"But, I wasn't looking at anything! I was just readjusting the window display!"

"Okay fine, but you can do that later. We really need to get these boxes out of the way so we can actually welcome the customers you're trying to attract with your incredible and enticing window display."

Valérie had a point. Plus, even though Didier had actually been busy spying out the window, he wasn't blind to the fact that her back had been troubling her more and more these days. Maybe it really was time to get a part-time assistant? But, could they afford to hire someone... with this new 'threat' that had just popped up down the street? Didier took one last peek before going to relieve Valérie of her unpacking duties. On the window above his head were the words: *Laborde, fils et fille. Maison fondée en 1925.* Laborde, son and daughter. Founded in 1925.

***

There was never any question whether Valérie and Didier would take over their family's wine shop when their father retired. It had always been a given, as far back as they could remember. Businesses naturally passed down in the family. It was tradition.

Hailing from the prestigious wine region of Bordeaux, their grandfather had worked as a *négociant en vin*, a wine merchant, traveling the country selling the fine wines of Bordeaux to wine shops. On one fateful trip to the capital he met and fell in love with *une belle Parisienne*, a beautiful Parisian, their grandmother. He was so enamored with Célestine, he'd have moved mountains for her. Fortunately, simply moving to Paris was much easier than trying to budge the Pyrénées, the closest mountain range to Bordeaux.

He convinced his parents to give him a loan so he could open his own shop, but in the 'big city' his money didn't go as far as it could down in the southwest. So, he eventually had to settle on the more working-class 11th district. Thanks to his professional contacts, he was able to stock his *cave à vin* with a notable selection of excellent quality Bordeaux wines that complimented the various needs and budgets of the neighborhood, from everyday wines to top quality *grands crus* wines for special occasions.

Didier and Valérie's father took over the shop from their grandfather in 1960. The period of their father's ownership saw many social changes in France, often sparked in part by the tumultuous protests of May 1968 that brought about labor reforms and more equal rights for women. These reforms didn't bother Mr Laborde; on the contrary, he was proud that both his son and his daughter showed an interest in their family's *savoir faire*, their know-how. Always the more scholarly of the two, Valérie had pursued a university degree in Wine Sales and Business Management. Walking back with her family to their shop after her graduation ceremony, Valerie suddenly stopped, completely surprised and absolutely thrilled when she saw their storefront. Her father had already added the word 'daughter' to the shop's signage and handed her a small box containing her very own business cards.

The two siblings worked alongside their father until he too retired in 1995, and they were each given half; partners with equal ownership of the shop. Business-minded Valérie had taken over handling the shop's overall management and stock. And charismatic Didier was the main sales consultant, wooing everyone from older ladies out with their trolley carts for their daily shopping excursions to office workers stopping in on their way home from work for a bottle to drink with that night's dinner.

The siblings had both married and had families, yet, as hard as they'd tried, a passion for wine didn't seem to flow in the veins of any of their children. Valérie's daughter Elodie had pursued architecture studies and seemed to have gotten lost in the depths of the Opéra Garnier, conducting research for her Ph.D. Didier's son, Stéphane, who was a personal trainer, taught bootcamps and led jogging clubs in the city's parks. He personally would cringe at the sight of a glass of wine, filled with senseless calories. That meant it was down to their two youngest, Valérie's son Gabriel and Didier's daughter Katherine. Although, both were still in their first year at the Sorbonne and very much on the fence about what they wanted to do professionally speaking. Young people these days!

***

Young people, Didier grumbled to himself, as his eyes drifted once again towards the window across the street. He could tell they were young. It was obvious. One just had to look at the wacky colors of the facade of this new shop (bright pink and lime green?!). But, it wasn't this new shop's decor that was disturbing him. It was something else, something much, much more serious. And it was eating away at Didier at a much more ferocious rate than the epidemic of phylloxera, tiny insects which ravaged 40% of French grape vines back in the late 1800s. It was something that could be equally devastating, so catastrophic that it could affect not only their livelihood, but also the very future of their shop!

Even though he needed to update his glasses prescription, he was quite sure he'd seen a customer leaving the new shop carrying a distinctly shaped paper bag. A long thin one designed for one thing and one thing only. A bottle. A bottle of wine. Obsessed, he simply had to know if his hunch was right. Was there another wine shop opening, right there, on *their* street? Anxious to continue his investigation, he unpacked and shelved the new cases of inventory faster than the best picker could work through a row of grapes during the harvest.

Didier snuck a glance over at Valérie. She'd sat down at the computer after Didier had taken over the unpacking and seemed deeply engrossed in her monthly accounting. Perfect timing.

"Um, I'm just going out, um, to the bank. Those kids of mine are a constant drain on my finances."

"Okay, but if I smell even the slightest whiff of tobacco on you when you return, I'm telling your wife," she threatened, giving him a stern look as he slipped out the front door.

She worried about her little brother. He could easily fall to temptation, especially when he was stressed out. She was surprised that he'd managed to stay strong when he finally quit smoking, but that was just before the quarantine. Since they also sold a few specialty food items from the Bordeaux region, they'd been allowed to stay open during the lockdown. However, with a huge number of Parisians fleeing the city for those first two months, and a good number staying away afterwards, this year's sales were down by at least 20%. Being in constant contact with so many different people also added to both of their anxiety levels, considering their ages were edging closer and closer to 60. Not exactly the Covid high-risk danger zone, but not far off.

Valérie leaned over to watch him as he strode down the street. He hadn't removed anything from his pocket, but she was still suspicious about the motives of his outing. She returned to her accounting, making a mental note to do a smell test when he got back from his supposed trip to 'the bank.'

***

Didier knew very well that Valérie would be watching him from inside the shop, so he casually walked in the other direction of the new shop until he was quite sure he was safely out of her line of sight. Then he jogged around the block circling back to the other end of their street, Rue des Boulets. He knew the neighborhood was continuously evolving, especially on neighboring Rue de Charonne. The former working-class families of the district were increasingly being replaced with these trendy young people. What was the word used to describe them today? Ah yes. Bobos, which was short for bourgeois bohemians. Or was it hipsters? He kept getting the two confused. No matter what they were called, he didn't like them.

Their street had miraculously remained virtually unscathed by the wave of eco-friendly clothing shops, Australian coffee places and vegetarian cafés that were infiltrating the area to suit the lifestyle of these bobo-hipsters. But Didier's worst fears might, finally and irrevocably, have come true. He really shouldn't be that surprised. He did get a sinking feeling when their street's newsagent didn't reopen after the quarantine. Some of the newspaper vendors in Paris doubled as tobacco shops, another type of 'essential' goods vendor, like food shops, that were allowed to stay open during the lockdown. But this neighborhood news shop only sold newsprint, magazines and basic stationery. And, in addition to the mandatory two-month closure, fewer and fewer people were buying print media, opting for online options instead. It seemed to be a dying business. *Was it simply a matter of time before all of these press shops would disappear?* Didier regrettably pondered. *Would wine shops be next?*

He bottled up this train of thought as he reached the other side of their street. He peered stealthily around the corner. The coast seemed clear. As nonchalantly as he could, hands in his pockets and whistling, he slowly ambled up the street, almost as if he'd happened upon it by chance. As he inched closer and closer to the pink and green *monster*, his heart rate increased. His pace was reduced to that of someone savoring a prized bottle of vintage Château Margaux. How could he get a proper look without being recognized?

"*Yoo-hoo, Monsieur Laborde! Monsieur Laborde!*" called a shrill voice from across the street.

Didier jumped back with the force of a popping champagne bottle, or more appropriately, a crémant de Bordeaux, his region's own bubbly wine. He flattened himself as best he could against the building he was standing next to, two doors down from the new shop, and shot a glance in the direction of the heart-attack rendering voice.

"*Ah, Bonjour, Madame Leroy.*" It was one of their regulars.

"*Ca va?*" she asked how he was, noticeably puzzled by his peculiarly skittish behavior.

"*Oui, oui, oui, ca va. Ca va très bien,*" he stuttered unconvincingly 'I'm good.'

A widow, Madame Leroy came into the shop far too often. Whether it was to bask in Didier's overly generous attention and compliments or that she drank an entire bottle of wine almost nightly, either reason was worrying as far as he was concerned.

However, judging by her deep frown, Didier was definitely not up to his usual charming self enough today to satisfy her.

"I'll stop by later!" she announced, when he hadn't returned her friendly greeting. She adjusted her autumnal hat, returned her grip on her shopping cart and went on her way. Most likely she was off to the Aligre Market, located a few streets away in the neighboring 12th district.

Close call! Didier thought, a drop of sweat slowly ran from his forehead down his cheek. Still plastered to the building he'd flung himself against, Didier titled his head forward in an attempt to peer into the new shop. But as he turned his head he got a fright. There, 'staring' at him straight in the eye, was the image of Bacchus, the Roman God of Wine, or rather a painting of a statue of Bacchus. He had grapes in his hair which helped Didier quickly identify it. He leaned out so he could get a better look. Bacchus held a wine goblet up to his lips, but couldn't take a sip because he was wearing a gas mask. Out of his cup were floating small virus symbols, which lofted off into the air. In addition to all those new hip shops and cafés, Didier had also noticed some street art popping up in the neighborhood, this must be the latest in the trend. He looked down to the 'statue's' feet where the artwork seemed to be signed D-Zyne. Just like society was trying to combat the virus, Didier wasn't going to give up on his battle against their shop's potential deadly threat. He got back to the task at hand: to find out more about that new boutique.

He leaned out as far as he was able to in order to see into the shop's front window. *Darn!* From his current position, he didn't have the right perspective. So, he took a deep breath and slowly slinked out into the street. He would have a better view from there. Yes, this new vantage point provided a better view... but also confirmed his worst nightmares!

Lining one wall were indeed bottles. There was no mistaking it, bottles were bottles! Fuming, Didier's eyes scanned the rest of the shop, well, what he could take in from his clandestine perspective. *Ah ha!* Just as he'd thought... it was indeed run by young people! Those hipster types! And girls to boot!

Yikes! One of them was walking towards the door and another followed close behind. Panic-stricken, Didier's first instinct was to hide, so he ducked between the two cars next to where he was standing. Finally, he built up enough courage to peek over the car's trunk.

Standing outside the shop, were the same two girls... laughing and smoking those vaporizer cigarettes! Not only did this inflame Didier's fury, it also really sparked his own urge for a cigarette! This infuriating situation felt like it was going to push him over the edge!

He crouched back down and tried to contain his anger. This glance though, was long enough for him to catch part of the shop's name. He could have sworn it had the word *naturel* in it. *Humph!* How natural were those modern cigarettes?

Didier raised his head high enough over the car's trunk to check on the action in front of the shop. Just then a car engine sprung to life, giving Didier an even bigger fright than Bacchus had. Didier was relieved when he realized it wasn't the car he'd taken refuge behind, but the one in front of it. After it had pulled away and driven up the street, Didier risked taking another peek. One of those hipster girls had gone inside and was coming back out with a wooden chair she used to block off the newly liberated parking spot. The girls gave each other a high five and went back inside.

He waited a minute before daring to stand up from his impromptu hiding spot and shake out the kinks from the uncomfortable position he had been in. He went to turn around to get one last look, plus there seemed to be some smaller print writing in the window he wanted to check.

Ding, ding, ding!

Didier's spying was rudely interrupted by a speeding *Vélib*, a bicycle from Paris's bike-share program, which he dodged by jumping back behind the parked car. The increasing number of bikes being ridden now, which resulted in less noise from car traffic, was a current trend he didn't mind. Nevertheless, he felt some of these bikers were careless daredevils. Okay, he admitted to himself he did deserve and need the warning of the dinging bell since he was standing in the street's bike lane, which were also on the rise in Paris.

Ding, ding, ding!

Just as he stepped back into the street to cross it, something else dinged while whizzing by. This time it was one of those electric foot scooters! *Mon dieu!* Forget the daredevil cyclists, these scooter riders seemed to come out of nowhere! Didier was not very fond of them. Since they didn't need to be left at a particular station, like *Vélibs* needed to be, abandoned scooters could occasionally be found in the middle of the sidewalk. These provided an annoying obstruction to the wine shop's deliveries.

With all these stressful events combined, Didier was about to cave into his burning desire to have a cigarette. Then he remembered Valérie's last words. Plus, he'd already been gone much longer than it would normally have taken to go to the bank. He didn't want to give her the satisfaction of being 'right' about her suspicions over his real intention for going out.

He managed to get across the street safely without any further incidents and made his way towards the shop. He tried to act as naturally as possible as he pushed open the door and strolled inside. Valérie looked up from her computer with a raised eyebrow.

"Long line at the bank?" she asked, her question covered in a thick layer of doubt.

"You can't even imagine!" he said, countering her distrust with his charisma. "I first spotted Madame Leroy and I let her go ahead of me, then Madame Vincent came in, so I felt obligated to do the same for her." Part of this fib was vaguely true, he had *seen* Madame Leroy, just not at the bank.

As he gave further false details about his outing to 'the bank,' Didier walked up close to Valérie so she could smell the lack of any tobacco odor on him.

"Just before the bank closes at 1 pm isn't exactly the best time to go," she replied sarcastically.

"Oh, is it 1 already?" he said, trying to change the subject. "The morning flew by so quickly!"

"Well, it's now practically 1:20. You kept those poor bank staff into their lunch break," she countered, trying to call him out.

"Oh no, I was out of there by 1, however, on my way back I ran into Mr Chevalier who asked if we'd received a new stock of Pauillac. I told him he was in luck; it had just arrived this morning!" Didier's little white lie was getting somewhat out of control, so he changed tactics. "Listen, it's lunchtime and all, but I don't feel like going to the bistro today. I'm not very hungry, so why don't you go out for lunch and I'll go out for a sandwich or something when you get back?"

Several days a week they ate at their 'cantine,' the old school bistro found a few doors down on their side of the street. Valerie tended to order à la carte, but Didier always got the two-course lunch menu, with a glass of Bordeaux, of course.

"Okay, in that case I might actually slip home for a bite, but I'll be back by 2:30," she said. For the time being, she didn't mention her true thoughts; that there was something very fishy about all of this. Her brother wasn't one for skipping out or skimping on meals. She couldn't remember the last time he'd had a sandwich, perhaps on a scout excursion when he was a kid? "Are you sure you don't want me to pick something up for you on my way back?"

"No, no. I'll be fine! I had a huge helping of coq au vin for dinner last night, I'm still stuffed!" he added, which was the first true statement that had come out of his mouth all day.

"Alright then, suit yourself. See you later."

"Bon appétit!" he exclaimed with a big smile as Valérie took her purse and left the shop. He crept up to the door and watched her until she reached the end of the street, then he swung his head around in the other direction.

The car he'd been hiding behind had since also driven off and the new shop owners were outside setting up some tables. *Tables??* Didier knew that the city had temporarily loosened the regulations on outdoor seating, allowing restaurants and delicatessens to use public parking spots as makeshift terraces. But did that mean they also served food? The possibility did nothing but further fuel Didier's animosity.

He began pacing back and forth alongside the shop's rows of perfectly aligned bottles of Saint-Emilion, Margaux, Haut-Médoc, Saint-Estèphe, Graves, Entre-deux-Mers and Côtes-de-Blaye. On the top shelves were the more prestigious bottles of Château Lafite, Château Mouton-Rothschild and Château Latour. They didn't bother stocking the absolute highest in the Bordeaux range or very old vintages, as they knew these were generally not in the budget of their regular clients. Nevertheless, Didier knew how to pull some strings to get a bottle of Petrus, if a client was really serious.

His pacing was interrupted by Madame Leroy, who'd returned from the market. She was so bubbly as she chatted away, simultaneously batting her eyelashes. Didier tried to turn his charm back on, but he knew there was no way he'd be at his best today. She eventually settled on her regular bottle of mid-range Côtes-de-Bourg and went on her way. Before Didier could return his attention to what his undesirable neighbors were up to, a series of regular clients came in one after the other.

"Is everything okay?" seemed to be the common question they each asked. Didier was definitely not himself and it showed. When the last customer finally left, Didier gave a big sigh of relief and snuck back up to the window. The girls had been busy. In addition to being fitted out with around six tables, well-spaced out for social distancing, the terrace had been festooned with streamers and balloons. *The nerve!* Didier was glaring at this scene so intently that he didn't notice someone approaching from the left. Then, all of a sudden, his view was blocked... by Valérie. Bearing a frosty glare, she raised a finger and pointed it menacingly at her brother, before pushing open the front door with a forceful whoosh.

"What exactly were you looking at? Don't even try repeating this morning's 'nothing,' because I'm not letting you off the hook this time," she growled, hands on her hips.

"Haven't you noticed?! Those imposters, across the road!"

"It's a new shop... and so?"

"It's run by two girls! A couple!"

"How do you know they're a couple? And besides, why would that even matter?"

"They are those hipster kinds! Covered in tattoos!"

"And so, I still don't get your point. Your daughter has a tattoo, doesn't she? Why are you so upset?"

"But it's not just any new shop... they are selling... WINE!"

"Are you so sure about that?"

"Yes! Well, about 99.99999 percent sure! They're going to steal our business! We'll have to close down! We'll be out on the street in no time!"

"Maybe there's room for two wine shops on this street! For heaven's sake, snap out of it, Didier! Put things into perspective for a minute. First of all, there's no way this other shop could specialize in Bordeaux wines and, secondly, we have a very loyal client base. One that's been maintained thanks to you, your charm and vast knowledge, but your new mysterious behavior is hardly becoming. If you're not careful, you're going to scare all our customers away and they'll go running into the tattooed arms of those hipster girls!"

Knock! Knock!

The knock on the door brought Valérie's tirade to an abrupt end. They both swung around to find the two hipster girls waving at them from the other side of the window. Frozen, it took the siblings an instant to react, but before they could, the girls cheerfully paraded into the shop.

"*Bonjour!*" they chimed in unison.

"*Bonjour...*" only Valérie managed to sputter in return.

"We wanted to come over and introduce ourselves," said the one with bleach blonde hair.

"We're from *Au Naturel*, the new boutique down the street," said the other one with dark hair and purple streaks, this was spoken with a slight hint of an accent.

"You probably don't recognize me, with this mask on and all, plus it's also been a while since we last saw each other, but I'm the daughter of Gilles Moreau, who used to own the press shop," said the blonde.

"Ah yes, Maïa, isn't it?" said Valérie. "I think you went to school with my son."

"Yes, that's right! I hope Gabriel is doing well! So, papa decided to retire. He moved back to the 5th after he and mom got divorced. It was a bit of a hassle for him to come all the way over here from the Left Bank every day, plus he was due to retire, so he gave us the lease of his shop. As you may have noticed, we've gone in the complete opposite direction of his business. We wanted to show you what we have on offer, so we brought you a present." She energetically held up one of those tall paper bag's Didier had previously observed and forced it into his hands.

For a long moment, Didier couldn't move, but he eventually regained control of his hands to tilt the bag and reluctantly peer inside it. Sure enough, the object in it was the shape of a wine bottle, as he'd rightfully observed on his reconnaissance mission. He slowly removed the bottle from the bag, dreading the worst. But no. He was wrong. It was not a bottle of wine. It was a bottle of cider. Organic cider from Normandy.

"We specialize in natural beverages, a passion I acquired when I worked a year in Australia. But my fascination for wine and fermented beverages actually goes back to my childhood. I'd always peek into your store after school on my way to my dad's shop. For hours I'd wonder how this mysterious wine was made. Fate would have it that while I was in Australia I got a job on a natural wine estate. The experience taught me a lot and inspired me to return to a natural approach of production. And, that's when

I met Katia. At the end of my year in Australia, I convinced her to move back to France and together develop the idea for the new shop. Please don't worry, wine isn't our main focus."

"In fact, the wine section is actually very small," added the Australian, sensing Valérie and Didier's reticence. "We have a wide range of craft beers, artisanal ciders, kombucha and pure fruit juices—those are more our focus. We serve these with small snacks, all made with 100% natural ingredients, hence the tables out front."

"Tonight's our grand opening and we'd love to have you there," said Maïa.

Valérie and Didier stared blankly at the two girls.

"Of course, we'd be honored," Valérie eventually accepted. "What time?"

"Great! It starts at 7 pm."

"Wonderful, we'll drop by after we close the shop," replied Valérie.

The hipster girls looked at each other with the same glee Didier had witnessed earlier during his spying. Contagious glee. The innocent and optimistic glee of these '*young people.*'

The girls bid the wine merchants *bon après-midi*, good afternoon, and bounced out of the store. Valérie and Didier watched as they cheerfully ambled, arm-in-arm and high on their youthful euphoria, back over to their pink and green *monster*. They hadn't even locked their door when they came over. They perfectly embodied the name of the venue. *Au Naturel.* They were today's *natural*. To move forward they were, in essence, taking a step backwards. Returning to tradition.

Valérie turned to Didier and poked him in the side.

"If none of our kids end up taking over the shop, we're calling those girls!"

Rata-toille at the Promenade Plantée & Viaduc des Arts

"*Magnifique!*"

"I'm so glad you like the photos I sent."

"I can't wait to see the works in person."

"Oh, yes. You'll love them even more when you see them in person at the gallery."

"The exhibit opening is on Thursday, right?"

"Yes, from 6 pm."

"I'll be there at 6 on the dot!"

"Excellent! I look forward to seeing you then!"

"*A jeudi!* See you Thursday!"

Yannick hung up the phone and did a little happy dance. Since representing Yoshi Karakami, he'd been wooing Lady de Bourg, the heiress of a Bordeaux wine dynasty and perhaps *the* most influential private collector of contemporary paper sculpture in France.

It had been a gamble when he'd agreed to represent Yoshi. However, the innovative artist had gradually been making headway and a recent glowing critique in *Art News* had stoked interest in his work. Selling a few pieces to Lady de Bourg would bolster Yoshi's profile, but it would also elevate Yannick's own prominence in the art world.

Yannick was relieved. He loved his gallery and would loathe to give it up. However, if he didn't make some big sales—and fast—he might. The thought of it made him cringe. He looked up at its soaring arched ceiling and thanked God for the luck he'd had in landing the unique space. He would do almost anything to keep it. Yes, just about anything.

***

Yannick had put in his time, blood, sweat and tears to get where he was today. Although he didn't share his father and brother's artist talent, a love of art had been fostered in him since he was a small child. This is what compelled him to study art history at the Sorbonne. After completing his undergraduate degree, he decided to apply his knowledge and passion towards a Master's in arts and cultural management. This helped him land a highly coveted, yet poorly paid, internship at one of the Upper Marais's top contemporary art galleries. He'd risen in the ranks at that renowned gallery, going from photocopying minion to assistant manager. But, after eight years, Yannick knew he couldn't rise any higher. Forget about a mere pandemic, it would take a true apocalypse for the power-hungry *directrice* to release her clutches on the gallery, despite the fact that she'd surpassed France's official retirement age. She'd be puffing away on her *Gauloises* and ordering around her staff until she was 100—unless her lungs gave up on her first.

When Yannick had come to this realization, he shifted strategies. Instead of catering to the *directrice*'s every whim, he carefully fostered relationships with the gallery's clients, art critics and artists. It wasn't until he'd built up a very solid professional reputation, and impressive contact list, that he felt ready to take the plunge and open a gallery in his own name.

***

As soon as he arrived at the address provided by the real estate agent, Yannick knew it was perfect. In front of him was a towering wall of glass set within a colossal brick archway. He was at the Viaduc des Arts.

In the mid-19th century, a vast network of rail lines was created in and around Paris. Some were built for intercity travel, others to transport suburban commuters in and out of the city center. Certain sections of the latter are still in use, nevertheless, when the *RER* suburban train network was developed in the 1960s, and tunnels for it were dug under the city's streets, most of its above-ground tracks within the city's limits were phased out. Over the past few decades parts of these have been rehabilitated, starting with an impressive 1.5 kilometer (1 mile) long viaduct located just east of Place de la Bastille.

In the late 1980s an urban garden and walkway was created atop the viaduct's 64 vaults while the large spaces beneath each arch were encased in huge panels of glass. These attractive spaces were then designated for the businesses in the arts, from artisanal workshops to innovative design boutiques. A beautiful example of architectural preservation and repurposing, it was the inspiration for other similar projects around the world, including the High Line in New York. The venues at the Viaduc des Arts hardly ever came up for rent, so it seemed like such perfect timing to Yannick. Where did he sign?

***

Or, was the timing really all that perfect? Within months of opening, Yannick had to contend with a two-month long transit strike which virtually paralyzed the city. This prevented people from attending a much-anticipated art show in December and reduced his visitors to a meager trickle throughout January and February. He was very eager to bounce back from this lag and had an excellent street art exhibit lined up for April, which even had a few works of his brother's. Again, more bad timing as it had to be canceled because of the Coronavirus. A lot was riding on this new show. It would not only launch the new season, it would make or break his entire career.

***

Yannick slid his cell phone into his pocket and went back to installing the exhibit. It was Tuesday so he had three full days to finish up. That was plenty of time. Plus, he'd already hung the most difficult pieces, so setting up the rest should be a walk in the park.

He gazed up at Yoshi's marvels. Suspended from the ceiling were several delicate paper sculptures. Although they were abstract, the sculptures were akin to lofty, dreamy clouds. They were made of natural materials and pigments using ingredients the Japanese artist had foraged himself in the forests around Paris. Yoshi shared his time between Paris and Tokyo, where he was currently stranded, having gone there just before the lockdown. However, the specific works for the exhibit had been created before he'd left, and his assistant had delivered them to the gallery on Monday.

Hey wait a second, Yannick did a double take as he was gazing up at the hanging artworks. *Are those spots?*

He could have sworn there weren't any dark marks in the pieces when he'd installed them. Yoshi had provided very detailed instructions for their installation and Yannick had followed them to a T. Perhaps some dust had fallen on them overnight?

He got out his extra tall ladder and climbed up to investigate. He squinted to scrutinize the works. His eyes immediately widened. No. It wasn't dust. There were small holes in the sculptures. Could they be tiny bite marks? *Impossible!* They were hanging in mid-air! His eyes followed the meandering path of holes all the way to the last sculpture. Just then it shook. Yannick's eyes widened even further and his mouth dropped as a small creature hopped off the sculpture and onto an industrial looking air vent.

"Hey you!" he shouted. The creature's small head turned back to look at him, its beady pupils locking with Yannick's hazel ones. It then darted along the vent, long thin tail trailing behind. A mouse!

Yannick watched, horrified, as it zoomed to the end of the vent and slid into a grate at the top of the wall. Yannick scrambled down the ladder and raced to the back door of the gallery. Luckily, there was a stairwell nearby which led to the upper level. He bounded up it two steps at a time, arriving at the top just as the little rodent squeezed through the other side of the grate. Seeing him, it bolted into some greenery.

Yannick chased after it, diving heroically into the bushes. Alas, he was no Zorro. He didn't have a sword to cut through the thick bamboo he suddenly found himself in. He attempted to weed through the shoots as best he could, but the minuscule menace was nowhere in sight. Defeated, Yannick tried to clear a path through the thicket in an attempt to find his way out.

"Hey!! What are you doing in here?" hollered a woman who was crouching down at the base of the bamboo.

"What are *you* doing here?" Yannick spit out in return.

"I work here!" she yelled at him.

"So do I!" he shouted back. "Well, I mean downstairs."

"Oh, isn't that nice," she said, mockingly. "By the looks of your outfit, at one of the fancy schmancy art galleries, huh? Well, I work right *here* and this area is normally off limits."

The woman stood up and brushed the dirt off her green uniform.

"Um, ah…" Yannick was flustered. She was obviously a gardener… and was obviously right. "I was chasing a mouse."

"Chasing a mouse?" She questioned, raising an eyebrow. "Are you sure it was a mouse?"

"What do you mean?" he asked, perplexed.

"Well, it might have been a rat," she replied. "I don't think there are any mice up here. Some breeds of rats look like mice. But that's totally besides the point. Why were you chasing it?"

"It was damaging some very valuable artwork."

The gardener sighed. "I'm not sure that's a valid reason to harm it."

"But... I..." Yannick started.

"Come with me," she cut him off, clearing the way through the bamboo.

"But ..." Yannick tried again.

"Let's go to my office, I've got a booklet of all the flora and fauna found up here. That way we can cross check what you saw."

Yannick obeyed, mainly because he wanted to get out of the greenery and back to the gallery.

"Look, that's very nice of you and all, but I really don't know if that's necessary," he said a little arrogantly.

"If you want to prevent it from 'damaging' any more of your precious artwork, it is," she replied in an equally smug tone.

The gardener deftly maneuvered through the tall shoots and soon they were on the Coulée Verte René Dumont. Also known as la Promenade Plantée, it was the walkway found above the viaduct. It was like a secret garden that Paris was hiding... in plain sight.

High above the street and removed from the noisy traffic, the Promenade was a lovely green space filled with trees, budding bushes, hedges, and a profusion of different varieties of flowers. In some sections there were trellises adorned with climbing roses. In other areas there were groves of bamboo, whose shoots were so tall they bent in a curved archway, like where the mismatched pair had just exited. Ignoring whether Yannick was following or not, the gardener turned right out of the bamboo grove. Yannick brushed the leaves and dirt off his suit pants, readjusted his slim fitting dress shirt and marched after her.

"Thank you for helping me," he said, deciding it was in his better interest to change his tune a little.

"No problem," she replied, also softening her stance. "I've had some issues with these rodents and I think you might have spotted a foreign one that's been invading the Promenade. It would be useful for our stats to know what exactly it was you saw."

"Ah I see, Madame...." Yannick said, fishing for her name.

"Margot. And you?" she answered, opting to go straight for first names since they seemed about the same age.

"Yannick. It's nice to meet you, Margot," he said, extending his hand.

"Same, but I don't think we're supposed to shake hands anymore, with the virus and all. Besides, you wouldn't want to shake these hands," she said, holding up her dirty fingers.

"Oh dear! My mask! I'd rushed out of the gallery so quickly I'd forgotten!" Yannick fumbled in his pocket and removed a stylish black one which he promptly put on. Margot gave Yannick a wink and on they proceeded along the Promenade.

At the end of the bamboo archway they reached a section which had an elongated water pool and fountain. Beyond this, Margot led Yannick over a small footbridge and past a grassy area where a few people were reading or taking in the sun. The beautiful and tranquil walkway was quite popular with the locals of eastern Paris. As Yannick scuttled after Margot, he noticed all kinds of people: walkers, joggers, kids eating ice cream, little old ladies strolling very slowly, huddling lovers, bird watchers and a group of school kids singing their hearts out.

"It's so pretty up here," said Yannick, taking in their surroundings. "I don't come up to the Promenade often."

"It's a great place to work," she replied. "It really feels like a completely different world up here. Like it's been touched by a more celestial or heavenly spirit compared to the busy city down below."

"I guess that's thanks to you and the other gardeners," Yannick complimented sweetly.

"It's really all nature's doing," said Margot modestly. "We just give it a small helping hand."

The walkway's route took them through building complexes and even through a couple of tunnels. From up here, one could see Parisian buildings, their rooftops and chimneys, from a different and very unique vantage point.

This part of the Promenade would be perfect for a romantic stroll, thought Yannick, sneaking a peek at Margot out of the corner of his eye. *No! No!* he scolded. He had to concentrate on the issue at hand: that troublesome rodent!

They arrived at one of the stairwells that led down to the street level. Beside this was a door to which Margot produced a key and opened. A cross between an office and a garden shed, the room was filled with all kinds of gardening equipment. On the left were two desks and a bookcase. Margot scanned the collection of books until she found a thin soft-covered booklet. She set it down on her desk and flipped through its pages.

"Ah ha, here's the right section," she said. "Can you identify which one of these creatures it might have been?"

Yannick examined the 'lineup' of potential suspects. Indeed, there were subtle differences between the rodents. Different tones of fur, smaller or bigger noses, pointy or rounded ears and shorter or longer tails.

"I think it could have been this one," he finally decided, finger stabbing one of the images.

"Just as I thought," she declared. "The Marsh Rice Rat. Since they are small and more brownish than grey, they resemble what we 'think' a mouse should look like. They are native to the Florida Keys and the Gulf Coast, and we believe someone here in Paris had one as a pet, but set it free. They are now breeding like crazy up here because they like the swampy sections of the Promenade."

"I see," said Yannick, completely lost on the details of this rat-mouse.

"If it comes back to your gallery would you call me?" she asked. "That way, I can properly add it to our stats. And, if luck's on our side, I could catch it and put a tracker on it. Then we would be able to find their main nest."

THERE'S ONLY *One* PARIS

"Sure, of course," he replied. "I'll do anything to help get rid of it."

"Great," she said, handing him her business card. "I gotta get back to work, I have a lot to finish before nightfall."

"I need to go as well. I have a lot to do to finish installing our next art exhibit," he countered. "You might actually like it, it's very nature oriented."

"Oh really?" she said. "Maybe I'll stop by some day."

"That'd be great," he said, perhaps a little too keenly. "In the meantime, I'll let you know if I have another sighting."

"*Parfait.* Perfect, have a nice day!" she said.

***

Yannick hurried back to the gallery. He had to keep things on track. Everything had to be perfect for Thursday. Slipping inside via the back door, he saw someone peering into the gallery's gigantic front windows. *Merde! Damn! It was Lady de Bourg! What was she doing here?!*

The elegant fifty-something knocked on the window and waved. *Double Merde!* She'd seen him. There was no way he could hide with the gallery's humongous windows. He had no choice but to go over and open the door.

"Madame de Bourg, how nice…"

"*Yannnnicccckkk….* I just couldn't resist," she screeched, barging past the stunned, helpless gallery owner. "I was in the neighborhood so I just had to come by to get a sneak peek. I'm dying to see Yoshi's new pieces."

"Um, ah," he stammered. "But I haven't finished installing them yet!"

"*Ohhhh, incroyable!* Incredible!" she gushed, already standing beneath the works. "*J'adore! J'adore! J'adore!* I simply adore them! I see that Yoshi has incorporated something new. Those holes… *magnifique! Magn-i-fique!!*"

211

Triple Merde! thought Yannick. *What was he going to do now?* Lady de Bourg had fallen in love with the mouse's, no, the rat's, handiwork.

"I hope he has many, many more of those!" she cooed, flipping around to face Yannick. "I will want to buy them all! Don't let anyone else lay claims on them! I'll be here on Thursday at 6 pm, sharp!"

And with that she turned around and sauntered in her impeccable Chanel suit out the front door and into her awaiting, chauffeured, black sedan.

Yannick stared at the door, in a state of shock mixed with panic. After a minute he looked back up to the artworks. He could think of no other solution. He had to get the *rat-iste* back.

***

Yannick pondered how he could lure the rodent back. *Cheese!* Yes, that's it! Didn't rats like cheese? No, he was getting confused with mice. But then again, maybe rats also liked cheese. Maybe his critter wasn't even a rat. It was entirely possible it was a mouse like he'd originally thought and could thus be tempted back by some fine French cheese.

He headed out the gallery's back door once again. This time he didn't take the stairs up, but instead went down the street, perpendicular to the viaduct. He walked with purpose through the back streets of the 12th district until he reached his intended destination, Place d'Aligre, home to one of Paris's historic covered market halls, le Marché Beauvau. Although part of the building had been damaged by fire a few years ago, it still retained its classic appeal. In the mornings, the market spilled out into some of the neighboring streets, where open air vendors can then also be found, however, in the afternoons only the covered hall was open. That's all he needed. Inside was a *fromagerie*.

What kind of cheese would a rat-mouse like? Yannick wondered as he entered the food emporium and was instantly hit by an intense melange of aromas and colors. *Gruyère, of course!* The hole-ridden cheese was usually associated with its small furry fans. Yannick strode over to the cheese counter, ordered some gruyère, then added in two other hard cheeses, some expensive beaufort and some 36-month aged comté. Maybe an art gallery rat-mouse had a more refined palate than regular ones.

He paid up and took the bag of carefully wrapped cheese from the counter. But before leaving it struck Yannick that since he was already at the market, he might as well pick up some supplies for Thursday's opening. So he quickly went over to the Italian deli stand to get some olives, a variety of nuts and some chic breadsticks. He then nipped over to the wine stand and bought a case of Graves from the Bordeaux region. Alas, he really didn't have time to go a few blocks further to where his favorite Bordeaux wine shop was located. This would have to do!

Arms loaded down with supplies, Yannick teetered back to the gallery and got down to his important task: Mission Rata-*toile*. *Toile* was the French word for canvas. Yoshi's modern natural canvasses now needed to be dotted with chew marks. And not made by any rodent—ones made by *le rat-iste*. The rat-artist. Yannick didn't have time to get his plans okayed by Yoshi, it was already late over in Japan. Besides, if chew marks were what would make Madame de Bourg pull out her checkbook, chew marks she would have!

He began by unpacking the other sculptures. He would place them strategically hoping to attract *le rat-iste*. Just then he had a brainwave and took out his phone.

"*Allô?*"

"*Oui, allô, Margot?*"

"*Oui.* Yes, this is Margot."

"It's Yannick, from earlier today. The art gallery owner."

"Oh yes, has the rat returned?" she asked excitedly.

"Well, not exactly," he started. "I was hoping I could get your help with something. A way to get it to come back. Would you mind stopping by later?"

"Ummm, okay, I guess," she replied somewhat hesitantly. "I usually finish around 6 pm, would that be okay?"

"Perfect!" he said. "Do you know where the gallery is?"

"Just under the bamboo grove, right?"

"Right."

"Okay, see you later!"

"*Au revoir*! Bye!"

He had just over an hour before Margot would arrive, so Yannick returned to his unpacking. Once finished, he unwrapped the three cheeses and meticulously cut them up into rat-mouse bite-sized pieces.

***

Knock! Knock!

Yannick put down his cheese knife. It was 6:10. On the other side of the door was a waving Margot, who'd changed out of her work clothes and into a pair of jeans and a T-shirt emblazoned with the words 'WE LOVE GREEN,' the name of an eco-friendly festival which took place in Paris every June. She was proving to be a staunch environmentalist through and through.

"*Bonsoir!*" greeted Yannick as he swung open the door.

"*Salut!*" she cheered. "Wow, nice space!"

"Thank you!" he said, with a hint of pride. "I've been here for a year."

"Ouch, tough first year I imagine," she replied thoughtfully.

Yannick gave her a brief overview of the gallery's backstory, its current woes and what the *rat-iste* had done. He then explained why it was so important for it to come back and get to work on the other pieces.

"So I've prepared all this cheese to lure..."

"Stop right there, Yannick," she ordered. "Rats and mice don't actually like cheese. It's just a myth!"

"Oh no!"

"Oh yes! But don't worry, because I know what they *do* like, especially this particular breed," she said. "I'll be back in a few minutes."

Before he could say anything, she jogged out of the gallery. Nevertheless, as promised, she was back in a flash, clutching something green.

"What's that?"

"Very special marsh grass," she answered.

"Marsh grass?" Yannick asked, confused.

"Yes, remember I told you the culprit is likely a Marsh Rice Rat?"

"Yes."

"Well, we think they are attracted to the Promenade because it has this specific marsh grass, which they adore. If something is going to bait your gluttonous rat, it's this."

"Wow, that's genius!" he beamed. "And it also explains a lot! I know the artist uses all-natural ingredients... I thought he got them from the forests outside Paris. Maybe, he was actually slyly picking them from the Promenade right above us!"

"I did notice patches of this grass going missing earlier this year. There was no evidence of chew marks, which really had me puzzled!"

"Then we've solved two mysteries!"

"Now let's solve a third! I think I know just how to lure in the creative rat."

Over the next hour Yannick assisted Margot as she carefully rigged the marsh grass to tempt the *rat-iste* into the gallery and over the works.

"That should do it!" she said.

"Great! Now what?" he asked.

"We wait," she answered. "After it's done its handiwork on the art, I want to try to catch it so I can put on that tracker I mentioned. Plus, it might not like cheese, but I certainly do!"

"Sounds like a plan, do you like wine too? I have some Bordeaux."

"Is it natural wine?" she asked, garnering a quizzical look from Yannick. She really was an eco-warrior. "You know, like no preservatives and chemicals. If not, it's okay! I'll take what you've got."

Yannick got two glasses from his kitchen area and opened up the wine.

"Maybe we should dim the lights and hide over on the other side of the gallery, behind those empty boxes," she suggested. "So it doesn't see us."

"Yes, good idea," Yannick agreed.

Hiding behind the large cardboard boxes, which had previously contained the sculptures, in hushed voices Yannick and Margot exchanged life stories while nibbling on *le fromage* and sipping on their glasses of Graves. Margot told Yannick how she'd discovered her calling during the endless hours of playing in the Palais-Royal Garden as a child, her grandmother supposedly supervising Margot and her sister from her favorite bench, although she always seemed more focused on her latest book. Yannick told her how his art history thesis supervisor, Professor Conroy, cried bittersweet tears at the inauguration of his art gallery. Sadly, she'd lost her protégé to the contemporary art world years before when he'd gone to work for the *Gauloises*-puffing gallerist. She was very proud of all he'd achieved nevertheless.

They each took turns 'on watch' for the *rat-iste*, but after a while they were so engrossed in conversation, they'd almost forgotten about their original mission. Margot was just telling Yannick about a clever crow who'd figured out how to turn on the Promenade's fizzy water dispenser and now came to drink from it every day, when they heard some scratching noises.

"That must be it!" Yannick whispered.

The two simultaneously peered over the box.

RATS!

It seemed like they were too late. High up on the other side of the gallery, all they could see was the shadow of a small creature zooming along the vent and sneaking out through the grate. They jumped up to go and examine the artwork.

"That little pest!" admonished Yannick. "He's gone and eaten just the marsh grass and hasn't touched the artwork at all!"

"Sneaky rat-scal!" exclaimed Margot. They turned to each other and could only laugh at their failure. "Well, there's always tomorrow."

"Yes, as long as you come and help me again," Yannick added.

"I will. As long as you pick up some more cheese... and a bottle of natural wine," she said with a sly smile. "There's a great new place just a few blocks from here. I also have some organic fresh vegetables from the community garden I volunteer at. Maybe I can make some ratatouille to go with our rata-*toile?*"

"I'm in!" agreed Yannick, with a twinkle in his eye.

On the surface it might seem like *Mission Rata-toile* hadn't been a success. However, the *rat-iste* had created an entirely different canvas, one bringing together art, nature—and possibly a bit of romance.

Le Métro

13th, 14th & 15th Arrondissements

Sasha couldn't believe his eyes. Nor his ears. On played Petite Piaf, completely oblivious to her new threat. She was in the middle of the car, eyes squinted shut as she emphatically stretched out her accordion for the grand finale of her song. The southbound Line 6 went above ground shortly after Bercy and was scuttling along the second of the iron bridges that spanned the Seine in eastern Paris. The River's waters were shimmering in the gentle September sunshine. Although no famous sites were visible from this bridge, the panorama was still lovely.

"Paris... Paris...!"

On either end of the train car stood two other musicians. Another accordion player and a clarinetist who was also pulling a portable sound system on a fold-up cart. Gypsies. Rough and tough looking ones. Although not all gypsies were deviants, some worked in strategically organized criminal gangs on the *Métro*. The teens were pickpocketing, the middle-agers were playing music, like these ones who'd gotten on their train, and the elderly sat in the corridors of stations begging, usually accompanied by a drugged up dog for additional sympathy. They could put on their best smile to pilfer coinage from innocent tourists. Most Parisians though could smell them from a mile away and therefore, didn't fall for their ruses. They must have been really hurting from the lack of tourists due to the pandemic. This meant that they were likely extra zealous right now.

Petite Piaf was playing her last notes. Sasha had to disguise himself, it was too risky for her to see him. But how? *Oh yes!* He had a black scarf in his bag, it was September after all. It might be sunny and mild during the day, but it was generally cool in the mornings and evenings. Trying not to attract the attention of the angry looking gypsy standing a mere few feet from him, Sasha pulled the scarf out slowly and flung it over his head *à la* glamorous Hollywood actress, or actually, gypsy lady, then turned his back to Petite Piaf.

She opened her eyes and pulled out her little pouch. As soon as she turned around and saw the menacing gypsies, her happy-go-lucky composure vanished.

"*Cette ligne, c'est à nous!* This is our line!" He gruffly informed her. "And if you don't get moving along, we'll prove it to you!"

The smaller younger one smacked his clarinet like a baton against his other palm, to reinforce the threats of the gruff accordionist. Even though he was terrified, Sasha had to do something. He was so close. He couldn't lose Petite Piaf. Plus, he feared they might actually hurt her, he couldn't just stand by and let that happen, despite the agony she'd caused him. He looked down at his shaking hands. His left hand was still gripping the 50-euro bill he'd been planning to offer Petite Piaf to get her to stop and talk to him. The train rattled to the other end of the bridge. They would soon once again be on the Left Bank.

"*Psst! Psst!*" Sasha hissed at the accordion-wielding gypsy. He thrust out the bill. The thuggish gypsy furrowed his brow and leaned in towards Sasha.

"Hey look, how about I give you this 50 and you lay off her. Just this once," whispered Sasha. "Take it, tell her to carry on and then you get off at the next station. But if you see her again, that's another story. Deal?"

The gypsy looked down at the 50 euros. That was definitely much more than he and his associate would make on this entire train line, and possibly even over the course of the whole day. He thought about it for a second, then took the orange-colored note and motioned to his sidekick. The train was about to stop at Quai de la Gare. Fortunately for Sasha, it was not an interchange station.

"Fine, little accordion girl, you keep on playing on this train. But if we see you again, you're in for it!" he spat out, then he looked back at Sasha. "Thanks, pal."

The train zoomed down the platform.

"Move along to the next carriage, girl. And remember, after this train, never again on Line 6... or else!"

Like a frightened little bird, Petite Piaf scurried up to the next car and the gypsies got off and waited on the platform. As the train pulled out of the station, Sasha could see them laughing over the 50 euros. *Whew!* That was a close one. He peered into the next car. *What? Where was she?* He hadn't noticed anything red bopping along the platform they'd just left, so he hoped and prayed she just jumped ahead to the second car.

Once again he had to play cat and mouse with Petite Piaf, this time through the 13th arrondissement, which one could see from the train as Line 6 was mostly above ground over here on the Left Bank. Chevaleret, Nationale, Place d'Italie. Sasha eventually caught up to her. She was in the second carriage from the front. Only one more car that she could play in, if she abided by the gypsy's threat. Therefore, Sasha was keeping an extra attentive eye on her. Stopping her at the end of this song would be ideal.

After they left Corvisart Station Sasha stood back from the window, relieved at the thought of having this whole ordeal over with, or at least he hoped very soon. He sighed. What an afternoon he was having! And all of this after what had happened last night. He was playing it over in his mind when something happening in his own carriage grabbed his attention.

More gypsies! The whole gang must work the line together! This time it was three scrawny teenage girls. They were buzzing around two 50-something ladies in the middle section of the carriage. The ladies were standing around a pole, deep in gossipy conversation. One of the teens opened up a map and rudely thrust it between the ladies, just above their purses. While she feigned asking for directions, the two other girls slid their hands into the ladies' purses.

"Hey! What do you think you're doing?" Sasha shouted without thinking.

The three girls and two ladies flung their heads around in his direction. Another passenger sounded the train's emergency alarm. This caused the train to come to a screeching halt. The three girls fled to the far end of the car, pretending as if they'd done no wrong.

Their carriage's speaker came alive with the driver's scratchy voice requesting information on what was going on. The passenger who'd also witnessed the attempted theft, and had subsequently pulled the alarm, was the closest to the intercom. She gave a quick report of the incident to the driver. A thick layer of tension descended upon the carriage. The smug girls, sitting crossed-armed at the back of the car, weren't having any of this. The would-be victims were sifting through their bags, checking to see if anything was missing. Sasha's blood pressure was going through the roof.

The last thing he wanted was another delay. He pulled out his phone. It was 2:50. He had a little more than an hour and a half to retrieve his object and then go drop it off. That seemed like enough time, as long as he could catch up with Petite Piaf, and soon.

After a few minutes, the train sprang back to life and advanced extremely slowly up to the next station, Glacière. It was at the edge of the charming Butte-aux-Cailles neighborhood, a former village and one of the prettiest areas of the 13th district.

"There's only one Paris…!"

Petite Piaf must be giving her audience an encore. She probably had no idea why the train had stopped… nor what probably awaited them at the upcoming station.

They pulled into Glacière, but there weren't just passengers standing on the platform. There were around five police officers. Two must have spotted Petite Piaf through the window of the train and went after her. While the others were waved down by the good Samaritan from Sasha's carriage. The train driver only released the locks when the police were in position. They deftly hauled the resistant gypsy girls off the car, knowing full well that it wouldn't do any good, they were certainly under-aged and without papers. There would be little they could do except hold them for a little while. The police also requested the ladies get off the train too, then asked if there were any witnesses who could come forward.

The good Samaritan quickly raised her hand, but before she got off to give her testimony of the events, she turned back.

"That man saw what happened too!" she stated, pointing straight at Sasha.

Oh brother! bemoaned Sasha. He really didn't want to get involved, plus, he'd already had his fill of dealing with the police in this 24-hour time frame. And, of course he had to keep an eye on Petite Piaf, who was in the middle of trying to sweet talk the other police officers into *not* giving her a fine for playing on the *Métro* without a permit. She wasn't pulling a repeat of the whole Revolutionary manifesto with them. Sasha slinked towards the back wall of the *Métro* station, in order to keep a low profile—and keep a hawk eye on his target.

The train set off again, leaving the cluster of people around 'the incidents' on the platform. Another train chugged up soon afterwards. This one held the same gypsy musicians. The police were too busy to bother with them, but the gypsies did manage to notice whom the police had cornered. As that train left the station, the burly accordionist sneered at Sasha. He definitely wasn't someone to mess with.

Another train came and went. Sasha was rather proud of Petite Piaf, whose charm and persuasion appeared to be working on the police. It looked like they were going to let her go. As such, Sasha had to be on his guard, ready to make a move as soon as she did. To get a better, yet discreet vantage point, Sasha drifted over to a nearby vending machine. One of the cops attending to the attempted robbery looked over at him suspiciously.

To make his actions seem legit, Sasha punched some buttons on the machine. He didn't mind buying something to get the cop off his scent. He put his hand into his pocket. *But of course!* He didn't have any change. He looked back at the machine; luckily, it accepted credit cards. He took his wallet out to pay for the randomly selected snack. The officer went back to filling in his incident report.

Sasha reached in and grabbed his undesired purchase. A bag of Maltesers®. He wasn't even a big chocolate fan, he nevertheless stuffed the bag into his satchel and went back to spying on Petite Piaf from behind the vending machine. In the distance he heard a low rumble.

"*Monsieur*, would you be willing to come to the station to provide a statement on what you saw?" Sasha flipped his head around to see one of the officers standing next to him. Piaf pulled her mask out and put it on to appease the two policemen who'd accosted her. She gave them a little wave and started towards the far end of the platform. Sasha crouched behind the officer who'd asked him the question so she wouldn't see him when she walked past.

"*Um uh.* Actually… I'm not sure I really saw anything, you know… these things happen so fast." he fumbled, stepping as nonchalantly as possible away from the group. He could see a green and white train coming up to the station. "I think the very observant lady saw everything."

The train darted into the station. Petite Piaf got on it and took a seat, pretending like she wasn't going to be carrying on with her musical act.

"Good luck with your investigation!" Sasha bid as he gave them a little salute and hopped into the closest carriage just as the doors were closing. Dumbfounded, the police officers gawked at him, shook their heads and then returned their attention to the pickpockets. The good Samaritan glared at Sasha as he drifted away on the train.

Saint-Jacques, Denfert-Rochereau, Raspail, Edgar Quinet; Line 6 trundled under the 14th arrondissement. Alongside the *Métro*'s tunnel were those of the Catacombs, filled with their millions of bones. Sasha feared he would also be dead if he didn't retrieve that essential object. He was once again ever so close. Once again, he'd finally caught up with and stop Petite Piaf. She was in the next car.

Sasha approached the door of his carriage, self-assured and ready to launch into her car. No more fiddling around. He was going to get straight to the point with her. The train zoomed up to the platform at Montparnasse-Bienvenüe. This mid-sized station had several intersecting *Métro* lines, but, like Austerlitz, it also served an intercity train station. That's where their similarities ended as Montparnasse was much busier than Austerlitz. Much, much busier.

Sasha's confidence rapidly disappeared upon seeing the barrage awaiting on the platform. An intercity train must have just arrived… and all its passengers seemed to want to take Line 6. The door lock released and a tsunami of travelers, and their huge suitcases, flooded the carriage. Sasha was pushed up against the back window. He was about to try to paddle his way through their masses, when he looked into the next carriage. Petite Piaf had also been hit by this sudden wave and was beached against the back wall of the middle section of her carriage.

As long as she was still there, he could stay put. Due to the sardine-like state of the train, there was also no way she could play. It looked like she was planning on waiting it out. Indeed, a small school of these commuter sharks swam off at the next station, Pasteur, which connected with Line 12.

The train crept into the sleepy 15th arrondissement. The largest district in the city, it was mainly residential, popular with middle-class Parisian families. The next station, Sèvres-Lecourbe, wasn't a very busy one, so only a few people got off. Among these was an exhausted looking tourist, made obvious, that is, thanks to her frazzled look and scarf emblazoned with little Eiffel Towers. *Watch out for your bags!* Sasha wanted to shout after her. *There are cunning pickpockets working this line!*

The next station, Cambronne, was also not very frequented. However, the following stop, La Motte-Picquet-Grenelle, was southwestern Paris's busiest interchange station. Much of the train emptied out there. Sasha had been ready to hop over to the next carriage, but decided to change strategies. With a careful eye on his prize, he stayed put; it would actually come straight to him. Petite Piaf was ready to shift cars and her destination was exactly where Sasha was.

Knowing she would be heading for the central section of the carriage, Sasha quickly sat down on a folding seat in the far end of the car and with its back to her. That way she wouldn't spot him. Sure, that meant that he too couldn't see her either. However, the only sense he needed to rely on at that very moment was his hearing. And his instincts.

"Il n'y a qu'un seul Paris..."

They were off.

The train tooted along on its raised tracks. Until now, Sasha had been much too busy to look out the window. However, the passing cityscape gave him something to concentrate on, something to calm his overworked nerves.

Dupleix Station was next. It went by without incident. Sasha's attention was caught by the train whizzing by in the other direction. On it were the gypsy musicians. The bulky one caught sight of Petite Piaf and scowled. Sasha hoped he'd never have to see him ever again. As long as he and Petite Piaf avoided Line 6, they should be safe. Nevertheless, the sighting sent Sasha's anxiety surging.

"There's only one Paris…!"

A few people got off and got on at the next station, Bir Hakeim. Sasha knew Petite Piaf was nearing the finale of her song. As soon as she would utter her last *Paris!*, he'd pounce on her.

The train chugged out of the station and in seconds they were flying once again over the Seine. However, unlike the previous times, which had pretty yet unceremonious views of Paris, this west end bridge of Line 6 featured an exceptional view of the city's star attraction: the Eiffel Tower. It felt close enough to touch. He could hear some oohing and aahing from some of the other passengers, delighted by this surprising sight of the iconic Paris landmark.

"Paris… Paris…"

The train was approaching the end of the bridge and Petite Piaf was nearing the end of her tune. Ever so slowly Sasha rose from his folding seat. The train decreased its speed as it entered Passy Station.

"Paris!"

Sasha flipped around. The doors flung open. Petite Piaf opened her eyes upon concluding her dramatic finale. Then they widened in terror—but not only by the sight of persistent Sasha. The doors snapped shut.

"Mesdames, Messieurs, vérification des titres de transport."

Out of the Oven and Onto the Streets
of the Butte-Aux-Cailles

Amine wiped his hands on his apron and set the timer on his phone. He could finally take a break and escape the stifling heat. He needed some fresh air.

He slowly climbed the back staircase and pushed open the door. He was instantly hit by the cool late night, or rather early morning, air. Despite being almost 5 am, there were still a few revelers overflowing from the late-night bar located a few doors down.

Their laughter didn't bother Amine, though. It reminded him nostalgically of his youth when he too spent some late nights out with friends. It wasn't that long ago, but still, now married with three small kids, Amine certainly didn't have much time for going out. Actually, more to the point, his job also forced him to go to bed early. In turn, his schedule dramatically limited his evening socializing.

Amine started to crouch down so that he could sit on the back doorstep, as he usually did during his breaks. Since his job involved a lot of standing, he relished a chance to rest his feet.

"Hey! What are you doing there?" he sternly questioned the stooped-over figure occupying his break-time perch. Startled, the figure quickly lifted its head gawking, surprised and wide-eyed, up at Amine. Even in the lowlight, as she swung her head up, he could easily see that it belonged to a petite young woman and not the burly homeless drunks that Amine was trying to discourage from creating a home in the doorway's alcove.

"*Pardon, pardon...*" she uttered, unsteadily rising to her feet. She wiped at her eyes, sniffed and teetered back and forth in front of the door. "I'm terribly sorry to bother you."

"You aren't bothering me, but what are you doing sitting here on the step?" he asked, softening his tone when he realized she'd been crying.

"I... I just needed to... to rest for a little while," she managed between stifled sobs. She put up a hand to support herself against the wall.

Upset... and a little drunk, deducted Amine, taking a better look at the dark-haired girl. *She couldn't be more than 20,* he thought with a sigh.

"Sit down, I'll be back in a minute," he ordered. She obeyed, flopping down on the stoop and sinking her head back into her hands.

Amine went inside and, as promised, returned shortly, two small paper cups in hand.

"Here, drink this," he commanded, handing her one of the cups before sitting down next to her. "It'll help clear your head."

Just then a group of university-aged partiers tumbled out of the bar, singing obnoxiously at the top of their lungs.

"*Ta gueule!* Shut up!" shouted a neighbor out of a window in the building across the street.

While the Rue de la Butte-aux-Cailles was certainly picturesque, it was far from sleepy, especially on Friday and Saturday nights. The mild late-September weather also contributed to the party mood, beckoning the bar-goers outdoors.

The Butte-aux-Cailles could be translated as 'quail hill,' however, the neighborhood in the southeastern 13th arrondissement actually got its name from a certain Pierre Caille who'd owned the surrounding land back in the mid-1500s. A village later formed here and the area still retained its charming small-town feel. The area's narrow streets, lined with quaint houses, were mostly peaceful. The exception being its main street, where Amine's business was found, which was packed with laid-back restaurants and lively bars, popular with students who attended the neighboring campuses of the University of Paris. Perhaps owing to its young spirit, the area also attracted street artists, whose ephemeral creations were scattered around the district's walls.

The angry neighbor's words fell on deaf ears or simply weren't audible over the rowdy group's singing. Luckily, the boisterous bunch soon stumbled down the cobblestoned street in the other direction, carrying on with their off-key tune as they went.

Amine took a sip of his espresso and turned to the girl.

"So what's troubling you?" This question sparked renewed sniffles in the distressed young stranger. "Now, now, none of that. What's your name?"

"Sylvie, and yours?"

"Amine," he replied. "So what are all the tears about, Sylvie?"

She took a deep breath in an attempt to pull herself together and downed the rest of her coffee. "I didn't get into the university program I'd applied to."

"Hasn't the new term already start or is starting soon?" he asked, puzzled by her answer.

"Yes, that's part of the problem," Sylvie added. "I was on a waiting list and I found out this afternoon that I didn't get in. Now, the other programs I was interested in are all full. My parents are going to kill me!" This last statement triggered a new wave of tears. Amine's phone alarm buzzed.

"I'll be right back, but try to stop crying!" he commanded as he rose to go back inside. Around five minutes later he returned, holding a croissant wrapped in a white paper napkin.

"Here, eat this, it's fresh out of the oven," said Amine, handing her the piping hot pastry. Sylvie's eyes lit up as she eagerly accepted the buttery delight. It created a momentary distraction from her woes.

"Why would your parents kill you? Don't you think that's a bit extreme?"

"Okay, they might not kill me, but they're going to be furious, super furious," she declared in between bites. "You see, they run a tea shop over in Chinatown. They immigrated here from China to escape the Maoist regime. As a university student, my father was accused of being against the Cultural Revolution and was going to be sent to a work camp. Before they could arrest him, he managed to flee with his new wife to France. However, when he got here, he couldn't pursue his studies since he didn't speak French and the studies he'd already completed in China weren't recognized. So he started working at a tea import business run by someone from his village back in Zhejiang Province. For many years he worked night and day to learn the trade. He saved every *centime* he could and eventually he was able to open his own shop. The only thing he wants is for his kids to get the university degree he couldn't."

"I totally get it, my parents were immigrants as well, from Morocco," said Amine. "They always wanted the best for me too, but just because you didn't get into that one program, it doesn't mean that you won't get into another one."

"My two brothers are super bright, they both got into *Grandes Ecoles*, Ivy League Schools, which is why there's even more pressure on me to succeed," Sylvie said. "And which is why I went out drinking with my friends after I found out the bad news. I'm too afraid to go home and face them."

"Success is in the eye of the beholder," Amine replied. "I was always passionate about cooking, especially baking. I went to a professional high school which put me on track to go to chef's school. I did really well, but it still took a few years of experience before I was able to land a job in a reputable bakery, not very far from here, over on Rue Mouffetard. I worked hard to perfect my craft and build a name for myself. Then, I heard there was a bakery for sale over here. It wasn't easy to get a loan, I had to try several

232

different banks. I got rejected by five different ones. The figures obtained by their computerized simulators didn't add up to amount I would need. Their mortgage advisors wouldn't hear me out and see that I could make this work. I kept trying and finally got accepted by the sixth. Now I have my own place and it's one of the most popular bakeries in the whole Butte-aux-Cailles."

"Your croissant was amazing," she complimented.

"Thank you, it's almost an award-winning croissant, *almost*," he replied. "Every year there's a contest for the best croissant in the city, just like there is for the best baguette and for some other pastries. I entered it for the first time last year and was really hoping to win. My excitement was growing as the contest approached. I felt like I'd finally come up with the perfect recipe, choice of ingredients and technique.

"When the results were announced, I was so disappointed to see the name of another baker in the number one spot, but then I scanned the rest of the list and saw I'd ranked 4th. Not first, nevertheless I was in the top five. I wasn't just going to throw in the towel because I came in fourth! At the time I thought, there's always next year... but then Covid hit and the contest was canceled this year."

"I'm really sorry to hear that," Sylvie said, looking down at the crumb-filled napkin that was now crumpled up in her hands.

"It's okay," he answered. "I kept on making my croissants and other pastries during the lockdown. I knew they brought joy to all our clients stuck at home. I told the hospital workers to come here and knock on the back door so they could get a croissant on their way to work. They needed that fuel to get through their arduous and perilous days. That became more important to me than winning a contest."

"Oh, I see what you mean," she said. "Nonetheless, I hope the contest will be running next year so you can enter again."

"Me too, but if it isn't, that's okay because I know that I tried and that I tried my best," Amine replied philosophically. "I'm sure you did too."

Sylvie smiled at Amine and then gazed up at the night's sky. It was gradually lightening as they inched towards dawn, yet there were still a few tiny stars illuminating the vast stretch of indigo.

"Maybe it was destiny speaking?" Amine suggested. "Perhaps that program wasn't for you. You might be meant to take another path in life."

"Well, to tell you the truth, I didn't really want to study business anyway," she admitted.

"There you go! It really was fate!"

"You could be right."

"What is it that you really want to do?" he asked.

"Actually, I love my parents' tea shop. Ever since I was a kid, I'd spend hours after school browsing the aisles, examining all the exotic labels, trying to connect the Mandarin characters to the words my parents spoke. I would eavesdrop on their conversations with regular clients, little old ladies who would shuffle in with their large grocery trolleys on their way back home from the Chinese supermarkets. When mom and dad weren't looking, I'd carefully pick up the delicate tea cups off the shelf and make up stories about the miniature scenes of a distant China that decorated them. This year hasn't been very easy for them. Even before having to close for the two-month lockdown, sales were down because some people feared we might have Covid just because we're Chinese. However, things are slowly bouncing back. My parents have worked so hard, I'd love to keep their legacy going, but I'd also like to create more of a bridge between my family's heritage and the country which hosted them, my country."

"Well, you should explain this to your parents. Hopefully they'll see this as a positive thing and be proud of the esteem you have for what they've achieved."

"I guess you have a point. Perhaps they'll look on the bright side."

"You go home, get a few hours' sleep and tell them tomorrow after you've rested up," said Amine. "But before you go, I've got something that'll soften them up. Wait here."

234

Amine stood up and opened the bakery's back door. The smell of the freshly baked pastries wafted out. Sylvie inhaled deeply, the fragrant air helped sober her up even more. Looking across the street from the bakery, some street art caught Sylvie's eye. The work depicted a statue she vaguely recognized from visiting the Louvre back in middle school. It was a headless sculpture with wings. Greek perhaps? Both her wings and her flowing robe were filled in with tiny green virus symbols which were cascading off her as she took flight. She was overcoming the virus and leaving it behind. At the bottom was a signature. Did it say D-Zyne? She smiled. If the whole world could get over such a serious crisis, she too could get over her own personal one. And she too could take flight. To fly with her own two wings.

A few minutes later Amine came out of the bakery's back door, this time he was bearing a brown paper bag. Sylvie stood up and he gave it to her.

"What's this?" she asked, curiously peering inside.

"It's something I've been experimenting with," he replied. "A modern take on a *pain au chocolat*, a chocolate croissant. I've substituted the traditional dark chocolate with white chocolate mixed with green tea powder."

"Wow, that's such a good idea! I'm sure my parents will love them!" Sylvie beamed. "They'll go perfectly with some tea from their shop!"

"You'll have to come back to let me know what they think of the pastries... and your suggested new path."

"Deal!" she exclaimed. "*Merci beaucoup,* Amine."

"Take care of yourself... and stick to drinking tea instead of all those cocktails!" he added teasingly.

"I'll be back soon, but hopefully not at 5 am!" she joked as she turned to go.

A smile appeared on Amine's face as he watched her walk down the cobbled village street and towards Paris's modern Chinatown. That section of the 13th district was a lot less picturesque than the Butte-aux-Cailles. It was filled with tall towers built in the 1960s and 70s, however, it was still very vibrant and held a lot of promise, especially for Sylvie. She'd lost the unsteadiness she'd had when he'd first encountered her. There was now confidence in her straightened steps. She had regained her balance.

He knew she would be fine, just fine.

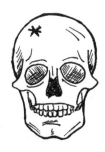

The Secrets of the Catacombs

"One at a time down the steps... ONE. At. A. Time!" shouted Madame Artois.

"How many steps are there?" Laure asked hesitantly.

"131!" replied Jérémie exuberantly.

"What?!" exclaimed Laure, freezing on step number 22.

Behind them the daylight, and their only chance of escaping their current fate, vanished with the closing of the creaky entrance door.

"Well, you should have been listening earlier when the guide told us all this," admonished Flora.

"You were too busy on your phone!" Pascal chimed in. "TikTok again?"

"No! I wanted to check my messages one last time!" grumbled Laure in self defense. "Geez, I really should have pretended to be sick this morning and skipped out on this altogether."

"Afraid of the dark, baby?" taunted Jérémie.

"Does your mom still tuck you in?" added Pascal.

"Of course not! Shut up... both of you!" growled Laure, punching the arms of the teasing boys.

"*Shhhhhhhhh! Les enfants, arrêtez de crier!* Stop shouting!" shouted Madame Artois from the bottom of the stairs.

"Just leave her alone! Come on, we're falling behind!" ordered Flora as she motioned her friends to follow her and the rest of the 14-year-old herd of students, down the steps.

Down, down, down they marched. The 131 steps would take them 20 meters (22 yards) below the street level and into the weakly lit tunnels of the Paris Catacombs.

School was definitely not on the top of most teens' lists of favorite things to do, however, after all those months of online classes and not seeing their friends, it had suddenly become highly desirable. Nevertheless, as the initial excitement wore off, Back to School had started to lose its appeal. The students were now eager to leave those classroom walls. However, they thought the merits of Madame Artois's choice of such a macabre and claustrophobic place for their first field trip, were a matter of debate. As they neared the bottom of the dimly lit stairs of the Catacombs, they realized… it was now too late.

"Bonjour and thank you for visiting the Catacombs," the tour guide began, once the students were herded together and shushed again by Madame Artois. "Even though you are my last tour of the day, we need to move along safely, stick to our schedule and stay together at all times. It's easy to get lost in here. If you have any questions, please ask."

The four friends naturally drifted to the back of the small side room they were gathered in.

"The Paris Catacombs are among the most famous underground sites in the world," continued their guide. "Since opening in 1786 they have attracted millions of visitors including the future King Charles X, Napoléon III, the Holy Roman Emperor Francis II and even Otto von Bismarck."

"Otta von Wizmark?" whispered Jérémie.

"**Bis**marck! The first chancellor of German, dummy!" Flora hissed. "No wonder you failed history class!"

"Cut him some slack, it isn't like Monsieur Leclerc's history lessons are very exciting," said Laure, defending Pascal.

"You have a point," noted Flora. "He must be even older than the Catacombs." Her cheeky comment even got a giggle out of petrified Laure.

"*Shhhhhh! Les enfants!* Children, quiet!" Madame Artois admonished.

"Underneath Paris there are over 300 kilometers of tunnels, but today, we'll only visit part of the 1.7 kilometers, which are open to the public. This site actually dates back 2,000 years when the Romans...."

"Boo!" Jérémie whispered into Laure's ear, simultaneously poking her side.

"*Ahhh!*" she screeched.

"*LES ENFANTS! Arretez!* Children! Stop it!" hollered Madame Artois, her anger mounting. "Pay attention!"

"Yes, we sure wouldn't want to be sent to detention right here and now!" said Pascal under his breath.

"That's for sure, imagine getting locked in down here!" added Flora.

"Cool!" enthused Jérémie.

"Terrifying!" whimpered Laure, as she scanned the room. All around them was the beige limestone upon which Paris sat. Some sections were supported by neatly carved blocks while others were roughly dug out and topped with pebbled rubble. Here and there were some dusty panels displaying facts, maps and vintage photographs of this peculiar place.

"After the fall of the Roman empire, this area was still used as an open stone quarry until the 1300s. From then onwards, the limestone started to be excavated by digging underground tunnels, like the one we are standing in. You've been to the Louvre and to Notre-Dame, haven't you?"

"Yes..." replied some of the keener students at the front of the group.

"Well, some of the stone used to build the Cathedral and other medieval buildings in Paris likely came from these very tunnels," informed the guide. "The quarry…"

"If it was a stone quarry, why are there a bunch of bones down here?" asked Jérémie.

"Don't interrupt the guide, Jérémie," Laure reprimanded.

"Let's move along first and I'll answer your question at the next stop," replied the guide politely. He then led the students towards a long corridor.

"*Arrête! C'est ici L'Empire de la Mort!*" said Pascal reading the words carved into the stone above the entrance.

"'Stop! This is the Empire of the Dead'… we're totally done for!" croaked Laure, gripping Pascal's arm.

"It'll be alright, Laure!" Pascal reassured her. "We won't be staying down here in the 'Empire of the Dead' for very long. We will all get out of here alive at the end of the tour."

Reaching the other side of the hallway, the guide stopped and gathered them in another rounded alcove. Here, the descriptive panels had been replaced with bones, row upon row of femurs and the occasional skull.

"By the mid-1700s the cemeteries of Paris were overflowing," explained the guide. "Many were simply huge mass graves that were literally packed to capacity after century upon century of use. So local sanitation authorities decided to close down the cemeteries in the city center and put all the bones in one common place. Back then, where we're standing was actually outside of the city limits of Paris. It was decided that these empty mining tunnels would be a convenient place to put the bones.

"Between 1785 and 1787 over six million bones were transferred here. Crews often had to work at night so Parisians wouldn't see them and cause a fuss about moving the bones from their intended final resting place. Instead of merely filling the tunnels with piles of bones, the man in charge, Héricart de Thury, decided to create a museum-like site. As you can see, he arranged the bones in original patterns…"

"Original? They're downright weird," Flora judged.

"Come on, Flora, I thought you were into art?" teased Pascal.

"I am, but I'm not sure if I'd qualify this as 'art'," she replied.

"Follow me, I'll show you some of the most unique of these," said the guide who turned down another tunnel; the group shuffling behind.

"*Pstt*, guys... I'll show you something 'unique'," said Jérémie. "Come have a look over here."

"Okay, but quickly, we don't want to fall behind!" pleaded Laure. The three others followed their wise-cracking friend to a small nook.

"Look at this skull," Jérémie instructed. "Don't you think it's a little different from the others?"

"Different, how so?" questioned Pascal.

"Look, there's a symbol carved in the top," said Jérémie.

"What are you talking about?" huffed Laure, impatient to catch up with the class.

"Come closer, Scaredy Cat!" teased Jérémie. Not wanting to completely lose face, Laure reluctantly took a few paces forward.

"Where? I don't see anything."

"Right here!" said Jérémie, poking the star-shaped symbol with his index finger. Suddenly, with a snap, a section of the bones opened.

"*Woahhhhhh*! That's totally mental!" said Pascal in awe. It was a hidden door to a secret passageway.

"What's down there?" asked Flora, peering past the door. "It looks like there are some stairs." I wonder where they go?"

"Well, only one way to find out!" declared Jérémie as he started down the steps.

"I'm not sure this is such a good idea..." Laure's voice wavered. "Someone will notice we're gone."

"How? The lighting is terrible down here. No one will notice we're missing until the end of the tour," said Pascal.

"Come on. Chicken?!" taunted Jérémie. "We'll just have a quick peek, then go back and join the others."

"I'm game!" said the more daring Flora.

"Well, alright, but just a super fast look," said Laure, caving to peer pressure.

The four friends tippy-toed down a few of the dark steps.

"Okay, I think this is far enough," moaned Laure. "There's nothing here, let's turn back."

"I think I see something down there," said Jérémie.

"I don't care, I'm heading back," stated Laure, in an increasingly panicked tone.

"Wait!" exclaimed Pascal. A lightbulb had gone off in his head. He pulled out his phone." I'll turn on my phone's flashlight so we can see better."

"Come on! We'll just go to the bottom then go right back up," said Flora in an attempt to persuade Laure.

"*Finnnnnnnne*," she accepted, very reluctantly.

Sure enough, once they reached the bottom of the short stairwell, they could make out a room to the right. They stepped inside and Pascal shined his light slowly around the mid-sized cavern. Roughly carved out of the stone, the room was spartan, save for a few piles of crates caked in a thick layer of dust.

"Hey what's this?" asked Jérémie, picking up a crumbling leaflet that was sitting on the top crate.

"Let me see," said Pascal. "Journal des Débats, October 13th, 1870."

"Wow!" marvelled Flora. "It's from the Siege of Paris!"

"The Siege of Paris?" repeat Jérémie, confused.

"Don't you remember?" asked Flora. "Mr Leclerc covered it at the end of last term."

"Mr Leclerc's online history classes were even worse than his in-person ones!" complained Jérémie.

"I was asleep half the time too," confessed Laure.

"Guys! The Franco-Prussian War!" reproached Flora. "Remember Napoléon III and Bismarck from the beginning of the tour?"

"Yah, sort of," said Jérémie sheepishly.

"Well, after only two months of battle, Napoléon III was captured by the Prussians, who then came to attack Paris," added Pascal, who'd obviously not been daydreaming in class, like the other two.

"Precisely," continued Flora. "However, the Parisians weren't going to give in that easily. They managed to hold out for four months while the Prussians bombarded the city."

"I've actually read that many Parisians took refuge underground!" said Pascal. "Some set up temporary bunkers in the cellars of their buildings, while others hid out in the city's stone quarries, like in the Buttes-Chaumont, in Montmartre and well, down here in the south. There were even people hiding out in the crypt of the Pantheon!"

"*Coooool!*" said Jérémie. "Imagine sleeping next to Victor Hugo."

"Dude, he wasn't dead yet!" corrected Laure.

"Details, details," scoffed Jérémie.

"This must be one of those hideouts!" declared Pascal.

"Yes!" said Flora. "Look! There are some bowls and some kind of wash basin."

"Hey, look over there, some blankets!" said Jérémie. "This takes the 'quarantine' to a whole new level!"

"And we thought we had it bad!" said Pascal. "At least we had the internet and Netflix to keep us entertained. They only had these crummy leaflets."

"Yah, but if my parents made me watch another episode of *Inspector Marcel*, I thought I was going to shoot myself!" added Jérémie.

"But I like *Inspecteur Marcel!*" admitted Flora.

"Dork!" teased Jérémie.

"Hey you two, stop it! Look at this," ordered Pascal who was shining his phone flashlight a little higher up the wall.

"'*La République ou la mort.*' The Republic or death," Jérémie read out. "Cool, they were into graffiti, even back then."

"This wasn't just any hideaway," noted Flora. "That's the slogan of the Commune of Paris! This was used by Les Communards, the leftist rebels who were defending the city."

"The same people who then led their own siege on the city a few months after the Franco-Prussian War ended," added Pascal. "There was virtually a two-month long civil war in Paris."

"Okay, you guys might think this is cool and all, but this place gives me the creeps," Laure declared. "I'd rather be up there with all those bones. You can stay here, *and* get in trouble, but I'm going back up."

Without waiting for a reply from the others, Laure turned and made for the staircase. As she placed her foot on the first step, the secret door slammed shut.

"Oh great!" wailed Laure. "Now look what's happened!"

"We probably just need to give it a push and it'll open," suggested Flora, trying to calm down her fearful friend.

"I'll go and check," offered Pascal as he raced up the stairs guided by his phone's flashlight. He gave the door a push, then a bigger one. "Oh geez, the door won't budge."

"See! We're stuck down here.... forever!" howled Laure. "We're going to *diiiiiiieeeee!*"

"Oh come on, Laure, stop being so melodramatic!" scoffed Jérémie.

"Hey, cut her some slack, she's been through a lot this year," hissed Flora. "Remember her grandpa, the bookseller, who died at hospital from… well, you know what."

"Okay fine, but still, I don't think *we* are going to die." Jérémie was trying not to lose his patience.

"We just might if we don't put our heads together and find a solution," replied Flora.

"There's got to be another way out," said Pascal. "Besides, if we're not there at the end, Madame Artois will send someone to search for us."

"Yes, but can you imagine how much trouble we're going to be in?" whimpered Laure.

"Which is exactly why we need to find our own way back to the group!" insisted Jérémie.

"Come on! We have nothing to lose!" said Pascal.

"There are two directions we could go along this tunnel, left or right," noted Jérémie.

"Didn't the guide say there were 300 kilometers of tunnels?" Laure commented hopelessly. "How are we ever going to figure out which way to go?"

"Didn't Madame Artois say we'd be finishing the tour near the school?" remembered Flora.

"Yes, so in the direction of Montparnasse, but how does that help us?" asked Jérémie doubtfully.

"Well, if that's the case, then we know which direction to go in," rationalized Flora. "See, it is worthwhile to watch *Inspecteur Marcel!*"

"Okay, *Madame l'Inspectrice*, but how do we know which direction that is from where we are?"

"Well, the Catacombs entrance is in Place Denfert-Rochereau and Montparnasse is to the west, so we just need to figure out which way that is."

"I know how!" declared Pascal, proudly waving his phone. "Last year in Scouts we learned that most cell phones have a compass on them!"

"Bravo, however, your magic compass isn't going to work now, since we are 20 meters below the street!" said Jérémie. With that pronouncement, Laure broke out in tears.

"It's going to be okay, Laure," consoled Pascal, putting his arm around her shoulder. In doing so, his hand hit something metal attached to the wall.

"Hey wait a sec, what's that?" he said, flipping his phone light towards the wall. "Look, some metal bars."

"It seems to be some kind of ladder," observed Flora. Pascal shined his light up the wall.

"Yes, which goes into a vertical passageway," concluded Pascal. "There doesn't appear to be an exit at the top, but I bet if I climb up as far as I can, I'll be close enough to the street level and the compass will work."

"If you're willing to try it, I'll use my phone light to help guide you," offered Flora.

"Great! Jérémie, give me a boost," said Pascal.

"Why am I the one who always gets walked all over?" Jérémie complained.

"Come on, lean over, Jérémie," ordered Laure, now getting back involved. He reluctantly obliged and leaned over for Pascal to climb onto his back. He was then able to pull himself up onto the bar ladder. Flora stepped back to shine the light as he climbed higher and higher.

"This is as far as I can go," called down Pascal. One hand gripping the bar, he pulled out his phone and opened the compass app.

"Does it work?" asked Laure anxiously.

"Give it a sec," said Pascal. "Yes! That way is west!" He said pointing to the left before scrambling back down and hopping to the ground triumphantly.

"Wait," said Flora. "Before we leave here, let's take those leaflets and scatter them along the way. In case we need to backtrack."

"Okay, good idea!" agreed Laure. The two girls grabbed a dusty stack each.

"Let's go!" said Jérémie. "Or else we'll be in detention for the rest of the entire year and it's only September!"

The four friends zoomed down the tunnel with the girls dropping a leaflet every few feet. Soon they came to a fork in the tunnel.

"Oh man, which way now??" blubbered Laure, her panic resurfacing.

Pascal flashed his phone over the walls. The light came across some more writing.

"Hey look!" said Flora, she read out loud the words drawn on the wall in charcoal: "Montparnasse!"

That's right," remembered Pascal. "I heard there were indicators down here, like road signs. Some of them are more recent, added by people who come down here to explore or even throw parties."

"Cool, I wanna go to one of those!" said Jérémie.

"Those fans of the Catacombs are called Cataphiles," said Flora.

"I'm never going to accept an invitation to one of their parties!" blurted Laure.

"Well, it's not time to 'celebrate' quite yet, we gotta get outta here first!" said Pascal. The gang raced down the tunnel on the left. After a few minutes they spotted something lying on the ground.

"Hey what's that?" asked Laure.

"Looks like some bottles of wine," guessed Pascal.

Maybe they are left from those partying Cadophiles," suggested Jérémie.

"CaTAphiles," corrected Flora.

Jérémie picked up one of the bottles and dusted off the label: "1940. Was that a good vintage?"

"People must have been hiding out down here during the Occupation as well," said Pascal.

"I hope they made it out... alive," Flora said, wincing.

"I hope *we* make it out alive!" cried Laure. "Let's get a move on!"

Jérémie put the bottle back and the pack carried on down the tunnel, picking up their pace.

"Hey wait!" shouted Jérémie. "Stop!"

The three others whipped around and started back to where Jérémie was standing, looking up to the left.

"Stairs!"

"Oh my god, Jérémie, you're our hero!" cried Laure, hugging him.

"So, I'm the good guy all the sudden?" he joked.

"Let's not get too excited, just yet." said Flora. "We'd better hope there's a door at the top."

They crept up to the stairs. Sure enough, when they reached the top, there seemed to be some kind of handleless door.

"Wait!" hissed Flora just as Pascal was about to heave it with his shoulder.

"What is it?" asked Pascal.

"*Shhhhh*! Voices!" she said in a hushed tone. The four friends became as silent as the sleeping souls of the Catacombs.

"We have one more room before the end of the tour," said the muffled voice of the tour guide.

"It's our class!" whispered Laure gleefully. "We're saved! We're saved from the Empire of the Dead!"

"Let's wait a minute, until they've gone past so they don't see us," suggested Pascal. "But if the door doesn't budge, we can yell our heads off and they'll still hear us, well, hopefully."

"Okay, sounds like a plan," the others agreed.

When they could no longer hear the guide nor their classmates, Pascal gave the door a big shove.

"It's moving a little, but it seems to be stuck," he said.

"Let's all help, maybe our combined strength will do the trick," proposed Flora.

The four friends fell into a line in at the door, like brave Communards defending the city from the Prussians.

"One, two, three!" commanded Pascal. They pushed with all their might. The door swung open with a giant whoosh. The four friends stumbled into a bone-lined alcove, similar to the one where their subterranean adventure had begun.

"We did it!" cheered Laure, hugging Pascal.

"*Shhhh*! We'd better keep it down," recommended Flora. The three others obeyed. They snuck to the end of the tunnel and peered their heads around the corner.

"The coast looks clear," said Flora.

"They must be in that room on the right," said Pascal.

Careful to not make a noise, they crept down the tunnel. As they approached the room, the lights suddenly went out. Shrieks echoed up ahead.

"Hurry, now's our chance!" exclaimed Flora. The four of them slid into the darkened room just as the guide turned the lights back on.

"See how dark it gets?" The guide was smiling. "That's why you should never sneak into any of the off limit sections of the Catacombs. You might not be able to find your way back out."

"*Exactement!* Exactly!" concurred Madame Artois who started clapping with the students following suit. "*Merci beaucoup! Quelle visite fascinante!* What a fascinating tour!"

The guide smiled and went to the far end of the room where there was a gate. The students could see a set of stairs leading up to the street. Madame Artois stood at the base, checking that all her students filed past one by one.

"Oh my God, freedom!" gasped Laure as they neared the steps.

"Hey, wait a second!" ordered Madame Artois, stopping the foursome. "What do you have in your hands?"

Laure and Flora froze. They were still clutching some of the leaflets they'd picked up in the secret hideout.

"Oh these?" said Flora, feigning innocence. "*Ummm*, they are just some brochures we picked up at the entrance. For the, *ummm*, the Speleology Club."

"Yes, the tour was so fascinating, we can't wait to become members and discover more underground places!" added Pascal. "Ones that we're allowed to visit, of course."

"Right guys?" said Flora, turning frantically and wide-eyed to Jérémie and Laure.

"You bet!" chimed in Jérémie.

"Yes... I can't wait," forced Laure, much less enthusiastically.

Madame Artois gave them a puzzled look, but let them go past. Up to freedom they went, and with an original souvenir of their adventures in the catacombs of the Catacombs.

A Very Special View of the Eiffel Tower

"I don't get it! It's supposed to be here…" whimpered Maddie. "Right here!"

She stared straight ahead down the empty street, immobile and stupefied. Suddenly someone on a little electric foot scooter whizzed by, inches from Maddie's bewildered face. This broke her spell of disbelief and forced her back onto the safety of the sidewalk.

How is this possible? Where is it??

It wasn't here in front of her, as she so meticulously planned, but the picture of it was crystal clear in her mind's eye. She'd memorized every last detail of it.

The studied snapshot was framed on both sides by two elegant turn-of-the-century Parisian buildings. Their facades of beige limestone were glowing in the late afternoon light. In the foreground was a glamorous curvaceous iron gate. However lovely these items were, they were not the star attraction of the image. Perfectly centered between the buildings, just beyond the gorgeous gate, was an even more seductive iron structure: the Eiffel Tower.

***

Forget spending hours researching which Paris restaurants she would dine at. Nor did Maddie put much attention to the museums and other attractions. She booked guided tours at the Louvre and the Musée d'Orsay tour and ticked 'museums' off her trip-planning checklist. She downloaded a self-guided tour of Montmartre; exploring a neighborhood—check! She'd sensibly allocated a block of time for sitting on a café terrace, as one does when one is in Paris. She would let everything else fall into place. Everything except one thing. It was what had inspired her trip and would be its sole, set-in-stone mission. She had to find that 'view.'

***

"Maddie, you're going to lose your extra vacation days if you don't use them," her boss reminded her after their first team meeting back at the office. Her first-year anniversary was fast approaching. One of the reasons Maddie had taken the job in the first place was its additional week of vacation. Now, she found herself neglecting this highly coveted perk. Her boss's comment was the wakeup call she needed.

Ever since she'd signed the contract, this job had been her main focus. She'd wanted to prove herself so much, she'd turned into a self-proclaimed workaholic. Covid had only made this worse! Working from home for months, she'd been glued to her computer during almost all of her waking hours. On the positive side, her social life in deficit led to a substantial increase in her savings account. She could actually afford a little getaway. Plus, time away would also give Maddie a chance to reflect on her life, goals and dreams. She seemed to have lost sight of these all too long ago. There was more to life than work, work, work. Could she let herself live a little and even try to pursue her dreams? One thing at a time. And that first thing would be the vacation. But, where to go?

***

That night provided Maddie with the answer, or rather, Instagram did. Until her boss's reminder, she hadn't considered what to do during that extra week. Perhaps she could ask some of her colleagues for ideas? She had an Irish passport thanks to her grandfather, but she'd already visited the homeland a few times. It would make sense to go somewhere different this time and that Irish passport would allow her easy entry into Europe in these times of the lingering virus. She would, of course, follow all recommended health and safety precautionary measures. That only narrowed down the selection to a certain degree. The pool of potential destinations was still extremely vast.

Then, as she was perusing Instagram on her commute home, it hit her. Never had she been this struck by an image. It was so powerful that she had stopped dead in her scrolling tracks. She was immediately entranced. One could even say it was love at first sight. That was it, she decided immediately. She would go to Paris. She would find this bewitching sight of the Eiffel Tower.

***

The Instagrammer hadn't put a location on the photo, but that wasn't going to stop Maddie. Before letting her brain over-analyze her decision she promptly went onto a flight booking website and purchased a round-trip ticket to Paris. Since fewer people were flying these days, she also got it at an excellent rate. Then she spent the rest of her evening scouring the internet trying to find that particular viewpoint. However, no matter what word combination web search she tried, and she tried them all, she couldn't find it. Even keywords like 'Eiffel Tower views' or 'Eiffel Tower shot between buildings' were leading her down one virtual dead end road after another. *Uh oh!* Maybe she shouldn't have been so hasty to buy that plane ticket after all.

The next day at work, Maddie was casually lamenting over her predicament at the coffee machine. Umberto, a tech-savvy colleague, suggested she do a reverse image search. *Brilliant!* Sure enough, on the website of Cohen & Sons, Real Estate & Notary Experts, there it was. Her precious view. Practically the exact same captivating perspective that had first mesmerized her on Instagram. Now she had all she needed. The website listed the stunning view's magical address.

Maddie wondered, why was she so drawn to the tower? Why had it captured her so? Possibly because it reminded her of her own town's famous monument: the Gateway Arch. The Eiffel Tower seemed to be omnipresent in Paris, just like the Arch was in Saint Louis. In Paris, she imagined one could round *any* corner and see the tower peek through and say: '*Bonjour!* Here I am!' The tower was like a guide, like a North Star. Similarly, the Arch also served as a beacon for residents of 'The Lou,' it signified that you were home. Maddie was compelled to seek out that image of the Tower because she needed a new North Star to guide her. Now more than ever.

***

Since savoring that particular perspective of the Eiffel Tower in person was the primary architect of her trip, Maddie wanted to stay nearby. She found a great deal on a deluxe room at Le Grand Hôtel Eiffel. Surely with such a name, she concluded, it would be close to the Tower. Hotel booked, she felt ready for her trip and her excitement grew exponentially with the decreasing days until her departure.

During her mid-morning coffee breaks, Umberto, a fan of all things Parisian and regular visitor to the City of Light, mentioned that if she was only bringing a small piece of luggage, which was the case, and since her hotel was right outside the *Métro*, at a station called Sèvres-Lecourbe, she could easily get from Charles de Gaulle airport to her hotel by public transit. That sounded perfect. Plus, this plan would mean she wouldn't risk seeing the Eiffel Tower from the window of a taxi. She wanted to save the big reveal for that magic spot she'd found on Instagram. After checking into the hotel, the plan was to take a short nap, freshen up and then deploy on her mission to seek out her Parisian North Star.

Sure enough, just as Umberto had promised, it was relatively easy to take the *RER* suburban train into Paris from the airport, even in her drowsy, jet-lagged state. She didn't run into any issues changing at Denfert-Rochereau onto the *Métro* Line 6. She did notice a sign at that station for the Catacombs, perhaps she would try to squeeze in a visit there during her stay.

Line 6 got really packed at Montparnasse-Bienvenüe, nevertheless, Maddie took this in stride. A crowded *Métro* journey was all part of the Paris experience! Wasn't it?Stumbling out of the train at Sèvres-Lecourbe, Le Grand Hôtel Eiffel was indeed right outside the station, just as its description had promised. It had all been so easy, she didn't even need to use the expressions she's learned on her French 101 app to ask for directions.

The hotel wasn't exactly 'grand,' as its name advertised, but it would serve her purposes, including that planned nap. She was asleep before she hit the pillow. Unfortunately though, 4:30 pm came all too quickly. Good thing she'd set her alarm or else she might have slept right on through to the following morning and failed at her most important mission. Maddie showered and made a cup of hotel instant coffee; a real Parisian *café* would have to wait until the next day. Reinvigorated, Maddie entered the fateful address and pushed the 'directions' icon.

"Twenty minutes?!" she exclaimed when she saw the estimated time it would take to get to her destination. Maybe the word 'Eiffel' could join the word 'grand' in the hotel's misleading name. Maddie shrugged it all off, discovering Paris along the way would be part of the fun. Right? It looked like all she needed to do was turn left out of the hotel and keep walking down that large street for a while, then make a few other turns and *voilà!*

She set down her phone, took a sip of the insipid coffee and finished getting ready. She was full of anticipation and excited smiles. A few minutes later, she laced up her shoes and put on her sweet 'bon voyage' gift from Umberto. He had surprised her with a

French scarf, embroidered in little Eiffel Towers, as a good luck token. Looking oh so chic, she scooped up her phone.

"Forty percent?" she gasped. "I guess I should have been charging my phone during my nap."

Oops! Just then Maddie remembered another wise piece of advice Umberto had given her: turn off your apps to save on battery power. So, she proceeded to flick up all of the active apps. Proud of applying what she'd learned, she threw on her jacket. Off she went, out of her room, down the stairs, exiting Le Grand Hôtel Eiffel, and joyfully bounding, to the right.

The sun was shining brightly and a warm breeze was gently lofting through the air on this idyllic September day. Maddie was soaking everything in. Parisians coming out of the bakery armed with fresh *baguettes*. Bunches of colorful roses meticulously lined up outside the flower shop. Waiters skillfully maneuvering teetering trays topped with glasses of wine. Sure, it was a little strange to see everyone wearing masks, but it didn't matter! She was in Paris! This terribly *Parisienne* ambiance added an extra spring to her step.

After around 10 minutes, Maddie reached a major intersection. *Wait,* she said to herself, *I think I was supposed to turn left here. I'd better check.*

Pulling out her phone, she first noticed that the battery had somehow dwindled to 30%. She cringed slightly and clicked on the maps app.

Hey, where are my directions? she puzzled, staring wide-eyed down at the maze of foreign-named streets, minus that blue line that was meant to be guiding her to her destination. The route she'd previously plugged in was gone, eradicated with that careless app closing she did back at the hotel.

Why hadn't I activated that foreign data plan? Maddie silently whimpered.

She hadn't because tech-savvy Umberto, with all of his wise advice, had said all she needed to do was load the address into her phone's maps app when she was connected to her hotel's WiFi. He had assured her it would continue to work no matter how far from the hotel her journey would take her. Plus, he said it would still work once she was offline. He was right. However, he failed to tell her she had to leave the app active in order to view the directions. This one fatal mistake made her mission go completely awry.

Okay, Maddie, remain calm, she heaved in deep breaths of air, trying not to panic. *Think. Hard. What was the street called? Didn't it start with R? Yes, it was an R.*

She zoomed in on the map, searching for possible suspects.

Ah ha! Here's a street that begins with an R. Rue Rapin. That sounds right, plus, it's not far from the Eiffel Tower. Yes, that must be it. Satisfied with her find, Maddie forced herself to smile and turned in the direction of Rue Rapin, cell phone firmly in hand, whose battery notification had just turned orange and read 20% battery power.

She turned onto a quiet side street and tried once again *to* soak in the legendary Parisian scenes. Around her she noticed parents escorting their kids home from school, a gaggle of teens giggling over their phones, and a food delivery guy on his bike.

It's still light out, but I guess it's nearing dinner time, Maddie decided. *I'd better hurry up to catch the light just right, before the sun sets.*

She checked her phone. The time flashed 6:20 pm and her phone battery shifted to red, signally a new low of 10% left of its battery.

As Maddie went down another street and rounded yet another bend, her anxiety went up several notches. She had come face to face with something behemoth... and it wasn't the Eiffel Tower.

"What are... *those*?!" she blurted out loud, horrified at the sight before her. "High rises?? These are the wrong kind of towers! They don't belong in Paris! Where am I??"

Dumbfounded, Maddie looked back down at her phone and zoomed out on the map to try to get a better idea of her approximate location. This confirmed that, yes, she was indeed still in Paris, despite the panorama of 1970s residential towers.

Where were the classy stone buildings and wrought iron gates she'd been expecting?

Zooming back in on her location, Maddie tried to find the fastest way to Rue Rapin, which, dreadfully, seemed to be on the other side of those mammoth buildings. She took a deep breath and forged ahead down a pedestrian walkway through the concrete and glass jungle.

The westerly facing modern towers glistened in the descending sun's rays. She hoped she had enough time to reach her destination during this golden hour. She immediately quickened her pace.

Then, just like that, the pedestrian path came to an end. *Are you kidding me?* Which way now? She pulled out her phone, only to find the screen... black.

An uncontrollable and chilling gasp left Maddie frozen in her tracks. Then, after a few minutes had passed, she began pulling herself together.

"You can do this," she said, giving herself a pep talk. "You've made it this far, it can't be that much further." Encouraged, she started off once again.

She turned right, then left, then right again. She pushed on, determined, even though these incognito streets were hiding any clues as to where she might actually be.

Suddenly, the image of the Gateway Arch flashed in her mind. A guide. A North Star. Come on Eiffel Tower, be my North Star. This thought gave her some renewed momentum. She had a good feeling, it had to be just around the next bend. She could even see a cluster of those classic stone buildings, obviously a promising sign. Then, at that very moment, the sunlight reached its pinnacle, its peak. She shuddered with anticipation. She turned the corner triumphantly.

"It's supposed to be here. Right here!"

It was not. The Eiffel Tower was, ever so sadly, nowhere in sight. And it was so that Maddie found herself in the middle of a nondescript Parisian street, as the young man, wearing a camouflage hoodie and sporting a backwards baseball cap, sped past on the electric foot scooter, inches from her nose. She wanted to cry, but was distracted with saving herself from being run over first.

Wallowing in despair, safely on the sidewalk, her stomach grumbled. It was only then that Maddie remembered she hadn't eaten since the mediocre 'breakfast' she'd been served on the airplane. She'd worked up quite an appetite with all the walking she'd done while trying to accomplish her mission. Her one and only true goal for the trip, at which she had failed so miserably.

Maddie looked around. Across the street was a little restaurant called *La Dame de Fer*. She didn't care what kind of restaurant it was. Sullen and famished, anything would do right now!

"*Bonsoir, Madame!* Good evening!" greeted a waiter as she entered. "*Une personne?*"

She'd gotten far enough in her French 101 app to grasp what he had asked, but she was only able to nod her head in reply. Yes, one person.

She was escorted to a small table near the back of the restaurant, a few seats over from the only other customers in the restaurant, a couple well into their meal.

Taking off her jacket and not-so-lucky scarf, she sat down. The first thing she wanted to order was a glass of bubbly. That would brighten her spirits.

"English?" the waiter offered, holding out one of two menus in his hands.

"Yes, please." At that very moment, she really wasn't in the mood for practicing her few phrases of French. "May I have a glass of champagne?"

"*Madame*, I am so sorry, this is a *crêperie*. We do not serve champagne. But we do have cider and it's bubbly."

She stared at him, desperately trying to hold back her tears. She barely managed to murmur some form of acceptance to his suggestion. She didn't really know what the cider would be like, however, within a champagne glass, she could fool herself into imagining it was the real McCoy.

She turned her attention to the menu. Gazing up at her, on its front cover was a jolly man in a chef's hat, enthusiastically flipping a *crêpe* from a flat pan, and, in the background, was none other than... The. Eiffel. Tower.

Aghast, Maddie's eyes darted around the room. The Tower wasn't only on the menu... it was everywhere! The placemats, the napkins, the salt shakers, the coat rack, the artwork on the walls... Absolutely everywhere!

As panic was quickly taking hold of her, the waiter returned, plunking a small ceramic bowl in front of her.

"*Voilà, Madame!*" he said before disappearing as quickly as he had appeared. The odd bowl was filled with bubbly liquid. Her eyes began welling up again, she'd reached her breaking point.

"Isn't this place delightfully charming?" asked the kind voice of a stranger, yanking Maddie back from the precipice of her misery. She turned to the other occupied table to find the soothing face of a woman smiling warmly at her.

"We first discovered this darling *crêperie* back in 1995," carried on the unbeknownst good Samaritan. "My husband proposed to me on top of the Eiffel Tower while we were backpacking across Europe. It's our tenth wedding anniversary and he reenacted the scene!"

"We just can't get enough of the Eiffel Tower," admitted the lady's dining companion, obviously the romantic husband from her story. "It's so special. Every time we admire it from different angles. The perspective from the carousel next to the bridge and the views from across the river in the 16th district are some of our favorites."

Maddie's downed spirits already began to lift. Maybe she didn't need to find that one exact spot to enjoy the Eiffel Tower. She picked up her bowl of cider, a gesture mirrored by the friendly couple.

"*Santé!*" the three of them cheered in unison.

"To *la Dame de Fer!*" added the woman. *La Dame de Fer…* *La Dame de Fer*, pondered Maddie. Of course. The Iron Lady, the Eiffel Tower's nickname.

Everything would be alright. Apparently she had actually 'found' *La Dame de Fer* today, just not in the way she'd meticulously planned out. There was always tomorrow.

She returned her focus to the menu. When the waiter came back, she ordered the 'Gustave' set menu and another bowl of cider, which wasn't so bad after all. Her dinner was wonderful and by the end of her meal she was scrapping the very last drizzles of *caramel au beurre salé* off her plate. Satiated, she was positively glowing after her glorious first meal in Paris, and maybe also from the cider.

"*Où est le Métro?*" Maddie succeeded in asking the waiter after paying her check. At least she could remember which *Métro* station to take to get back to Le Grand Hôtel Eiffel.

"Just turn right, then turn left and you can't miss it," he replied.

Maddie pushed open the door and turned right as instructed. The air had cooled, making her glad to have Umberto's 'French' scarf, with its dancing Eiffel Towers, to keep her warm. Although her step wasn't as gleeful as earlier in the day, it was self-assured and ready to tackle all of the new adventures her trip would surely present.

Carefully following the waiter's directions, at the end of the street she turned left, but came to a sudden grinding halt.

Straight ahead of her was the gleaming Eiffel Tower.

A split second later it broke out in a sparking frenzy of lights which literally took Maddie's breath away. This perspective may have been framed by tall modern buildings instead of stylish limestone ones, nevertheless, she was in awe.

Sometimes we just have to go with the flow and follow our own North Star. This kind of reasoning was even more true in difficult times, when trying too hard and falling prey to anxiety's powers only leads us down one dark path after another.

The tower had guided her to it, in its own way. Her Parisian North Star, and the experience in finding it, might have more lessons to teach her than she could have ever imagined.

Le Métro
16th, 17th & 18th Arrondissements

CONTROLLERS!

And not just any controllers, it was the same crew as before! Sasha couldn't believe it! But then again, they probably worked several lines in one day. And, via the speedy *Métro*, they weren't actually all that far from where Sasha and Petite Piaf had ditched them earlier on.

"So, you thought you could evade us, huh?" The bulky controller went straight for Petite Piaf. "Not this time! And we'll have none of that Revolutionary nonsense! You're getting two fines! One from before and one for now."

Sasha doubted she could talk her way out of this one as agilely as she'd done with the police.

"Monsieur, votre titre de transport. Sir, your ticket," the short female controller who'd asked him before barked at Sasha. She narrowed her eyes. Had she recognized him?

Sasha fumbled through the pockets of his bag and produced his ticket. She pressed it up against her verification machine. The train journeyed beneath the 16th arrondissement. Paris's ritziest district, it was popular with celebrities and *nouveau riche* Parisians who lived in its gorgeous Art Nouveau buildings and spacious mansions. The train approached Trocadero. Two of the other controllers were blocking the door of the section Petite Piaf was in to prevent her from trying to escape again.

"Sir, this ticket is past its validity," she informed him with a raised eyebrow. "Tickets are valid for a period of 90 minutes. According to this, you got on the *Métro* at 12:30 pm and it's now 3:10. You've been on the *Métro* for 200 minutes. What could you have possibly been doing for that long?"

"Um, well, I got a little turned around..." Sasha stuttered, a liberal interpretation of the truth.

"Oh, sure you did," she replied sarcastically. "You got off to do something and sneaked back on, didn't you?"

"No, no! Not at all!" Sasha stammered in his defense.

"I'm going to have to fine you," she stated with determination.

"But I've been on the *Métro* the whole time!" His words had no impact on the steadfast, by-the-book controller. She'd heard it all before.

A barely audible announcement came through the speakers. The next station, Boissière, was closed for renovations, so the train would be skipping it and journeying onward.

The more robust group of controllers were trying to get Petite Piaf's ID card from her, but she wouldn't comply.

"You can take me to the police station if you want," she said defiantly.

"Sir, your ID card." Sasha's controller requested, pulling out her fine pad.

At Kléber Station, Sasha could sense that Petite Piaf must have something up her sleeve. *She's biding her time.* Sasha concluded. He was getting to know her habits.

"Sir, your ID card. Now," the controller demanded more sternly.

"Yes, yes, of course," Sasha pretended to obliged. He too could play the stalling game. He opened up his bag and made as if he was looking for it. The train slowed as it approached the next station, the end of the line. Charles-de-Gaulle-Etoile. This interchange station sat beneath two other top tourist sites of Paris: the Arc de Triomphe and the Champs Elysées. More importantly for Sasha and Petite' Piaf's purposes, it was home to two other *Métro* lines and *RER* A.

The tracks curved as they neared the station. The way to exit here wasn't like other stations—and Petite Piaf certainly knew this. When the train came to a stop at the platform, the two controllers blocking the doors on the right, reinforced their stance. But the little click of the lock being released, didn't come from the doors on the right here. It came from the left. And upon hearing that magic click, Petite Piaf bolted for those doors and was out of there in a flash. Sasha didn't waste any time to follow suit.

She raced down a stairwell. Sasha was close behind. Rounding the corner, he almost tripped on an older gypsy sitting with his legs straight out on the ground, drugged-up dog on his lap. He was on the phone, although he was keeping a sly keen eye on his surroundings and sized up Sasha. *As if he really needed donations, since he could afford a cell phone!* Sasha huffed, judging the beggar. A deep voice bellowed from the top of the stairs. It must have been the hefty controller. He wasn't going to give up that easily—especially after their second escape.

The tunnel they were running down led to only one place, the eastbound platform of Line 2. Sasha could hear the train breeze into the station. Petite Piaf sped up, Sasha did the best he could, but she still proved to be the fastest and had already turned onto the platform. Sasha arrived just as the buzzer started ringing. He leaped through the last doorway of the train. Swinging around as the door slammed, he could see the gorilla-like controller charge onto the platform, panting and snarling.

"Just you wait!" he shouted after the train.

Sasha was also panting heavily. Not only was he not used to all this running, he wasn't used to evading the law. As soon as he got his object back, he would return to being, himself, a model citizen.

Until it was in his hands, Sasha thought he was capable of almost anything. Well, within reason.

He allowed himself a few stations to catch his breath. He knew Petite Piaf was still on the train. Line 2 also had modern full-train-length cars, so, since it currently wasn't very full, and lacking the buzz of passenger chatter, Sasha could hear her melody all the way in the back of the train.

Maybe I should wait for her to reach the center of the train? wondering Sasha. *It would be harder for her to escape that way.* He walked past a few seat sections, then flopped himself down on a two-person bench seat. This way he could remain less visible, as his back was against the wall, but could then lean over to peer down the train and check on her every now and then.

"There's only one Paris…!"

The train trundled along. Line 2 mirrored Line 6. Its route also formed an archway, this time around the northern districts of the city. Above ground was the 17th arrondissement. The southwest half of the 17th, the part that extended from l'Arc de Triomphe to the Parc Monceau, was particularly posh whereas the northeast half contained mainly working to middle-class housing with a scattering of quaint village-like pockets.

"Paris… Paris…"

It wasn't uncommon for glamour to rub shoulders with grunge in Paris. This was also the case for the district they were approaching, the 18th. That arrondissement was like a gourmet baguette sandwich, with postcard perfect Montmartre as the filling squashed between the shady Red Light district of Pigalle and a huge swath of very working-class housing to the north and east. The train was nearing this district and Petite Piaf was also getting closer and closer to Sasha's location.

A crowd of people got on the train at Place de Clichy, where Line 2 met number 13. Sasha noticed the platform clock. Its bright yellow lights told him it was 3:35. He now had less than an hour to achieve his mission. Once he, hopefully, retrieved his crucial object, he still needed to get it to the drop-off site.

"Il n'y a qu'un seul Paris…"

Petite Piaf was still able to play on despite the influx of passengers, luckily fewer people than had bombarded them at Montparnasse. The train breezed through Blanche Station. Only a few tourists got off. Most of them probably wanted to see the Moulin Rouge, located just outside the station. The train then slowed into Pigalle. Here they would intersect with Line 12. Among the new arrivals who'd gotten on at the back of the train, two caught Sasha's eye.

Oh no! The gypsies!

How did they get up here? Sasha was flabbergasted. Then he remembered that older gypsy he'd almost tripped on… or was it he who'd tried to trip Sasha?? He'd been right at the end of Line 6 and talking on the phone. He could be their informer; one of their sentinels. The important question wasn't *how*… but *why*? What were they doing here? They weren't playing music. They were moving through the train with conviction.

As determined as they were, the train had gotten relatively crowded between the last two stations. The portly gypsy's size and the smaller one's portable sound system slowed them down a little as they tried to maneuver around the other passengers. Despite their hurdles, they were still advancing. He had to warn Petite Piaf. She definitely seemed to be their target and they definitely looked like they meant business. Serious business.

Sasha stood up at the next station, Anvers. It was the closest station to Sacré-Coeur. At this stop a large family of German or Austrian tourists piled on. Sasha was barely able to squeeze by them. They would provide a handy obstacle for the gypsies. Sasha stood on his tippy toes to look ahead down the train. Petite Piaf wasn't all that far up ahead.

The train climbed above ground in its ascent to Barbès-Rochechouart, another very popular two-line interchange station. Here a number of passengers got off and on. Among these was a

whole cluster of people who entered at the front of the train. There
was something familiar about them. Sasha narrowed his eyes. He
swallowed. Hard.

Seriously? It was the controllers!

They must have taken a shortcut over to reach them. This
would have entirely been possible by taking the *RER* A, when
they'd slipped away from them at Charles-de-Gaulle-Etoile, and
then up to here via the Line 4 at Châtelet-Les-Halles. They too
looked extremely focused on a specific target.

Could Sasha reach Petite Piaf before her adversaries?

'Crazy' Times at the Castel Béranger

Dingue, complement dingue. Man, that's one crazy looking place.
thought Sacko.

He was standing on the sidewalk, gawking up at the designated address. He'd never seen a building quite like it. Even though it was nighttime, the lamplight provided just enough illumination so he was able to see that the building was made of red and beige brick. That was weird in itself considering that the majority of Paris buildings were made of stone. Materials aside, it was the decorated features on this particular structure that were downright wacky. Around the windows, and especially on the main door, there was the quirkiest ironwork. To Sacko it seemed as if the designer had let his pen go wild on his drafting papers. Actually, the more he looked at it, the more it reminded him of something else in Paris, yet he couldn't quite put his finger on what.

Rich nutcases, he grumbled, shaking his head. He looked back down at his phone. Yes, it was indeed the right address. He punched in the door code included in the information he'd been given and pushed open the funky door. The foyer was even stranger than the exterior! He'd never done any hallucinogenic drugs, but this was the sort of thing he figured people on a trip might envision. Everything looked like it was moving, courtesy of the same undulating pale green ironwork that Sacko had observed on the facade. Its movement compelled your eyes to follow it up to the arched ceiling. Was it made of copper? The walls were also sculpted with curvaceous motifs. Possibly flowers? It was hard to tell, but Sacko was sure of one thing though—that he wanted to be in and out of there as fast as possible! It was that crazy!

He went over to the intercom and pushed the button marked R.V.V., as indicated in his notes. It was one of those high-tech systems with a video camera. This new technology didn't quite fit in with this old building, which Sacko figured must be at least 100 years old.

"*Montez au sixième,*" ordered a rushed voice through the speaker. This was followed by a long buzz indicating that the lock on the interior glass door had been released and he could enter.

"Go up to the sixth floor," Sacko repeated mockingly. *Can't even come down and get it? These darn rich folk can't make any effort, can they?* he went on complaining as he proceeded inside. He stopped his griping when he saw that there was at least an elevator. That convenience would help get him in and out faster.

An old-fashioned metal cage lift, it slowly chugged upwards. Along the way, Sacko noticed more of those psychedelic decorative flowers as well as stained glass windows in between each floor. He actually kind of liked those.

Arriving on the sixth floor, the elevator doors squeaked open and he stepped out. He looked down the sage-colored hallway. There were only two doors, which were directly opposite each other. One of these was slightly ajar. *That must be it*, reckoned Sacko. He took the package out of his bag and leaned down to set it on the doormat, following the new Covid policy of no direct contact. Just then the door swung open, a slender hand reached out and yanked him inside, slamming the door behind them.

"Hey! What the…" The twin to the kidnapping hand covered his mouth to stifle his protests.

"*Shhhhh!!!!*" his abductor hissed, putting the red-nail polished index finger of the other hand up to her lips. When Sacko saw that his kidnapper looked quite harmless, at least in size, he let down his guard. She kept her hand over his mouth for another minute then slowly removed it.

"We don't want him to hear us," she finally said in a hushed voice as she crept over to the door and looked cautiously through the peephole.

"Don't want whom to hear us?" asked Sacko, totally confused.

"Richard!"

"Listen lady, I don't know who Richard is nor do I want to know. I just came to deliver your food. I don't want to get wrapped up in some personal saga."

Man! did Sacko ever regret listening to his buddy Amadou. He had never had any problems with the 'normal' people who used the mass-market food delivery apps. In fact, he'd done extremely well during the lockdown when the use of home delivery services skyrocketed. Some days it felt like he was working round the clock. He was tired, but he was young and had a good level of stamina. Now was the time to work hard and save up.

However, when the quarantine was lifted and people gradually returned to restaurants in person, his work diminished. So when Amadou told him about a new app, *Chez Gourmand*, which only featured gourmet food shops and restaurants, he thought he would give it a try. It paid a higher per-delivery rate than most of the other apps. In addition, Amadou assured him he'd get much better tips from those wealthy Parisians ordering their caviar, foie gras, filet mignon or whatever they ate in their big apartments and mansions in western Paris. It sounded like it was worth a try—a decision he was now regretting in his current hostage situation in this crazy building in the 16th arrondissement.

"I need your help," she begged. Seeing that Sacko wasn't moved by her plea, she added: "Wait."

She hastened in her high heels and chic skirt and blouse ensemble into the next room and returned moments later, giant designer purse in hand. Rummaging through it, she retrieved her wallet from which she withdrew a single bill. A green bill. 100 euros.

"I just need you to stay for a little bit, maybe 15 to 20 minutes," she said, extending the bill in his direction. Sacko stared at it, shocked. This wasn't exactly the amount which had come to mind when Amadou had alluded to big tips! Just then his phone buzzed with an alert. He pulled it out to check. It was from *Chez Gourmand*, offering him a delivery which would probably take him the same amount of time as she'd suggested, yet would only earn him eight euros. He looked back at the green bill.

"As long as it doesn't involve anything kinky," he agreed cautiously.

"Oh, nothing of the sort!" she assured him, pressing the bill into his hand. "Deal?"

"Okay, lady. Deal. But 20 minutes max."

"Come," she ordered, ushering him into the next room; a sprawling living room about 20 times bigger than the 13th district shoebox apartment he was sharing with his cousin in the high-rise towers of Chinatown. It was also the polar opposite to where he currently was, geographically and stylistically speaking. This large room had similar decorative details that he'd noticed on his way up. The more he observed its intricacies, the more this peculiar style was actually growing on him.

She gestured to an immaculate egg-shell white sofa and beckoned him to take a seat. He placed the food bag on the nearby glass coffee table and sat down as instructed.

"So, here's the thing," she started, sitting down on a matching armchair. My husband and I couldn't handle living together during the lockdown. He used to always be busy with work, especially in the evenings, so we managed to get along fine until we were stuck with each other 24/7. One of us would have gone to our holiday home in Deauville, but he assured me that the lockdown was only going to be two weeks. Apparently, he had a tip-off from the friend of a friend who worked at the Ministry of the Interior. Some tip-off! We were at each other's throats after the second day."

"No offense, lady, but that doesn't sound like a great marriage."

"I should have divorced him years ago, but there was a hitch…" she said before pausing. "You don't recognize me?"

"Nope, can't say that I do."

"Vanessa Vavan. *The* Vanessa Vavan."

He gave her a blank look. She huffed.

"*Tu me rendes dingue… c'est toi, un-huh, c'est toiiii*, You drive me crazy, oh yah, it's you, it's you…." she spontaneously sang. "That doesn't ring a bell?"

Sacko shook his head.

"*L'Amour Dingue*. Crazy Love. It's only one of *the* biggest hits of the 1990s. You can't tell me you've never heard it!"

"I'm from Mali!" cried Sacko. *Crazy love! It wasn't just crazy love… this whole situation was crazy!* He thought. "There wasn't even electricity in the house I grew up in, let alone a stereo to listen to the radio! Besides I wasn't born until 1995."

"Okay fine, but it's still played all the time on the radio. Well, certain radio stations. Maybe only the classic stations now, but never mind. You've probably heard it at least at the supermarket or someplace like that." Sacko continued to give her a 'yah, so what?' look so she carried on. "I suppose I was a bit of a one-hit wonder, but back then I was a household name. I was invited on all the talk shows, I was the special guest at events, that sort of thing. And that's when I met Richard. He's a concert promoter. He swept me off my feet, I got pregnant unexpectedly and we had a shotgun wedding. The gossip magazines had a heyday, but that helped my album sales, for a little while. My second album was something of a flop, so I decided to take some time off from my artistic career and to focus on raising our son. It's a break that's now lasted 22 years. I still make good money from my royalties… but now that money is getting funneled to his new girlfriend!"

"Ouch! Back up a minute. Did you say your husband's 'girlfriend'?"

"Yes! Remember when I said we were driving each other crazy?"

"Yes."

"We somehow made it through the lockdown, but our neighbor couldn't hack being in Paris anymore. He decided to move to the French Riviera. My husband found out and he arranged to rent his apartment."

"Sounds like some time apart might do you good."

"Do *us* good? It's only done Richard any good! And I'm the one footing the bill! You see, the big issue is... since concert halls still haven't reopened due to the pandemic, he hasn't made a dime in months. He's all but drained our joint-bank account!"

"Can't you just cut off his access?"

"No, it's in both of our names. Plus, if we were to get a divorce, he'd get half my net worth, unless he chooses to ask for the divorce and I accept only under certain conditions. So instead of doing that, he's simply living the high life across the hall and has this floozy of a young girlfriend who sneaks over. And she came over just before you arrived! I saw her dark flowing mane through the peephole!"

"That really sucks, lady."

"Vanessa. Call me Vanessa. What's your name?"

"Sacko. So, what is it you want me to do?" he asked, looking at his watch.

"Well, there is one other way I might be able to get the divorce I want."

"And what way is that?"

"If I catch him red-handed with his bimbo girlfriend. I would have grounds for a more favorable divorce."

"And how do you intend to do that?"

"Well, I was thinking, you could pretend this delivery is for them and go ring their doorbell. When Richard comes to take it, you say it's for Tiffany, that's *her* name, I heard him call her that once. I'll be hiding ready to take a photo of them together!"

Sacko furrowed his brow and sighed.

"Look, Vanessa, I'd love to help you and all, but there is *no* way I'm doing anything that might get me involved with the law."

"What do you mean?"

"Well, the only way your evidence might stand up in court is if I am a witness."

"Good point, I could give you more money, if that's the problem."

No, that's not at all the problem… I don't have my papers in order and it's completely out of the question for me to go before a judge. I'd be deported the next day!"

"How did you get here?"

"Not by boat across the Mediterranean if that's what you're thinking, although I do have some friends who got here that. No, I came to visit my cousin two years ago and I just never left."

"How are you able to work?"

"Oh, easy enough. That's the thing with these new apps. Nobody does proper checks. I created my account with my cousin's ID card and details. He'll do anything for family, which is nice and all, however, I really need to get my situation sorted out. To do that, I first need to save up enough money for an immigration lawyer."

Now it was Vanessa's turn to sigh. She looked at Sacko and realized her dubious plan was as big of a flop as her second album.

"I need a cigarette," she declared. "Come, let's go out onto the balcony." Seeing his reluctance, she added: "We still have some time, right?"

"Yah, yah, it's fine." he conceded, following her across the room to a pair of French doors.

Once out on the balcony his eyes bulged in wonder. The apartment had a killer view. Right there, across the river, was the Eiffel Tower. It sported its evening glittering silvery glow. The large spotlight on its top whirled around and flew right above their heads.

"Pretty nice view, isn't it?" she commented, lighting up a slender menthol.

"You're telling me."

"It was one of the reasons I bought the place all those years ago. The building is quite famous for those who know architecture. It was designed by Hector Guimard, the architect behind the green iron and red glass *Métro* stations."

"Ah, that's it! I thought the style looked familiar."

"The building is called the Castel Béranger and was built shortly after the Eiffel Tower."

"It's certainly original, if not a little crazy."

"Sorry, I asked you to do that silly favor for me. It was a stupid plan," she said, taking a drag of her cigarette and slumping her elbows down on the balcony's railing.

"Nah, don't worry, I totally get why you're upset."

"And I totally get your situation. You see, I wasn't always rich. In fact, I grew up in northern France, in an old coal mining town. There was no work for a few generations and from a young age, all I ever wanted to do was get out of that dead-end town and make something of myself. After I graduated high school, I came to Paris to go to university. I was studying marketing and thought I'd go work for one of those big companies in the La Defense business district. I was living with a family friend over in the 11th district and had to tutor their kids in exchange for a tiny-closet sized room. I got a part-time job in a classy bar to have some spending money. It was there that I was discovered by a talent scout and the rest is history as they say."

"Oh man, now I see even more why you don't want that dog of a husband to get his hands on your money."

"I guess in the end it's only money. Speaking of which, I think I've kept you over the 20 minutes. Let me give you some more."

She butted out her cigarette and stepped back inside. Sacko hesitated before following her. He was enjoying the view, and besides, Vanessa's story was inspirational, in its own crazy way. This encounter gave him some much needed hope for his situation. Maybe he too could make it, really make it in Paris. He certainly had more ambitions than being a delivery guy all his life. As soon as he got his resident permit worked out, he was planning on returning to the journalism studies he'd started in Bamako. Then maybe he'd even get a chance to become a reporter and properly cover what was actually happening in his strife-ridden country.

The Eiffel Tower's spotlight flew by again, snapping him out of his daze. He took one last look over at the tower, at that guiding beacon, like a North Star, a guide. He sighed and went back inside. Vanessa was once again rifling through her enormous handbag.

"Listen, Vanessa, there's no need to give me any more cash. I hope you can get your situation all sorted out with your husband. I'm sure a good solution will come up."

She had her wallet in her hand, but she seemed to be looking for something besides money.

"If you really insist that I can't give you more money, then let me at least give you this," she said, handing him a business card. "I have a useful cousin too."

Sacko read the card: Maître Christophe Leclercq, Immigration Lawyer.

I'll ring Christophe up tomorrow and tell him that a certain Sacko will be in touch. So you'd better give him a call. He owes me big time! I let him stay here during his studies."

Sacko smiled. "Okay, Vanessa, I will. That's very nice of you."

"You were nice to me too, Sacko. Best of luck."

Same to you, Vanessa."

Before he turned towards the front door, he was struck with a beam of light. *La Dame de Fer.* Lady Luck had found him, this beacon of hope. And it had come in the most peculiar, or rather 'crazy,' way.

The Ghosts of la Cité des Fleurs

"*Ca va?*"

"*Ca va?*

"*Ca va?* Are you okay?"

Everything was dark. Nicolas's head was throbbing. The thought of opening his eyes, to see who the muffled voice belonged to, made it pound even more.

"Are you okay?" The voice seemed to be getting louder, but everything was still very fuzzy in his head.

Nicolas mustered up enough energy to open his eyes, ever so slightly. He tried to focus, but all he could discern was a blurry, swaying midget gawking down at him. It felt and looked like the effect you get from a curved mirror at a fair. *Am I trapped in a warped David Lynch movie?* he wondered hazily.

The ground began to vibrate with rapid, dull thuds. These got louder and sharper as they neared his pounding head. Footsteps? Women's heels?

"His eyes are opening!" screeched the small person. Its voice was also becoming clearer and was noticeably high pitched. Now, in addition to his splitting headache, Nicolas's eardrums were exploding with the shrieking voice and booming footfalls.

"*Dieu merci!* Thank God!" exclaimed the previously distant voice. This likely belonged to the wearer of the clip-clopping high heels. Those heels skidded to halt, to what seemed to Nicolas, right inside his left ear. He forced his eyes to open a little bit more. His vision was still foggy, but he was able to make out two people, or at least he thought there were two and that he wasn't actually stuck in some bizarre David Lynch-esque scenario or the Twilight Zone. Although the figures were very different sizes, their two faces were remarkably similar. Both had big olive-colored eyes and long auburn hair, which was now dangling above his face.

Nicolas blinked and pried his eyes fully open. The spinning in his head was diminishing and he'd almost regained his full vision. Yes, there were definitely two different people, an eight or nine year old girl and a woman in her mid to late-30s. Judging by their resemblance, he assumed they must be mother and daughter. He lifted his head in an attempt to rise, wincing in the process. This caused the pair to lean back and give him some space.

"Maybe we should call an ambulance," suggested the presumed mother, in a tone of urgent concern.

"No really, I'll be fine. I'm fine," he claimed, sitting up with some difficulty to reassure her. He put his hand up to his pounding forehead.

"Nina, I'm sending that scooter back with your dad when he comes to pick you up next weekend."

"I just need some more practice!"

"No, that's it!"

"Actually, I might have stepped out into the street without looking where I was going," admitted Nicolas, sensing the rising tension between the mother and daughter.

"It doesn't matter how the accident happened, Nina simply needs to be more careful," admonished the mother sternly, glaring at her daughter. "Just because this is a pedestrian street, it doesn't mean you can scoot down it at full speed."

Nina opened her mouth in an attempt to defend herself. She immediately snapped it shut, knowing wisely that there was no point in arguing with her mom, not right at that moment anyway with this poor dazed stranger sitting on the ground, at their feet.

"Are you really sure you're okay? You have a little cut on your forehead," she observed. "At the very least, let me disinfect it. Come, have a seat in our garden while I fetch the first aid kit."

She took Nicolas by the elbow to help him stand, which he did, albeit still somewhat wobbly. She let him adjust to this new vertical position, her brow furrowed with worry.

Come on, Nicolas, pull yourself together! He reprimanded. *Don't be such a wussy.* It really wasn't the poor chastised little girl's fault. Perhaps this incident happened to serve him a bit of a wake-up call. He hadn't been sleeping well for weeks. Nicolas either needed to shape up or go back to the doctor's to reassess his meds. He feared it might come down to the latter. But, one thing at a time.

He turned to the woman and gave her a weak smile. She took that as a sign they could start walking. She guided him about ten feet ahead and then steered him towards a gate on the left. She fumbled through her pocket for her keys, withdrew them and unlocked the metal door. Nicolas followed her inside.

Ahead of him was a small two-story house; such a rarity in Paris, otherwise densely packed with apartment buildings. Lanes lined with houses like this one were often called 'villa' streets. There were some nice examples of these in the Butte-aux-Cailles area, around the Buttes-Chaumont park and in the 16th arrondissement. Here in the 17th district, there weren't many villa streets, but they currently found themselves on one of the nicest: la Cité des Fleurs. Roughly translated as the 'city of flowers,' Nicolas noted that the street was true to its name, or at least this house was courtesy of its beguiling, flower-laden garden. Fuchsia bougainvillea, pale pink roses, pots of red geraniums, delicate yellow forsythia; their colors and fragrances further awakened Nicolas's senses as well as his memory.

The sleeping pills his doctor had prescribed were becoming less and less effective the longer he took them. Sleep deprived and consequently unable to concentrate on his work, Nicolas now recalled that he'd gone out for a stroll. After all, he could only stare at his empty computer screen for so long. He'd left his apartment in Montmartre and walked aimlessly down behind the hill. He had no idea how long he'd been wondering; such was his current zombie-like state. The last thing he could remember was that he'd looked to his right. He saw someone coming out of the iron gate of this country-style lane. Intrigued, he slid inside before the gate closed.

Nicolas slowly ambled down the street, gazing up at the different-styled houses. Bourgeois homes likely from the second half of the 19th century, they were attractive, but not as regal as the stately mansions in the Marais or bordering the Parc Monceau. Some Neo-Gothic decorative work around a window caught Nicolas's eye. In order to have a better look, he stepped down into the road, as it seemed to be closed to traffic. That was his last memory before he came to, flat out on the street's very hard cobblestones.

"Please sit," instructed the woman, guiding him into an old-fashioned iron garden chair. She made sure he was seated safely, before hurrying inside. Nicolas looked up at the pretty house. Made of creamy beige stone and slightly shorter than the houses on either side, there was something about it that exuded an aura of peacefulness. Nicolas's mind was now getting back up and running. Such a place must contain some fascinating stories.

"Our house is... haunted..." a voice whispered into Nicolas's left ear, hurling him back to the present moment. He turned around and came eye to eye with the very wide-eyed little girl.

"Oh really? Haunted, huh? How so?"

"There are ghosts."

"What kind of ghosts?"

"*Scarrrrrry* ones!"

"No I meant, ghosts that look like people or like Casper the ghost? Was it wearing a sheet over its head?"

"Oh, you've never seen ghosts quite like these..."

"Well, I can't say that I've ever seen a ghost, so I have nothing to compare your ghosts against."

"The one ghost that...."

"Nina! I can't leave you alone for one second! Stop with your stories!" admonished her mom, who'd just returned bearing a small first aid kit. "I know you're watching too much TV at your dad's. I just know it. He's got everything over there, Apple TV, Amazon Prime, Netflix, all those different cable channels... Too much TV isn't good for you, don't you agree, Mr...?"

"Mr... just call me Nicolas. And you?"

"Rachael, and this is..."

"Nina," he replied before she could get a chance.

Rachael smiled, realizing that she'd probably been shouting a little too much at her daughter. She missed her terribly when she was at her father's. Still, she wished Nina would spend more time down on earth rather than frolicking up in the clouds of her overactive imagination.

"What's your job, Mr Nicolas? Or maybe you don't have one since you're out and about in the middle of the day on a weekday."

Rachael shot Nina a '*zip it!*' look. Nina just couldn't help herself! There was no containing her curiosity. Rachael opened up the first aid kit and squirted some disinfectant onto a small cotton wipe. She began dapping the cut on Nicolas's forehead gently.

"Well, I'm actually a screenwriter. For TV shows, the kind on all those channels your mom doesn't approve of." At this revelation, Rachael dabbed a little harder at the cut, causing Nicolas to wince from the disinfectant. On the other hand, Nina was ecstatic. Forget hanging out on the clouds of her imagination, she was now completely over the moon.

"*Woooooow!* That's *sooooo* cool!" she exclaimed exuberantly. "What show did you write? What show?"

"*L'Inspecteur Marcel.*"

"*L'Inspecteur Marcel?* For REAL?!" Her eyes were popping out of their sockets as she started bouncing up and down all over.

This kid certainly didn't need any sugar to transform herself into the Energizer Bunny. "Mom, mom! *L'Inspecteur Marcel!*"

"I have no idea who or what *L'Inspecteur Marcel* is… and neither should you! I really need to talk to your father about what he's letting you watch!" This statement fell upon deaf ears; Nina was far away in another galaxy. Her bounce had accelerated into a gallop around poor helpless Nicolas. He was held captive by Rachael and her stringing swab and the intergalactic cowgirl Nina doing rounds around him on an imaginary horse.

"We watched every episode during the lockdown. Ev-er-y single one of ev-er-y single season! Twice!" Nina squealed.

"I hope you were watching all those dozens of episodes in the evenings or weekends and **not** during the day when you should have been giving your undivided attention to your teacher's online classes," Rachael scolded as she finished up cleaning Nicolas's head. Still on cloud nine million, Nina ignored her mother and carried on with her commentary.

"I think my favorite episode was the one with that burglar who was robbing all those mansions around Parc Monceau. He thinks he'll escape through the other side of the park… but *nooooo…* Inspector Marcel is already there, waiting for him outside the gate! You totally had me!"

"You probably liked that one because your dad allows you to poke around in those mansions and apartments over by the park after one of his clients has passed away and before he gives the keys to their heir or heiress. That's something else I have to tell him not to do! I don't care how glitzy those places are, snooping through them is downright creepy. That's likely where you get these silly ghost ideas," Rachael rolled her eyes as she packed up the first aid kit. She closed it, picked up the used wipe with her fingertips and went back inside.

Nina stopped her skipping and peered over to watch her mother retreat into the house. When the coast seemed clear, she leaned closely towards Nicolas.

"But there really are ghosts here," she claimed in a hushed tone. "You see our house? It used to be a hideout of ... the Resistance!"

"Is that so?" Nicolas commented with some trepidation.

"Yes. A hundred million gazillion percent true," she assured him, nodding her head. "Some mean neighbor ratted them out to the... Gestapo. Maybe they were tortured. Inside the house... or maybe right here. In the garden. On this very spot!" Her olive eyes, now a mere inch or two from Nicolas's were once again bulging.

Nicolas cautiously looked around the garden, which suddenly felt a lot less tranquil. A chill trailed up his spine and a gust of wind shook the garden's leafy fruit trees.

"Ahem..." the eerie moment was broken by Rachael clearing her throat. Nina and Nicolas simultaneously turned their heads around to find Rachael standing next to them, her hands firmly on her hips. "Last week it was Revolutionaries from the Paris Commune revolt of 1871 who'd gotten trapped in the tunnels beneath the house. The week before it was soldiers who'd been billeted here during WWI... for some peculiar reason or another. Nina, honestly. I don't know where you get all these ideas if it isn't for all those TV shows or creepy mansions which probably really are haunted. Do you need an apprentice, Nicolas?"

Nina's face lit up and she started shaking his arms.

"Oh yes! Yes! Yes! Come on, Nicolas. *Pleeeeeeeaaasssse!*"

Nicolas smiled, exhaled and released his clenched fists. That imaginative tyke had really got him going with her stories. Actually, that's what Nicolas needed right now. An overactive imagination. He felt like his mind had been on pause ever since the outbreak of the pandemic. He surmised his mental stock of creative juices had run dry. He'd been cut off, just like someone who hadn't paid their cable bill. No more ideas meant no more shows.

"When's the next season of *L'Inspecteur Marcel* coming out? Do you know? Do you know?" she asked impatiently.

"Well, you see. That's the bad news. It's been discontinued."

"WHAT?!" she shouted as if she'd just been told that Tooth Fairy wasn't real. "But how is that possible? It's the best show ever!"

"Unfortunately, the producers think this new reality show they're developing will be the best thing ever."

"Rubbish! I want *L'Inspecteur Marcel!* Or if not him, something else. Something by you."

"I'm trying to come up with a new concept, Nina. Online streaming did do exceptionally well when everyone was glued to their screens during the quarantine. But when mandatory confinement was lifted, viewership slumped. It isn't like I want people to be stuck inside again, but producers have since gotten really picky. I have to come up with something that will capture a wide audience, on evenings and weekends, that is," he added for Rachael's benefit.

"Nicolas, would you like something to drink, to give you a little energy boost?" offered Rachael. "We've got some fresh organic pear juice. It's from my little sister's new shop in the 11th arrondissement. No preservatives, no pesticides and it comes straight from a farm in Normandy."

"That sounds great, thank you." he accepted.

Nina watched her mother go up the steps and into the house. As soon as she thought she was out of earshot, she turned eagerly to Nicolas.

"So, that stuff about the Resistance, it's actually true! There's even a plaque outside our house!" she resumed excitedly. "Their leader was killed during the raid. Her name was Colette, like the writer. How could her ghost *not* be inhabiting our house... if this is where she... perished?"

Nicolas pondered this, but before he could come up with a clever response, she carried on.

"I think the whole street is haunted. The Impressionist painter Alfred Sisley used to live down the street and the actress Catherine Deneuve was born next door..."

"Hold on a second, did Sisley actually die in that house...? And Deneuve is still alive, right? So, her ghost can't be haunting the place, at least not just yet."

"That might all be true... But there are... *others!*" she managed to counter his objection.

As she opened her mouth to elaborate, she was interrupted by a clatter. This noise was courtesy of Rachael as she slammed down a tray containing three glasses and a large bottle of juice onto the round garden table. She then sat down on the garden chair opposite Nicolas.

"Seriously, Nina," she chided. "First you hurt Nicolas's head by knocking him over while riding your scooter, now you must certainly be making his headache worse with all of your tall tales!"

"Oh, I don't mind, really," he said. The outlandish stories were just the grease the wheels of his own imagination needed to start turning again. Well, and some sleep.

"Speaking of tall... a giant lived a little further down the street. I heard he was eight feet tall and that was a star attraction at the Moulin Rouge!"

"So Nicolas, do you live around here?" asked Rachael, trying to silence her daughter's stories by changing the subject.

"Actually, I live up in Montmartre, not too far from the Moulin Rouge. However, sadly I only live in an apartment. It must be so nice to have a garden. That's all I thought about during the lockdown."

"I have to admit, it was a real saving grace. I think we would have gone crazy otherwise, well, maybe just me. Nina would have kept busy tracking down the ghosts dwelling in all four corners of our house."

"Once I sell another show, I'm seriously going to look for a place with a garden, or at the very least a balcony."

"I can let you know if we see one come up for sale here."

"Yes! Yes! Yes!" squealed Nina. "Come live over here! Just imagine if we were neighbors?!"

"Well, I'm going to need to come up with an amazing new show idea to be able to afford a house over here."

"I totally understand. I could never afford this place now. I'm an elementary school teacher over by the Canal Saint Martin, it isn't like we're paid very well. I bought this house with my ex-husband. He got a good deal on it as one of his client's heirs couldn't afford to keep it and needed cash quickly. Now he lives over in the chicer part of the 17th, near the Parc Monceau, but I prefer it over here. This is a very special street. It seems that as soon as you step over that gate, you're transported into another realm. Well, that's sort of what happened to you today, Nicolas!"

"Yes, that's for sure. It's actually got me thinking... about my next show," said Nicolas.

"Sometimes we just need to let go of our regular habits and thoughts. Then all kinds of new perspectives will suddenly appear," philosophized Rachael.

"That's true," Nicolas contemplated. He finished up the pear juice and set his glass back down on the table. "Well, I shouldn't take up any more of your time, but it would be great to exchange numbers. Um, in case you see a house come up for sale around here."

"Oh, I'm sure Nina would be happy to see you back here any time! Speaking of the devil, where did that little rascal go?" They hadn't noticed, but while they were talking Nina had mysteriously drifted off.

"Nina! Come say goodbye to Nicolas!" shouted Rachael. "Perhaps she's back to chasing ghosts already. Anyway, let me go get my phone and I'll see if she's inside."

Rachael picked up the drinks tray and walked inside. Nicolas stood up and looked back up at the charming house. An intriguing house on an even more intriguing street... there was definitely something very special going on.

I wonder what it looks like on the inside? Was it really filled with ghosts? thought Nicolas. He crept up to the door to have a quick peek.

"Boo!!!"

"Nina!!!!!"

The Magic of Montmartre

"That's a wrap!" said Elin as she set her armful of bags down on an armchair in their hotel lobby.

"Whew, I'm pooped!" Bente exclaimed collapsing into an adjacent chair.

"We did pretty good though, didn't we?" declared Elin. She sifted through the contents of her bags, stopping here and there to admire a newly acquired treasure.

"Yes, I'm very content with this year's finds!" Bente agreed. "We can add the Paris Jewelry and Gem Show 2019 to our list of successful fairs!"

"Indeed!" said Elin. "Are you still interested in going up to Montmartre tonight?"

Suddenly, Bente, perked up from her previously fatigued state at the suggestion of a new Paris adventure; "I can't wait!"

"Great! Let's get freshened up and meet back down here, say, at 7?" Suggested Elin as she gathered up her bags.

"Sounds good!" confirmed Bente. She peeled herself out of the cushy seat and felt around in her pockets for her key card. "See you then!"

Elin and Bente had been coming to the Paris Jewelry and Gem Show for years. It had become an annual tradition for the two friends, who were both jewelry designers back in Denmark. Although they came for work, and had busy days making purchases and contacts at the fair, they always tried to eke out a little time in their schedule for taking in Paris. They hadn't been up to Montmartre in a while, so when Bente had proposed they spend their last evening there, Elin instantly agreed.

***

"Don't you look nice!" complimented Elin when the two ladies reunited in the foyer.

"As do you!" said Bente. "Let's go out and really make the most of our evening, we're in Paris after all!"

"And it's our last night!" added Elin. "You never know what the evening could have in store!"

"Precisely!" said Bente. "Let the magic of Paris decide!"

"*Allons-y!* Let's go!" cheered Elin. And with that the two friends exited their hotel near the Musée d'Orsay and made their way towards the Solférino *Métro* Station.

"I have an idea," started Bente when they were seated on the the *Métro* train.

"What's that?" asked Elin.

"I've never been to the Moulin Rouge," confessed Bente.

"Neither have I," seconded Elin.

"Why don't we give it a try?" suggested Bente. "We look dressed up enough. It could be a nice way to cap off our stay."

"Why not?" agreed Elin. "Plus, I spent less at the fair than I'd budgeted. I have all these leftover euros. I suppose I could save them for next time, but you just never know. There's always a chance we won't make it to the next fair and the money would simply be collecting dust in my wallet."

"A friend of mine just went to the Moulin Rouge," Bente elaborated. "She said she was mesmerized watching the singers and dancers in their fabulous costumes. The show has other talented performers, like ventriloquists, magicians and clowns, but the dancers were her absolute favorite. She said they were simply exquisite in their flowing chiffons, feathered headpieces and dazzling jewelry. Perhaps the show could give us inspiration for our own creations?"

"Shall we put this down as research?" proposed Elin. "Maybe we can claim the tickets as a business expense?"

The two friends giggled. The old-fashioned train serving *Métro* Line 12 carried on with its journey north. The closer they got to their destination, the more excited they became. *Oh, the anticipation!*

Elin had always been interested in art and, in particular, the prints and posters of Toulouse-Lautrec, many of which starred the multifaceted characters of the Moulin Rouge. For as long as she could remember she'd wanted to go to the place that had inspired him to paint and draw those eccentric women and men. One can only imagine the incredible stories of the performers who have graced the cabaret's stage over the decades—stories about love, lust, loss and adventure. Elin wondered if their ghosts were dancing in the wings or, at the very least, floating nearby in the streets of Montmartre.

Elin was dragged out of her thoughts when they arrived at Pigalle Station, they'd walk the rest of the way from there. Reaching the street level, they noticed it had rained while they'd been on the *Métro*. The damp pedestrian median which dissected the wide Boulevard de Clichy was cast in the hazy reflections of the bright neon signs of the street's racy shop fronts. Over the course of the 20th century, the area's Belle Epoque cabarets and cafés, were mostly replaced with seedier boutiques and evening entertainment venues. Now, into the 21st century, this 'Red Light District' was gradually gentrifying. Despite all of these changes, le Moulin Rouge, the 'red windmill,' was still standing. The historic cabaret had prevailed and was a testament to the area's heritage. While it evoked a certain nostalgia of the late-19th century heyday of cabarets, in many ways it also perfectly embodied the magic of Paris, both past and present.

"That's quite the line…" noted Elin as they arrived in front of the Moulin Rouge.

"I hadn't really thought that we'd need to buy tickets in advance," admitted Bente.

"I doubt that was required of the patrons who came here 100 years ago!"

"Most certainly not!" Despite the seemingly unfavorable odds, the two Danes went up to the ticket booth to check.

"Désolée Mesdames, on est complet. I'm sorry, ladies. We're sold out," announced the ticket vendor.

"Oh drat!" said Bente, noticeably disappointed.

"Ah, it's okay. We can always go next time, right?" Elin suggested consolingly. She always tried to look on the bright side.

"Yes, that's true," conceded Bente. "Well, since we're in Montmartre, let's go for that stroll around the hill that we'd originally intended to take."

"Perfect!" Elin replied cheerfully. Arm in arm, the two friends embarked up Rue Lepic, its shops now closed and its residents snug at home on this misty autumn evening.

No need for a map when you can simply lose yourself in the back streets of Paris, especially the ones in Montmartre. Its lovely lanes were exceedingly picturesque in the evenings, when they were clear of the tourist masses that traipsed around this popular former village during the day. The ladies enjoyed their leisurely wander around its cobblestoned streets, now glistening in the glow cast by the occasional lamppost.

As they ambled, savoring the silence, Bente thought about the many generations of Parisians who had lived, and those who probably still lived, on *la Butte*, as locals referred to the hilly neighborhood. They passed the former homes of great painters, the art studio where early 20th-century art was born and a windmill, this time not red, but instead one that had been immortalized by the brushstrokes of Impressionists painters. She marveled at the fact they were walking, right then and there, in the footsteps of legendary artists, many of whom, like Toulouse-Lautrec, van Gogh and Modigliani, would not see or enjoy the fame that would sadly come to them posthumously. Now their works hung in the world's top museums, like Paris's very own Musée d'Orsay.

One their explorations, they also discovered some works by modern-day artists. Street artists. Plastered here and there on larger walls, these works showed how the neighborhood still attracted and fostered creativity.

Their stroll eventually led them to Place du Tertre. Once the main town square of the historic village, it was another place in Montmartre where artists congregated, that is, to sell paintings depicting Paris scenes or sketch portraits of tourists. However, on this drizzling evening, they'd already packed up their easels, palettes and paint sets. Despite its emptiness, the square still had a special allure... a certain magic.

"*Mesdames, venez, venez!* Come in!"

The two women turned around to find the beaming face of a waiter, holding open the front door to La Bohème, a restaurant bordering the square. The ladies looked at each other.

"Well, we haven't had dinner yet," said Elin. "It's almost 10."

"Already? No wonder I was feeling peckish," responded Bente. "I know these places are a bit touristy, but one can't go wrong with a *soupe à l'oignon*?"

"French onion soup! That's perfect for this weather!" Elin concurred. "*D'accord, monsieur, une table pour deux.* A table for two."

Stepping inside, the two friends were instantly enveloped by the restaurant's warmth and its cozy decor, a welcome respite from the cool evening air. The waiter escorted them to a table next to the window overlooking the square. They wouldn't be needing to spend their time gazing outside though; they quickly realized there was a much livelier ambiance *inside* the restaurant. Not far from where they were seated was a raised stage area. A lively gypsy jazz band was playing and, although the restaurant wasn't too busy, a few of the other customers were even up dancing.

"How fun!" enthused Bente.

"Yes, I would have never expected this!" added Elin.

"Me neither!" said Bente. "The surprises of our evening continue!"

When the waiter returned, Bente and Elin ordered their two soups and *un pichet de vin rouge*, a pitcher of red wine.

"*Santé! Skål!*" the ladies gleefully toasted when their wine arrived.

Just as they set down their glasses, the restaurant's door swung open in great pomp. In waltzed a woman, extravagantly dressed 'to the nines,' in pure Parisian black. She was of a certain age, although it was difficult to place what that could be... 60... 70... 80... 90? Whether it was thanks to her large diamond studded sunglasses (yes even at 10 at night) or her fur-trimmed cape, she was both timeless and over the top. The waiter rushed to fawn over her.

"Madame Mimi! *Bienvenue!* Welcome! Your table is awaiting!"

Madame Mimi's designated table, perfectly positioned to view the stage, most of the restaurant and the square beyond, turned out to be next to Elin and Bente's. When they'd finished playing their song, the lead musician gave a little bow to welcome Madame Mimi. Moments later, without even having placed an order, the attentive waiter reappeared with a glass of champagne for *la madame*.

"*Merci Rodolfo, tu es adorable!* You're adorable!" she cooed.

The waiter returned shortly bearing two steaming bowls of French onion soup for Elin and Bente. These looked divinely delicious with their generous layer of gooey gruyère cheese blanketing thick chunks of bread and dense broth loaded with large slices of caramelized onions.

"*Bon appétit!*"

They stopped simultaneously, their spoons poised and ready to dig into their piping hot bowls. The two Danes turned towards the lyrical voice. There was Madame Mimi, smiling and raising her glass in their direction.

"*Merci!*" they replied cheerfully before devouring their satisfying soup all the while swaying to the classic jazz tunes of the modern-day Django Reinhardt and his band. Then, as soon as they finished and set down their spoons, Madame Mimi returned her attention to the two accidental tourists.

"Are you visiting Paris?" Madame Mimi asked them in English with a French accent thicker than the French onion soup.

"Yes, we're from Denmark, but we come to Paris often," said Bente. "We were hoping to go to the Moulin Rouge tonight, but it was sold out."

"*Ah, le Moulin Rouge!* I know it all too well," reminisced Madame Mimi theatrically.

"Oh really, how so?" asked Elin.

"I was the star dancer there for almost a decade!" she announced proudly. "Those were the good old days…"

Just then the waiter returned to remove their bowls.

"*Rodolfo, trois coupes de champagne!*" Madame Mimi ordered flamboyantly before Elin and Bente could utter a word of protest. Soon the Danes were being entertained by both La Bohème's music and Madame Mimi's vivid tales of her life and times at the Moulin Rouge.

The band members set down their instruments. It was the end of their last set. Madame Mimi elegantly sipped the last drops from her coupe.

Dong! Dong! Dong!

France's largest church bell, hanging not even right around the corner in the tower of Sacré-Coeur, thunderously tolled twelve times.

"How is it midnight already?" exclaimed Elin.

"It's the magic of Montmartre," replied Madame Mimi. "It's a timeless place."

Montmartre was timeless, Mimi was timeless, but the *Métro* service was not.

"We'd better get going if we want to catch the *Métro*," said Bente as she flagged the waiter for their check. "Unfortunately, we have an early flight tomorrow."

"Please, come up to see us again when you return to Paris," ordered Madame Mimi. "The 'real' show is here, not at le Moulin Rouge!"

"Yes, we certainly found that out tonight," confirmed Bente. The two ladies hurriedly put down twenty euros each to cover the bill and waved *au revoir* to Madame Mimi as they rushed out the door, jackets in hand.

"Quick, I think there's a *Métro* station over this way," said Elin. They scurried down a street that looped around the white-domed basilica. Something twinkling to the right caught their eyes, causing the ladies to stop in their rushed tracks. In the distance was the Eiffel Tower whose hourly evening sparkle-fest was just finishing up.

"Gorgeous!" gasped Bente.

"More of the magic of Montmartre," noted Elin. The neighborhood was the highest location in Paris and its views of the sparkling city were rivalled by few other vantage points. However, on that particular night, the ladies didn't have the luxury to linger and soak up the vista. They had to hustle if they were going to catch the *Métro*.

In seconds they reached the staircase in front of Sacré-Coeur, which seemingly went on forever and ever down the Rue Foyatier. The steps were still glistening from the early evening rain, so the ladies tried their best to descend both quickly and carefully, eyes glued to their feet to avoid slipping. All of the sudden the steps were illuminated with flashes of orange and red. They'd reached one of the landings that were found every dozen or so steps on that endless staircase. They stopped wide-eyed in their tracks. Standing on this small space was... a fire-breather!

He raised his smoldering stick up to his lips and huffed out a giant gust of fire which lit up the sky in front of the Danes and the few other passers-by who'd gathered to witness the awesome spectacle.

Elin was captivated. This wasn't any ordinary fire-breather either, he was truly amazing. She noticed a donation hat on the ground, so she hastily opened her wallet to give him some money. All she had was a 100-euro bill and a few *centimes*. She hesitated for a split second, then removed the crisp green note.

"*Kom nu!* Come on, Elin, are you crazy?" Bente hissed in Danish.

"I have to," replied Elin with conviction. "I don't know why, but I just have to. Besides, that's what we would have spent had we gone to the Moulin Rouge... I'm much happier with the alternative show we got tonight!"

Elin put the large note in the hat and looked back up at the fire-breather. In the low light, she could hardly see his face, nevertheless, their eyes met and he made a gesture of thanks.

"*Lad os gå!* Let's go!" commanded Bente. "We have to get a move on... now we won't have money to take a taxi if we miss the *Métro!*"

The ladies raced the rest of the way down the stairs. On their left, inside the dark park, was the shadow of a vintage carousel. The merry-go-round added a last dash of whimsical allure to their evening of magic in Montmartre.

How were they to guess that a mere few months later an international pandemic would drastically change all travel? There was no way they could have ever imagined that this trip might be the last time the two friends would experience the magic of Paris for the unforeseeable future.

Or, was it?

***

"It's official," announced Bente over the phone to Elin. "The Jewelry and Gem Show 2020 has been canceled, as has Minéral Expo."

As the virus spread and travel was dramatically restricted, Elin had the uneasy feeling that their annual trip to Paris would be canceled. She consoled herself by keeping busy with her jewelry creations. After some time, her shop in Århus was able to reopen. Freedom of movement was slowly re-established, however, with their two favorite trade shows canceled, the women had less of a reason to trek to Paris. Yet, deep inside them, the city still beckoned... and they yearned to answer its call.

***

It was 6 pm on a mild late-September day. Elin turned the sign on her door to 'closed' and went back to run her end of day accounting.

Knock! Knock!

"Ah, that's probably Bente," Elin said to herself as she returned to the door. But no. The person standing on the other side of the glass was not her dear friend. It was a tall dark stranger.

Caught off guard, Elin fumbled for the door handle.

"*Hej, kan jeg hjælpe dig?*" she greeted.

"Do you speak English?" asked the stranger.

"Of course, what can I do for you?" she responded.

"Make a necklace for me, please," he quickly begged and then added in the same breath, "I know it's last minute, but I leave Aarhus in the morning. I'm passing through on my way to Copenhagen. Just now, as I was walking around, your beautiful jewelry caught my attention. I decided to take a chance and ask for this favor."

Times had been tough since the crisis and Elin couldn't really refuse the unexpected sale. Plus, there was something about this mysterious stranger, something that made Elin feel like she'd met him before. She opened the door to let him in. The two sat down at her counter where he explained his ideas for the design and the colors he wanted to be included.

"How much would that be?" he asked.

"A hundred euros?" replied Elin.

"Okay, that's fine," agreed the stranger, pulling out a crisp 100-euro note from his wallet. "I'll pay you right now."

"Excellent, it'll be ready by 10 tomorrow morning." They went to shake hands, then stopped midway. No shaking hands these days. Their hands hadn't locked, but their eyes had. Yes, Elin did know these eyes, eyes which had shone under an orangy-red flare...

"It *was* you..." he said, his sentence trailing off.

Yes. And it *was* him. The fire-breather.

Incredible! What had brought him here, to Aarhus, to her shop? The fire-breather went on to explain.

As it turned out, back when Elin and Bente had fatefully descended those Montmartre steps and encountered the fire-breather, whose name was Damien, he was totally broke. Despite his dismal finances, he was still hoping to collect enough money to make a video of his fire-breathing skills. This video was a requirement to get invited to a prestigious competition in Spain. If his application was shortlisted, he'd be invited to the event, all expenses paid. This deadline was fast approaching and Damien didn't think he would be able to raise enough money in time.

Then, like a sign from Vulcan, the God of Fire, he received Elin's 100-euro note. This was just enough for him to rent a professional video camera. A friend filmed the video, he sent it in and was invited to the competition. Once there, he ended up winning the top prize: a two-month live 'Tour of Europe' gig, which was accompanied by a very generous travel allowance. Originally scheduled for April and May, the tour had to be postponed due to the pandemic, but was eventually moved to August and September. Denmark was the last stop on his tour. At

10:30 the next morning, he would be on a train back to the Danish capital to catch his flight back to Paris.

"How did you know it was me," questioned Elin after hearing his amazing story.

"I noticed the jewelry in your window display," he explained. "You were wearing a similar necklace that night. It flickered like a sparkler in the light of my fire. It gave me hope. The thought of it, and your generous gesture, were my good luck charms. Now I'll have this physical one to accompany me wherever I go."

When Damien left, Elin marveled over his story as she took special care in making his necklace. His new good luck charm.

Her 100 euros had returned. The City of Light had found her. The flame, and the magic of Paris, would forever burn brightly, no matter where she was. And provide a certain amount of magical good luck. *Le coup de chance de Paris*. The good luck of Paris.

Le Métro
19th & 20th Arrondissements

The train jetted forward on its above ground tracks. By the time they arrived at La Chapelle Station, he'd almost reached Petite Piaf.

"There's only one Paris…!"

He didn't know how many times she'd gone through her signature song today, however, this might be the last time she ever sang it if she was caught by either the controllers or the gypsies. Sasha was one seat section away from her. Both nemeses were held up behind clusters of passengers, around four seat sections away. Sasha didn't want to risk her dashing off the train at the next station, Stalingrad, so he waited it out, praying that the others didn't get there by the time they got to Jaurès.

The train was cruising along the border between the working-class 19th district, home to the beautiful Buttes-Chaumont park, and the gentrifying 10th arrondissement. On his right, Sasha noticed the sparkling waters of the Canal Saint-Martin. Normally, it was a delight to see, however, today, seeing a few boats bobbing up and down in its waters added to the sinking feeling of dread in his stomach. How could he save Petite Piaf *and* get his valuable object back? *Come on Sasha, think!* he commanded desperately.

"Il n'y a qu'un seul Paris..."

As they pulled into Jaurès Station a red object garnered his attention and for once it wasn't Petite Piaf's hat. *Yes!* That might just work. It just might.

He inched closer to Petite Piaf. Her eyes were scrunched closed and her head was thrown back passionately leading up to her finale. Some nearby passengers left at the last station, so Sasha leaned up against a closed folding seat, right near the door. He was a mere few feet away from Petite Piaf. He slid his nervous hand in his bag and rustled around for something inside it.

"Paris... Paris..."

Petite Piaf's enemies were so intently focused on her that neither seemed to notice Sasha.

"Paris!"

She drew out that last note on her accordion and opened her eyes as the train went back underground and pulled into Colonel Fabien Station.

The burly gypsy started clapping, slowly. She hesitantly turned her head in his direction.

"Remember, little girl, I tell you no more singing on my line. You got off train. That should be end of story. Then I see you back on another train. You know what this means? End of playing for you," he threatened menacingly. "That accordion you have, it's ours."

His sidekick set his portable sound system to the side and moved over in front of the door to block her from fleeing. He was waving his clarinet in the air, like he was practicing his bat swing. Sensing there was trouble, the other *Métro* passengers within their vicinity cautiously drifted to other sections of the train.

"*Ahem,*" the brawny controller cleared his throat. He and his team were standing, arms folded, on the other side of Petite Piaf.

"Now that will be three fines for you and we're going to confiscate your accordion," he announced, in a condescending tone.

Belleville Station was just up ahead. Sasha had to have perfect timing for his ploy.

"As for you two, I'd like to see your permit to perform, that is, if you even have one," the uppity female controller who'd tried to fine Sasha informed the gypsies. She still hadn't noticed Sasha. They now had bigger fish to fry anyway.

The train slowed as it cruised down the platform at Belleville.

"But that accordion belongs to us now," the beefy gypsy declared to the head controller. Like on cue, the clarinetist stepped menacing towards the controller, 'bat' clarinet in hand.

"Oh, you really think so?" mocked the arrogant controller.

"Yes, and we'll prove it to you." He started towards Petite Piaf. The controllers also stepped forward, fearless to the clarinetist's threats.

Sasha pulled his hand out of his bag and emptied the contents of a small red bag onto the train car's floor. Malteser® balls cascaded all around them, sending Petite Piaf's band of adversaries skidding and slipping all over the section they were in.

"Come!" Sasha reached over and yanked Petite Piaf by the arm. The two of them dashed off the train. The buzzer sounded.

Breathless in the Buttes-Chaumont

"*Attend!* Wait!" Dimitri wheezed, breathless. "Karine, wait!"

Karine stopped and looked in Dimitri's direction. Seeing him collapse on a bench, and huffing and puffing like a 19th-century steam train, she circled back.

"I can't do it," he managed to spit out in between heaving breaths.

"But what about the rest of the group? They're going to wonder what happened to us," she said, jogging in place in front of Dimitri.

"I don't give a flying hoot if they wonder what happened to us," he exclaimed. "I think I'm going to die! If I keep on jogging, everyone will be held up waiting for the paramedics to arrive to revive me from my ensuing heart attack!"

Just then a troop of firemen appeared over the crest of the hill, jogging in perfect unison wearing matching little blue and red shorts. A fire station was right next to the park and the firemen also used the large green space for their exercise routines. Karine suddenly had a sneaking suspicion that this was the first, and last, time she and Dimitri would be using the park as their outdoor gym together.

"See! They've already come to get me!" Dimitri joked as this group of firemen, the first responder paramedics in France, sped past. Dimitri might have lost his breath on the agonizing jog up the hill, but not his sense of humor.

"It's okay, I'll send Stéphane a message to say we had to bail early," she said, conceding to defeat. Maybe encouraging Dimitri to join her runners' group hadn't been such a good idea. It definitely wasn't the right fit for him. But what would be? Karine wondered, as she sighed and plunked herself down on the bench next to him.

They sat there for a few minutes in silence, well, in relative silence, save for Dimitri's panting and some birds chirping in trees behind them. Dimitri gazed down at the pretty view, the one and only advantage he could associate with their current location and situation. Sloping from their perch was a large section of the Buttes-Chaumont's extensive lawns. Covered in a thin layer of dew, the blades of grass glistened in the mellow, early-morning sunlight. There was a slight chill to the air on this late-September Saturday. It was perfect weather for jogging, at least, those who enjoyed the sport would likely concur.

Karine and Dimitri were lucky to live near the beautiful Buttes-Chaumont Park. Well, actually, truth be told, luck had nothing to do with it. They hadn't moved to the 19th arrondissement by choice. It was one of the few districts in Paris that was still affordable.

***

The couple had met in their mid-twenties when they were both working in the tour department of the Louvre. Since then they'd both moved onto other jobs in the Paris museum world; Karine was in charge of thematic tours at the Musée d'Orsay and Dimitri was a tour guide on staff at the Catacombs. They had comfortable jobs with good benefits and a generous amount of paid vacation, but they were hardly the most lucrative. This mattered a lot less when they were younger, but when it came time to think about buying an apartment, their meagre salaries had a big impact on available and affordable choices.

After they'd paid off their wedding bills, Dimitri and Karine started squirreling away all their extra income. They cancelled the trip to Sri Lanka they'd been dreaming of, they didn't renew their season passes to the Opéra Garnier and they reduced their theater and restaurant outings. Their efforts eventually paid off and after five years, they'd managed to save 50,000 euros.

Proud of themselves, their optimism was quickly deflated during their much-anticipated meeting with the mortgage broker when he announced that they could get a loan for no more than 350,000 euros. That amount was definitely not enough to buy the two-bedroom apartment they'd been hoping for. In fact, it was barely enough for a one-bedroom. They knew they could not survive in anything smaller than that. A studio would simply not be possible. They would end up killing each other.

The finances vs space dilemma is what compels many young Parisian couples to move out to the suburbs. Suburban living wouldn't have bothered Karine. She'd grown up in the southern Paris suburb of Gentilly. Dimitri, however, was a Parisian through and through. It was out of the question for him to live on the side of the *Peripherique*, the circular expressway which acted as the border between Paris's official 20 arrondissements and the burbs.

Therefore, in order to get more for their money, they decided to search for a fixer-upper. They were both into DIY, plus Dimitri's dad was an electrician and had offered to give them a hand. What's more, they were eager to embrace the challenge. It would be fun! It would be a bonding experience!

Karine signed up for email alerts on various real estate agency websites. They spent most of their Saturdays visiting apartments. However, time and again the places would inevitably be too dark, too damp or too dingy. As much as these visits were discouraging, they did help the couple narrow down what they were looking for, or rather, what they would be willing to settle for. After having visited over 40 places, they also knew they would have to be ready to make an offer virtually on the spot, when they found the 'right one.'

***

"I think I've found it!" exclaimed Karine as she popped her head over her laptop one night when they were still in their old rental in the Buttes-aux-Cailles area. Dimitri stopped making dinner and came over to Karine's makeshift desk area, aka the corner of the dining room table, to have a look.

There on the computer screen were very poor-quality photos of an apartment that seemed like it hadn't been renovated in 100 years and had an accumulation of 100 years of stuff. It looked like a total dive. Cringing, Dimitri looked at the size, 50 square meters (538 square feet), which was a good size for Paris standards. His eyes then drifted over to the price. 349,000 euros. He looked back at the photos. Maybe they weren't so bad after all...

"Yes, Karine, looks like you have!"

And it was so that Dimitri and Karine moved from the Butte-aux-Cailles to the Buttes-Chaumont—from one Parisian hill to another.

***

Les Buttes-Chaumont. The Bald Hills. It was probably the least poetic name of any place in Paris. A disheartening name for a (once) very dismal and well, bald, place. For centuries the hills on the northeast fringes of the city was used for public hangings. Its status wasn't much improved with its next incarnation in the 1760s: an open-air sewage dump. Deep beneath this was a gypsum quarry, similar to the quarries found in other former peripheral areas of what was then Paris, such as Montmartre and the site which became the Catacombs. The area's fate took on brighter perspectives when it was annexed into Paris in 1860 and transformed into one of the 26 parks commissioned by Baron Haussmann for his new and improved city.

Karine flexed her feet on the ground and stared out in the other direction to Dimitri. Her eyes drifted down to the park's lake and a suspension bridge. Haussmann's Director of Parks, Adolphe Alphand, took advantage of the site's morphology in the park's design. Instead of flattening the area, he dynamited the remains of the stone quarry and used the blasted stone to create a 50-meter (168-foot) high rocky cliff, crowned by a belvedere lookout. This was where Dimitri had his 'near heart-attack.'

An alluring rocky hill, rolling lawns and relaxed clusters of trees and flower beds; Alphand's handiwork had successfully converted a dismal dump into one of the loveliest parks in the city. Karine could only hope that, after all of their hard work, their own 'dump' would achieve the same fabulous finale.

***

The couple got the keys to the apartment last October. They didn't take a holiday in summer so they could put those vacation days towards time off to get the renovations underway. However, those three weeks didn't turn out to be enough to get all the initial base work completed. And, that was despite the generous help of Dimitri's dad and also that of various friends who stopped by sporadically to help. At least by the end of that three-week period, they had the bathroom installed and Dimitri's dad had finished the electrical rewiring. The walls weren't finished though. Actually, it looked like a stick of the dynamite that Alphand had used to destroy the Buttes-Chaumont's former stone quarry had been thrown into their place, too. Shambles was a kind description, in their opinion. They were sleeping on a mattress on the floor. Their 'home décor' consisted of stacks of unpacked boxes and large plastic bins. Karine couldn't wait to unpack these, and do some real decorating, especially with the lovely vintage homeware her mother had given them as a housewarming gift from her shop in the Marais.

Tired, but still on a DYI high, Karine would get up early every Saturday to join her running group in the beautiful park while Dimitri would stay behind and assess what projects they'd work on that particular weekend. They finished installing the kitchen in mid-November, which meant they could swap out the frozen meals they'd been reheating in the microwave for Dimitri's tasty cooking. This milestone brightened both of their spirits. For a time.

The drywall was meant to be their end-of-year holiday project. However, they didn't quite have enough time to finish it since they'd allowed themselves a teeny weeny bit of a break to simply enjoy the festive season. They were planning on taking time off around Easter to complete the walls. But then the quarantine was announced. In the mad rush to stock up on food, they didn't have the foresight to do the same for DIY supplies.

***

"Which color do you prefer?"

"I don't see any difference," Dimitri answered honestly, examining the two samples before handing them back to Karine. It was now several months after the lockdown and they were on what seemed to be their trillionth visit to the hardware store. Their loyalty card was racking up some serious points, however, Dimitri's interest, and patience levels, had hit an all-time low. His and Karine's both.

"No, they are not the same. This one is Jasmine white and this one is Almond. So, which one?"

"You choose!"

"Dimitri, this is supposed to be a team effort, remember?"

"Almond then!"

"But you didn't even really look at it!"

"So make it Jasmine!"

Forget all those Saturdays they'd spent visiting potential apartments. Since getting those keys, they'd spent every Saturday, Sunday *and* several evenings per week working on their apartment, and now for nearly a year. Any 'fun' the project might have initially entailed had worn off like the faint vanish on their parquet floor… which, they may never get around to resurfacing at the snail pace of their do-it-yourself renovations.

***

Neither of their jobs could be done virtually. Therefore, it would seem that the two-month quarantine would have been the perfect opportunity for Dimitri and Karine to complete the renovations. BUT, there was one colossal catch: there were absolutely no hardware stores within the one-kilometer radius they were allotted for the 'essential' outings as per the lockdown's regulations.

They did all they could with what they had on hand. Nevertheless, many of the tasks they still had to do were simply not possible. They were stuck in their apartment 24/7 or rather 23/7, since they were allowed outside for one hour of 'essential exercise' per day. Karine made use of this quarantine privilege by going out for a jog a few times per week. However, since the park was closed, she could only jog around its locked fence, gazing longingly through the iron bars at its pathways, trees and lawns. She couldn't even meet with any of her running buddies since it was forbidden to gather with anyone outside your household and, even though she'd asked him time and time again, Dimitri wouldn't join her.

In fact, he was staying inside to watch baking tutorials. He started by learning how to make croissants, claiming he missed the ones from their favorite bakery down in their old neighborhood. Talk about time consuming! But even Karine had to admit, he was getting pretty good, although she did not want to know how much butter went into his flaky delights. With each passing week of the quarantine, he added several new recipes to his repertoire, many courtesy of Chef Lise's online classes. *Tarte au citron, crème brûlée, madeleines, tarte tatin…* it seemed like he learned how to make every pastry and dessert imaginable! He perfected his *lava cake* recipe while Karine did her online strength training classes. Karine's respite from their dump of an apartment, and the bizarre World climate they were living through, was exercise while Dimitri's was baking. By the end of confinement, these activities had two very different results... on their physiques.

***

"Do you really need *two* sugars?"

"But I always take two sugars in my coffee!" Dimitri said in an attempt to defend himself. They'd stopped for a coffee after their DIY shopping excursion. At their feet were two large bags filled with painters' tape, stir sticks, paint trays, rollers, brushes and two large containers of Almond White, not Jasmine, paint.

"Maybe it wouldn't hurt to cut that down to one," she suggested. Dimitri was about to toss the wrapped sugar cube on the café table.

"Well, I've already touched it," he said. "They'll just have to throw it out with these new Covid regulations, so there's no point in wasting."

At that, he defiantly unwrapped and dropped it into his coffee.

Karine bit her tongue. She'd been trying to drop subtle hints about Dimitri's 'quarantine 10,' the 10 pounds many people had put on during the lockdown. But in the case of Dimitri, this 10 pounds was more likely 20! She feared it might even be more than that, however, whenever she asked Dimitri to locate the scale from within their packed-up boxes, he found something 'more important' to do. He hadn't, however, had any trouble in tracking down the kitchen scale so he could do his baking.

He stirred his coffee, clanked his spoon on the side of his cup to knock off any remaining liquid and then loudly sipped his sweet espresso.

"Do you really have to make so much noise? Can't you just drink your coffee like a normal person?"

"What's the big deal? There's tons of space between us and the next table. Who could I be bothering?"

"ME!" she shouted, attracting much more attention from patrons seated at the neighboring tables than Dimitri had with his slurping. He set his cup down and stared out the window. Realizing she'd overreacted, Karine's cheeks flushed in embarrassment. She looked the other way to avoid Dimitri's sullen face. The tension between them was thicker than his new chocolate mousse recipe.

"Alright. How about I join you and your running group next Saturday?" Dimitri meekly suggested, breaking the uncomfortable silence.

"Okay, that'd be great. I'll sign you up," Karine agreed, her mood noticeably improved—but not for very long.

***

"What are you doing? We have to get going!" chastised Karine. She checked the time on her watch again. It was 7:45 am.

"I'm nearly ready!" Dimitri shouted from the kitchen. Some clattering of crockery followed.

"What are you eating? I already told you! We'll have breakfast when we get back!" Karine yelled, glaring towards the kitchen, as she waited next to the front door. She was used to getting up at 7:30, throwing on her workout clothes and jogging out to meet the running group for its 8 am departure. Today Dimitri was already awake by the time she got up. Was he that anguished about going out for a run?

A moment later he exited the kitchen and jogged over to her. *Was that butter on his cheek?* Karine wondered as she opened the front door for him. *He seriously couldn't even wait till we got back?!*

This is what was whirling through Karine's head as they sat on the hill in the park. The more she stewed about it, the more her blood boiled. *That's why he couldn't make it up the hill! He was full from sneaking breakfast before we left!* she huffed with disappointment, staring out at the suspension bridge. Their relationship seemed to be hanging precariously on a wire these days.

She didn't really mind the love handles he'd put on during the quarantine, she was more worried about his health. Diabetes ran in his family. She knew this was one of the specific reasons he'd also preferred to stay inside during the lockdown, to avoid falling ill, but never once had he tried to prevent her from going out. Maybe she should have paid a little more attention to this concern, and the potential germs she was bringing back after every run.

"Well, we might as well go back home," she acquiesced.

"Wait, before we do, come over here," he said, leading her up to the lookout. It wasn't just any viewpoint. It was the pinnacle of the Buttes-Chaumont's fake hill, the Temple de la Sibylle, honoring Sibyl, an ancient Greek oracle. The romantic structure was made up of columns and had a conically arched roof. It sat on the very top of the hill, granting it an exceptional panorama over the north of the city. Dimitri led Karine up into the temple, void of any other people due to the early morning hour. They both leaned onto the balustrade and looked out at the panorama.

"Remember the first time we came up to this spot together?" he asked. "After we'd visited the apartment?"

"Yes, and we were debating over if we should call the real estate agent back right away to say we wanted to take it."

"Remember how we looked out from here and over to Montmartre? How we said we were much better over on this *Butte*. On our Bald Hills?"

Karine smiled and gazed over at Sacré-Coeur, proudly sitting on its high perch. That day seemed distant now, yet it had only been a little over a year ago. And what a year it had been. They'd been so much happier then. Would their happiness return once they'd finally finished the endless renovations? And once they didn't need to worry about the virus anymore? Once things got back to 'normal'?

"Yes, I remember," she finally replied wistfully. "But that wasn't the first time we came here. That was on our third or fourth date. It was a balmy September day, just like today. You'd suggested a little picnic here in the park and said you'd take care of everything. I hadn't had lunch. You laid out a blanket, pulled out a bottle of champagne and several plastic containers… each holding a different dessert you'd made!"

"I didn't know what your favorite was yet! I didn't want to get it wrong!"

"We were totally buzzing from the sugar high…"

"And the champagne!"

"And that's when you walked me up here, and kissed me for the first time. With this perfect Paris backdrop."

"The sweetest kiss ever! And not because of the chocolate icing sticking to your lips!"

They both laughed, savoring the delicious memory.

"We should do those sorts of things more often."

"Yes, screw the Jasmine White paint!"

They laughed again and lingered over the view for a moment in silence.

"Shall we head back?" suggested Karine. Dimitri looked at his watch.

"Yes, it's time to go back to our little dump."

***

When Karine approached the door, she could swear she smelled fresh baking. It must be coming from a neighbor's apartment. But when she turned the key in the lock and opened the door, the aroma was much stronger.

"Just a second!" shouted Dimitri, as he raced to the kitchen. "Don't come in here!"

Karine obeyed and plopped herself down on a dusty pile of boxes.

"Close your eyes!" he commanded from the other room. She obeyed, although she had no idea what he could be up to. A few minutes later, she heard his footsteps scuffling across their creaky parquet floor and come to a halt in front of her. "Okay, open them!"

When she did, she was surprised to find a white frosted cake in front of her with a number 7 candle on it.

"Happy seventh anniversary!" he cheered. "It's a vegan zucchini-carrot cake. I made it this morning before we went out and put it in the oven on the timer. It has half the calories as the chocolate cake I usually make. I might not be cut out for jogging, but I can make other cuts."

"Dimitri, I love you just the way you are, love handles and all." she said, poking him in the side. "I think the best anniversary present we could give each other is to pay for someone to finish the renovations for us."

"I couldn't agree more!"

Aux Folies de Belleville

That must be her, he decided, peeking over the heads of the crowded terrace and in through the bar's vast front window. *Come on, Pierre. You can do this!*

Despite this pep talk, Pierre took a few steps backwards, trying to avoid her line of sight. He fumbled through his pockets in search of his inhaler. He found it and brought it to his lips. He was so nervous his hands were visibly shaking. He opened his mouth and inhaled the medication deeply. He always turned bright red when he was stressed out, but right then his usual flushed cheeks were an even brighter red under the glow of the large neon sign he was standing under. Its fluorescent red letters were beaming the bar's name: Aux Folies.

She's even prettier in person, he thought leaning over to the right just enough so he could catch another glimpse. *She's never going to like me...*

There was really no need for Pierre's nervousness. He felt he resembled his photos closely enough. Okay, some of them might have been a few years old and he'd put on a little weight since the beginning of the year, but hadn't everyone due to the lockdown?

He'd 'met' Kim on a dating app back in late February. They'd hit it off right away and, after a couple of weeks of chatting, they decided to set a date to meet up in person. But then, the quarantine was announced. The pandemic put their first date on hold, and then on hold again and again with every extension of the lockdown. Even after the quarantine was finally lifted, Pierre took extra precautions and extended his own confinement because of his asthma. He continued to work from home and limit his outings. When summer arrived, they both took holidays, but at different times and to different places. This further delayed their 'in person' meeting. Now, suddenly, it was September.

Although six months had passed, not a day had gone by without some form of communication between the two of them. Over 180 days, 250,000 minutes… 15 million seconds… and now the moment had finally come! They were only separated by a pane of glass… and Pierre's towering wall of fear. At that very instant, he just couldn't muster up enough courage to step inside that bar.

He anxiously glanced up Rue de Belleville, the 20th district's main street and apparently where Edith Piaf was born, at number 72, a myth she enjoyed propagating during her lifetime, which bolstered her 'kid of the street' persona. Legends aside, the working-class area hadn't changed all that much since the famous songstress got her start singing in this hilly neighborhood of northeastern Paris.

Pierre's gaze was locked on the sloping street; buzzing with people going home from work or going out for the evening. Among the throngs, a face pulled him out of his hypnotic state. *Yikes!* Was that Rose? The last person Pierre wanted to run into was his gossipy Corsican colleague. If she had spotted him then the whole office would know about his rendezvous before he could even put his 50 *centimes* in the coffee machine on Monday morning. This mortifying thought was enough motivation for Pierre to duck inside Aux Folies *toute suite,* right away.

"Salut, Kim?" he managed to squeak out as he arrived at her table.

"Pierre, bon soir! Enchantée! Good evening! It's so nice to meet you!" she said, enthusiastically hopping up to greet him. The force of her movement, and the weight of her jacket and purse, propelled her chair backwards, tumbling in a gigantic clatter across the bar's classic tiled floor.

"Oh la la! I'm so clumsy!" she declared. Her face turning an even brighter shade of red than Pierre's face had been standing outside under the Aux Folies sign. Pierre gentlemanly bent down to pick up her chair and held it out for her. At the same moment, she leaned towards Pierre to give him *la bise*, the French cheek kiss, the whole reason for her jumping up in the first place. But, he immediately recoiled.

"Oh right, we're not supposed to be giving *la bise* right now," she said, realizing why Pierre was being so standoffish. *What an idiot!* Kim admonished silently. So far, she felt this meeting had totally gotten off on the wrong foot. *First, I arrive 'early,' then I commit a huge social faux pas! Deep breath, Kim, deep breath.*

"No worries, all of this is taking some getting used to," he said, sitting down opposite the lovely blonde.

"Did you find the place alright?" she asked, in an attempt to diffuse her embarrassment.

"Oh yes, no problem," he said. "I don't cross the Seine much, unless it's for a good cause."

"Well, I'm honored," Kim said, her cheeks flushing once again. "I hope I can tempt you over to the Right Bank more often. I've been getting to know my new neighborhood and there are plenty of cool places around here that I'd love to show you... street art, hip hangouts, art studios, that sort of thing."

"Um... great," Pierre replied, not entirely mirroring her eagerness. He hadn't exactly jumped for joy when he'd read Kim's ecstatic message announcing she'd finally found a new place... in Belleville. He'd grown up and still lived in the 15th arrondissement. His parent's *crêperie* was there, first opened by his grandparents after WWII. The Tanguys fit in perfectly to that very family oriented, tranquil and tidy district. It was the polar opposite to Belleville and not just geographically speaking. Artsy, cosmopolitan and on the somewhat grungy side, Belleville had been slowly gentrifying, nevertheless, it still retained an edgy vibe. Pierre was willing to travel across the city, to put his preconceived notions aside, for this one very specific good cause: Kim.

"*Qu'est ce que je vous sers?*" asked the waiter, when he arrived at their table.

"What would you like, Kim?" Pierre asked even though he knew her French was next to perfect and she could easily order for herself.

"I think I'll have a glass of rosé, since the weather is so nice."

"Good idea. Let's revive the summer *apéro* we weren't able to have. *Allez. Deux verres de rosé s'il vous plaît.*" The waiter left to fetch their order, leaving the duo alone.

"Wow, it's hard to believe we're finally meeting," said Kim. "In person."

"Yes, after all this time! Where to start…"

Actually, they'd already covered so much via their messaging. She knew that as a kid he'd hated spending his summer holidays at his great aunt's home in Brittany, but he now went every chance he could. He knew she'd grown up near Bath, and yet had never visited the inside of the famous Roman baths which had given the city its name. She knew he didn't like camembert (sacrilege!). He knew she didn't like marmite (understandable). Sometimes they would chat for hours, other times they simply exchanged a cute emoji or goofy meme. It didn't matter what the message was about, this daily contact had helped both of them get through those mandatory self-quarantine days. Now, meeting face to face after all these months, they were tongue-tied.

"Umm, so how was your day?" Kim asked, taking the plunge into their murky conversational waters.

"Fine, it's a little strange being back at the office with the new Covid regulations and all. But it's nice to see my colleagues again, or at least some of them."

"Agreed, maybe even the difficult ones aren't as bad as we previously thought!"

"Yes, perhaps," Pierre said. Although he was not convinced seeing his gossipy colleague Rose would ever be a good thing inside, but most especially by chance outside the office.

"*Et voilà!*" announced the waiter as he placed two frosty glasses on their table before floating off to deliver the remaining contents of his tray to nearby tables.

"*Santé!*" cheered Pierre, raising his glass.

"Yes *santé!* To our health!" echoed Kim, clinking her glass lightly against Pierre's. They each took a sip of their rosé. Maybe the cool liquid would activate their vocal cords? As they set their glasses back on the table, their hands brushed ever so slightly. Pierre uncontrollable went to reach out for Kim's long elegant fingers, which he so longed to touch.

"*Cacahuètes?*" Pierre rapidly retracted his hand, as if he'd been caught with his fingers in his great aunt's candy dish. He looked up to find an elderly African man. On his head was a knit kufi cap and in his hands was a squat cardboard box, like an old-fashioned cigarette tray. It was loaded with home-prepared plastic baggies of unshelled peanuts. Belleville didn't seem to follow the same rules as the rest of Paris. It had something of a Revolutionary spirit. Its residents had been heavily involved in the Commune de Paris revolt of 1871. So important was their involvement, a recent campaign tried to get the words 'Commune de Paris 1871' added as a subtitle to the signage of the Belleville *Métro* Station.

"Actually, I came straight here from work and I'm famished," said Kim. "*C'est combien?*" How much?"

"*Un euro,*" replied the entrepreneurial retiree.

Kim rummaged through her purse and exchanged a one-euro coin for a packet of peanuts. Content with his sale, the man shuffled off to tout his homemade wares to the next table.

"I hope you don't mind," said Kim as she tore into the bag. "Do you like peanuts?"

"Um... they're... alright," Pierre said hesitantly.

"Here, I unshelled some for you," she sweetly offered in her outstretched hand. Pierre stared at her irresistibly fingers... now filled with potential lethal contents. He knew he probably shouldn't eat her generous token, but he didn't want to seem impolite or contrary.

"Don't worry, I washed my hands as soon as I arrived," Kim added, mistaking his concern for hygiene rather than the substance she was offering. Pierre gave himself another pep talk: *Come on, Pierre! Don't be, well, nuts. You'll be fine!*

Admittedly, he wasn't officially allergic to peanuts, but he hadn't tempted fate since he was a kid. Honestly, in these last months, Pierre now felt he had played things all too safely in every aspect of his life. He was surprised Kim had waited around. She might not for much longer, especially if he carried on with this wishy-washy behavior. He caved, wanting to please her. He accepted her kind gesture and popped a peanut into his mouth.

"So, how was your trip back home?" he asked, taking a sip of rosé to wash down the bits of nut.

"It was really nice to see my family after so long," she said. "England isn't that far, but with the travel ban, then the reduced number of trains, it was complicated."

"I can imagine," he replied nervously, munching away on the remaining peanuts.

"Did you have a nice holiday?"

"Well, it rained a lot and we were stuck inside for days, the last place we wanted to be after the lockdown, but it was still great to be back in Brittany," he answered before taking a big chug of wine. *Is it just me or is it getting hot in there?* Pierre thought.

"Pierre, are you alright?" asked Kim, brow furrowed with concern.

"I'm not so sure..."

"Your face is all splotchy," she commented, in the nicest way possible. "And I think you're sweating."

"Maybe it's from the peanuts, I have allergies, or rather intolerances," he confessed, picking up the menu to fan his face.

"Do you need to go to the hospital? Shall I call an ambulance?"

"No, no!" he managed to spit out despite his tightening throat. "I think… I… just… need… some air."

"Of course!" she agreed without hesitation. She pulled a 10-euro bill out of her wallet, much more than was needed to cover the cost of two drinks in this unpretentious bar. She placed it under her half-finished glass of rosé and jumped out of her seat. It fortunately didn't go crashing down to the floor this time. "Come on, let's go."

Exiting the bar via its side door, they found themselves in a long, dimly lit alley. Pierre took some deep breaths. Then he remembered his inhaler, his saviour.

How could I have screwed this up so royally! thought Kim frantically. *I've been dying to meet Pierre and then I go and almost kill him! I'm a total disaster! Maybe it's too soon to date again. Forget self-isolation, I should head straight to a convent and lock myself up forever!*

Just as Pierre's breathing seemed to be returning to a normal rhythm, an enormous cloud of cigarette smoke wafted into the alleyway from the bar's terrace.

"Come on, let's move down the street," suggested Kim, pulling at his sleeve. The terrace was packed, evidence that some things had finally returned to normal, or at least for these seemingly footloose and fancy-free Friday night revelers. Soon, Kim and Pierre were out of harm's way, and all alone midway down the dark lane.

"Whew! You seem to be doing better," said Kim, relieved.

"Yes, thank you, I really did just need some air," Pierre murmured.

"You had me worried. I wasn't sure if I was going to have to give you mouth to mouth," Kim added flirtatiously.

"I wouldn't have objected to that," he replied with a sly grin, finally letting down his guard. She still had his sleeve, which he used as leverage to move in closer to her. The motion caused Kim to fall gently back against the building they were standing next to.

"Being here, with you, is magic," Pierre whispered. He leaned in even closer and put his hand up against the wall to support himself.

That doesn't feel right, thought Pierre. *Was the wall... wet?*

"Doesn't it smell a little funny right here?" asked Kim, scrunching up her nose. "Hey wait, I'm stuck!"

Pierre stepped back, removing his hand from the wall. He held it up to the lamplight to find his palm smudged in a rainbow of pink, green, yellow and purple. Fresh paint.

"Oh my god, that's right!" Kim exclaimed, peeling her hair off the wall. "This road is chocked full of street art. I think we may have just added our own touch to a freshly made work of art."

Sure enough, they looked closer at the wall and could make out the image of a couple, a couple in stone. Pierre vaguely recalled it from the Louvre. It was Canova's sculpture *Psyche Revived by Cupid's Kiss*, except that the couple, on the verge of kissing, were wearing gas masks. Cupid's wings were filled with small green virus symbols which were flying off them and dotting the wall in a trail behind the couple. Another work by D-Zyne, whom Pierre and Kim appeared to have just missed. Love in the time of Corona. The virus had been thwarting Kim and Pierre's own attempts at romance, well, Pierre's feeble health and low self-confidence were also partially to blame.

"I'd always thought about dying my hair, but green wasn't exactly the color I'd had in mind!" chuckled Kim, taking the incident in stride. Her positive outlook was contagious and Pierre couldn't help but laugh too, which rapidly spiraled into a fit of coughs. Kim shot him a renewed look of panic.

"I'm fine, I'm fine!" he said, regaining control of his breathing. "Laughter is the best medicine, right?"

"That's true, but we still have to deal with this paint," she said. "Of course I've got some antibacterial hand gel in my purse, but I don't think it'll be enough to clean this up. I recall that there's a fountain up ahead. We can get washed up there. Oh, we'd better put our masks on as well."

"Oh right," said Pierre, reaching into his pocket. Being asthmatic, he wasn't terribly fond of wearing one, but he knew it would help keep him and others safe.

The quiet side streets of Belleville might otherwise have been the perfect setting for a romantic stroll hand-in-hand. The paint mishap had gotten in the way of this, however, it didn't stop them from gravitating close and closer together.

"Drat, the fountain is actually up a little further," she said, once they'd reached the end of the lane. "You don't mind, do you?"

"No, no, that's fine," Pierre said before realizing that the direction she was referring to... was up.

Do we really need to trek up the Belleville Hill? Weren't there other places down here where they could wash up? Pierre grumbled in his head. *Things are getting back on track. Don't mess it up again with your respiratory problems and anxiety. Just let her do the talking as you climb this... flipping mountain... and you'll be fine.*

Luckily for Pierre, Kim launched into a detailed description of her weekend plans, so he didn't have to say much. Besides trying to save his breath, literally speaking, he was lapping up her sparkling optimism. She was truly radiant. This had even come across in her text messages. She was always looking on the bright side, forging fearlessly ahead into the unknown. Her motivating energy was exactly what he needed right now, tonight and in his life. But could he relinquish his fears and go outside of his comfort zone?

And just like that, before he knew it, they were nearing the summit of the hill. But before reaching the very top, Kim led him down a small street to the right, which was, much to Pierre's and his lung's delight, flat.

"Ah, there it is," said Kim, pointing ahead. Sure enough, she'd located the promised water source. Despite the low light, Pierre could see that it was a Wallace Fountain. Following the Franco-Prussian War and the Commune of Paris, in the 1870s British philanthropist Sir Richard Wallace donated dozens of these lovely fountains to provide fresh water to the city, as it struggled to recover from war and internal strife. In recent years, the City Hall had started installing modern water fountains around the city, some of these even dispensed fizzy water, like the one over on the Promenade Plantée. As nifty as they were, what would happen to these beautiful classical fountains? At that very moment, the historic fountain was much more useful in Pierre's efforts to scrub his hands and Kim's own to de-punkify her hair.

"How are you getting on?" Pierre asked after his hands had only a small trace of the paint.

"I got most of the paint out and the rest should come out when I wash my hair," she said, yet another illustration of her idealistic outlook. "In the meantime, I might just look a little funny."

"Not at all. You're incredibly beautiful just the way you are," Pierre dared. Although his hand was now mostly clean, he was still too nervous to reach out to her.

"You're pretty cute yourself," Kim returned bashfully. "Come over here. There's something I want to show you." She added, tugging at his sleeve once again. Up ahead was a little plaza, bordered by a few bar terraces on one side and a large opening on the other.

"Close your eyes," she ordered coyly.

"Alright." Pierre wasn't one for surprises, but he complied nevertheless. He was learning to trust her, and to trust his own instincts. Mind over matter. He could do it, or at least try. She guided him a dozen or so paces forward, then swung him 45 degrees to the right.

"Okay, open your eyes!"

He obeyed. There, in front of him, was a vast panorama of sparkling lights. They were now above the Parc de Belleville, whose heights offered one of the most spectacular views of the city. The Eiffel Tower rose in the center of this twinkling plain, as its queen, its goddess, its beacon, its North Star. So close, yet so far away. Mesmerized, Pierre considered, did he really need to look so far ahead? Did he constantly need to worry about what if this and what if that? All he needed was right there, in the present. Could he just seize the moment?

"It's a stunning sight," he said, turning to Kim. "But you're all the sparkle I need."

He raised his tie-dyed hand to Kim's cheek and leaned down to kiss her. Kim moved in closer, bridging the gap between them and that special moment they'd both been dreaming of for what now seemed like an eternity. They stopped.

Those darn protective masks!

All they could do was giggle.

Life seemed to be on hold right now. But one could still attempt to move forward in other ways. To overcome fears and anxiety. To embark down new paths. To take steps into the great unknown. To advance towards a new, brighter future. It was there. Sparkling, like the City of Light, in the near distance.

Le Metro
The End of the Line

Sasha and Petite Piaf ran through a passageway and entered a tunnel leading to Belleville's other *Métro* Line, number 11. They heard some shouting behind them, but tore on ahead. An arriving train rumbled above their heads.

"This way!" shouted Sasha, leading them up to the platform heading southwest. They hopped on just in time and, fortunately, without any dangerous tag-alongs. Breathless, they collapsed into a section of empty seats.

"I give up," said Petite Piaf once she'd managed to get her panting under control. "Why precisely have you been chasing me?"

"I accidentally tossed something very important into your change pouch earlier on and I desperately need it back," he answered between gasps.

"What is it?"

"Empty out your change, here, onto the back of my bag. I promise, I'm not going to take any of your money."

She did as he instructed. Amidst the tumbling coins of various denominations, was a small, black disk. A memory card. Sasha's hands trembled as he reached down and extracted it. He held it up slowly.

"You see, I'm a photographer. While most people were confined to their homes during the lockdown, I could move around freely thanks to my press card. I used this privilege to capture Paris during that period. At first, I took photos of empty streets and historic sites void of their tourists. But then I turned my focus to the people keeping society going. The nurses, bakers, grocery store employees, food delivery guys, *Métro* drivers, even police officers!

"A publisher, who'd discovered my work, contacted me and offered me a book deal. The images were due next week, but then she called me yesterday to say they were also going to submit the project to a very prestigious contest run by a major photography magazine. The winning selection would be put on the front cover of the magazine, which would then be distributed around the globe. If I were to win, it would life-changing.

"However, my publisher said they'd need two of the best images today, by 4:30 pm, so they could meet the application deadline which is at 5:00. I spent all yesterday editing them, but then last night I went out to walk my dog and when I got back home, I found my door smashed in. All my valuables were gone. Including my cameras, my computer and my backup hard drives. The police came. They took fingerprints. I had to go to the station. All that.

"Sure, insurance will cover most of the cost of the goods, but those images are priceless and irreplaceable. I thought I was completely ruined. That that was going to be the end of the book deal and the contest as well. I could barely sleep last night. I was worried about what I was going to tell my publisher, but I was really grieving over all the work I'd lost and was so regretful for not being able to commemorate those courageous people in the images, as they so deserved to be honored.

"Then, this morning, when I was tidying up the papers the robbers had scattered over my desk, I spotted something black in a small dish I toss my spare change into. It was the memory card I'd been using during all those months of the quarantine. I had taken it out of my camera when I'd uploaded the photos to my computer. I couldn't believe it. It was a true godsend. That said, with barely sleeping a wink, and with all the mounting stress, I was a complete wreck today. That's how I accidentally threw it, along with that previously lucky spare change, into your pouch."

Petite Piaf stared at him. A tear ran down her cheek.

"I'm so sorry I gave you such a hard time."

"Please, don't worry about it. I totally get it. I must have looked like a total lunatic. I didn't want you to think I was stalking you, but I really, really needed to get that card back."

The train had been rolling along during Sasha's explanation and they were approaching Châtelet Station. The end of the line.

Petite Piaf gathered up all her change and the two dragged themselves to their feet, completely wiped out from their afternoon filled with unexpected exertion and anxiety. They stepped down onto the platform. The *Métro* clock flashed 4:15 pm. Sasha had 15 minutes, but from here he wasn't too far from his publisher's office. He should make it just in time. Well, as long as he didn't have any more unexpected, hair-raising hold-ups.

"Please don't play in the *Métro* anymore," requested Sasha. "I'd hate for you to run into those nasty gypsies, or those intimidating controllers, again."

"Well, there's this café up in Montmartre whose manager keeps trying to recruit me. I always thought the place was a tourist trap, but I went by the other evening and it's actually quite eccentric. Maybe I'll finally accept his offer. Although I have to say, I'd miss the *Métro*."

Sasha certainly wouldn't. After he reached his publisher's office and made sure she had the contest photos safely copied on her computer, he was planning on taking a taxi home. He wouldn't be setting a foot down here for a very, very long time.

"Good luck, Petite Piaf," he said, calling her by the nickname he'd given her.

"That's cute! Maybe I'll use it as my new stage name!"

"I'll ask around for you at the cafés the next time I'm up in Montmartre."

"And I'll look out for your book in a few months' time at my favorite bookstore in the Galerie Vivienne!"

They gave each other a little wave and set off in opposite directions.

"Wait!" Sasha suddenly called after her. Petite Piaf turned around. "I've been wondering, where does your song come from? I don't know if I'll ever get it out of my head."

"It's from a quote by the artist Vincent Van Gogh," she answered. "There's only one Paris, and however hard living here may be, and if it became worse and even harder, the city does a world of good. True, isn't it?"

"Yes. Very true. There really is only one Paris."

La Fin

Thank you for reading There's Only One Paris!

If you enjoyed the book, it would be wonderful if you could post a quick review on Amazon, Goodreads ... or simply help spread the word by telling your friends or family about it!

Merci beaucoup!

Enjoy more of Lily's writings on Paris on her site:
jetaimemeneither.com

About the Project

There's Only One Paris was born in the early days of the Covid-19 pandemic. When international travel was restricted in mid-March 2020, millions of Paris lovers were kept from coming to their favorite city. To help transport them to it virtually, while also getting involved in the process, I started writing weekly 'participatory' short stories. At the beginning of the project, readers sent in their favorite places and things to do in Paris. One of these locations was selected every week and readers once again had the chance to share their impressions or memories of it, whether it be their favorite artworks at the Louvre or the Musée d'Orsay or what they love about Montmartre or the Marais. These would then serve as the inspiration for the fictive tales. The project has evolved greatly since its incarnation, however, the initial objective always remained the same; to bring Paris vividly to life while providing inspiration and motivation during these very peculiar and difficult times. Paris can be our beacon, our guide, our North Star to get through the pandemic.

Acknowledgements

This book wouldn't have been possible without my editor, and dear friend, Susan Romig. She believed in and dedicated herself to the project since day one. I am also extremely grateful to Karin Lynn Bates, Karina Clarke, Alisa Morov, Blaise Alexander and Bronwen Leslie who assisted with proofing the final manuscript and to Lauren Sarazen for diverse editorial advice. The stories themselves wouldn't have been possible without the enthusiasm and love of Paris shared by hundreds of people on the posts I put up on Facebook over the course of the project. Their commentary is peppered throughout the book. Among these, an extra special *merci* goes to Jeanie Meyer, who contributed beautiful and descriptive memories of various venues in the book, some of which specifically inspired story #3. I would also like to thank Mona Sonderborg Tompkins who sent in a magical personal story which was used as the base for story #18. A number of other people contributed along the way as sounding boards for the stories, these include Joshua Heise, Gail Boisclair, Pascale Vincent Marquis, Jeremy Wolf, Katrin Holt, Georgina Weavers, Pandora Boudrahem, Mats Haglund, Evelyne Rose, Denise Powers and Philip Ditchfield. A shoutout goes to Zavier and Skyler for naming a number of the characters. I am also very thankful to the members of my Patreon club who helped support the project and see it to fruition, in particular the club's *grands et royals amoureux* Corianna Heise, Shaina Brady, Rebecca Stranberg, Ann Kirsebom, Dolores Heide, Andi Fisher, Kathryn Reichert, Margaret Hope, Andrea Yates, Clara Borges, Cheryl Matzker, Tracy Miller, Véronique Savoye and Lachlan Cooke. As always, a big thank you goes to my family for encouraging, and putting up with, my overactive imagination. Lastly, although I wouldn't have thought it at the time, I'm grateful to LN for unintentionally inspiring the whole project back at the beginning of the pandemic.

About the Author

Originally from Canada, (April) Lily Heise has been living in Paris since 2000. Her travel writing has appeared in *The Huffington Post, Business Insider, Conde Nast Traveler, Frommer's, Playboy, Fodor's*, among others. In addition to *There's Only One Paris*, she is the author of two books on looking for romance in Paris, *Je T'Aime, Me Neither* and *Je T'Aime... Maybe?*, which was shortlisted in the best new book category in the Best of Paris contest 2017. She also runs an award-winning blog on Paris, www.jetaimemeneither.com.

Made in the USA
Las Vegas, NV
05 February 2021

17243897R00193